Forced To Fight:
Book One

Trials of the Chosen

Stephen Snyder

Printed in the United States.
ISBN: 979-8-9921457-2-4
Publisher: Stephen Snyder

DEDICATION

To Lois Bolster Charlebois,
You were not just a teacher; you were my guide, my encourager, and my inspiration. In high school, you helped me focus, believe in myself, and achieve what I never thought possible. Because of you, I passed 9th grade with confidence and grades I was proud of for the very first time. I'll never forget the handwritten story I gave you to type up all those years ago, and how you took the time to nurture my creativity. You didn't just teach me how to study or prepare for exams—you taught me that I was capable of so much more.

Thank you for believing in me when I didn't yet believe in myself. This book is a small testament to the difference you made in my life.

With endless gratitude,
Stephen Snyder

PROLOGUE

Tucked into my bed, I stared at the shadows on the wall when, out of nowhere, something moved. My heart pounded, and a chill ran down my spine. I tried to convince myself it was just my imagination, but the fear wouldn't go away.

"Daddy! I saw something in my room!" I screamed.

Mom's voice echoed from down the hall, sounding annoyed and weary. "I told you we shouldn't have let him watch Nightmare on Elm Street! Now you can try to calm him down!"

"All right! All right! I'll go, but I'm sure it's nothing," Dad replied, jumping out of bed. His usually comforting voice carried a hint of frustration. The sound of his footsteps grew closer, each one making my heart beat faster. He opened the door slowly and flicked on the light. The room flooded with brightness, but I was already hiding in the closet, peeking through the slats.

"Jack! Where are you?" Dad called out, now sounding worried.

I didn't answer. Too scared to move, I could barely breathe as I watched the bedroom door slam shut behind him. A stranger, dressed in a tattered red and black plaid shirt and dirty blue jeans, stepped out of the shadows. Mud covered his worn boots. He muttered something inaudible, then pulled out a gun and pointed it at Dad. I wanted to scream, to do something, but I froze.

The gun went off with a loud bang, echoing in the small room. Dad fell to the floor, blood pouring from his head. He didn't move. He didn't even make a sound. My world shattered in an instant.

"Jack! What in the hell is going on?" Mom screamed from down the hall. She burst into the room, tripping over Dad's body and crashing into the dresser. She looked around, confused, and then saw the open window. The curtain fluttered in the breeze, a stark contrast to the horror within those walls.

Mom turned back and saw Dad on the floor. Her face twisted in horror as she dropped to her knees beside him, shaking him, trying to wake him up, but it was too late. Her screams filled the entire room, a sound I would never forget.

"Jack…" she gasped, crawling toward the closet. She looked so tired, so broken. I just sat there, not moving, not saying anything, feeling an overwhelming sense of helplessness.

Hours seemed to pass before the police arrived. I stayed in my spot, hidden but watching. The more I realized what had happened, the angrier I got. I didn't feel scared anymore. I felt something new, something dark and cold. Clenching my fists, my tears turned into silent rage. The world had let this happen, and I was mad. I just sat there, waiting, as the night dragged on.

The days after were a blur. Mom and I stayed at a neighbor's house while the police investigated. I heard the adults talking in hushed voices about the "intruder" and "murder," but it made little sense to me. All I knew was that Dad was gone, and everything felt wrong. The weight of loss was crushing, an ever-present ache I couldn't escape.

CHAPTER 1

The hot water from the shower cascaded down my body, but it did little to wash away the heaviness that clung to me. Steam filled the bathroom as I leaned against the cool tile, letting the water beat against my back. My thoughts swirled, tangled in the relentless cycle of nightmares and memories I couldn't shake—no matter how hard I tried. My mind, like the bathroom's fogged mirror, was clouded with flashes of my past.

I remembered sitting in Dr. Evans' office. He was the kind of man who made you feel both scrutinized and safe at the same time. His salt-and-pepper hair was always neatly combed, a sharp contrast to the softness of his hazel eyes, which seemed to hold an endless well of patience. His glasses, thin and rectangular, rested on the bridge of his nose, giving him the look of someone who had spent too many nights reading by lamplight. He dressed in the kind of muted tones—grays and navy blues—that made him blend into the background, as if he wanted the focus to be on you instead of him. But he stayed with me: calm, steady, and frustratingly knowing, like he'd already seen the walls I was building before I had even finished laying the bricks.

"How are the nightmares?" he'd asked, his pen poised, waiting for my response. I had rubbed my hands over my jeans, trying to keep my frustration at bay, though I knew it would come out eventually.

"Same as always," I muttered. He'd nodded, gently prodding, as therapists did.

"Tell me about last night's dream." I hadn't wanted to. Talking made it feel more real, but I promised to try. I'd told him about my father—how I'd watched him fall, helpless to save him.

The sharpness of the memory brought me back to the present, and I turned off the water, the sensation of the cool tile under my palm grounding me. Stepping out, I dried myself mechanically, the mirror now completely fogged over. Maybe it was better that way. I didn't want to see the exhaustion etched into my face.

Wiping a small section of the mirror, I glimpsed my reflection. I never liked looking at myself for too long, but when I did, I couldn't help but think I looked like someone trying too hard to hold it all together. My dark brown hair was perpetually messy, as if it couldn't decide whether to stand up in defiance or lay flat in surrender.

My face bore the sharp angles of someone who had been through too much, too fast—cheekbones more prominent than they should have been, jawline hard, like I was always gritting my teeth. My eyes, once vibrant, had dulled to a tired, haunted green that didn't seem to belong to someone my age.

The stubble on my face was uneven, a half-hearted attempt to mask the weariness that no amount of sleep—or lack thereof—could fix. I carried myself like someone always on edge, shoulders tense, like the weight of my past was pressing down on me, no matter how hard I tried to shake it off. My thoughts, like stubborn ghosts, refused to be banished.

"You couldn't have saved him," Dr. Evans had said, his voice patient yet firm. The memory of his words followed me like a shadow as I pulled on my jeans. He always said the same thing—that I was just a kid, that it wasn't my fault. But no matter how many times I heard it, it never stuck. I should have done something. Anything.

It wasn't until years later that I found a way to channel some of that guilt, anger, and helplessness. Mom had pushed me to join karate when I was a teenager, thinking it might be good for me to have an outlet. "You need to focus your energy on something healthy," she'd said. At first, I resisted—it felt like just another chore. But as the weeks turned into months, karate became more than just a hobby. It was therapy. Every punch, every block, every kata became a way to work through the pain I couldn't put into words.

I poured myself into it, training harder than anyone in my class, eventually earning my black belt. The sense of control, of being able to fight back—against anything—was something I hadn't realized I was missing. Now, years later, I helped teach a class a few times a week at a local dojo. Seeing the kids focus, watching them learn discipline and strength, reminded me of where I'd started. It didn't erase the pain, but it helped. In a way, it kept me grounded. I tore my gaze away.

Before I could move to grab my clothes, a pair of arms slipped around my waist from behind. Warmth replaced the cold in an instant, her embrace chasing away the lingering tension in my shoulders.

"Good morning, sleepyhead," Tiffany murmured, her cheek resting against my back. Her voice was soft, teasing, the perfect contrast to the heaviness in my chest.

I let out a breath I hadn't realized I was holding. "You always know how to sneak up on me."

She chuckled, her grip tightening for a brief moment before she stepped back slightly, turning me to face her. Tiffany was shorter than me by at least a head, her blonde hair pulled into a ponytail that swayed with her movements. Her hazel eyes sparkled with a playful glint, and her gym clothes—sleek black leggings and a fitted tank top—clung to her like a second skin, emphasizing her athletic build.

"You seemed like you could use a good hug. Or some coffee," she said, her smile widening as she scanned my face.

I smiled faintly, reaching up to tuck a stray lock of hair behind her ear. "Coffee sounds good."

Her lips quirked into a mischievous grin. "Hurry up and get dressed, then. Unless you'd prefer I join you back in here."

I raised an eyebrow at her teasing tone. "Tempting, but I think we'd be late for… everything."

She laughed, standing on her tiptoes to press a quick kiss to my cheek. "Well, don't keep me waiting too long." With a wink, she grabbed a towel from the counter and tossed it at me before heading for the door. "Coffee's downstairs when you're ready."

I watched her leave, a small smile tugging at my lips despite myself. Tiffany had a way of making the world feel just a little less heavy.

The smell of freshly brewed coffee pulled me out of my head as I made my way downstairs. Tiffany's morning rituals, something so normal, had a way of grounding me. The kitchen was bathed in soft morning light, and I found her by the coffee machine, pouring herself a cup. She looked up as I entered, her smile lighting up the room.

"See? I knew you couldn't resist," she teased, holding up a second mug. "Thought I'd save you the trouble."

"Thanks," I said, taking the mug from her. My fingers brushed against hers, the small touch lingering for just a moment longer than necessary.

She tilted her head, studying me as she leaned against the counter. "Did you sleep any better?"

I shrugged, taking a sip of coffee. "Not really."

She frowned slightly but didn't push. Instead, she set her mug down and crossed the room, wrapping her arms around me. Her warmth seeped into me, her presence steady and unwavering. "You're not allowed to let today get the better of you," she murmured, her voice firm but gentle. "Not while I'm around."

I huffed a small laugh. "You always seem to know what to say."

"Comes with the territory," she replied with a grin, pulling back just enough to meet my eyes. "Now, let's see that smile."

I gave her a faint smirk. "You're relentless, you know that?"

"Only because I know you can take it." She reached up, brushing her thumb lightly over my cheek before stepping back. "Alright, Mr. Grumpy, I'm off to the gym. Don't let the coffee get cold."

I caught her hand before she could grab her bag, pulling her back into a brief hug. "Thanks, Tiff."

She leaned into me for a moment, her arms around my waist. "Always, Jack." With a quick kiss to my chin, she grabbed her bag and headed for the door. "Don't mope too much while I'm gone!"

She flashed me one last smile before slipping out the door, leaving behind an emptiness that felt heavier without her presence. But her words lingered, anchoring me, keeping the darkness at bay just a little longer. And for now, that was enough. I couldn't keep running from these memories. Yet no matter how much I tried to push them away, they clawed their way back, as vivid as the night they had happened.

The doorbell rang, jolting me from my thoughts. I wasn't expecting anyone. When I answered, a delivery man handed me a small package.

"Delivery for Jack Shaw."

I signed for it, the unease that had followed me all morning creeping back. Inside the box was a folder and a hastily written note. My eyes scanned the words, my heart raced.

Jack,

The nightmares are only the beginning. You've been chosen for something greater, something that will test your strength and resolve. The truth behind your father's death is more complex than you know. Prepare yourself.

-Queen

The cryptic message rattled me, dredging up feelings I had tried to bury. I couldn't shake the cold, unsettling sense that my past wasn't finished with me—that something, or someone, was pulling me toward a truth I wasn't ready to face.

Once outside, I noticed a white van parked on the other side of the street. It was an unremarkable vehicle, nondescript and plain, but something about it made me pause. The van's tinted windows gave it a sense of being out of place in our quiet neighborhood. I watched as the van idled for a moment, but then it pulled out quickly. I shrugged it off—it was probably just a coincidence, nothing more. With the van now out of sight, I focused on my walk.

As I walked down the street, the letter consumed my thoughts. My route took me past the local convenience store. On a whim, I stopped in, hoping a brief distraction might help me calm down.

As I wandered the aisles of the store, the fluorescent lights seemed to buzz more than usual. My thoughts kept drifting back to the strange letter. I just wandered around from aisle to aisle, lost in thought. In the back corner, near the stockroom, I overheard a conversation that snagged my attention. A stock clerk, a lanky young guy with a scruffy beard that looked like it was trying and failing to connect, was ranting to his co-worker. His tired eyes, shadowed with the unmistakable heaviness of sleepless nights, darted between the box of canned goods he was unloading and the older man beside him. He tossed the box onto the shelf with more force than necessary, his frustration evident.

"Man, you won't believe this," he said, his voice tinged with annoyance as he grabbed another box. "I found this note on my door this morning. It just said, 'You're invited!'"

The older man, stocky and balding, paused mid-motion with a stack of cereal boxes in his arms. His deeply lined face carried the weary expression of someone who'd seen enough in life not to be easily surprised, but the puzzled look in his tired brown eyes betrayed a flicker of curiosity. He adjusted his glasses, perched slightly askew on his nose, and frowned.

"Invited to what?" the older man asked, his gravelly voice carrying a tone of mild skepticism. "That's not exactly informative."

"Exactly!" the younger man replied, slapping a can of soup onto the shelf with an exaggerated motion. "No address, no details. Just that cryptic message. I thought it was some kind of prank at first."

The older man grunted as he set the cereal boxes down, dusting off his hands. "Sounds like a prank to me," he said, shaking his head. "Either that or someone's got a weird sense of humor."

The stock clerk sighed, running a hand through his unkempt hair. "Yeah, maybe. Still… it's unsettling, you know?"

The older man shrugged, his expression softening into something more thoughtful. "These days, kid, unsettling's just the price of admission." With a weary chuckle, he returned to stocking the shelves, leaving the younger man to brood over his mysterious invitation.

At that moment, I realized something bigger was happening, and it wasn't just about me. I stood there, still processing the conversation, when a different stock clerk approached me. She was a petite woman with shoulder-length auburn hair that framed her heart-shaped face. Her kind hazel eyes seemed to study me for a moment before she offered a warm, genuine smile. Her nametag read "Sarah," and her demeanor was as welcoming as the sunshine spilling through the store windows.

"Hi there, can I help you find anything?" she asked, her voice gentle and calming.

Startled, I turned to face her, my thoughts still tangled. "Oh, um, no thanks. I'm just looking around."

She tilted her head slightly, her expression soft but inquisitive. "Are you sure? You seem a bit lost. Anything I can do to help?"

I forced a smile, trying to appear more composed. "I'm fine, really. Just had a lot on my mind lately."

Sarah nodded, her brows knitting slightly in sympathy. "I get it. Life can be overwhelming sometimes. If you need anything, just let me know."

"Thanks," I replied, appreciating her kindness but eager to escape the conversation.

As she walked away, I noticed the way she carried herself—calm, unhurried, as if she'd mastered the art of finding peace in chaos. Her green apron swayed slightly as she moved down the aisle, and for a fleeting moment, I envied her apparent ease with the world.

I forced myself to ignore it and continued to the checkout. After paying for a few items, I left the store, my mind racing with the implications of what I had overheard. As I walked, I glanced over my shoulder. The white van I had noticed parked near my house was here too, its driver's seat now empty but the van itself still giving off an ominous vibe.

I quickened my pace, unease growing with every step. The combination of the letter and the overheard conversation left me with a deep sense of foreboding.

CHAPTER 2

I walked with heightened alertness, my eyes darting around, scanning every shadow and movement for any sign of danger or surveillance. The crunch of leaves beneath my feet seemed louder, amplified by the tense silence. Every passerby appeared suspicious; every rustle of wind felt like a potential threat. The world around me seemed to shift, the familiar rhythm of daily life replaced by an ominous undertone.

By noon, hunger reminded me of its presence. I glanced at my watch—already past noon. My walk had taken longer than I realized. Deciding to indulge in a momentary distraction, I headed to the local pizzeria for a couple of slices of BBQ chicken pizza.

As I stood in line, I noticed another white van driving past. I dismissed it, figuring it was just another of the many white vans in the area, and didn't let it add to my growing list of concerns.

As I settled into a booth at the pizzeria, the warm, comforting aroma of pizza offered a brief escape from the swirling chaos in my mind. I took a bite of my BBQ chicken pizza, savoring the flavors, but the uneasy feeling in my stomach remained. My phone buzzed with a text from Tiffany.

"Where are you?" she asked, her concern clear even in the brief message.

I sighed and called her, cradling the phone between my shoulder and ear as I took another bite of pizza.

"Hey, sorry. I got caught up in something," I said, trying to sound casual but feeling the tension in my voice.

Tiffany expressed worry in her voice. "I came home, and the apartment was empty. What's going on? You were supposed to be back by now."

Unsure of how much to reveal, I hesitated. "I ended up going for a walk, but things took a strange turn. I saw something at the store that didn't sit right with me. A stock clerk was talking about receiving a note just like mine. It seems like it's not just us getting these weird invites."

I frowned, trying to piece together the sense of dread. "I've been seeing white vans everywhere I go, and I'm not sure what the connection is. It feels like something is seriously off."

Tiffany's concern deepened. "That's unsettling. You're not the only one seeing white vans, either. I've noticed them too, and I thought it was just my imagination."

Tiffany filled with anxiety. "This is getting serious. You need to come home right away. I don't want you out there alone with all this happening."

I agreed, though my mind was still reeling from the day's events. "All right, I'll head back as soon as I'm done eating. I'll be careful."

After ending the call, each bite now feeling like a forced distraction rather than a comfort.

After finishing my pizza, I felt a slight sense of relief, though my mind remained troubled. Tiffany's call had added a layer of urgency to my already fraught day. I hurried out of the pizzeria, hoping to get home quickly.

Glancing around as I walked, my heightened alertness made every shadow and movement seem suspicious. My footsteps on the crunchy leaves felt louder, more pronounced as I scanned the surroundings. The unsettling note and the clerk's odd conversation made me believe they were connected to the white van I had seen earlier.

With my thoughts racing, I took a detour, hoping to avoid any unexpected encounters on the opposite side of the road. The call with Tiffany and the strange sense of dread that had settled over me continued to occupy my mind. I was determined to get home, yet I couldn't ignore the nagging feeling that something was amiss.

That was when I spotted it: the same white van, parked on the opposite side of the street from where I had been walking earlier. My stomach churned with unease. I ducked behind two large trash containers lined up for pickup, their gritty gravel shifting beneath my feet.

Peering around the containers, I saw a disheveled man struggling with a large flat-screen TV. His rumpled clothes, bushy beard, and greasy hair emphasized his unkempt appearance. He grumbled under his breath as he loaded the TV into the van, his frustration clear.

"Goddammit," he muttered, glancing around nervously. "People just don't cooperate. If they won't pay attention to the invites, maybe they'll notice this."

The man stowed the TV in the van's back and muttered about needing a break. He walked back into the house, giving me a fleeting chance to investigate. Quietly, I approached the open passenger door of the van. Inside, a small tackle box caught my eye. I opened it cautiously, revealing photos, notes, a journal, and more of those cryptic invites.

As I was examining the contents, I heard a rustling behind me. My heart raced, and I quickly shut the tackle box and ducked back behind the trash containers. I glimpsed a squirrel darting out of the bushes, offering a moment of relief.

The man returned, entered the van, and drove off, leaving me hidden and bewildered. I exhaled sharply, grappling with the weight of the situation. The sense of dread I had felt all day seemed to crystallize into a more concrete fear.

I emerged from my hiding spot, feeling the oppressive weight of the day's events. The familiar streets of my neighborhood now felt eerily menacing. Every house and corner seemed more ominous, each step toward home laden with the unsettling feeling that something was terribly wrong.

As I walked home, my mind churned with questions and uncertainties. The man's muttered words replayed in my thoughts. What did he mean by "invites"? What was the significance of the TV? The more I pondered, the more tangled the threads of this mystery seemed.

The fall air felt colder against my skin, as if mirroring the chill that had settled in my chest. The rustling leaves and distant sounds of the neighborhood seemed to blur into an indistinct hum, the familiar comforts of home replaced by an overwhelming sense of dread.

What were we being invited to? The question gnawed at me with increasing intensity. Was it a gathering, a confrontation, or something else entirely? The cryptic nature of the invitations, combined with the man's frustrated comments, suggested something far more sinister than a simple prank.

Attending or confronting whatever it was the invitations were leading to filled me with anxiety. Did I even want to know what was going on? The thought of facing whatever lay behind this made me hesitant. The comfort of ignorance, however unsettling, seemed preferable to the potential horrors that might await.

I felt the weight of the day's events heavy on my shoulders as I neared my apartment. The once-familiar surroundings now seemed cloaked in an eerie, unsettling atmosphere. The white van, the disheveled man, the stolen TV—it all pointed to something much larger and more threatening than I had initially imagined.

With each step, I grappled with my fears and uncertainties. The sense of being watched, the cryptic messages, and the strange behavior of the man left me questioning my next move. It wasn't just the strange white van or the strange letter; it was the culmination of years of feeling like life was teetering on the edge of something I couldn't quite grasp. I had always been cautious, ever since my father's death had left me with a sense of dread that never quite faded.

As I approached my apartment, I noticed my neighbors, Linda and Phil, the older Asian couple who usually carried an air of quiet contentment. Linda, a petite woman with silver-streaked black hair neatly pinned back, clutched her purse tightly to her chest. Her dark eyes darted nervously, a stark contrast to the usual warmth they held when she greeted me with a kind smile. Her husband, Phil, stood tall beside her, his broad shoulders slightly hunched. His salt-and-pepper hair was disheveled, and the furrow in his brow deepened as he glanced around the parking lot, his typically steady demeanor now tinged with unease.

The visible distress on their faces immediately replaced their usual calm demeanor, drawing my concern. It wasn't like them to look so shaken, and the weight of their worry was obvious, as though it had followed them home.

"Hey, what's wrong?" I called out, my voice filled with genuine worry.

Phil, usually so warm and welcoming, looked anxious. "We got another letter," he said, his voice trembling slightly.

My stomach dropped at the news. "Really? Can I saw it?"

Linda, her face pale and her hands shaking, handed me a crumpled note. The paper felt cold and heavy in my hand. The message read "You're Invited!" in jagged, unsettling letters, with an added scrawl below: "Can't wait to see you!"

A shiver ran down my spine. The note was disturbingly similar to the one I had received earlier. "I got something like that this morning. It's definitely not a good sign."

Linda's eyes welled up with tears. "Oh, that's terrible," she whispered, cracking with fear.

Phil wrapped a protective arm around Linda, his face a mask of frustration and helplessness. "This has been going on for a long time now," he admitted, heavily. "He's been sending these letters and breaking into our place for years."

I thought back to what I had witnessed earlier. "I saw a man with a TV. He was acting suspiciously and seemed to steal things," I said, holding up the tackle box I had found. Inside were photos, notes, and more invitations. This seemed to make things worse for them.

Linda sobbed, her shoulders shaking. "What else is going on?" I pressed, trying to understand their situation better. "What's really happening?"

Phil hesitated, glancing at Linda before answering. "We know who he is. He's a thief," he said reluctantly. "He breaks into our home and steals things."

Linda's tears flowed freely. "I think the invitation is just a sick joke. It's like he's inviting himself to take whatever he wants."

Phil let out a sharp sigh, rubbing his temple as though the conversation had worn him thin. "His name is Jim," he said, his tone clipped and edged with frustration. "That's all we know." A wave of concern washed over me.

"Have you thought about calling the police?" I asked, though I already feared I knew the answer.

"We've been too scared," Linda replied.

Their helplessness was palpable, and it mirrored my growing anxiety. The late afternoon fall wind added a somber chill to the atmosphere. Phil paced restlessly while Linda clutched the letter tightly, her eyes red and swollen.

"You mentioned you know him," I said, trying to understand more. "Do you have any idea why he's targeting you?"

Phil shook his head in frustration. "No, we've tried to figure it out, but there's no pattern. It's always random and unsettling."

Linda looked at me with pleading eyes. "We're afraid to stay here, but we don't know where else to go."

The sense of dread grew stronger. The neighborhood, once so peaceful, now felt like a stage for a disturbing drama. I glanced at the letter again, its message "Can't wait to see you!" taking on a menacing tone.

"Have you reached out to other neighbors?" I asked. "Maybe they've seen or heard something that could help."

Phil shook his head. "We've kept to ourselves mostly. We didn't want to alarm anyone."

Understanding their desire for privacy, I still felt a need to sort this out. "Maybe you should tell others."

As Phil continued to pace, his face a mix of frustration and fear, Linda's voice cracked. "We're just so tired of being targeted. It's like there's no escape."

The constant stress had clearly taken a toll on them. As I was about to offer some words of comfort, a white van pulled up and parked in front of their house. My heart pounded as I recognized the driver—it was Jim, the same man I had seen earlier carrying a TV.

Jim stumbled out of the van and lurched toward Linda. He wrapped her in a tight, almost suffocating hug, his hands lingering inappropriately. Linda stiffened, clearly uncomfortable, as she tried to pull away. Phil started yelling, but Jim ignored him.

My irritation boiled over. I walked up to Jim and pulled him away from Linda. "Maybe you should, asshole," I said.

Jim pushed me away, visibly upset by the interruption. He glanced at the tackle box I was holding, his demeanor changing instantly. Without another word, he swiftly returned to his van and drove off.

As I hurriedly said my goodbyes to Linda and Phil, a sense of urgency gripped me. The unsettling encounter with Jim and the disturbing revelations about the letters had left me on edge. My phone buzzed repeatedly with missed texts from Tiffany. I glanced at the screen, seeing her mounting concern. I had promised to return home after lunch, but the day's events had pulled me deeper into a troubling mystery.

I quickly made my way back to my apartment, my thoughts racing. The white van, the cryptic notes, and Jim's alarming behavior all painted a disturbing picture. The vulnerability in my apartment felt more pronounced than ever. As I reached my building, I couldn't shake the feeling that something ominous was closing in.

The lack of Tiffany's presence heightened my anxiety. I frantically searched the apartment, checking every room and corner, but she was nowhere to be found. Her last text, sent thirty minutes ago, was a growing source of panic. I had been so absorbed in the situation with Linda and Phil that I had missed her repeated attempts to reach me.

I tried calling her several times, but each call went straight to voicemail. My worry deepened.

Returning to the tackle box, I dumped its contents out, hoping it might provide some clue to Tiffany's whereabouts. Inside, I found a stack of grim photographs and a small, worn journal. The photos depicted various scenes taken from surveillance footage. Each image was grainy but unmistakably captured moments from people's daily lives, including Linda and Phil. The thought that someone had been watching them—and possibly me—made my skin crawl.

I set the photos aside and examined the journal. I found the cover of the journal scuffed, and the pages filled with erratic handwriting. The entries detailed unsettling observations and bizarre ramblings about various people, including the couple from earlier. Mentions of "inviting" people and disturbing notes about their behavior further deepened my unease.

As I flipped through the journal, a small USB fell out. I connected it to my laptop, hoping it would shed light on the situation. The USB contained a file labeled "Security Footage." My heart raced as I clicked on the first video.

The footage showed the exterior of Linda and Phil's house at night. A figure dressed in dark clothing approached the front door. The figure glanced around nervously before using a key to unlock the door. My breath caught when I recognized the figure as Jim.

The next clip made my stomach tighten. Tiffany stepped outside; her gym bag slung over her shoulder. She paused on the porch, her head turning sharply as if listening to something. Her eyes darted to the street, scanning it quickly before she adjusted her bag and hurried down the steps. Even as she walked, her shoulders were tense, and every few steps, she glanced back over her shoulder. The unease in her movements was unmistakable, a silent scream that something—or someone—was making her feel unsafe.

Before I could process everything, my phone rang. It was a blocked number. Hesitant but determined, I answered, "Hello?"

A distorted and menacing voice came from the other end. "Jack, you think you're so clever. But you're in over your head. You can't win."

The line went dead, and a chill ran down my spine.

I set the phone down, my hands trembling with a mix of fear and anger. The distorted voice echoed in my mind, taunting me, daring me to fight back.

I glanced back at the tackle box, its contents sprawled across the table. The photos, the journal, the USB—all of it pointed to a larger puzzle, one I couldn't ignore.

My thoughts turned to Tiffany. Her absence gnawed at me like a wound, and the memory of her anxious glances over her shoulder only sharpened my resolve. Whatever this was, it had come too close.

The Queen's note replayed in my mind. "The nightmares are only the beginning…"

Maybe it was time I stopped running from those nightmares. If someone wanted me in this game, they'd get me—but on my terms. I wouldn't let them hurt Tiffany, Linda, or Phil. Not while I could fight back.

I grabbed the tackle box, shoving everything back inside, and headed for the door. This wasn't over—not yet.

CHAPTER 3

The night air bit sharply at my face as I stepped outside, my coat wrapped tightly around me. A strange tension settled in my chest, propelling me forward with purpose. The faint hum of distant crickets was drowned out by the echo of my boots crunching against the gravel.

When I reached the driveway, my gaze locked on the white van parked under the dim glow of the streetlight. Its silhouette loomed like a silent predator. Taking a deep breath, I moved toward it, each step deliberate. At the back, I slipped inside, shutting the doors behind me as quietly as I could. The stale air inside reeked of grease and gasoline. I crouched low, waiting, the sound of my heartbeat pounding in my ears.

A gruff voice muttered nearby, breaking the silence. "Lost the evidence again... Dammit." Heavy boots stomped closer, and the driver's door creaked open. The engine roared to life, sending a shudder through the van as it lurched forward.

The van weaved through countless streets, taking sharp turns that threw me against the walls. The tires screeched occasionally, and the uneven roads jostled me enough to bruise. After what felt like an eternity, the van came to an abrupt stop. I braced myself as the engine died, and the muffled sounds of voices drifted away.

Sliding the door open just enough, I slipped out and scanned my surroundings. The faint smell of pine hung in the air, mingling with the faint metallic tang of rust. A decrepit garage stood nearby, its chipped paint and broken windows a testament to years of neglect. The men disappeared inside, their laughter fading as the door shut behind them.

I crept toward the entrance, each step precise. My hand brushed against the rough wooden door as I slipped inside. The interior was dim, shadows stretching across the cracked floor and peeling walls. The faint hum of conversation guided me through the labyrinth of hallways.

At one turn, my breath hitched. A room filled with chairs lined the far wall, each one occupied. Gags silenced the captives, and thick ropes bound their arms. My stomach twisted as I recognized Linda and Phil among them. My gaze shifted, and my chest tightened when I spotted Tiffany. Her head hung low, a bruise blooming across her cheek.

I leaned against the wall, forcing myself to stay hidden. A rush of footsteps echoed down the hall. Ducking into a janitor's closet, I left the door ajar, holding my breath as the voices grew louder.

"Get them ready," Jim barked. "The Queen doesn't like delays."

One of his men hesitated. "What about the last invite?"

Jim's laughter rang out, sharp and cold. "We'll have him soon enough."

The footsteps faded, and silence filled the air once more. I slipped out of the closet and hurried back toward the captives. Tiffany's eyes widened when they met mine. I pressed a finger to my lips and began untying her ropes. She whispered my name, the relief in her voice almost breaking my focus.

Linda's soft sobs drew my attention next. As I worked to free her and Phil, the door slammed open. I froze as a group of thugs stormed in, their eyes narrowing. One lunged at me, but I sidestepped, striking him hard in the ribs. He crumpled to the floor with a wheeze.

Another swung wildly, his fist barely missing my face. I grabbed his arm, twisting it until he dropped to his knees with a grunt. The commotion was enough to set off an alarm, its blaring screech echoing through the building.

I darted into the hallway, my chest heaving. The distant pounding of boots on the floor grew louder, and I ducked into a narrow side corridor. Every step felt like a gamble, the stakes rising with each turn.

Footsteps pounded through the building, their echoes sharp and chaotic. Shouts followed, growing louder with every second. I grabbed a mop handle from the janitor's closet, my grip tightening around its worn wood. Hugging the wall, I positioned myself at the corner, muscles tense, waiting.

The first thug stormed into view. Without hesitation, I swung hard, the mop handle connecting with his head in a dull thud. He crumpled instantly. Before I could catch my breath, the second man charged. I sidestepped his lunge, kicking his hand with enough force to send his gun clattering across the floor. He stumbled, and I finished him with a swift elbow to his temple.

Adrenaline surging, I snatched the fallen gun, its weight cold and unfamiliar in my hand. Moving forward, I kept low, each step cautious. The dim, flickering lights cast erratic shadows across the maze-like corridors. My breath came shallow, every sound sharpening my focus. I had to reach the exit and ensure Tiffany, Linda, and Phil were safe.

A gunshot shattered the silence. I ducked instinctively, pressing myself against a concrete pillar as fragments of plaster rained down. Returning fire, I forced my attackers to scatter, their shouts filling the space. The standoff didn't leave room to linger. I darted from cover to cover, each movement calculated, every shot deliberate.

The exit loomed ahead, but just as hope surged, more men burst through the doors. My pulse hammered. No escape that way. I spun toward the stairwell beside me and sprinted upward, taking steps two at a time, the gunfire below driving me forward.

At the top, I burst into a large conference room. My eyes darted around, searching for another exit, but the only options were the massive windows lining one wall. I moved to the nearest window, glancing outside. The ground below wasn't far, but it wasn't close enough either.

Dammit.

I upturned a desk, crouching behind it as the door slammed open. Bullets tore through the room, splintering wood and shattering glass. The acrid smell of gunpowder stung my nose. Pinned down, I clenched the useless gun, its empty magazine a cruel reminder of my dwindling options.

Through the chaos, Jim's voice cut through. "There's no way out, Jack," he said, his tone almost amused. I peeked over the desk to see him stepping into the room, his smug grin framed by the barrel of his cronies' weapons.

Rising slowly, I faced him, my body coiled with adrenaline. "Who is the Queen? What's this about a tournament?" I demanded, my voice steady despite the pounding in my chest. "I won't let you keep abducting people."

Jim's smirk widened. "The Queen? You'll meet her soon enough." He gestured toward the room as though unveiling a grand plan. "She's handpicked every contestant. And congratulations, Jack. You're the final invite."

The weight of his words hit like a punch. Before I could react, he signaled his men to move in. I gripped the mop handle like a lifeline, swinging it hard as the first man lunged. He crumpled to the floor, but another took his place. A shot rang out, narrowly missing my shoulder and shattering the window behind me. Acting on instinct, I turned the gun on its wielder, disarming him with a sharp twist and knocking him unconscious.

"Impressive," Jim said, watching with cold detachment. "The Queen will enjoy breaking you."

As his remaining men closed in, desperation overtook reason. I turned and dove through the shattered window, the rush of night air stealing my breath. Glass sliced at my skin as the ground rushed to meet me. I landed hard, the impact jarring every bone. Pain flared in my side, but I rolled to my feet, adrenaline numbing the worst of it.

Gunfire erupted behind me, bullets tearing through the night. Jim's voice echoed faintly. "I need him alive, you idiots!" But I didn't stop. With no sign of anyone I rescued, I made my way around the building. There had to be other exits where they might have fled.

I moved swiftly but cautiously, keeping to the shadows and using the trees for cover. The building was large, and I knew it was risky, but I couldn't leave without ensuring everyone was safe. As I circled back, I noticed a side entrance, slightly ajar, that led into a dimly lit corridor.

I slipped inside, my senses on high alert. The hallway was eerily quiet, and I moved quickly but silently, listening for any sounds that might show where Tiffany, Linda, and Phil had gone. I crept through the corridors, avoiding any patrolling guards. With every step, I could feel my heart pounding, as I was conscious of the possibility of being discovered at any moment.

Suddenly, I heard muffled voices coming from a room down the hall. I inched closer and peered through the small window in the door. To my immense relief, I saw Linda and Phil huddled together, looking frightened but unharmed. I carefully opened the door and slipped inside. They looked up, their faces lighting up with relief when they saw me.

"Where's Tiffany?" Linda stammered, her hands trembling as she clutched Phil's arm, her wide eyes glistening with barely contained tears.

"We separated during the escape. We don't know where she went," Phil added, his face pale with worry.

Frustration covered my face. "We need to move, now," I whispered. "There are more guards around. Follow me and stay close."

We dashed through the corridors, avoiding detection as best as we could. As we neared an exit, I could hear footsteps and voices approaching. I motioned for everyone to hide behind a stack of crates.

The guards passed by without noticing us, and we made our way to the exit. Just as we were about to step outside, we heard a voice behind us.

"Going somewhere?" It was Jim, flanked by several of his men, all armed and ready.

My heart sank, but I knew we couldn't give up now. "Get out of here, now!" I shouted to the others as I lunged at Jim, using every bit of my training to fight off the attackers.

Linda and Phil ran toward the woods, and I fought desperately to hold off Jim and his men. The fight was brutal. I ducked under a wild punch, delivering a solid kick to the first thug's ribs. He crumpled to the ground, gasping for air. Another man swung at me with a baton, but I blocked his strike with my forearm and retaliated with a quick jab to his throat.

Jim came at me with a fierce look in his eyes. "You should have stayed out of this, Jack!" he snarled, throwing a powerful punch. I had to resort to dodging and countering with a series of rapid blows, each one driven by the need to protect my friends.

But the numbers were against me. Someone hit me from behind, causing an explosion of pain in my side as a baton connected. I stumbled, and Jim took advantage, landing a punch to my jaw that sent me reeling. I fought back, fueled by adrenaline and determination, but more men joined the fray, overwhelming me with sheer force.

Eventually, a few tasers hit me, and I convulsed in agony. My energy drained, and I had no choice but to surrender. They tied my hands behind me and dragged me back inside.

Linda and Phil were already bound and forcefully brought into the room, their faces displaying fear and despair. There was no sign of Tiffany.

"Where's Tiffany?" I demanded, struggling against my restraints.

Jim yanked me forward, forcing me to walk. "Don't worry about her. She's safe with us," he said, laughing at his own joke.

My heart ached with fear for Tiffany, but I couldn't do anything now. We were all recaptured and thrown into the back of the van. Our next stop? Who knows? The only certainty was that the fight wasn't over. We had to escape again and put an end to this nightmare.

As the van rattled down the bumpy road, I tried to think of a way out. Jim and his men had us under tight control, but there had to be an opportunity to escape. I noticed Linda and Phil huddled together, their faces etched with fear and exhaustion.

Jim's voice broke the silence. "Enjoy the ride. It's gonna be a long night."

I focused on the bindings around my wrists, testing their strength. If I could just loosen them a bit, I might have a chance. While the van continued its journey through the dark woods, I concentrated on the sounds outside, attempting to get a sense of where we are headed.

Eventually, the van came to a stop. The doors swung open, and harsh light flooded in, momentarily blinding us. We are roughly pulled out and forced to stand in a clearing surrounded by dense trees. Jim and his cronies stood in a circle around us, their weapons trained on us.

"We're here," Jim announced with a smug grin. "Welcome to the actual game."

Before I could react, someone threw a hood over my head and shoved me forward. The next thing I knew, I was being dragged along a rough path. My mind raced, trying to figure out a plan. I had to find Tiffany and get us all out of here.

CHAPTER 4

After what felt like an eternity, they forced me to sit in a chair, forcefully removed the hood, untied my arms, and I realized I was in a small, enclosed area with white walls and a TV connected to the wall in front of me. I looked over to my left and could see Linda and Phil, just as confused as me, sitting on similar chairs. On my right, Tiffany got her hood taken off just as I looked her way. I'm relieved when I saw her, and I stand up to hug her, but I'm shoved back down by a big, burly man.

"Hey, get your fucking hands off me, man!" I exclaimed, my attention drawn to a guy in a corner. I recognized him from the store—the store clerk who complained about the letter he got. From my count, there are about five of us in this room. I didn't recognize the fifth guy. Where did everyone else go that I untied earlier?

A TV flickered to life in front of me, revealing a shadowy figure whose presence was both captivating and terrifying. The woman's laughter was like nails on a chalkboard. "Welcome, everyone, and thank you for answering your invite!" More like forced to play your stupid fucking games. "Congratulations, you are now part of my exclusive Trials of the Chosen."

The words echoed in my head. "Trials of the Chosen? What are you talking about?" My voice trembled with fear and confusion.

The woman's voice dripped with malevolence. "Ah, the Trials of the Chosen. One hundred of you have been craftily and specially chosen by me, your queen. You'll be split into groups to make things more interesting. The Trials will continue until only one survivor remains—the ultimate champion. And that champion won't just win; they will become a warrior in my army."

Despair mingled with my anger. "What do we have to do?" I shouted, trying to hold onto my composure.

The woman became menacing. "The rules are simple. Survive!"

"Fuck you!" My voice cracked with defiance and desperation. "I'll get you!"

"You will?" The woman seemed intrigued but determined. "Good, keep that motivation and you may just get out of this alive!" With that, the TV abruptly shut off.

Tiffany's voice, choked with tears, "Jack!"

"Are you okay?" My voice broke, desperation and anguish flooding through me.

"Shut up!" Jim barked, irritated by her cries. "You have until dawn."

My eyes turned cold. "Fuck you! Get me out of here!"

Jim, undeterred, smiled. "Good luck!" With that, he and most of his men left, leaving only two big muscle men behind to make sure we didn't get out. Escaping was inevitable, no matter what Jim believed.

I looked around at the others, determination hardening my resolve. "We're getting out of here," I whispered. "No matter what."

The burly guards stood by the door; their faces expressionless. I knew it would be a challenge, but I had to overcome them. I took a deep breath, my mind racing with strategies. This was our only chance, and I couldn't afford to fail.

"Listen," I said quietly to the group, "we need to work together. When I give the signal, we'll take them down. Be ready."

They nodded, their fear replaced by a flicker of hope. I tensed, waiting for the right moment. The guards exchanged a glance, momentarily distracted.

"Now!" I shouted, springing into action.

We surged forward as a unit. I went straight for the guard on the left, aiming a punch at his jaw. He staggered back, and I followed up with a swift kick to his midsection. Linda and Phil tackled the second guard from behind, throwing him off balance after he swung at me. The second guard stood back up and took out a big knife hidden in a holder on his belt. The second guard stabbed the unknown fifth guy through the chest as he ran at him, causing him to fall to the ground immediately.

Cold and calculating, the first guard drew his own knife. The room became more intense with the fear of dying, and I could see the desperation in everyone's eyes. The stakes had never been higher.

"Stay back!" I shouted to Linda, Phil, and Tiffany. "I'll handle this!"

The first guard lunged at me, his knife gleaming under the harsh lights. I dodged to the side, grabbed a metal chair and swung it forcefully. The chair connected with the guard's arm, causing him to drop the knife with a grunt of pain. I didn't give him a chance to recover. I swung again, this time aiming for his head. He went down, unconscious.

The second guard, seeing his comrade fall, roared in anger and charged at me. I braced myself, waiting for the right moment. As he closed in, I sidestepped and kicked him hard on the knee, making him stumble. Phil and Linda joined in, grabbing anything they could find to hit the guard with. Together, we overwhelmed him, and he soon lay on the ground, unconscious, next to his partner.

I bent over, panting, my heart pounding in my chest. The room was eerily silent, save for our heavy breathing and the distant, dying gurgles of the fifth guy.

"Is everyone okay?" I asked, looking around. They nodded, though their faces were pale with fear and adrenaline. "We need to move. We don't have much time."

We quickly searched the guards, taking their weapons and anything else useful. Tiffany grabbed a set of keys from one of the guards' belts, her hands shaking.

"Let's go," I urged, leading the way to the door.

We moved swiftly down the corridors; the keys jingling softly in Tiffany's hand. Every shadow seemed to hold a threat, and every sound made us jump. But we couldn't stop. Not now.

A group of men started running down the hallway after us. I turned to the group and told them to get out of here, that I would distract them. Tiffany protested, her eyes wide with fear and concern, but I insisted. "Go! I'll catch up. Just get to safety!"

The store clerk didn't even wait; he just kept running. Tiffany, Linda, and Phil hesitated for a moment, their eyes pleading with me, but I gave them a stern look. "Now!" I barked. Reluctantly, they turned and fled down the hallway.

With a deep breath, I directed my gaze toward the group of men rushing in my direction.

The sound of gunshots grew louder, and my anxiety mounted. With them on my tail, I burst through a set of double doors into a dilapidated basketball gym. The faded paint and broken windows gave it an eerie, abandoned feel. Before I could process the scene, a fist collided with my face, sending me crashing to the floor. Pain exploded in my mouth as blood trickled down my chin.

Looking up, I saw five men encircling me, their laughter harsh and mocking. Fury surged within me, eclipsing the pain. My adrenaline was a roaring blaze, dulling the agony. I rose with renewed strength, my anger transforming into a potent force.

"You think you can take us all on?" one man sneered, cracking his knuckles.

"You have no idea what I'm capable of," I growled, wiping the blood from my chin.

With quick, decisive movements, I uppercut the man on my left. His teeth shattered, and he flew backward, landing with a bone-jarring thud. The man on my right swung at me, but I ducked and grabbed his arm, twisting it with brutal force. A sickening crack echoed as the bone broke, and he screamed in pain. I followed up with a fierce kick to his face, his nose splintering with a spray of blood.

Two more men lunged at me. I spotted a push broom lying nearby and grabbed it. Swinging it with all my might, I struck one man in the head. He flipped through the air at the same time I spun and jabbed the broom handle into the other man's stomach, the sharp end piercing his flesh. He crumpled, clutching his injury, as his friend landed with a thump. To the guy clutching his stomach, I delivered a powerful kick to his face, breaking his jaw.

The last attacker, visibly terrified, backed away, his fear uncontrolled. "Oh, shit! Oh, shit!" he muttered, running away, his panic clear. I hurled the sharpened broom handle at him, impaling his shoulder. He stumbled, tripping on a deflated basketball, and crashed to the floor, unconscious.

Breathing heavily, I looked around the gym, now eerily silent except for the occasional groan from the fallen men. My body ached, but the adrenaline kept me moving. I bent down and retrieved a knife from one of the unconscious men, gripping it tightly.

Leaving the gym, I made my way down another hallway. The oppressive silence of the building pressed in on me, heightening my sense of isolation. The dangerous game I had become entangled in was a constant reminder, as every step ominously echoed.

Lost and alone, I was determined to survive. The fight wasn't over, and I had to stay sharp if I wanted to find my friends and end this nightmare.

As I crept through the dimly lit corridors, the walls seemed to close in around me. My breathing was heavy, each exhale a reminder of the pain and exhaustion setting in. I couldn't afford to stop. The stakes were too high.

A voice echoed through the hallway. "You can't run forever, Jack!" Jim's voice dripped with sadistic amusement, the sound bouncing off the walls.

My knuckles turned white as I tightened my grip on the knife. "I'm not running," I muttered under my breath. "I'm coming for you."

Navigating through the labyrinthine corridors, I came upon another set of double doors. I pushed them open cautiously, revealing a large storage room filled with crates and shelves. The smell of dust and decay was overwhelming, mixing with the acrid scent of sweat and fear.

As I stepped inside, I heard a faint rustling. I froze, my heart pounding in my ears. The sound grew louder, and I realized it was coming from behind a stack of crates. I crept closer, knife at the ready.

"Jack?" A whisper broke the silence, and I exhaled in relief.

"Tiffany!" I rushed forward, pulling her into a tight embrace. "Thank God you're okay."

Her body trembled against mine, and I felt her tears soaking into my shirt. "I was so scared," she whispered, her voice breaking. "I thought I'd never see you again."

"I thought I'd lost you," I said, my voice heavy with emotion. I cupped her face in my hands, forcing her to look at me. "We need to get out of here. I can't lose you, Tiffany."

"We have little time," I said, with fear and determination. "We need to find Linda and Phil and—"

"They're here," she cut in, her voice urgent. "They're safe."

I nodded, wiping her tears. As if on cue, Linda and Phil emerged from behind another stack of crates. They looked exhausted but relieved to see me.

"We're all together again," Phil said, his voice shaking with emotion. "Now let's get the hell out of here."

The words barely registered in my mind. I could see the raw fear in her eyes mingled with the anger of feeling trapped and helpless. We moved quickly, navigating through the building with newfound determination.

Finally, we found an exit at the end of the hallway. The metal door was slightly ajar, and a sliver of moonlight cut through the darkness.

"We're almost there," I said, urging everyone forward.

Just then, Jim and his men appeared at the other end of the hallway, blocking our path. Their faces were grim and menacing, and Jim's cruel smile only made the situation worse.

"Going somewhere?" Jim drawled, a twisted grin spreading across his face as his eyes narrowed, his words slicing through the tense air like a predator toying with its prey.

CHAPTER 5

I glanced slightly to my left and noticed a door leading to another hallway. I quietly signaled Tiffany. "That way," I mouthed, hoping she understood.

Her eyes met mine, and she gave a subtle nod.

I stepped forward, knife in hand, ready to fight. "This ends now."

Jim laughed, a cold, menacing sound. "You think you can survive?"

Just before I made a move, Jim's voice became commanding. "TAKE THEM ALL OUT! DON'T COME BACK UNTIL THEY ARE ALL DEAD!"

With that, his men charged with deadly force. We ran as fast as we could through the door. I wedged my knife into the door frame, creating a temporary barricade. The sound of splintering wood and angry shouts echoed behind us.

Eventually, I caught up to Tiffany, Linda, and Phil, my breath coming in ragged gasps. We found a small, dusty room, temporary refuge from the chaos. Old, forgotten furniture and cobwebs filled the room, but it provided us with a momentary shield.

"I'm going to stay here," I said, determined. "I'll buy you enough time to escape."

Tiffany's eyes widened with disbelief. "No, Jack. We can't just leave you behind!"

Assertively, I stated, "I need to do this. I have to make sure you get to safety. I can't lose you all now."

Her face crumpled with anguish. She reached out, clutching my arm with a fierce grip. "We were supposed to build a life together, Jack. We were supposed to make it out of this. Don't you dare leave me now."

The intensity of her words, the pain in her eyes, were like a knife to my heart. "Tiffany, I'm doing this because I love you. Because you matter to me more than anything else. If I don't do this, I'll never forgive myself."

Tiffany's tears fell freely now. "I love you too, Jack. More than you'll ever know. But I can't stand the thought of losing you. We had plans... dreams. I want that future. I need that future."

I pulled her into a tight embrace, holding her as if it was the last thing I would ever do. "We will have that future, Tiffany. I promise you that. But right now, you need to get out of here. Live for both of us. Live and make those dreams come true."

She clung to me. "I'll do whatever it takes. I'll make sure we have that future. But please, come back to me."

"I will," I said, my voice cracking with emotion. "I'll find a way. Just promise me you'll stay safe."

With one last, lingering hug, we pulled apart. Tiffany, Linda, and Phil slipped out of the room and into the darkness, their silhouettes disappearing into the night. I took a deep breath, steeling myself for the challenges ahead.

Alone now, I stood there in silence. The empty room seemed to amplify the solitude I felt, a stark contrast to the desperate rush of emotions moments earlier. Jim's men would search for us, and I needed to buy as much time as possible. I couldn't afford to fail. The stakes were too high, and I had to see this through to the end. I never had a plan. I never do.

Focusing my mind, I took another deep breath. The burden of uncertainty couldn't consume me. I needed to act quickly. I forced my thoughts away from the fear gnawing at the edges of my consciousness and focused on the task at hand. My only chance of survival was to stay unpredictable and relentless.

Moving cautiously through the dimly lit corridors, I followed the distant echoes of gunfire. Each shot reverberated through the building, a grim reminder of the danger closing in. My footsteps were careful, each sound amplified in the tense silence. The fear of being discovered kept me on edge.

Suddenly, I spotted two men ahead, their backs turned as they chatted in low, urgent tones. I gripped the gun tightly, taking a deep breath to steady my nerves. With practiced stealth, I approached them from behind; the darkness cloaking my movements.

In one swift, decisive action, I pulled the trigger. With a muffled groan, the first man collapsed. The second man turned, shock etched on his face, but before he could react, I took him out with another shot. The quiet thud of their bodies hitting the floor was the only sound in the tense silence.

I stepped over their bodies, the gun feeling like a heavy, reassuring weight in my hand. The risk of being discovered was too high. I needed to keep moving, to stay one step ahead of Jim's men.

As I pressed forward, the faint sounds of distant conversations and the occasional burst of gunfire guided me. I briefly wondered how the other groups of survivors were faring. The uncertainty gnawed at me, but I forced myself to focus on the immediate task.

The building's layout was a maze, and I navigated through the labyrinthine corridors with a mix of instinct and desperation. Each turn, each step, felt like a gamble against the unknown. The gunfire grew louder, signaling I was getting closer to the source of the conflict.

I finally reached a small alcove overlooking a large open area. Below, I could see several men moving about, their attention focused on their search. I took a moment to survey the scene, strategizing my next move. My heart raced as I weighed my options. The only way through would be to create a diversion.

I noticed a stack of flammable materials near the far end of the room. With grim determination, I made my way over, carefully avoiding the scattered patrols. I set up a makeshift trap, positioning a few items to create a minor explosion. Once everything was in place, I set it off, the sudden burst of fire and noise drawing attention away from my path.

Using the chaos to my advantage, I slipped past the distracted guards and snatched a knife from a nearby table, feeling its cold metal in my hand. The excitement coursed through my veins as I moved deeper into the building, navigating the dimly lit corridors with urgency. Every second mattered; Tiffany and the others needed to be safe, and I had to stay focused.

The gunfire grew louder as I approached a door. I burst through it, only to find my mother hiding behind a wall, her gun shaking in her grip. The shock of seeing her made my heart pound harder. I quickly took cover on the opposite side of the room.

"Jack!" she cried out, her eyes wide with fear and relief.

"Mom, what are you doing here?" I shouted, but the sound of gunfire drowned out my words.

My mind raced, anger and confusion mingled. The realization that this was now personal, driven by the cruel "Queen's" schemes, fueled my resolve. I had to end this nightmare.

Pushing aside my concern for my mother, I moved into the adjoining room where the shots were coming from. The sight of Jim smirking with a sadistic glee ignited a burning rage within me.

"Finally, you and I," I growled, my voice trembling with fury.

Jim's laughter was chilling. "You think you can take me on?" he taunted, his eyes glinting with malice.

I aimed my gun at him, but the familiar CLICK of an empty chamber sent a wave of frustration to me. I threw the gun at him, lunging with my knife. Jim ducked, expertly dodging my attack, causing me to stumble forward. I quickly recovered, my anger giving me renewed strength.

Jim hurled a knife at me, which I dodged by a hair's breadth. I spun to face him; the hallway echoing with the sounds of our combat. He moved with a fluid grace, his strikes precise but his arrogance clear. Our brawl was a flurry of movement—punches, kicks, and parries. Each hit was a burst of raw emotion, a manifestation of my rage and desperation.

Jim's face contorted with annoyance as I landed a solid punch to his midsection, driving him back. He retaliated with a vicious elbow to my ribs, pain radiating through me, but I pushed through it. My focus was laser-sharp, fueled by a need for justice and survival.

I grabbed a metal pipe from the ground, swinging it hard. Jim blocked the strike with his forearm, but the impact forced him to stagger. Seizing the opportunity, I followed up with a barrage of quick strikes, each one landing with satisfying thuds. Jim's smirk faltered, replaced by a grimace of pain.

In a final, desperate move, I threw a powerful kick at Jim's head, sending him crashing against the wall. He slumped to the floor, unconscious, his reign of terror ending with a resounding thud.

Breathing heavily, I turned to find my mother standing nearby; her face was pale and tear-streaked. I rushed over and enveloped her in a tight hug, feeling the warmth of her body and the familiarity of her presence.

"Mom, I've missed you," I said, the words catching in my throat, thick with emotion.

"I'm so sorry, Jack," she replied, her words trembling like a fragile thread. "I missed you too."

Tears welled up in my eyes as I held her close. "I was angry and hurt after you disappeared, but seeing you again… I'm just so relieved."

She pulled back slightly, looking at me with a mix of regret and love. "I just wanted to keep you safe, but I saw now that I should've stayed in contact."

"Mom, why are you here?" I asked, the weight of desperation tightening my chest. "How did you end up in this hell?"

Her eyes filled with pain as she tried to explain. "I got an invitation. At first, I thought it was some sort of mistake or a cruel joke. But then, they came for me. They forced me into their van and brought me here with another group of people. If I wanted to, I wouldn't be able to fight. I thought… I thought maybe if I played along, I could find a way out."

My anger flared. "So, you're part of that sick and twisted queen's tournament too? Why would she put you in this nightmare with me?"

She looked down, her shoulders slumped. "I'm so sorry, Jack. I didn't want any of this."

Calming down a bit, I needed Mom to know this has nothing to do with her. "Mom, I need to tell you something," I said, my voice trembling. "I got an invitation, too. That's how I ended up here. That's how we all got here."

Her eyes widened in shock. "You got an invitation?"

I nodded, cutting her off gently. "Yeah, I received one just like you. They brought me here the same way, after I was abducted. I tried to fight my way out; I was so close until I was overpowered."

She looked down; her face a mixture of sadness and disbelief. "I thought it was a mistake. I didn't know they were targeting you too."

"They did, plus many more," I said, my voice filled with urgency. "They've been playing this sick game with all of us."

"I think one hundred people, according to what that lady on the TV said—the Queen, is it?"

"Yeah, all we have to do is survive her games, no matter what. What will she do if we all survive? Make us fight each other?" I laughed at the absurd thought before quickly getting back on track. "But we have to stay focused."

She nodded, her resolve hardening. "You're right. We need to escape. I just wish I had known you were here sooner."

"We'll figure it out," I assured her. "Right now, we need to keep moving. We're getting out."

We moved through the corridors, my determination to protect her only grew stronger. We ran into many lifeless bodies that didn't make it, including that stocking clerk. Each body was a stark reminder of the stakes and the brutality of the tournament. My mother gripped my arm tightly, her eyes wide with a mix of fear and determination.

Finally, we stepped outside. As we navigated the stuffy corridors, the cold night air hit us, creating a stark contrast. The first light of dawn broke on the horizon, casting a faint glow over the landscape. The sun would be up at any moment. We had beaten the deadline set by the Queen.

CHAPTER 6

I took a deep breath, feeling a small sense of relief. "We made it out, Mom. But we're not safe yet."

I scanned the area, my eyes searching for any sign of them. The silence was unsettling, broken only by the distant sounds of the forest waking up. Every second felt like an eternity, the uncertainty gnawing at me.

"Stay close," I whispered to my mother, guiding her toward a path that led away from the building.

We moved quickly and quietly toward the tree line up ahead, my senses on high alert. Every rustle in the bushes, every shadow, seemed like a potential threat. My mind raced with thoughts of getting to safety. Were Tiffany and the others safe? Had they found a place to hide? Suddenly, Tiffany jumped out from behind a tree.

My heart leaped. "Tiffany!"

"Jack! You made it!" She ran to me, and we embraced in a tight, desperate hug that lingered. The relief and joy of seeing her safe overwhelmed us both. The warmth of her body against mine was a stark contrast to the cold fear that had gripped me moments before. Still hugging and kissing Tiffany, I noticed Linda and Phil standing up from their hiding spots, looking equally relieved. We all embraced the weight of our ordeal momentarily lifting. It felt surreal, like a fleeting moment of peace amidst chaos.

"We were so worried," Tiffany said, her voice shaking with emotion. "We didn't know if you'd make it out."

"I didn't think I was going to, either," I replied, my voice firm. "My motivation to be with you drove me."

Phil looked at my mother, his expression was curious. "Is this…?"

"This is my mom, Marishka," I explained, holding her hand. "She was taken here too, just like us. Mom, these are my neighbors, Phil and Linda." My mom said hello while shaking their hands. Her grip was firm, but I could feel her trembling. "And this is my girlfriend, Tiffany." My mom smiled through her tears.

"Oh, you're so pretty." Mom gave her a hug.

"Thanks." Tiffany giggled, but her eyes were still clouded with fear.

"We're all in this together," Linda said with a determined smile, her voice steady. "And we're going to get out—"

A shot fired from the distance cut Linda off. We were all shocked and confused at first, before we saw Phil falling to the ground, dead. Another shot rang out, and that's when we finally snapped back to reality and ducked for cover.

Linda started screaming, crawled over to her husband, held him, and cried while he slowly passed. Her sobs were gut-wrenching, echoing the pain we all felt.

I wanted to calm her down, but with bullets flying, there was no way at this point. "Linda, we have to move! We can't stay here!"

Tiffany tugged at my arm, her eyes wide with fear. "Jack, what do we do?"

I scanned the area, trying to spot the shooter. "We need to find better cover. Stay low and move quickly."

We crawled toward thicker underbrush, every muscle tensed for the next shot. The air was thick with fear and desperation. My mother clung to my arm; her eyes filled with terror. "Jack, what if we don't make it?"

"Just let me think, Mom," I said firmly, though my mind was racing. The shooter could be anywhere, and we were out in the open. I needed to get us to safety, and fast.

Linda, through her sobs, nodded and reluctantly let go of Phil's lifeless body. But then, with a final act of defiance, Linda stood up, her tears turning into rage. She screamed bloody murder before running as fast as her older body would let her toward the shooting.

Within seconds, someone shot her in the head, causing her body to swiftly slide across the tall grass before coming to a stop. We were mortified, but deep down inside, we understood the pain and anger she felt.

Tiffany's panic escalated, her breathing becoming erratic. She clung to me, her body shaking uncontrollably. "Jack, what are we going to do? They're all dead! We're going to die too!"

I pulled her close, trying to steady my breathing. "We have to keep moving. We can't let their deaths be in vain."

"But... but... Phil... Linda!" Tiffany's sobs were uncontrollable. "I can't do this, Jack. I can't! We're going to die!"

My mother looked at me, her eyes filled with a mixture of terror and determination. "Jack, I believe in you. Lead us out of here."

I nodded, swallowing the lump in my throat. "Stay low and follow me."

Tiffany's sobbing made it harder for us to move quietly. Each step felt like a struggle against the rising tide of fear. I tried to soothe her, but the sheer terror in her eyes mirrored my inner turmoil.

"We need to keep moving, Tiffany," I urged, my voice firm but gentle. "I know it's hard, but we can't stop now."

Through her tears, she nodded, but her body continued to be wracked with sobs. "I'm sorry, Jack. I'm so scared."

"I know," I whispered, squeezing her hand. "But I'm here. We're going to get through this."

We crawled through the underbrush, every sound amplified in the forest's silence. The weight of loss pressed heavily on us, but the need to survive pushed us forward. My mother, ever the pillar of strength, kept her focus, her grip on my arm reassuring.

As we reached a denser part of the forest near a roadway, I motioned for everyone to stop. "We need to find a safer place to regroup and figure out our next move. Maybe, if we're careful, we could flag someone down driving by."

Taking a step onto the road, Tiffany's tears turned into frustration, her voice filled with pain. "What's the point to all of this? They're just gonna drag us into another sick game. Remember, we are in a tournament? We will have to keep fighting no matter what!"

I was silent. I had no words, no rebuttal. She was right; this nightmare would not end soon.

My mother placed a comforting hand on Tiffany's shoulder, her voice soft yet resolute. "Tiffany, I know it's hard. We're all scared. But we have to believe there's a way out of this. We have to keep fighting—"

In frustration, Tiffany pushed my mom away from her, the situation coming to a boil. "Fuck that, bitch!" Tiffany screamed in anger, as I helped my mom up off the ground. "I'll kill that stupid 'Queen' myself!"

I didn't have any time to react when a white van came out of nowhere and hit Tiffany hard. The sound of the impact was sickening. The van came out of nowhere and hit Tiffany hard, tossing her body like a rag doll. Then it dragged her underneath as it kept going, eventually stopping down the road a few hundred yards.

Mom and I screamed at the impact, our emotions high and raw. I couldn't think, only react. I ran to Tiffany, holding her broken body, crying as I held her tight. The world around me faded, her life slipping away in my arms. The anguish was unbearable, a tearing, gut-wrenching pain that consumed me.

"Tiffany, no! Please, no!" I sobbed, my voice breaking with despair. Her eyes were wide open, staring at nothing, and I could feel the warmth leaving her body. "Stay with me, please! I need you!"

Her blood was everywhere, soaking my clothes, my hands. I could feel her last, shallow breaths against my neck, and then there was nothing. Just silence. The finality of it hit me like a tidal wave, crashing over me, drowning me in sorrow.

"Tiffany, I love you," I whispered, my voice choked with tears. "I love you so much. Please, don't leave me." But she was gone, and the emptiness that filled me was unbearable.

When I finally came to my senses, my mother was frantically pulling at my shirt, her face a mask of terror and urgency. The van had turned around and was hurtling back toward us, its engine roaring like a predator on the hunt. I barely shoved her aside, rolling over her as the van sped past, the whoosh of its tires stirring up the dust and dirt around us.

My eyes darted back to Tiffany's lifeless body lying motionless on the road. A wave of devastation crashed over me. I clutched her cold, lifeless form as I kneeled beside her. Through choked sobs, my voice barely audible, I whispered, "I love you." "I'm so sorry I couldn't keep my promise to you. I failed you."

My mother's frantic voice cut through the haze of my grief. "Jack, we have to move! We can't stay here!" She pulled me to my feet, her own eyes filled with tears and desperation. The urgency in her voice pierced through my sorrow, forcing me to focus.

The van's engine roared again, its monstrous presence creeping closer. I glanced at my mother, my heart pounding with a fierce, burning rage. "Stay down," I ordered, my voice strained but resolute.

I stepped out onto the road, positioning myself in front of Tiffany's lifeless body. The van skidded to a stop, its headlights blinding. Jim's face appeared at the driver's window; blood smeared across his features. His eyes were cold, a cruel smile playing on his lips.

"Hey, Jack," he sneered, glancing at his watch. "You've got about twenty minutes left before dawn. Looks like you will not make it." His laughter was a jarring, sadistic sound, a mockery of our suffering.

Anger surged through me, hot and raw, mingling with my grief. Every injustice, every moment of helplessness, crystallized into a single, explosive emotion. My chest tightened with rage, and I felt a fierce, primal scream rising from the depths of my soul. "I'm done with this shit! Come at me, motherfucker!"

Fueled by a torrent of fury and sorrow, I ran toward the van, every step driven by a desperate need to end this nightmare. The vehicle roared toward me, its headlights cutting through the darkness like a blade. My heart raced; my muscles burned with the intensity of my emotions.

A single, focused purpose emerged because of the pain of losing Tiffany, the anger at the Queen's twisted game, and the sheer frustration of being trapped in this hellish situation. The van closed in, its engine a deafening roar that filled the night. The world narrowed to the van and me, a brutal clash of wills.

As the van hurtled toward me, I held onto the hope that my act of defiance might break the cycle of torment, that somehow, my sacrifice would make a difference. I could hear my mother's voice screaming out, but it felt distant from my rage-filled mind. If it was to be the end, I would meet it with a fire in my heart, determined to fight against the darkness that had claimed so much from me.

With a surge of adrenaline and determination, I leaped onto the front of the van, my fingers gripping the cold metal of the hood. The impact jolted me, but I held on as Jim's erratic steering threatened to throw me off. The van swerved violently, tires screeching against the asphalt as it veered left and right, desperately trying to shake me loose.

Jim's face was a mask of twisted satisfaction as he grabbed his gun, aiming wildly at me through the windshield. The gunshots rang out, deafening and close, each bullet ricocheting off the metal with a sharp, echoing clang. The van's interior became a chaotic storm of noise and danger as Jim's erratic movements made his aim imprecise. Bullets pierced the thin metal of the van's exterior, narrowly missing me as I clung to the front.

Fighting against the wind that battered me, I scrambled up onto the roof of the van. The gusts made it a struggle to maintain my balance, but I pushed through the disorientation and fear. The top of the van was a narrow, unstable platform, but it offered a brief reprieve from Jim's frantic gunfire.

I crawled forward; the wind teared at my clothes and hair, my eyes stinging with the rush of air. I spotted the side door of the van, slightly ajar from the wind's pressure. With a last burst of strength, I reached the edge of the roof and pried open the sliding door.

The door slid open with a groan, pushed by the relentless wind. Inside, the van's interior was a chaotic mess, with bags and equipment scattered around. Jim, still struggling to control the vehicle, shot at me with increasing desperation, his aim still off.

"Jack, you're too late!" Jim shouted over the roar of the engine, his voice tinged with both irritation and cruel amusement. "You think you can stop me? This is just the beginning!"

I ducked and rolled inside the van, narrowly avoiding another round of bullets. "You think this is a game? People are dead because of you. Tiffany is dead!" My voice filled with raw anger and grief. "I'm ending this now!"

Once inside, the van lurched and swayed as Jim fought to regain control. I glanced around, assessing my surroundings. The van was a cramped, disorganized space, but I needed to end this fight quickly.

With renewed determination, I moved toward Jim. He focused his attention on the road but kept glancing at me with a mix of annoyance and malevolence.

"You think you're some kind of hero?" Jim sneered, his hands shaking slightly as he continued to steer erratically. "You're just another pawn in her sick game!"

"You're wrong," I said through gritted teeth, closing in on him. "I'm not a pawn. I'm the one who's going to make sure you pay for everything you've done."

As I reached Jim, he whirled around, his face twisted in anger. "You think you can stop me? I'm not afraid of you!"

I grabbed Jim by the collar, my fury unrestrained. "You should be afraid. This ends now!"

Jim struggled against me, his attempts to wriggle free only making him more desperate. The van swerved dangerously, but I held firmly.

As I shouted, "This ends here!" my voice cracked with the weight of every loss, every betrayal. The fury I felt was a wild, blazing fire, and I was determined to see it through. Jim's face, contorted in rage, was almost unrecognizable as he wrestled with the steering wheel, the van swerving wildly beneath us.

In a moment of desperation, Jim slammed the gas pedal, his eyes leaving the road. The van lurched forward, hurtling toward the bridge embankment with terrifying speed. The impact was brutal, the metal frame groaning and twisting as we both went through the windshield in a shower of glass and debris.

The world became a chaotic blur as we plummeted into the cold, dark water below. The force of the fall was a shocking jolt, the water slapping against me with icy ferocity. I struggled to regain my senses, pushing through the disorienting rush of the fall.

Breaking the surface, I gasped for air, my lungs burning. Jim surfaced nearby, his expression a mix of fury and confusion. I glanced up to see the van precariously perched on the edge of the embankment, its position shifting dangerously. The sounds of metal creaking and the van's groans were ominous, signaling an imminent collapse.

Jim's anger was palpable as he splashed through the water, trying to yell at me. The water and the surrounding chaos choked his voice, though full of venom. "You think you've won, Jack? This isn't over!"

Before he could say more, the van, unable to hold on any longer, finally gave way. With a thunderous crash, it fell from the embankment, its metal frame colliding with the water and Jim's body with a sickening impact. The sound of the van hitting the water was a brutal finale, the metal and water clashing together in a chaotic explosion of noise and debris.

I swam to the shore, my movements heavy with exhaustion and a profound sense of relief. The adrenaline was fading, leaving me shivering and spent. As I crawled out of the water, I took a moment to breathe deeply, my chest heaving with each breath. The sight of the van sinking beneath the water was a grim reminder of the battle that had just ended, but the victory felt hollow against the backdrop of the losses I've endured.

As I lay next to the water, exhausted and battered, Jim's watch floated past me, its alarm beeping intermittently. The dawn's early light painted the world in hues of gray and gold, a cruel reminder of my survival amid the relentless pain. The fleeting sense of victory felt hollow, overshadowed by the grim reality of the situation and the uncertainty of my mother's fate.

Summoning every ounce of strength left, I dragged myself up the embankment. My body was a cascade of aches and pains, each movement a battle against fatigue and worry. I scanned the road desperately, hoping to spot my mother, but the distance rendered my search futile. The weight of her potential danger pressed heavily on my heart.

A white van rolled up with a menacing rumble, its tires crunching against the gravel. A man in a suit emerged from the driver's side, opening the sliding door with a practiced ease. He stood silently to the side, his expression unreadable as if he were a mere spectator to the unfolding horror. My drenched and shivering body felt as though it was moving through a thick, molasses-like sludge as I approached the van, each step sapping what little strength I had left.

The Queen's sinister laugh rang out, slicing through the morning stillness with a chilling echo. The sound sent shivers down my spine, and I glanced inside to see her seated on a throne-like chair, her posture exuding both regal authority and malevolent intent. Her eyes gleamed with a twisted delight, and her laughter was a maddening melody that seemed to penetrate my very soul.

"Congratulations, Jack. You've survived the first Trial!" Her voice dripped with twisted satisfaction, each syllable a reminder of the cruelty and perversion of this game. "You've shown quite a lot of tenacity. I admire that in a contestant."

A sharp sting seared through my neck. My hand flew to the source, finding a dart embedded in my skin. Panic surged through me, but a suffocating drowsiness swiftly overtook it. My vision blurred, the edges of my world dimming as my limbs grew heavy and unresponsive.

The Queen's laughter receded into the background; her voice now tinged with a mocking playfulness. "Oh, and don't think you're off the hook just yet. This is only the beginning. The real challenge is yet to come. I hope you're ready for the next Trials of the Chosen. You will face even greater perils, and remember, the ultimate champion will be chosen to join my army."

As the darkness enveloped me, the man in the suit moved toward me with an unsettling calmness. His grip was cold and unfeeling as he caught me, his touch was a stark contrast to the warmth I yearned for. He lowered me gently to the ground, the rough texture of his suit pressing against my skin.

The last image burned into my fading consciousness was the Queen's satisfied smirk, her eyes glinting with a malevolent promise of more torment. Her last words echoed in my mind, a haunting reminder that the nightmare was far from over and that the true extent of the Trials was yet to be revealed.

CHAPTER 7

When I was eight years old, life was already hard without my dad. He had passed away a few years earlier, leaving a void in our lives that was impossible to fill. It was just Mom and me, trying to navigate a world that felt colder and lonelier without him. She was resilient and did her best to make life as normal as possible. We found joy in the little things, like watching movies together or going to the park. But everything changed when she married Kyle.

At first, Kyle seemed nice enough. He smiled, laughed, and even brought me toys. But soon, his true colors showed. The hitting started almost immediately after the wedding, and it quickly escalated into brutal beatings. He never needed a reason to lash out; any small inconvenience would set him off. Mom tried to shield me from his anger, but sometimes, I endured it, too.

Kyle moved us across the country to a rundown trailer in a desolate area. We were cut off from family and friends. Mom got pregnant shortly after the move. She was afraid to tell Kyle at first, fearing his reaction. She waited until her belly showed, hoping that maybe the news of a baby would soften him.

Having a sibling excited me. I would rub Mom's tummy, feeling the tiny kicks, and we would talk about names and plans. But the day Kyle found out about the baby, everything changed.

He had been drinking heavily that night, his anger brewing with every sip. When he saw her growing belly, he erupted. His fury was terrifying. He screamed obscenities, calling her names, and then he attacked. His fists flew, landing on her face, stomach, and back. I watched in horror, unable to do anything.

Desperate to protect her, I grabbed a bottle from the kitchen counter and smashed it over his head. The glass shattered, cutting my hand, but I didn't care. Blood streamed down Kyle's face, mingling with the alcohol, and he stumbled back, momentarily stunned.

I was crying, trying to hold Mom and keep her conscious. But Kyle wasn't done. He grabbed the back of my shirt and flung me across the living room. I landed on the couch, dazed and terrified. Kyle grabbed a knife from the kitchen, his eyes wild with rage, and started walking toward me.

Mom, bleeding and desperate, got up and grabbed his knife-wielding arm. She tried to push him away, but he was too strong. As he reached me, she did the only thing a loving mother would do—she threw herself over me, shielding me from the blade. The knife plunged into her back. She squeezed me tightly, her body shaking with pain.

I knew something was wrong, but my sobs drowned out my understanding. Kyle yanked the knife out and dropped it, his face twisted in a mixture of rage and fear. He stormed out, slamming the door behind him, and I heard his truck speed away. Blood drained from Mom's mouth.

"I love you," she whispered, before collapsing to the floor. A pool of blood formed around her. Remembering the emergency plan Mom had always gone over with me, I grabbed the phone and called 911 with trembling hands.

The police arrived quickly, their lights flashing through the windows. Paramedics rushed in; their faces grim as they assessed the situation. I felt sick from the blood loss and the overwhelming fear. I was told to lie down in the ambulance.

The doctor informed me that Mom was stable but needed rest when I woke up in the hospital. I could still see her. I pulled a chair up to her bedside, rested my head on her arm, and cried until I couldn't anymore.

The doctor burst into the room, waking us both. Mom, still groggy, rubbed my head and looked up at the doctor, her eyes wide with fear. "Where am I? What happened?"

"Ma'am, you're in the hospital. You were severely stabbed in the back. If it wasn't for your son calling 911, you might not have made it," the concerned doctor explained.

Mom looked at me, pulling me close. She kissed my forehead and hugged me tightly, tears streaming down her face. "Thank you, Jack. You saved my life."

She then asked the question I knew was coming, but dreaded hearing. "Is the baby all right?"

The doctor frowned; his expression was heavy with sorrow. "Ma'am, I'm going to be honest with you. It was an extremely severe stab wound. The knife went through your abdomen. The baby didn't make it. It was already gone by the time you arrived. I'm really sorry."

Mom held me tighter, a guttural scream escaping her lips before she broke down into sobs. I cried with her, devastated by the loss. Her anguish was palpable, a raw, aching wound that I felt deep in my heart.

In the months that followed, we attended counseling sessions. With time, we moved past the trauma, though the pain lingered like a shadow over our lives. We clung to each other for support, finding solace in our shared grief and love. Eventually, we found happiness again, a fragile but beautiful thing that we nurtured together.

As I grew older and moved out, life took over, and we drifted apart. But the bond we shared, and the memories of those dark times remained, shaping who I am today. Even now, I can feel the strength of her love and the depth of her sacrifice, a constant reminder of what we endured and overcame together. The events of my childhood left scars that would never fully heal, but they also taught me the value of resilience, courage, and the fierce, unbreakable love of a mother for her child.

CHAPTER 8

I woke up. It was daytime. I could tell because the light was shining through the window with bars. Bars? What was going on? Where was I?

I sat up, my head spinning. The room was bare and sterile, with a small cot and a toilet in the corner. My memories were still fuzzy, and I struggled to piece together what happened. My heart skipped a beat as I remembered my mom. Where was she? Was she safe? It had been seven years since I had seen her.

Tears blurred my vision as I tried to recall anything about a mysterious woman. My body felt strangely better, no longer wracked with pain. What was going on? The cell door creaked open, interrupting my frantic thoughts.

Three men dressed like soldiers march in, their faces cold and unfeeling. One of them yanked me up roughly, slapping handcuffs on my wrists. "All right, get up. It's time!" he barks.

"Am I in jail?" I asked, my voice trembling. The soldier just laughed, a cruel sound that echoed in the small space. He shoved me forward, and I almost tripped from the force. We walked down a dimly lit corridor lined with empty cells. Questions raced through my mind, but I doubted anyone would answer them.

The corridor seemed endless, but finally, one soldier walked ahead and unlocked a heavy door. They pushed me through, and I stumbled into an enormous room. It looked like a miniature arena, with other people emerging from various doors around the room.

Mirrors lined the walls, reflecting our confused and frightened faces. I reached the center of the room, and the soldiers uncuffed me. The soldiers pushed more people into the middle, joining us in this twisted spectacle.

A booming voice echoed throughout the arena, sounding like an older woman. "Welcome to Beast Island!" she announced with false cheer. "We are so glad you could make it!"

As if I had a choice! I gritted my teeth, annoyed but trying to stay calm.

"We have a wonderful day planned, another exciting event for you! For those of you who made it this far, congratulations! That means you have passed the first Trial. The challenge was to simply survive until dawn. Fifty-nine of you made it through that event. But only a very select few did an extraordinary job, like Jack, who ended the Trial with only seconds to spare after a grueling fight inside a runaway van that crashed into a river. It was truly remarkable. It surpassed our expectations. So, we are very excited about the next Trial! And remember, this tournament ends when there's only one left. Good luck!"

Her words sank in, and an icy dread filled me. I noticed someone in the crowd. My heart skipped a beat. It looked like my mom! I pushed through the crowd, my mind set on reaching her.

"Mom!" I called out, my voice breaking.

"Jack! Is that you?" She pulled me into a tight hug, her tears soaking my shoulder. "Oh God, I thought I lost you!"

"I'm still alive, but this is so messed up," I said, holding her as tightly as I could. The crushing weight of my grief shattered the brief relief of finding my mom. I remembered Tiffany, and my chest tightened with sorrow.

My eyes scanned the crowd desperately. Tiffany... where is she? My heart ached with every passing second. The realization hit me like a physical blow. She's gone. The memory of her death was too vivid, too horrific. I couldn't bear it. My breath came in ragged gasps as panic engulfed me.

Soldiers stepped in, tearing us apart. Despite my resistance, a taser struck me, causing me to collapse onto the ground. I struggled to get up, my body trembling, my thoughts consumed by the anguish of losing Tiffany. I saw my mom, crying and helpless, and it only deepened the pit of despair in my heart.

The woman's voice boomed again, mocking us. "For the next Trial, we are going to set you all free in the surrounding area! There's no hope of getting away! HAHAHAHAHAHA! Good luck!"

Someone threw a dark cloth sack over my head, and panic surged through me. Now I remembered! She was the same woman who tormented us before everything went dark. Her cruel laughter echoed in my mind. I struggled, but the taser hit me again, and the electricity overwhelmed me. I passed out, my last thoughts consumed by the horror of Tiffany's death and the desperate need to survive.

I woke up, the light filtering through the sack over my head. My hands were still bound, but the ground beneath me felt rough and uneven. As the sack was yanked off, I blinked against the sudden brightness.

I was in a forest clearing. The air was thick with the scent of pine and damp earth. Around me, others were waking up, looking as disoriented as I felt. I spotted my mom nearby, and my heart sank further.

"Mom," I whispered, crawling over to her.

She looked up, her eyes red and swollen from crying. "Jack, what's happening? Where are we?"

"I don't know, but we need to stick together," I said, my voice strained as I tried to suppress the grief threatening to overwhelm me.

The woman's voice crackled through hidden speakers. "Welcome to the next Trial! Survive or die. The choice is yours!"

I helped my mom to her feet, my heart heavy with grief and fear. Every step forward is a reminder of the violence that brought us here, a cruel echo of my father's death, and losing Tiffany.

"Jack, what do we do?" my mom asked, her voice small and frightened.

"We survive," I said. "We find a way out of this nightmare."

I stopped, hearing something that chilled me to the bone. I turned around, and everyone else heard it too. The sound was bloodcurdling, like a scream torn from the depths of a nightmare, and it was getting closer now.

"ROAR!!"

It leaped into the open—a beast, towering and monstrous, covered in matted fur with rows of gleaming teeth. Panic erupted, people scattered in all directions. Fear clutched my chest as I joined the stampede, running toward any semblance of safety.

A woman fell, and several others tripped over her. I heard their screams as the beast tore into them, but I couldn't look back. In the chaos, my mom and I got separated, and panic tightened its grip on my heart. I scanned the crowd frantically, but she was nowhere in sight. Ahead, I spotted a broken-down barn with one of its enormous doors missing.

I pointed toward it. "To the barn!" I screamed, my voice cracking with fear.

Only a couple of people heard me. I couldn't see my mom, but I have to keep moving. Survival is the only goal now.

Most people scattered in different directions, some heading toward the woods, others circling the barn. The beast roared, its attention shifting to the fallen. It's already tearing them apart. My heart pounded as I pushed myself harder, sprinting toward the barn.

I reached the barn just as another person rushed inside. I tried to close the door behind us, but it was too heavy. The other person grabbed a thick wooden board.

"Hey, just go! I got this!" he shouted, urgency and fear in his eyes.

I abandoned my efforts and ran down the stairs. His screams echoed through the barn as I descend. Fear gripped me tighter. I heard the beast gaining on me. At the bottom, I sprinted toward the back doors, bursting through them without slowing down.

The beast's presence loomed behind me, a terrifying shadow. I saw another person sprawled on the ground, blood pooling around him. He must have fallen on some rusty nails jutting from broken boards. Panic propelled me forward, past his prone form. More screams pierced the air.

I darted behind a huge rock, pressing myself against it, trying to make myself as small as possible. The beast's heavy breathing was close, too close. it stood on the rock above me. I hunched down, squeezing my eyes shut, hoping against hope it wouldn't see me.

I'm going to die. The thought was clear in my mind. The beast sniffed the air, then suddenly it bound away. I opened my eyes, my breath hitching in my throat. I looked around, half expecting it to return, but there was no sign of it.

What just happened? More screams in the distance pulled me back to reality. This is a nightmare. How do I get out of this?

I needed to leave this place, find my mom, and survive. I ran away from the screams, my mind a whirlwind of fear and determination. Every step was a struggle, every breath a victory. I wouldn't let this place break me. Not now, not ever.

The forest was a maze of shadows and tangled roots. Each step was careful, deliberate, as I navigated through the underbrush. The distant screams faded, replaced by an eerie silence that made my skin crawl. I kept moving, my senses on high alert.

I heard a rustling to my left and froze. The sound was faint, but it's enough to send a spike of fear through me. Slowly, I inched forward, keeping my eyes peeled for any sign of movement. A twig snapped underfoot, and the rustling grew louder. My breath caught in my throat as I braced myself for whatever might come next.

A deer bolted out from the bushes, startled by my presence. I exhaled, relieved, but the moment of calm was short-lived. The beast's roar echoed through the trees, closer than before. I broke into a run.

I weaved through the forest, branches scratching my face and arms. My legs burned with exertion, but I couldn't afford to slow down. I glanced back, and through the trees, I glimpsed the beast charging after me, its eyes wild and hungry.

Up ahead, I saw a rocky outcrop, a potential hiding spot. I pushed myself harder, desperate to reach it before the beast closed the distance. I scrambled up the rocks, my fingers slipping on the damp surface. Just as I hauled myself over the edge, the beast's massive paw swiped at my feet, missing by inches.

I tumbled to the ground on the other side, gasping for breath. The beast roared in frustration, its claws scraping against the rocks. I didn't wait to see if it found a way around. I get up and keep running, the adrenaline coursing through my veins.

The forest thinned, and I saw there was a clearing ahead. My heart lifted with hope. Maybe There was a way out. As I broke into the open, and spotted a small cabin nestled at the edge of the woods. It was old and weathered, but it might offer some shelter.

I sprinted toward it, my lungs burning with every breath. I reached the door and threw it open, rushing inside. The interior was dim and musty, but there was no time to be picky. I slammed the door shut and locked it, my hands trembling.

I leaned against the door, trying to catch my breath. The silence was oppressive, but at least for now, I was safe. I took a moment to gather my thoughts, but the reprieve is brief. The beast's roar pierces the air, and I hear it crashing through the trees outside.

While scanning the cabin, I search for any means of self-defense. I spotted an old hunting rifle mounted on the wall. I grabbed it, checking the chamber. It's loaded. I took a position near the window, monitoring the forest.

The beast emerged from the trees, its eyes scanning the clearing. It spots the cabin and advances, its growls low and menacing. My hands shake as I raise the rifle, aiming for the beast. My finger hovers over the trigger.

The beast crashes through the cabin with all its force. I shoot the rifle aimlessly, hitting its arm. The creature howled in pain, its massive form thrashing wildly. I backpedal, heart racing, as it tears apart the doorway.

Splinters flew, and the walls shuddered under the beast's assault. Amidst the deafening roars and the sound of my own panicked breathing, I could barely think. I still clutch the rifle in my hands, but my first shot only seemed to enrage it. I needed to aim better.

I took a deep breath, trying to steady my trembling hands. The beast's eyes locked on me, burning with fury. It lunged, and I fired again. The shot hit its shoulder, but it kept coming. I threw myself to the side, narrowly avoiding its claws.

The beast crashed into the wall, momentarily stunned. I scrambled to my feet, grabbing anything within reach to slow it down. A broken chair, an old lantern—anything to buy me more time. I threw them at the beast, but they barely faze it.

Desperation fuels my movements as I retreated further into the cabin. I spotted a trapdoor in the floor, partially hidden under a tattered rug. It was my only chance. I yanked it open and dove out, pulling the door shut behind me.

The darkness was suffocating, but I forced myself to stay calm. Above, I heard the beast's enraged roars as it tore through the cabin. The trapdoor creaked under its weight, but miraculously, it held. For now.

I stayed as silent as possible, my breath shallow. The beast's growls faded, but I knew it's still up there, waiting. I have to think of a plan. My mind raced, grasping for any solution.

I crawled out from the trapdoor; muscles were tense and ready to flee at any sign of danger. The cabin is in shambles; the walls torn apart and the floor littered with debris. I scan the wreckage for anything useful, but there's nothing. No more bullets, no weapons, nothing to defend myself with. I have to keep moving.

The forest felt even more oppressive now, each shadow and rustle a potential threat. I picked my way carefully through the underbrush, moving as quietly as I can. The beast could return at any moment, and I have to be ready.

Hours passed, the sun dipping low in the sky, casting long, eerie shadows. My legs ached, and my stomach rumbled, but I pushed on. I have to find my mom. She was out here somewhere, and she needed me.

I heard a noise up ahead and froze. Slowly, I crept forward, peering through the trees. A small shed came into view, its weathered boards blended into the surrounding forest. It looked abandoned, but it could be a place to rest, even if only for a moment.

I approached cautiously, every sense on high alert. The door stood ajar, creaking slightly in the breeze. I pushed it open and step inside, holding my breath. The interior was dark and musty, filled with old tools and broken furniture. It was much, but it was better than nothing.

I shut the door behind me and took a moment to gather my thoughts. Despite its cramped space, the shed felt safer than the open forest. I rummaged through the clutter, hoping to find something useful. An old hammer, some rusty nails, and a length of rope—it was better than nothing.

I sat down, leaning against the wall, and closed my eyes for a moment. Exhaustion tugged at me, but I couldn't afford to rest for long. I had to keep moving, keep searching. My mom was out there, and I couldn't let her down.

A distant roar echoed through the forest, sending a shiver down my spine. The beast was still hunting, still searching for me. Footsteps steps approached. My heart raced again. I peer through a crack in the door and see a woman stumbling toward me. She's small, Asian, with short brown hair and eyes that reflect a mix of fear and determination.

"Mom?" I called out, my voice wavering.

The woman looked up, her brown eyes wide. She wasn't my mom, but she was alive. I rushed outside to meet her.

"Hey, wait!" I shouted, raising my hands. "Are you okay?"

The woman looked at me with a mix of relief and confusion.

She said, "T—Tulong! Nasaan ako? Ano'ng nangyayari? Nakita mo ba si Anne? Kambal ko siya... hindi ko siya mahanap…" Her words came fast, each one trembling as if barely holding back a flood of panic. She clutched her chest, her wide eyes darting around like she was searching for someone.

I hesitated, unable to follow her. "I'm sorry, I—I don't understand. English?"

Her shoulders dropped as she seemed to gather herself. "I'm Diane," she said, switching to English with effort, her tone steadying. "I lost my twin sister, Anne, during the chaos. I don't know if she's still alive."

My heart ached for her as I saw the pain reflected in her eyes. "I'm Jack. I'm trying to find my mom. Have you seen anyone else?"

Diane shook her head, tears welling. "No, I haven't seen her. Anne and I were split up. I... I don't know if she made it."

Diane's expression tightened, her trembling hands clutching at nothing, as though trying to hold herself together. The weight of her fear and loss hung heavily in the air, reflecting the anguish gnawing at me. "I'm sorry about Anne," I said softly. "We need to stick together. It's too dangerous out here alone."

Diane nodded, wiping tears from her face. "You're right. Let's find a way out of this nightmare."

We stepped out of the shed together, moving cautiously through the underbrush. The sound of the beast's roars and distant screams were a constant reminder of the danger surrounding us. Diane's presence was a small comfort.

As we navigated through the forest, Diane's eyes caught my attention again. They were deep and brown, filled with both fear and resilience. For a moment, I was distracted by their intensity. I remembered Tiffany, the familiar warmth of her presence, and the grief of losing her. The thought of her brought a pang of sorrow, reminding me of the loved ones I was desperate to find.

As Diane and I carefully made our way to the edge of a rocky cliff, the view below brought a mix of relief and dread. The cliff isn't too high, but the wide expanse of grass and the cluster of trees hint at the danger still around. The distant screams pierced through the air, growing louder and more frantic.

Peering down, I spotted a man sprinting across the open space, his movements frantic as he tried to escape. The beast—an enormous, furry monster with razor-sharp teeth— burst onto the scene, chasing the man with terrifying speed. Diane flinched beside me, her eyes wide with fear.

I crouched lower, hoping the beast wouldn't notice us. The man's screams faded as he ran, eventually swallowed by the trees. The beast's form disappeared behind the foliage, giving me a fleeting moment of calm.

But then Diane's words broke through my thoughts, her tone sharp and trembling in Tagalog. "Ano ba ang ginagawa mo? Gusto mo bang mamatay?" ("What are you doing? Do you want to die?")

I stared at her, not understanding. Before I could respond, I made a split-second decision. I grabbed Diane's arm, pulling her with me. Without waiting for her reply, I leaped off the cliff. We slid down the rocky incline, the rough terrain scraping against our legs. As we hit the bottom, we rolled to absorb the impact, trying to avoid injury.

I scrambled to my feet, adrenaline surging through me. Diane, frustrated and out of breath, pushes me away but quickly realizes the urgency of the situation. We need to keep moving.

As we stood there, panting, I could see the panic in Diane's eyes mirroring my own. The forest around us felt less like a refuge and more like a trap. I met Diane's gaze, determined to keep pushing forward.

"We have to keep going," I said, my voice firm despite the exhaustion. "We can't stop now."

Diane nodded; her fear tempered by resolve. "You're right. Let's keep moving. We'll find a way out of this."

We pushed on, every step a fight against the growing despair. The distant roars of the beast, a constant reminder of the danger lurking just out of sight, punctuated the forest's oppressive silence.

As Diane and I pushed through the dense underbrush, the forest seemed to close in around us. We moved carefully, trying to avoid making any noise that might attract its attention.

Suddenly, the beast's massive form burst through the trees, its eyes glowing with malevolent intent. It was closer than I thought, and its roar was deafening. Panic surged through me as it charges in our direction.

"Takbo!" Diane yelled, grabbing my arm and pulling me along. We sprinted through the underbrush, branches slapping against our faces as we pushed through.

We ran until we reached a narrow gap between two large rocks. It wasn't ideal, but it was a potential hiding spot. We squeezed through the gap, pressing ourselves against the rocks, hoping the beast wouldn't see us.

I peered out cautiously, the beast's heavy breathing growing louder. Its massive form appeared at the edge of the rocks, sniffing the air. I could feel Diane's breath against my back, her body trembling. We held our breaths, barely daring to move.

The beast's glowing eyes swept across the gap, and I could see the sharp claws and teeth glinting in the dim light. It paused, its nostrils flaring as it sniffed the air. My heart pounded in my ears, and I knew it had spotted us.

Without warning, the beast's claws swiped at the gap, narrowly missing us. Diane let out a small gasp of fear. I turned to her, trying to keep my voice steady. "Stay calm. We need to stay quiet."

The beast roared in frustration, its claws scraping against the rocks. I knew we couldn't stay here for long. The gap was too narrow for us to escape easily, and the beast's patience was wearing thin.

I glanced around frantically, searching for any way to escape. My eyes fell on a loose boulder near the edge of the rocks. It was heavy, but if I could move it, we might create a diversion.

"Diane, hold on!" I whispered urgently, then made a quick decision. I waited for the beast's next swipe, then darted out from the gap, using all my strength to push the boulder down the slope.

The boulder tumbled and crashed down the rocks, creating a loud commotion. The beast turned its attention to the noise, roaring and charging after it. I raced back to Diane, grabbing her arm and pulling her out of the gap.

"Let's go!" I pulled her to her feet. We sprinted away from the rocks, making our way through the forest as quickly as possible. My breath was ragged, but I kept pushing forward, determined to find safety.

We continued through the forest, the night air thick with tension. The distant roars of the beast faded, but we knew it was still out there, searching for us. The forest felt endless, and each step is a battle against exhaustion and fear.

We'd been moving for hours, taking turns leading and navigating the treacherous terrain. The night was relentless, every rustle of leaves and snap of a twig heightened our anxiety. Exhaustion weighed heavily on us, and hunger gnawed at our stomachs.

We found a small, shaded area and decided to rest for a moment. Diane sat down on a fallen log, her face drawn and tired. I leaned against a tree, trying to steady my breathing. The distant howls of the beast had faded, but we knew better than to relax completely.

"Jack, we need to find somewhere safe," Diane said, her voice barely above a whisper. Her eyes were weary, but there was a fire in them that kept me going.

"I know," I replied, rubbing my sore legs. "We'll find a way out of this. We just have to keep moving."

As the first light of dawn broke through the canopy, we moved again. The forest looked different in the pale morning light—less menacing but still filled with hidden dangers. We stayed alert, scanning for any sign of the beast or other threats.

A low growl rumbled through the trees. Diane and I froze, our hearts racing. We glanced at each other, knowing we had no choice but to run.

We sprinted through the forest, the underbrush thick and unforgiving. The beast's growls grew louder, and the ground shook with its heavy footsteps. We pushed ourselves harder, but the forest is relentless. The growls grew nearer, and I could hear the beast's ragged breaths behind us.

Ahead, I saw a steep hill. "This way!" I shouted at Diane, pointing toward the slope. We scrambled up the hill, but it's slippery and treacherous. Just as we reached the top, the beast lunged at us, its claws swiping dangerously close.

Diane grabbed my arm and pulled me to safety, but we lost our footing on the loose gravel. We tumbled down the hill in a chaotic roll, the world spun around us. I landed heavily on top of Diane, our bodies tangled together in a heap.

For a moment, our faces were inches apart, our breaths mingling. The proximity was electrifying, and I couldn't help but noticed the softness of Diane's lips so close to mine.

Diane looked up at me with a teasing smile. "Ingat ka, Jack. Baka masyado kang masanay sa ganyan."

I blink, trying to understand. "Uh, what? "

Diane giggled. "It means be careful, Jack. You might get too comfortable up here."

I chuckled, feeling a bit more at ease despite the situation.

Diane's expression lit up with mischief as she leaned in closer. "Eh kung nandiyan ka na rin lang, baka naman puwedeng mas maging kapaki-pakinabang ka?" she teased with a grin. ("Well, since you're already here, maybe you could be more useful?")

I raised an eyebrow, still not entirely sure what she meant, though her playful tone gave me a hint.

"Huh?" I asked, tilting my head slightly.

We both got up, brushing off the dirt and leaves. We were tired and hungry, but there was a renewed determination in our eyes. Diane stretched, shaking off the last remnants of our tumble.

After some time, we noticed a small, dilapidated building through the trees. It was far from perfect, but it looked like it could offer some shelter and possibly supplies.

"There's something up ahead," I said, pointing toward the building. "We should check it out."

Diane nodded, her expression a mix of relief and determination. "Let's hope it's what we need."

We made our way toward the building, every step bringing us closer to potential safety and a much-needed respite from the relentless nightmare.

We stumbled toward the small building, its weathered exterior, a grim reminder of past sorrows. The beast's roars grew fainter but still disturbingly close. My heart raced as I scanned the area for any immediate threats. Diane, her face a mix of fear and determination, helped me check the surroundings.

The building's door stood slightly ajar. I pushed it open and step inside, the musty air heavy with the scent of old wood and dampness. Diane followed, her presence a minor comfort amid our terror. I glanced at her, seeking a fleeting sense of calm in her determined face.

A faint sound reached my ears—crying, muffled, and desperate. My heart leaped. I turned toward the back of the room and spot a woman huddled there, her body trembling. My breath caught.

"Mom!" I shouted, my voice cracking with a mix of relief and anxiety.

"Jack!" My mom's voice was weak, but unmistakable. Her tear-filled eyes met mine, and a wave of relief washed over me, mingling with a deep, gnawing worry.

I hurried over to her, pushing aside the chaos of the moment. "Mom, are you okay? What happened?" I ask urgently, my voice gentle.

"I—I was hiding," Mom stammered, her voice cracking. "But I think my leg is broken. I couldn't move. I thought I was finished."

"I'm here now," I said, trying to keep my voice steady. "We're going to get out of here."

Diane's hand found mine, her touch warm and reassuring, but the promise of safety felt hollow without Tiffany.

The minutes stretched into what felt like hours.

The building's dim interior was lit only by the faint light seeping through cracked windows. Diane and I sat close, our shoulders brushing. My mom clings to me, her hands trembling. Diane focuses, taking quick, shallow gasps of breath.

"I—I didn't expect this," Diane whispered, glancing at me with vulnerability. "I didn't think I'd end up in a place like this. Parang bangungot."

I nodded, my heart heavy. "None of us did. It's like a nightmare we can't wake up from."

Diane's gaze dropped, her fingers fidgeting with her shirt. "I was separated from my twin sister, Anne. We were running together, but we got split up. I don't know if she's alive or…"

Her voice trailed off, choked by emotion. I saw the pain in her eyes, and it made my heart ache. "I'm sorry, Diane. That must be so hard."

She swallowed hard, brimming with tears. "Yeah, it is. But you—" She paused, her gaze meeting mine with gratitude and sadness. "You found your mom. That's something. I'm glad you're together."

I glanced at my mom, who is now sitting beside me, her face a mix of relief and fear. "We're not out of danger yet," I said softly. "We need to stay vigilant."

Diane shifted slightly, her expression tight with worry. "You're right. It's just… I've been running and hiding. The letter, the woman with the laugh… it's all been so surreal. Parang panaginip lang." (It feels like a dream.)

Running a hand through my hair, I sighed. "I know. I got a letter too. It felt like we're trapped in a twisted game we didn't sign up for."

Diane's expression softened as she listened. "Did you have anyone else with you before this? Someone you were close to?"

I hesitated, my thoughts drifting back to Tiffany. "I had a girlfriend, Tiffany. We were close. But… she's dead. She was killed."

"I'm so sorry, Jack. I can't imagine what you're going through."

I nodded, the weight of grief pressing down on me. "Thank you. It's been incredibly hard. It felt like a part of me is missing."

There was a brief silence, the only sounds being our heavy breaths and the distant roars of the beast. Diane broke the stillness, her tone soft but sincere. "You know, despite everything, I'm glad I met you. It's comforting to have someone to talk to. Alam mo yun? You know what I mean?"

I turned to her, my expression sincere but conflicted. "I felt the same way. It's been tough, and having someone who understands… it helps. Even if it complicates things."

Diane nodded, understanding. "I'm from the Philippines. Tagalog is my first language. Sometimes, when I'm scared or stressed, it just comes out."

I smiled slightly, the mix of languages adding an exotic touch to her words. "It's okay. It's actually kind of nice. Makes you sound... unique."

The building felt like a fragile sanctuary amidst the chaos, but in this dim space, Diane and I found solace in each other's company. Afraid to do or say anything else, we sat in silence, awaiting our next move. Despite the danger that still lurked outside, there was a sense of safety in being here with my mom and Diane. For now, this small, dark room was our refuge from the storm.

CHAPTER 9

The shared fear and vulnerability between Diane and me forged an intense bond, a connection that grew stronger with each passing hour. In the dim, claustrophobic space of the small building, our survival instincts were in overdrive, but so was our reliance on each other. The beast's roar outside is a constant, chilling reminder of our precarious situation, its sound reverberating through the thin walls and amplifying our anxiety.

I stole glances at Diane and my mom, each a reminder of how dire our predicament had become. The small, flickering light bulb overhead cast long, jittery shadows, heightening the sense of dread that gripped us all. Diane's face mirrored my fear—her eyes wide and haunted, her hands trembling as she tried to keep herself steady. Her presence was a fragile thread of comfort amid the encroaching darkness.

We huddled together, exchanging hushed words of reassurance, our breaths coming in short, ragged gasps. I could see the worry etched deeply in Diane's features, and it tugged at my heart.

Through the grime-covered window, a glimpse of hope emerged—a dilapidated car, abandoned but possibly our last chance. I exchanged a desperate look with Diane and my mom, the urgency of our situation clear in my eyes.

"We need to go now," I said, my voice strained but resolute. Diane and my mom nodded, their faces a mix of fear and determination. We slipped out the back door, our steps muffled by the oppressive quiet that preceded the storm.

We reached the car just as the building shuddered from the beast's assault. I slammed the door shut. The beast's growls were almost deafening now, shaking the car as if trying to tear it apart.

I scanned the interior, my eyes landed on a dusty, forgotten key lying on the floorboard. It was a glimmer of hope amidst the terror. My hands shook as I brushed off the grime and fumbled with the key, slotting it into the ignition. Diane and Mom's nervous glances mirrored the fear in my chest.

"Hawak lang," Diane whispered, her voice slipping into Tagalog. I didn't understand, but her tone was enough to steady me. Later, I'd learn it meant, "Just hold on." We all buckle our seatbelts, each movement filled with frantic energy. Diane's hand found mine, her grip tight and reassuring.

I took a deep breath, trying to steady my shaking hands on the steering wheel. I turned the key, but the engine just sputtered. The beast's roar grew louder, a chilling reminder we were running out of time. I turned the key again, the engine coughing and sputtering with a life of its own.

The beast crashed against the car, its claws tearing at the metal, its breath hot and heavy against the glass. Diane and my mom screamed. I was thrown back against my seat as the car jolted and stalled, the beast's claws raked through the windshield.

"Dali na, dali na!" Diane muttered, frustration mounting as I turned the key again (Hurry up, hurry up!). The car stuttered, almost turning over, but it stalled again. The beast roared in fury, its claws ripping through the roof, shards of glass raining down on us.

Finally, with one last desperate twist of the key, the engine roared to life. The beast lunged, its claws swiping at the trunk. I slammed my foot on the gas pedal; the tires screeched as we lurched forward. The beast's claws raked against the rear of the car, a last, desperate swipe as we tore away from the building.

The car hurtled through the forest, the beast's enraged roars fading behind us. My heart pounded, the adrenaline making every nerve feel alive. Diane still gripped my hand, her fingers trembling, but her eyes, with fierce determination.

The car careened downhill, the landscape blurring into a chaotic mix of trees and rocks. I fought to maintain control, each violent jolt amplifying the peril. The steering wheel slipped through my sweaty palms, and before I could react, the car slammed into a tree with a bone-jarring impact. The force catapulted me out of the vehicle, my body soared through the air. I hit the ground hard, pain exploded through my back as I skidded through the dirt. The world spun around me, and I came to a stop, gasping for breath, my vision swimming with stars.

I struggled to push through the searing pain, my legs felt like lead. Diane, thrown from the car with me, stumbled over, panic and concern written all over her face. She knelt beside me, her hands shaking as she helped me up. Her touch was a slight comfort against the overwhelming peril.

"Jack!" she cried out, her voice trembling with raw fear.

"Are you okay?" I rasped through clenched teeth. Diane's eyes, though fierce, reveal her own turmoil. She steadied me, her determination unwavering despite the situation.

"I'm fine. We need to move—now!" Her voice was urgent, cutting through my disorientation.

My mom lay a few feet away; her face twisted in agony. My heart leaped into my throat as Diane and I stumbled toward her, each movement sending sharp pangs through my body. "Mom, are you okay?" I asked, desperation lacing my voice. Her leg was bent at an unnatural angle, the bone jutting out grotesquely.

"My leg!" she cried, her voice breaking. "It's broken! I can't move it!"

"Hold on, Mom. I'm here," I said, trying to sound calm despite the rising panic. We helped her to her feet, her weight pressing heavily on my shoulders. We stumbled back toward the wreckage of the car, the beast's roars grew louder, a menacing reminder of the danger closing in.

The beast appeared suddenly, emerging from the trees with a lumbering, predatory gait. Its eyes locked onto us with a chilling hunger, its massive frame imposing and terrifying. The beast's roar reverberated through the forest, shaking the very ground beneath us.

Diane's grip tightened on my arm, her face set in a grim mask of resolve. "We need to move, now!" she shouted, her voice barely audible over the beast's growl.

I gave my mom one last glance; her face etched with pain and fear, and then I pulled her along as Diane lead the way. We managed a few steps before the beast lunged forward, its massive claws swiping at the air with a terrifying screech.

Diane spotted a narrow opening between the trees and quickly yanked me and my mom toward it. We squeezed through; the branches scraping against our skin. As we pressed close together, Diane and I ended up with our faces inched apart. Our breaths were heavy, mingling in the tense silence. Diane's warmth radiated through the gaps in her torn clothes, making the proximity feel both comforting and intense.

We stay hidden, our bodies pressed together, hearts pounding in unison. The beast's roars faded, and the oppressive silence that followed was almost as unsettling. Diane's eyes locked with mine, and I saw a flicker of something lighter in her gaze, despite the dire situation.

She out a soft, nervous laugh, her voice dropping to a whisper. "Mukhang may bago tayong paraan para magpainit," she said, slipping into Tagalog. The mischievous glint in her eyes told me she'd tried to lighten the mood, but I didn't understand her words.

"What did you say?" I asked, my voice barely more than a breath as our faces remained close, the tension between us thick.

Diane's teasing smile softened, and she quickly translated, "I said, it seemed we've found a new way to keep warm." She leaned in slightly, our lips almost brushing, her breath warm against my face.

I heard the distant rumble of the car's engine still running. The sound snaps me back to reality. "We should get back to the car," I said, my voice a mix of relief and urgency.

Diane's smile faded into a more serious expression, her eyes reflecting the same mix of exhaustion and determination I felt. She nodded, stepping back and helping me and my mom through the foliage. We make our way back to the car, the weight of our predicament heavy on our shoulders, but a flicker of hope guiding our steps.

Just as we reached the car, the beast appeared limping toward us with a menacing gait. Its eyes locked onto us with predatory hunger. Suddenly, a shot rang out, and the beast collapsed, a howl of pain escaping its mouth.

A man with a gun strode into view, his face set in a determined, grim expression. Behind him, a woman with torn clothes emerged. Diane's face lights up with recognition and relief. "Anne!" Diane screamed. "Anne, ikaw ba 'yan?"

Anne, her face streaked with dirt and exhaustion, nodded vigorously. "Diane!" She rushes over, and they embraced tightly, tears streaming down their faces as they clung to each other.

The man with the gun turned to us, his voice urgent and commanding. "Get into the car, now!" His tone left no room for hesitation.

"What about you?" I shouted, panic rising as I glanced back at the beast's twitching form. "What are you going to do?"

"I'll handle this beast! Just get out of here!" he ordered, his eyes blazing with resolve.

Diane and I assisted my mom into the car's front seat, with Anne following closely behind, her eyes filled with a mix of gratitude and concern. Diane and Anne took the back seats, still clutching each other for comfort. I scrambled into the driver's seat, my hands trembling as I put the car in reverse.

As I backed up, maneuvering past the twisted tree that had initially blocked our path, I heard a horrifying scream echo behind us. The sound carried raw agony and desperation. I glanced back to see the beast gripping the man's head in its jaws, the man's body limp and lifeless. The sight was both horrific and heartbreaking. I turned my attention back to the road, my heart pounding as we sped away, leaving behind the chaos and terror. The car's tires spun wildly, but we were finally on the move, the night swallowing us as we drove into the uncertain darkness, hoping against hope that we've escaped the worst of the nightmare.

The roar of the beast fades into the distance, replaced by the eerie silence of the darkened road. My grip on the steering wheel tightened, exhaustion mixing with a gnawing grief that felt like a lead weight in my chest.

The narrow road ahead seemed like a distant beacon of hope. We were almost there. The promise of safety and the possibility of ending this nightmare surged within us, pushing us to press on through the darkness.

Diane and Anne finally reunited in the back seat. Anne, covered in dirt and with torn clothes, reached out to Diane. Their reunion was a mix of relief and overwhelming emotion, their tears mingling as they embraced.

"Oh, God, Anne, akala ko nawala ka na!" Diane's voice broke with sobs. "I thought I lost you!"

Anne clung to her sister. "Natakot ako! Akala ko… hindi na kita makikita ulit!" She then repeated, "I was so scared! I thought… I'd never see you again!" Their reunion was a small beacon of hope amidst the chaos, but it cut deeply. Diane's fingers combed through Anne's tangled hair. I felt a pang of envy as I watched them, a bitter reminder that I'd never experienced such a reunion with Tiffany.

Anne pulled back slightly, looking at Diane with tear-filled eyes. "Walang ideya kung gaano kita na-miss. Akala ko… akala ko pati ikaw nawala na." She then said, "You have no idea how much I missed you. I thought… I thought you were gone too."

Their shared grief is palpable, a stark contrast to the fear that drove us to this moment. Anne's gaze shifted to my mom, her concern clear. "Is she okay?" Anne asks in English, her voice trembling.

"She's hurt," I said, my voice strained. "Her leg is broken. We need to get her to safety."

Diane's expression softened, her tears continuing to flow. "Aayusin natin 'to," she said to Anne. Then, looking at me, she added in English, "We'll make it through this. What's important is that we're together."

My mom managed a weak, grateful smile. "Thank you," she whispered.

Anne nodded, her eyes reflecting the gravity of our situation. "We need to find a place to rest, somewhere safe where we can get medical help."

I focused on the road, my thoughts tangled in the aftermath of everything. "We'll keep driving," I said, trying to sound firm despite the weariness. "We'll find somewhere to stop and figure out our next move."

Diane's hand rested on my shoulder, her touch warm and reassuring. "Salamat sa lahat ng ginawa mo," she said softly. "Thank you for everything."

I nodded, forcing a small smile. "We just need to keep going. We'll get through this."

As the car rolled on into the night, their bond was a reminder of humanity and solidarity in the darkest moments, but it also underscored my loss.

The relentless hum of the engine was the only sound that kept me grounded. My eyes grew heavy, despite the adrenaline still surging through me. Diane and Anne were finally asleep. Their steady breathing was a bittersweet reminder of our fragility and fleeting comfort amidst the chaos.

Mom stirred slightly, noticing my fatigue. "Jack," she said softly, her voice filled with concern, "are you okay?"

Despite feeling weak, I forced a weary smile. "I'm fine, Mom. I just... need to keep going. We can't stop now. The beast could still be out there, and there's no telling what else that woman has planned."

She looked at me with understanding, her own exhaustion evident. "You need to rest too, Jack," she insists.

I shook my head, focusing on the road. "I can't afford to. Not now."

She seemed to sense my determination and closed her eyes, drifting off into sleep despite her discomfort.

I glanced at Diane and Anne in the rearview mirror. Their peaceful sleep is a small comfort but also a stark reminder of what I'd lost. The road ahead seemed endless, stretching into darkness.

As the hours passed, I fought to stay awake, my eyes burned with the effort. The clock on the dashboard was a constant reminder of my need for rest.

Thoughts of Tiffany invaded my mind. Her death was a sharp, relentless pain. I remembered her final moments, the look of fear and pain on her face. I'd never see her again, and the finality of it all was a crushing weight on my soul.

The darkness outside blurred, and despite my efforts, sleep overtook me. I gave in, pulling over to an abandoned factory. I parked the car and, overwhelmed by fatigue, and finally allowed myself to rest. The hum of the engine and the rhythmic motion of the car were the only anchors to the present as I drifted into a restless slumber, haunted by shadows and echoes of the day's terror.

CHAPTER 10

The dim light filtering through the cracked windows of the abandoned factory paints the space with long, eerie shadows. I stirred awake, the stiffness in my limbs a reminder of how deeply I slept. The cool air bites at my skin as I stretch, the tension in my muscles slowly unwinding. My eyes found my mom first—her leg still in a makeshift splint, her face a mask of worry despite her attempts to rest. Nearby, Diane and Anne huddled over a table, their focus intense as they whispered and worked on something that resembled a device.

I got out of the car where I'd been resting, rubbing sleep from my eyes, and walked toward my mom. The memory of her injury hit me hard, but so was the sight of Diane and Anne—especially Diane, whose presence pulled at something deep within me. I pushed the thoughts aside, focusing on what needed to be done.

"Mom," I said gently, masking my fear with a forced cheerfulness. "Are you okay?"

She looked up; her smile strained but sincere. "I'm fine, Jack. How do you feel?"

"Better," I replied, trying to convince both of us. "The sleep helped."

Her expression softened but worry lined her face. "Diane and Anne have been working on something important. Explosives, I think. They seem to know what they're doing."

My stomach tightened. "How long was I out?"

"A few hours. But time's running out, Jack. We need to stop that beast soon."

Her urgency snapped my attention back to Diane and Anne. Diane glanced up, catching me watching her. There was A smirk on her lips, a flicker of something between us I didn't have time to dissect. I cleared my throat and walked over to them.

"My mom says you've built explosives?" I asked, trying to keep the conversation professional, but the tension in my voice betrayed me.

"Yes," Diane said, a mix of pride and weariness in her tone. She shared a brief, unreadable look with Anne before turning back to me. "How was your sleep?"

"Good," I replied, too quickly, my thoughts veering back to Tiffany—her face, her laugh, the life we could have had. I shoved the thoughts away, focusing on the here and now.

"That's good," Diane murmured, her hand resting on my shoulder for a moment too long, a touch that both grounded and distracted me.

Anne stepped forward, her voice steady as she explained, "We built a bomb, but it's on a timer. Once you set it by pulling this lever, you'll have just enough time to get to safety before the timer hits zero and you push this button to detonate."

I frowned, feeling the weight of the situation pressing down on me. "What's the catch?"

Anne's expression darkened. "The timer won't start unless someone stays behind to push the button."

The words hit like a punch to the gut. "Dammit! There has to be another way!"

Diane stepped closer, her eyes meeting mine with a hard truth. "We've tried everything else. This is the only way to be sure it'll kill the beast."

A surge of anger and helplessness swelled within me, but I knew she's right. I looked at my mom, her face pale and stricken, and I felt the decision solidify within me.

"I'll do it," I said, my voice firm despite the fear clawing at my insides.

"No!" My mom's voice was a desperate plea. She grabbed my arm, her eyes wide with terror. "There has to be another way! Please, Jack!"

I took her hands, squeezing them gently. "Mom, I have to. If I don't, that thing will keep killing. I can't let that happen."

Her grip tightened, her eyes flooding with tears. "Please, Jack... I can't lose you too."

Her words cut deep, and for a moment, I wavered. But then I saw the determined faces of Diane and Anne, the reality of the situation crashed back in. We didn't have time to debate.

"I love you, Mom," I whispered, leaning in to kiss her forehead. "But this is the only way."

Her sobs were quiet, but they echoed in my ears as I stepped away, feeling the unbearable weight of what I was about to do. Diane and Anne complete the bomb, their movements quick and precise. The factory seemed even quieter; every sound amplified in the silence that followed.

Diane's hand finds mine, her touch warm and steadying. "Are you sure?" she asked, her voice soft, filled with something I can't quite name—something that both comforts and unnerves me.

I swallowed hard. "Yeah. I'm sure."

She gave me a long, searching look before pulling me into a brief, fierce hug. "You're braver than you know, Jack."

I held on to her, feeling the heat of her breath on my neck, the closeness of her body against mine. It's a moment that's both grounding and terrifying. When she pulled back, there was something unspoken between us, a connection forged in fire and fear.

Diane's voice dropped to a playful whisper as she teased, "Alam mo, dapat talagang itigil na natin ang ganito. Next time, let's aim for a less catastrophic setting."

Despite everything, I chuckled, shaking my head. "I'll hold you to that."

She smiled—a real, warm smile that made the impending danger seem momentarily distant. "Mabuti. Now, let's get through this so we can have that normal meeting."

Her words gave me the strength I needed, and I took a deep breath, ready for whatever came next.

As Anne gave us the final instructions, an almost suffocating silence shrouded the factory.

Diane and I found ourselves in a dimly lit corner, away from the others. The air was thick with the tension of what lay ahead, but for a moment, it felt like we were in our own little world.

I sit down, leaning against the crumbling wall, and Diane joins me, her presence a comforting balm to the chaos in my mind. I glanced at her, and she met my gaze, her eyes reflecting a depth of concern that touched something deep inside me.

Our hands find each other, and the simple act of holding on felt like a lifeline. "You're the bravest man I've ever met," Diane said softly. "At syempre, quite a catch, if I may say so. If only we had met under better circumstances…"

Her words stirred a bittersweet ache in my chest, a mix of pleasure and guilt. Tiffany's memory loomed large, her laughter and love now gone, making this moment feel more fragile. I swallowed hard, trying to push the guilt aside, but it clung to me like a shadow.

"I… I don't know what to say," I admitted, my voice trembling. "Everything's been so crazy. I'm not sure I'm handling any of it well."

Diane's thumb stroked the back of my hand, her touch soothing. "You've done more than anyone could have asked. Alam ko na ang lahat ng ito ay sobrang hirap—more than anyone should have to endure. But you're here, you're fighting, and that means something."

Her words resonate with me, easing some of the tension in my chest. "I just… I just wish I could've saved her," I confessed, the pain of losing Tiffany spilling over. "I keep seeing her face… I thought we had a future. Now, I'm just stuck with this image in my head."

Diane pulled me into her arms, holding me close as I finally let the tears fall. Her embrace was a safe harbor in the storm of grief and regret, and the world felt a little less harsh.

"It's okay to grieve," she murmured. "It's okay to feel this pain. You don't have to go through it alone."

I clung to her, finding some solace in her presence. We sat there, the cold, desolate factory around us, holding on to each other as if it was the only thing keeping us grounded in this nightmare.

After a long silence, Diane pulled back, her expression searching mine. "Remember when we almost kissed?" she asked, her tone light but with a serious undertone.

I nodded, a small smile tugging at my lips despite everything. "Yeah, I remember."

Diane's smile turned playful, but there was an intensity behind it. "If things were different, I wouldn't have let that moment slip away."

I chuckled, shaking my head. "You're impossible, you know that?"

She leaned in closer, her breath warm against my skin. "Maybe. But it's keeping us both sane, isn't it?"

I met her gaze, feeling the pull between us, the connection that had grown stronger with each passing moment. "Yeah. It is."

Diane's playful smirk carried a spark of mischief, but something in her demeanor hinted at a deeper emotion that made my heart skip a beat.

Diane's request, though unexpected, carried a mix of vulnerability and playful charm. "I need to pee," she said, her cheeks flushing. "Can you keep watch for me?"

A little thrown off by the request, I suggested, "Can't you ask your sister instead?"

But Diane's subtle expression conveyed a hint, and I sensed she wanted my company. I nodded, understanding. "Sure, I'll keep watch."

Diane's face lit up with a grateful smile. "Salamat, Jack. You're a lifesaver."

As Diane moved toward a nearby bush, I followed, trying to act nonchalant but feeling the weight of the moment. The rain drizzled, adding to the surreal atmosphere. Her movements were purposeful yet playful. She glanced back at me, a mischievous glint lighting up her expression.

"Don't let anyone sneak up on me," she joked in Tagalog, "Huwag mong hayaang may sumulpot sa'kin, ha? I trust you to be my guardian?"

I twisted my head, focusing on the surrounding area. The faint sound of the rain pattering against the ground and the rustling of leaves were the only things that broke the silence. I couldn't help but feel a twinge of embarrassment, my mind racing as Diane's laughter carried over to me. Amid the chaos of our current situation, a part of me felt this unexpected, awkward connection with Diane.

"Are you keeping a sharp lookout?" she calls out, her voice teasing. "O baka naman masyado kang abala sa iba?"

I tried to clear my head, forcing myself to concentrate on the task at hand. "I'm looking. Just... make it quick."

Her laughter was soft and light, carrying a hint of flirtation. "Don't worry, I'll be done soon. Baka magustuhan mo pa ang tanawin."

I shifted uncomfortably, my face growing warm. Diane continued her playful banter, the sounds of her adjusting her clothes punctuating her words. The laughter and teasing are a stark contrast to the heavy grief I felt, and I'm torn between the comfort she offers and the painful memories of Tiffany.

"All right, you can turn around now," she announces.

I turned to see Diane pulling her pants up, her underwear visible for a moment. Her smirk is clear as she caught me looking. "Did you enjoy the show?" she teased, her eyes twinkling with mischief. "O baka naman napansin mo lang na mabuti?"

I blushed deeply, my gaze shifting awkwardly. "Uh, I—"

Diane steps closer, her presence warm and undeniably intimate. "It's okay, Jack. Hindi araw-araw na makakita ka ng ganito." Her voice dropped to a conspiratorial whisper. "Lalo na kung may kagaya mo."

She inched closer, her breath mingling with mine. I was aware of her nearness, the way her clothes clung to her damp skin. She grabbed both of my arms. My heart felt conflicted. Diane's touch is both comforting and confusing, a source of solace and an unwanted reminder of my loss.

"If only we had met under different circumstances," Diane said softly, her words filled with an unspoken longing.

A lump formed in my throat, making it hard to speak. "Yeah, things would've been different."

Diane's smirk grew bolder, her eyes locked on mine. "You know, I could help you forget, even just for a moment." Her fingers trailed down my arm, sending shivers through me. "There's something about you, Jack. Something that makes me want to... explore."

My breath caught at her words; the intensity of the moment almost overwhelming. "Diane, this is... a lot."

"Is it?" she murmured, leaning in even closer. "O baka ito lang ang kailangan mo?" Her hand rested on my chest, her touch burned through the fabric of my shirt. "Sometimes, in the middle of all this chaos, you need a distraction. Something... or someone... to make you feel alive again."

Her words send a thrill through me, a dangerous mix of desire and hesitation. "Diane, I'm not sure if this is the right time..."

She smiled, her lips brushing my ear. "When is the right time, Jack? Life doesn't wait for perfect moments." Her hand slides down my chest, teasingly stopping just above my waistband. "And right now, I want to be your moment."

My heart pounded, the nearness of her driving me wild. "Diane..."

"Shh," she whispered, her breath hot against my skin. "Just feel."

Her boldness was intoxicating, her touch electric. As her hand moved lower, the air between us thickened with tension. We breathed raggedly, with the world outside fading away as we got lost in each other.

"Jack," she breathed, her voice a sultry whisper, "you drive me crazy. And I know I drive you crazy too."

My hands moved of their own accord, grasping her hips and pulling her closer. The heat of her body against mine is almost unbearable. "Diane, this..."

"This is exactly what we both need," she finished for me, her lips so close to mine I could almost taste her. "Don't fight it."

Just as our lips were about to meet, a heavy downpour began, drenching us both. We scrambled toward the shelter of the factory, our laughter ringing out.

We found a dry spot and huddled together; the air filled with the scent of rain and the lingering warmth of our shared moment. Diane's eyes sparkled as she looked at me, her smile infectious.

"You know, Jack," she said, her voice soft yet strong, "we can't change the past, but we can choose how we move forward."

Diane's shirt clung to her chest, accentuating every curve. I couldn't help but notice, and she caught me staring. Her eyes narrowed playfully.

"Enjoying the view again?" Diane laughed. "Or are you just fascinated by how rain makes everything cling?"

I shifted awkwardly, my face flushing. "Sorry, I—"

Diane placed a hand gently on my cheek, her touch tender despite the cold. "Relax, Jack. It's okay." Her eyes glinted mischievously as she added, "Plus, I like the attention."

Her words stirred a mixture of embarrassment and longing within me. Diane's closeness is a comfort and a distraction, but it also brings up the memory of Tiffany. Her presence reminds me of what I've lost, adding to my confusion.

"If only we had more time," Diane reaped.

Diane's kiss caught me off guard, a brief but electrifying contact that sent a jolt through me. I stood frozen for a moment, unsure of how to react. Diane was testing boundaries, seeing how far she can push, but There was sincerity in her actions—a longing that mirrored my own.

"Diane…" I started. Her eyes lock onto mine, a mixture of mischief and genuine affection swirling within them.

"I'm sorry," she said softly, though there was a playful glint that suggested she wasn't entirely regretful. "I just couldn't resist."

Anne let out a small laugh, breaking the tension, and suddenly the moment felt a little lighter, more manageable. "You should see your face, Jack," Anne teased. "You look like you've just been struck by lightning."

I managed to smile, rubbing the back of my neck awkwardly. "Well, it kind of feels like that," I admitted, trying to shake off the flustered feeling that's taken hold of me. "You two are a lot to handle."

Diane's expression softened, and she stepped back, giving me a bit of space. "I don't want to make you uncomfortable, Jack," she said, her tone more serious now. "But I want you to know that I'm here, for whatever you need. Whether it's just a friend, or something more… I'm here."

Her words hung in the air, filled with possibilities, and I could sense the sincerity behind them. But there was a part of me that was still hesitant, still caught in the web of my past grief. Tiffany's memory loomed large, and while I felt something for Diane, I wasn't sure I was ready to fully embrace it.

"I appreciate that, Diane," I said finally, my voice steadying. "But I think I need some time to figure things out. This is all… a lot to process."

Diane nodded, her understanding clear. "Of course, Jack. Take all the time you need. I'm not going anywhere."

Anne, sensing the shift in mood, lightened things up again. "All right, you two," she said with a mock sigh. "Enough of the serious talk. We've got more important things to worry about, like surviving this crazy situation."

I chuckled, grateful for the distraction. "Yeah, you're right. Let's focus on what's in front of us."

The rain had slowed to a gentle drizzle now, and the three of us move toward the factory again, our clothes still damp but our spirits lighter. Despite the chaos of the world, there was a small sense of peace that came from the connection we shared, a bond forged in the fires of hardship and uncertainty.

As we reached the entrance to the factory, Diane shot me a sidelong glance, a small smile playing on her lips. "You know, Jack," she said, her voice teasing but warm, "if you ever need another guardian while you're… occupied, you know where to find me."

I laughed, the sound genuine this time, and shook my head. "I'll keep that in mind."

Anne gave Diane a nudge, her tone equally teasing. "Better watch out, Diane. Jack might just take you up on that offer."

Diane grinned, her eyes twinkling with mischief. "I certainly hope so."

We stepped inside the factory, the air cooled and still, the echoes of our footsteps the only sound. The storm outside had passed, leaving behind a sense of calm, but I knew that the real storm—the challenges ahead—were still brewing. But with Diane and Anne by my side, I felt a little more prepared to face whatever came next.

And maybe, just maybe, I'd heal the wounds of the past and open myself up to the possibilities of the future.

Inside the factory, we settled around my mom, who was propped up on a makeshift bed of old factory equipment and rags. The dim light cast long shadows, and the soft hum of rain outside created an oddly soothing backdrop. Diane found a comfortable spot in my lap, displaying her ever bold and affectionate nature. Her breath was warm and steady against my neck, her body pressed close to mine as I tried to keep her warm despite our wet clothes.

"You're so tense, Jack," Diane murmured. She shifted slightly, snuggling even closer. The softness of her hair brushing against my cheek was both comforting and distracting.

My mom glanced up at us, raising an eyebrow with a hint of amusement. "Looked like Diane's found a cozy spot," she remarked in a playful tone. "Don't let her get too comfortable, Jack. We wouldn't want her to take up permanent residence."

I chuckled, trying to mask my embarrassment and the fluttering feeling in my chest. "Oh, don't worry, Mom. I'll make sure she doesn't get too used to this." I gave Diane a gentle nudge. "But it's not the worst company."

Diane's eyes sparkled with mischief as she leaned in closer, clearly enjoying the banter. Her hand rests lightly on my knee, her touch lingering. "I think Jack's just being modest. He loves the company, really."

Anne, seated closer than usual, watches with a mixture of curiosity and something more—perhaps a touch of sibling rivalry. Her eyes flick between Diane and me, then back to Diane. "Well, it looked like Diane's made herself quite at home," she said with a soft laugh, though there was a slight edge to her voice. "I'm just here for the company too."

I couldn't help but notice the subtle similarities between the twins—Anne's eyes, her smile, even her mannerisms. Despite their differences, the resemblance was undeniable. With everything going on, I struggled to process my feelings about either of them.

To shift the focus, I turned to my mom. "Mom, where have you been the last seven years?"

Her expression softened, and she looked away, as if gathering her thoughts. "It's a long story, Jack. After everything that happened, I had to leave to keep you safe. I didn't have a choice. I went into hiding, moving from place to place, always trying to stay one step ahead."

She paused, her eyes reflecting a deep sadness. "I had to do things I'm not proud of, just to survive. It wasn't safe for you or me. I tried to reach out, but it was too risky. I kept hoping that someday I could come back, that things would settle down."

Tears welled up in her eyes, and I reached out to take her hand. "I understand, Mom. I really do. It was hard but hearing this now... it helps. I just wish things had been different."

Anne, noticing the gravity of the conversation, subtly shifted closer, her curiosity clear. Diane, sensing the shift in mood, withdraws slightly but remains close, her hand still resting on my knee, though less assertively.

Continuing, my mom's voice trembling slightly, she said, "I did what I thought was best. I wanted to protect you, Jack. I didn't want you to be caught up in the dangers that followed."

We sat in silence for a moment, the weight of her words sinking in. The factory's eerie quiet contrasts with the emotional intensity of the conversation. Diane and Anne remain close, their presence a silent support.

Diane watches with concern as I converse with my mom, her fingers occasionally brushing against mine, grounding me in the present despite the chaos surrounding us.

Anne, who was sitting close by, noticed Diane's proximity and how I responded to her. Her gaze lingered on me, a subtle smirk on her lips. She shifted slightly, moving closer with a playful glint in her eyes. "You know, Jack," she began, her voice smooth, "how do you manage to stay so calm in all this chaos? It's impressive."

I glanced at Anne, sensing the flirtation in her tone. "Well, I guess it helps to have amazing people around me," I replied, trying to keep the conversation light.

Anne leaned in closer, her shoulder brushing against mine. "So, you're just doing your best to impress everyone around you? Charming strategy."

Diane tightened her hold around my waist, her voice playful but carrying a hint of challenge. "Or maybe Jack's just being his usual self—trying to keep everyone safe and happy. I'd say it's working; don't you think?"

Anne's eyes narrowed playfully as she met Diane's gaze. "Well, I suppose he's got a lot of practice. But I wouldn't mind seeing how he handles a little extra attention."

Diane's smile turned serious, though her tone remained light. "Careful, Anne. I don't think you want to start a competition here."

Anne let out a light laugh, her lips curling into a sly grin. "Oh, I'm just having a bit of fun. No need to get territorial," she said, her playful tone laced with a hint of mock innocence.

The playful exchange between Diane and Anne heated up, the underlying rivalry becoming more apparent. Diane's arm around my waist tightened, while Anne's proximity grew more intimate, her hand casually resting on my shoulder.

Noticing the growing tension, my mom steps in to lighten the mood. With a warm, teasing smile, she said, "Well, Jack, it seemed like you've become quite the center of attention tonight. I hope you're up for the challenge."

I let out a nervous laugh, trying to defuse the situation. "I guess I'm just lucky to have such... enthusiastic company."

Anne grins, giving me a playful wink. "See, Jack? Even your mom thinks you're doing a great job."

Diane leaned her head against my shoulder, her expression softening as she looked at me. "We all appreciate you, Jack. And if it means putting up with a bit of rivalry, I think you're handling it pretty well."

Annen laughed, her eyes dancing with amusement. "All right, all right. I'll ease up. Just couldn't resist having a little fun."

My mom, with a knowing smile, added, "Well, it's good to see everyone getting along, even with all the tension. We've got enough on our plates without adding any more drama."

As the day faded into darkness and the rain subsided, Diane and Anne headed out to gather wood for a fire.. I sat beside my mom, who was wrapped in a blanket with her injured leg propped up on a makeshift bed. Despite her effort to appear strong, the strain was clear.

"Jack," my mom said, her voice trembling. "I need to tell you everything that's happened since... since we were separated. It's important you understand."

I nodded, sitting close to her. "I'm listening, Mom."

She took a shuddering breath, her eyes clouded with memories. "When I received that letter, I was paralyzed with fear. It was so cryptic, yet it carried an urgency I couldn't ignore. Kyle had been stalking me for a while, lurking in the shadows. I knew I had to run, and keep moving. I couldn't let him find me, let alone find you."

I squeezed her hand, trying to offer comfort, but my heart ached with the weight of her words. "And then?"

Her eyes filled with tears, her voice cracking. "I ran from place to place, always on the edge of panic. I thought the gun would keep me safe, but it was a false sense of security. When you first saw me, I was so relieved to finally be near you, even if I was terrified. I didn't want you to see me like that—so broken and scared."

I looked at her with deep empathy, my own eyes misting over. "I understand, Mom. It was a lot to take in, but I'm just glad we're together now. I missed you so much."

She smiled through her tears, the weight of her sorrow palpable. "I'm sorry for everything you've been through because of me. I thought I was protecting us, but I only made things worse. And now, with this beast and everything we've faced... I felt so helpless. I don't know how we're going to get through this."

I pulled her into a gentle embrace, trying to convey all the comfort and reassurance I could. "We will get through it, Mom. We've faced so much already. Diane and Anne—they're good people. We're not alone."

She wiped her tears away, her expression softening with gratitude. "Thank you. It means everything to hear that. I just hope we can keep fighting. If we make it through this, I promise—I'll never leave your side again. We'll face everything together."

I held her close, the resolve in my voice steady. "I promise the same. No matter what happens, we stick together. We survive together."

There was a pause as my mom's gaze grew more intense, a mix of worry and urgency in her eyes. "Jack, I need to talk to you about Diane."

I looked at her, sensing the gravity in her tone. "What about Diane?"

She hesitated, then muttered, her voice trembling with concern. "I see how much Diane has been there for you. But... I've noticed something. Diane's feelings for you are deepening, and while her support is crucial, you need to be careful. She seems to want more. Her emotions are strong, and in the middle of this chaos, they could complicate things."

My heart sank as I thought about the truth in her words. "I know, Mom. Diane has been a lifeline for me, especially after... after Tiffany's death. I'm grateful for her, but it's all so overwhelming."

My mom's expression softened with understanding and a touch of sadness. "It's important to have that kind of support. But you need to stay aware, Jack. Emotions can cloud judgment. It's not just about surviving the beast; it's about making sure we're all clear-headed and focused."

As her advice sunk in, I nodded slowly, feeling its weight. "I appreciate you looking out for me. I need to find a balance between the danger, the emotions, and making sure we all stay strong."

My mom gives me a tearful, yet determined smile. "That's all anyone can ask for. This will be overcome by us. We have to. We have each other, and that's what matters most."

Diane and Anne return with an armful of wood. Diane's laughter cut through the tension as she headed over to the corner, her eyes alight with a renewed sense of purpose. She arranged the wood for the fire, and I watched her with a growing appreciation.

Anne followed behind, her gaze flicking between Diane and me with a hint of lingering jealousy. She set the wood down with a soft, almost resigned sigh and stacked it beside Diane.

Their conversation quickly shifted to Tagalog, and though I couldn't understand the words, the tension was clear.

"Si Jack na naman ang topic," Anne muttered, her tone edged with frustration. (It's about Jack again.)

Diane responded without missing a beat. "Ano bang problema mo, Anne?" she retorted. "Masyado ka namang nakikialam." (What's your problem, Anne? You're meddling too much.)

Anne huffed, clearly irritated. "Baka naman kasi masyado kang attached na sa kanya. Hindi mo ba napapansin?" (Maybe because you're getting too attached to him. Haven't you noticed?)

Diane paused, her eyes narrowing as she turned to face Anne. "At ano naman kung ganun? Alam kong naiinggit ka lang." (And so what if I am? I know you're just jealous.)

I couldn't understand their exact words, but the underlying tension is palpable. "Is everything okay?" I asked, trying to break the ice.

Diane quickly looked back at me, her expression softening. "Yes, Jack, everything's fine. Just a little sisterly disagreement."

Anne gave Diane a pointed look before turning back to the fire, her voice dropping to a near whisper. "Sana lang hindi ka magsisi sa huli, Diane." (I just hope you don't regret it in the end, Diane.)

Diane's eyes flashed with determination as she placed the last piece of wood. "Alam ko ang ginagawa ko," she said firmly. (I know what I'm doing.)

Anne just shook her head, a mixture of frustration and resignation in her expression. "Sana nga," she replied softly, almost to herself. (I hope so.)

The fire crackled to life, sending shadows dancing across the walls. Despite the warmth it provided, the coldness between Diane and Anne lingered, their unspoken rivalry simmering just beneath the surface.

After the brief altercation over the firewood, Diane finished setting up the flames and turned back to me with a soft sigh. Her eyes searched mine for reassurance as she slid into my lap, her body pressing against mine in a way that is both comforting and possessive. I could feel her heartbeat against my chest, steady but quickening with her emotions.

Anne, not to be outdone, strode over to where we sit, her steps deliberate and her presence almost challenging. She sat down beside me, so close that her shoulder brushed against mine. There was a fleeting look of defiance in her eyes as she glanced at Diane, as if daring her sister to push back. Diane subtly shifted into my lap, creating a barrier between us and Anne.

Diane's breath on my neck is warm and teasing, her closeness marked by an intimate, tender touch. Anne's jaw tightened, her fingers curling into the fabric of her pants, betraying her jealousy.

Anne broke the tense silence with a sarcastic laugh. "What the fuck ever," she muttered, her voice laced with bitterness. She abruptly moved to the other side of the fire, the flames casting harsh shadows on her face as she sat with a huff. "You win, for now."

Diane's laugh was soft but triumphant, and she nuzzled closer to me, her fingers trailing possessively down my skin. Anne glanced over, catching the movement, but quickly looked back at the fire, her expression darkening as she changed the subject. "This should keep us warm and give us a bit of light. We'll be okay for tonight."

Anne's voice was steady, but there was an undercurrent of hurt that I couldn't ignore. She sat facing the fire, her posture stiff and unyielding, trying to block out the scene behind her. The warmth of the flames contrasted with the coldness in her demeanor, and the guilt I felt gnawed at me. Anne was clearly hurting, and I was caught in the middle, torn between the two women who meant so much to me.

My mom, quietly observing the interaction, let out a light-hearted laugh. "Ah, to be young and silly again," she remarked, her words carrying a soft warmth that hinted at nostalgia and amusement. Though her comment briefly broke the tension, it couldn't fully dissolve the lingering unease.

Diane leans in, her body molding to mine as she seeks to deepen our connection. She rubbed my face, her touch gentle as she looked into my eyes. "How's everything going over here with your mom?" she asked, her tone soft but edged with concern.

"Just talking," I replied, my voice subdued. "Catching up on everything we've missed."

My mom looked at Diane and Anne, her gaze filled with gratitude despite the tension. "Thank you both. For everything you've done."

Anne forced a smile, though it didn't reach her eyes. "Just doing our part. And don't worry, Jack won't be the only one getting all the glory." Her words, intended to be light, carried a sharp edge, a reminder of her lingering hurt.

Diane laughed, nudging me playfully as if to defuse the tension. "Yeah, don't let it go to your head, Jack. We've still got a long road ahead."

I chuckled, though the sound felt empty. The fire's warmth offered comfort, but the sense of camaraderie felt fragile under the weight of the complex dynamics between us. With Diane in my lap, her breath warm against my neck and her hands trailing over my chest, the intimacy of the moment only emphasized the unspoken strain between us.

As I rubbed Diane's back, trying to provide warmth and comfort, my thoughts kept drifting to Anne. She sat by the fire, her posture rigid and her eyes fixed on the flames. Diane, sensing Anne's lingering gaze, shifted slightly in my lap but kept her arm possessively around me, her fingers tracing lazy circles on my chest.

"Anne, if you're cold, get closer to the fire," Diane said with a sweetness that barely concealed the edge in her tone. "I know you don't have a lap to sit in."

Anne's expression hardened briefly before she forced a neutral look. "I'm fine, thanks," she replied curtly. The unspoken conflict between the sisters was palpable, each glance and word a quiet battlefield of emotions.

The warmth of the fire and Diane's closeness should have been comforting, but they served as a reminder of the unspoken rivalry that has been festering for so long. I tried to focus on maintaining comfort and connection with Diane, but my thoughts strayed up to Anne, who sat by the fire, her posture rigid, her eyes fixed on the flames.

CHAPTER 11

As the night deepened and the fire's flickering glow danced across the factory walls, the unspoken strain between Diane and Anne hung heavy in the air. The crackling of the wood and the occasional rustle of the tarps added to the surreal stillness, but beneath the calm exterior, emotions churned, threatening to erupt.

Diane yawned, stretching her arms above her head. "We should lay down and get some rest," she said, her exhaustion clear in her voice.

My mom, scanning the room with concern, nodded. "Diane and Jack, you two should huddle under the tarps with your wet clothes. Try to get as dry as you can."

Diane's eyes briefly met mine, a playful glint in them. She then turned to Anne with a challenge in her gaze. "Sounds like a plan."

Anne forced a chuckle. "Looked like you two are getting cozy." Her tone was teasing but carried an edge.

Diane's smile tightened as she replied in Tagalog, her voice laced with a challenge. "Oo nga, Anne. Naiinggit ka ba?" (Yeah, Anne. Are you jealous?)

Anne's smile faltered. "Bakit naman ako maiinggit? Masaya ako na komportable kayo" (Why would I be jealous? I'm happy you're comfortable).

Sensing the tension, my mom attempted to lighten the mood with a chuckle. "We all need to stay warm and dry. Let's not let our pride get in the way of a good night's rest."

Diane's gaze softened as she looked at me, inviting. "Come on, Jack," she said, spreading out the tarps. "Let's get comfortable."

As I stood up, I noticed my pants had ridden down slightly, revealing my wet red boxers. Diane's teasing comment makes me flush with embarrassment. "Nice ass, Jack," she said with a wink.

"Aww, I missed it," Anne said, her frown barely hiding her annoyance.

I chuckled, the absurdity of the situation helping to ease the last of my nervousness. My mom joins in with a laugh. "All right, you two, don't get too excited—it's just a butt," she said, her laughter easing the tension.

Diane's embrace caught me off guard, her hug warm and comforting. Her hand playfully squeezed my ass. "Hmm, it's tight also."

Anne let out an exaggerated sigh, her gaze shifting back to the fire as though trying to block out the scene. Diane's expression locked with mine, radiating a mix of affection, longing, and a desperate need for connection. Her hand slid to the back of my head, gently drawing me closer, and for a moment, the world faded to just the two of us.

But a distant, guttural roar that sent a shiver down my spine abruptly shattered the moment. The unmistakable sound of the beast snaps me back to reality.

Diane's face paled as she gripped my arm tightly. "Jack, we need to hurry!" Her voice was urgent, filled with fear.

Her panic jolted me into action. We scramble, our previous warmth and connection replaced by the cold urgency of survival. "Diane, Anne, get my mom out of here!" I shouted, desperation edging my voice.

Diane and Anne spring into action, helping my mom out of her makeshift bed. Her frantic cries are a harsh reminder of the danger we're facing. The comforting glow of the fire becomes a backdrop to our grim reality, its warmth overshadowed by the immediate need to escape.

I dash to the control panel and pull the switch, starting the timer. "Hurry! Make sure you're clear before this goes off!" I shouted, my voice steady but my heart racing.

Diane and Anne nodded; their faces set with determination. They dragged my mom toward the opening, her protests echoing through the factory. Diane's strength and Anne's resolve are clear as they work together despite the chaos.

I glanced at the timer, watching the seconds tick down as I prepared for the next steps. The weight of our situation presses heavily on me, but the determination in Diane and the camaraderie of the group provides a sliver of hope amidst the chaos.

As the massive overhead door groaned open, Diane and Anne strained to pull my mom through the narrow gap. The factory's dim light flickered erratically, offering fragile hope as the door rose. The beast's roars grew louder, as Diane and Anne finally got my mom to the opening. With a final push, they help her through. Anne looked back at me, her eyes a mix of relief and fear.

"Go, Anne!" I urged, my voice strained. "I'll be right behind you!"

Anne hesitated, her lips parting as if to speak, but then she clenched her jaw and ducked under the door, pulling Diane and my mom with her. The door slammed shut with a deafening clang, its rusted gears grinding, trapping me inside. With a bone-jarring crash, the beast smashed through the factory wall, its yellow eyes blazing with unrestrained fury. The beast, still limping but driven by relentless rage, charges at me with terrifying speed.

I was momentarily frozen, my mind racing with horror and panic. The beast's roar was deafening, a primal sound that shook me to my core.

Desperation fueled my actions as I lunged for the control panel. "Come on!" I yelled, slamming my hand on the button. But the mechanism remained inert, and a sinking dread gripped me. I glanced at the timer: one minute left. I had forgotten about it entirely.

Before I could react, the beast was upon me. It swiped with a massive claw, and hurled me through the partially closed overhead door. The impact was brutal and unforgiving. I hit the ground outside, pain exploding through my body. The force of the throw left me gasping, my vision blurred as I struggled to comprehend the agony.

The beast roared triumphantly behind me; its growls reverberated through the factory. I lay on the cold ground, pain searing through every limb, as the factory door exploded into metal shards.

Through the haze of pain and disorientation, Diane and Anne's frantic voices reached me. "Jack!" Diane's cry carried fear and urgency." She let go of my mom, her eyes wide with terror.

Anne's shadow loomed over me as they both rushed to my side. "Hang on, Jack!" Anne's voice trembles as she kneels beside me. Diane was already by my side, her hands desperately checking for injuries.

I tried to focus, my breaths coming in ragged gasps. "The timer," I croak out, my voice barely audible. "It didn't go off. I messed up."

Her face pale, Diane looked at me with eyes filled with anguish. "It's okay, Jack. You're going to be okay. We're here with you."

Ignoring them, my attention turned back to the beast. It was coming for us. I pushed Diane and Anne away, ordering them to go! I spotted a big metal pipe on the ground. How convenient. I picked it up and swung it as the beast lunged at me. I hit it in the face, and it jerked sideways in the air, landing crookedly on the ground.

It was injured. I ran toward the bomb again, the beast right behind me. Just as I reached the bomb, the beast hit me from behind. It knocked me forward into a bunch of old computers sitting on a dusty table. I awkwardly tried to get up as the beast grabbed the table and hurled it into the side of the building, smashing it into pieces.

I jumped through its legs and went into a roll. Without hesitation, I snatched a sharp piece of debris and pounced toward its back. I stabbed it right in the middle of its upper back. It knocked me off, and I got thrown outside again. I get up, shaking my head to get my bearings straight. Dizzy, I half walked, half ran toward the beast.

As I charged, the beast swiped at me with its massive claw. I narrowly dodged, feeling the rush of wind from the near miss. I swung the metal pipe again, aiming for its injured leg. The pipe connected with a sickening crunch, and the beast howled in pain, momentarily staggering.

Seeing an opening, I leaped onto its back, grabbing onto its matted fur. The beast thrashed wildly, trying to throw me off. I held on with every ounce of strength, raising the sharp piece of debris and plunging it into its side. The beast roared in agony, its movements became frantic and desperate.

"Jack, look out!" Diane's voice pierced through the chaos, but I was too focused on the fight. The beast bucked hard, finally dislodging me and sending me crashing to the ground. I rolled to my feet, grabbing the metal pipe again just as the beast lunged at me with bare teeth.

I thrust the pipe upward, catching the beast in the throat. It gags, black blood pouring from the wound. I pulled the pipe free and swung again, hitting it across the snout. The beast stumbled back, disoriented and enraged.

The timer on the bomb continued to tick down. I needed to end this now. Summoning all my strength, I rushed at the beast, delivering a flurry of blows with the pipe. Each strike echoed through the factory, a desperate symphony of survival.

The beast swiped at me, catching me across the chest and sending me sprawling. Pain seared through my body, but I forced myself to stand. I couldn't give up now. I couldn't let this thing win.

I noticed a length of chain hanging from the ceiling, probably used for lifting heavy machinery. An idea forms in my mind. I grabbed the chain, wrapping it around my hand as I dodged another attack from the beast. With a quick maneuver, I looped the chain around the beast's neck and pulled tight.

The beast thrashed, trying to free itself, but I held on, using all my weight to keep the chain taut. The beast's movements were slow, its strength fading as the chain cut off its air supply. Finally, with one last roar, it collapsed to the ground, its body limp.

I released the chain, collapsing to the ground beside the beast. Pain wracked my body, but relief washed over me. It was over. I defeated the beast.

Diane and Anne rushed to my side, their faces etched with concern. "Jack, are you okay?" Diane asked, her voice trembling.

I managed a weak smile, my vision blurring. "We did it," I whispered. "It's over."

As they helped me to my feet, we walked out of the building. Behind us, a rattling noise stopped us in our tracks. We look back and see the beast slowly slashing its way back up, smashing and hitting anything nearby. Exhausted and hurt by the fight, I desperately searched for my mom. I couldn't find her.

Then I noticed something. "Oh, no!" I cried out, my heart sinking. My mom stood next to the bomb. The beast was still trying to get the sharp object out of its back. I realized what's happening. I forced myself to run. She was going to push the button.

"No! Mom, don't do it!" I screamed, my voice breaking.

She didn't say a word. As time seemed to slow down, my mom raised her hand at me. She formed the "I Love You" sign with her fingers.

I was flooded with flashbacks. She always did that with me. That was our thing. No matter what was going on in my life, she always made me feel special with that simple gesture.

I saw memories of her doing that at various stages of my life, of throwing herself in front of me to protect me from Kyle's attack, almost killing her. Still running toward her, I raise my hand up and make the "I Love You" sign as well. Tears stream down my face.

The beast gets the sharp piece out of its back. It turned its attention to my mom. I get even closer, my heart pounding.

I looked at my mom. A single tear fell down her face as she managed to smile. The beast leaped at her, its mouth opened wide with razor-sharp teeth. My mom pushed the button.

"BOOOMMM!"

The explosion was catastrophic. The blast hit me hard, knocking me off my feet. I felt the intense heat of the fire seared my face. I was thrown backward, the force of the explosion sending me crashing into debris. As I hit the ground, I smacked my head, and everything went black.

My memories flash through my mind as I slip into unconsciousness. I saw my father, his warm smile and strong embrace. Witnessing the moment, he was taken from me, I saw his body crumpling to the ground, along with my mother's helpless cries. I saw Kyle, the torment and fear he brought into our lives. And I saw my mom, always there, always protecting me, her love unwavering.

As I drifted further into the darkness, one last memory surfaces. It was my mom and me, in the backyard, her teaching me to make the "I Love You" sign with my fingers. "No matter what happens, Jack, always know that I love you," she said.

I woke up with a start, my body aching all over. The ground was cold and hard beneath me, and I could barely see through the haze of dust and smoke. I tried to sit up, but pain lances through my chest, making me gasp. I looked around frantically, searching for any sign of Diane, Anne, or my mom.

"Jack, over here!" Diane's voice was weak, but unmistakable. I saw her and Anne, battered and bruised, but alive, pulling themselves out of the wreckage. Relief flooded through me, but it was quickly overshadowed by the gut-wrenching realization of what my mom did.

"Mom…" I whispered, my voice breaking. Diane and Anne helped me to my feet, their faces etched with sorrow.

"We have to go," Anne said softly. "The beast is gone. Your mom… she saved us."

"Jack, come on!" Diane shouted again, her voice breaking with emotion.

"We have to go, now!" Anne yelled; her eyes wide with panic.

But I couldn't leave. I couldn't abandon my mom. My heart pounded, a mix of fear and determination driving me forward. "Mom!" I screamed, my voice raw with desperation. I stagger toward the burning building, my legs weak but my will strong. Flames danced at the edges of the structure, the heat intense, almost unbearable.

I heard Anne and Diane calling me back, their voices growing more frantic, but I couldn't stop. "Mom!" I screamed again, my voice breaking. The smoke stung my eyes, and I coughed, but I pushed forward, navigating through the wreckage. Each step was a struggle, the debris shifted under my feet, threatening to trip me.

"Mom!" I shouted, my voice hoarse. I saw a figure amidst the rubble, and my heart leaped. "Mom!" I rushed over, but as I got closer, I realized it was just a piece of twisted metal, not her.

Tears blurred my vision. Despair threatened to overwhelm me, but I couldn't give up. "Mom!" I shout again, lifting broken beams, pushing aside debris, refusing to believe she's gone.

Anne and Diane reached me, grabbing my arms, trying to pull me back. "Jack, it's too dangerous! We have to go!" Anne pleaded, her grip firm but gentle.

"No! I can't leave her!" I screamed, struggling against them. Diane wrapped her arms around me, trying to calm me down.

"We can't lose you too," she whispered, her voice choked with emotion. Her arms were strong and steady, anchoring me as my world fell apart.

I looked into Diane's eyes, seeing the fear and sadness there. I knew she was right, but it tore me apart. "Mom," I whispered, my voice cracking. The pain was almost too much to bear.

"We have to go," Anne repeated, her voice trembling. "Please, Jack."

Tears streamed down my face as I realized the truth. The building was a raging inferno, and my mom was gone. With one last look at the burning wreckage, I let out a sob, my heart shattering.

Diane pulled me into a tight hug, her warmth and strength enveloping me. "It's okay," she whispered. "It's going to be okay. We need to survive for her."

Her embrace finally broke me. I nodded slowly, the weight of reality crashing down on me. With Diane's arms around me, I found the strength to move. Together, we retreated from the burning building.

As we reached the edge of the destruction, I turned back one last time, whispering a silent promise to my mom. "I'll never forget you," I vowed, the pain of her loss etched into my soul.

Anne and Diane guided me toward the escape route they had discovered. At first, it looked like a cave entrance, but as we approached, it became apparent that it was a metal barrier. The surface of the metal barrier was scorched and pitted, with debris scattered around it. Like it had melted.

"It's a barrier," I said, wincing as I held the back of my throbbing head.

"That evil bitch is lying to us," Anne snapped. "She's had us trapped this whole time, stuck inside this enormous bubble."

"Yeah, well, we're getting out now." I stepped forward.

Diane tightened her grip on my arm. "Hold on. You don't even know what's on the other side. It could be just another trap set by that crazy woman."

"Bitch! That crazy bitch!" Anne yelled in agreement, taking a step toward the hole with anger in her eyes.

We all peered through the hole. The darkness on the other side was absolute, like staring into a void that swallows everything. Diane's hand clutched mine with a trembling grip. I tried to focus on her, but her presence was just a faint sensation in the overwhelming blackness. Her panic was palpable, her breaths quick and uneven.

The darkness shifted and churned around us, enveloping everything in an oppressive void. My stomach lurched as an unseen force yanked us forward, the sensation akin to being caught in the grip of a violent, invisible storm. My chest tightened as the air grew impossibly thick, every breath a struggle. An unbearable weight pressed against my body, squeezing from all sides, leaving me desperate to stay grounded in the chaos.

I tried to scream, but the oppressive force around me swallowed my voice. My mind raced, unable to process what happened. The pressure became unbearable, squeezing me until I was on the verge of losing consciousness.

Just as my vision dimmed, a faint light appeared in the distance. In an instant, everything went white. I was abruptly in a stark, sterile room. A TV on the wall flickered to life, and I sat alone, a profound sense of dread washing over me.

The TV screen lit up with the woman's face. Her laugh was unsettlingly cheerful, a cruel contrast to the despair I felt. "Congratulations, Jack! You made it through the third Trial. You fought bravely against that beast. Even though you didn't deliver the killing blow, you survived. Now, for the next Trial—you'll be sent two years into the future! How thrillingly unpredictable!"

My frustration exploded. "Where are Diane and Anne? What have you done to them? You monster! I swear I'll make you pay for this!"

The woman's smirk widened; her eyes gleaming with malevolence. "Oh, Jack, Diane and Anne will be sent to the same place you'll be going, but at different times. I want to see how you handle the loneliness and uncertainty of seeing them only when you least expect it. It's all part of making this Trial more... interesting."

Confusion and anguish churned inside me. "Why all this madness? You killed my mother!"

The woman's expression hardened. "You're the reason your mother is dead, Jack. Your failures and indecision are why she's gone. You didn't finish the job with the beast. You were lucky to survive this Trial, but don't expect any mercy. Greater challenges await you."

The TV abruptly shut off, leaving me in oppressive silence. My heart pounded painfully in my chest as despair overwhelmed me. I staggered to my feet, my anger blending with deep, unrelenting grief. The only light came from a blinking indicator on the far wall. I stumbled toward it, my mind reeling with loss and confusion. I pressed the button, and a blinding flash enveloped me. Everything went dark. I couldn't see or feel anything, as it felt as though I was falling into an abyss of despair.

CHAPTER 12

Without warning, I crashed onto a table; the impact was jarring. The table splintered beneath me, causing my body to be engulfed in pain. Darkness engulfed the room, and the stench of mildew permeated the air. Adding to the overall sense of decay is the wet and sticky floor.

I pushed myself up, my voice echoing in the emptiness as I muttered, "Where am I?" The isolation was maddening, and the woman's earlier laughter reverberated in my mind. I needed to find a way out and grasp what was happening.

I spotted a faint glimmer of light and crawled painfully across the floor until I reached a window. As my eyes adjusted to the dim light, I saw an abandoned street outside, illuminated only by flickering streetlights. The area was desolate, with broken windows and overturned cars. It looked like something out of a post-apocalyptic nightmare.

A wave of memories crashed over me. I recalled when streets like this were bustling with life, contrasting with the decay before me. The realization hit me hard: Tiffany was truly gone. My tears flowed uncontrollably.

"Mom!" I screamed, collapsing to the floor. My sobs are raw, my face drenched in tears. The weight of losing everyone I loved was almost too much to bear. I had promised to protect my mother, and now she was gone. The thought drove me into a seething rage.

My fists clenched tightly, the agony transforming into steely determination. Whoever orchestrated this nightmare would pay. I wasn't sure where Diane and Anne were, but I knew I must find them and end this hell. With resolve set, I dragged myself toward the window, searching for any sign of hope amidst the desolation.

SLAM!

I froze, the sound slicing through the haze of my confusion. My heart raced. I held my breath, straining to detect any other sounds. The silence stretched, almost unbearable.

Then, I heard it: faint, hurried footsteps echoing up the stairs. The footsteps grew louder, more distinct. I glanced around the dimly lit room, trying to make sense of my surroundings. My body still ached, my head throbbing from the earlier encounter. The desk in the corner seemed like the only piece of furniture, with any hope of providing cover.

Adrenaline surged through me, pushing me past the pain. I stumbled toward the desk, each step jarring my battered body. I got underneath it, positioning myself so that the back faced the door. My breath came in ragged gasps, and I tried to calm myself, but fear gnawed at my insides.

The footsteps grew louder, their rhythm almost palpable. I scrambled to search the surface of the desk, hoping to find something—anything—that I could use as a weapon. My hands trembled as I reached out, feeling around for a useful object. My fingers brushed over something, but it kept rolling away just as I tried to grasp it.

The footsteps were now so close that I could almost hear the person's breathing. Being found was not something I could afford. I continued my frantic search, my heart pounding. I felt something solid under my fingers and seized it, only to have it drop to the floor with a clatter.

BANG! BANG! BANG!!

The force of the banging made me jerk up, slamming my head painfully against the underside of the desk. Pain exploded in my skull, and I bit back a scream, covering my mouth with my hands. The banging intensified, becoming more frenzied and aggressive. My heart raced as panic gripped me.

I peered out from under the desk. The door cracked; the force of the banging split the wood. I spotted the object that fell—the pen—rolling slightly away. It was all I had. I stretch out as far as I can, finally grabbing it just as the door bursts open with a splintering crash.

Wood and debris flew everywhere. I clutched the pen tightly, my knuckles turned white, and I pulled myself back into hiding. I held my breath, hoping the chaos would provide enough cover. The room fell eerily silent except for the sound of footsteps drawing nearer.

A voice broke the silence, low and menacing. "Jack, I know you are here. I can smell you." The voice was unnaturally guttural, filled with a sinister undertone. "Come out and make this easy for me."

I risked a glance over the desk. The figure approaching was a man, but not an ordinary one. His eyes glowed with a hellish yellow-orange hue, a sight that sent chills down my spine. My heart raced, and I quickly ducked back down, trying to stay hidden.

"It's such a shame about your mother," the man taunted, his voice dripping with malicious delight. My throat tightened, and tears flowed uncontrollably. "Should've been you, but it was your mom who bit the dust instead. Her body blown to bits. Ha Ha Ha!"

The memory of the explosion flooded my mind, the image of my mother's death replaying vividly. The anger and grief merged into a searing rage. I couldn't let this monster get away with this. I clutched the pen, my resolve hardening. My fists clenched tightly as I prepared for a fight.

"I would have liked to taste her flesh, but I'll settle for yours!" The man's voice was a cruel promise. He moved closer, his presence overwhelming. I took a deep breath, forcing the tears back, and stood up. With a determined roar, I leaped over the desk, the pen aimed straight at him.

He blocked my attack with ease, his movements swift and almost inhuman. He countered with a swift punch to my stomach, doubling me over in pain. I could barely stay on my feet, swinging the pen wildly. He dodged each strike effortlessly, his yellow eyes gleamed with amusement.

With a growl, he lunged at me, but I ducked under his arm and stabbed the pen into his side. He howled in pain, but the wound only seemed to anger him further. He backhanded me with a force that sent me sprawling to the floor, the taste of blood filling my mouth.

I scrambled to my feet, my vision blurring. The man advanced, his movements predatory. Desperation fueled my actions. I grabbed a splintered piece of wood from the broken table and swung it at him. He caught it mid-air, yanking it from my grasp and tossing it aside.

Before I could react, he grabbed my throat with a grip of steel. I was lifted off the ground and slammed against the wall with bone-jarring force. The impact knocked the wind out of me, leaving me gasping for breath.

His eyes bored into mine, a dark abyss filled with malevolence. I struggled to breathe as his grip tightened, my vision narrowed. Desperation drove me to act. Without thinking, I thrust the pen upward, aiming for his eye.

The pen pierced his eye with a sickening squelch. The man howled in agony, his grip loosening as he stumbled back, clutching his injured face. He collapsed to the floor, writhing in pain. I dropped to the ground, gasping for air, my body trembling with exhaustion.

The room fell silent again. I pushed myself up, my body protesting with every movement. I crawled toward the doorway, but as I reached it, I was suddenly thrown back into the room. My body skidded across the floor, crashing into the wall.

Another figure appeared, charging at me with the same eerie yellow eyes. He lunged, and I barely dodged, rolling aside as he crashed into the floor, creating a loud crack. He roared in frustration, rising to his feet with a menacing glare.

"You can't escape me that easily!" he screamed, his voice a shrill snarl. He lunged again, and I'm hit hard, slamming into the wall. The impact is almost too much to bear, my vision swimming.

I spotted the man by the broken window, his figure silhouetted against the night sky. Desperation fuels my actions. I charged at him, tackling him with all the strength I could muster. We crashed through the window, falling through the air in a chaotic tumble. The rush of wind was both exhilarating and terrifying.

CRUNCH!

We landed on the top of a bus, the impact jarring and painful. The bus roof offered little protection, and I was left sprawled on top, my arms numb and aching. I glanced up at the building from which we fell, realizing with disbelief that I'd survived an eight-story plunge.

I tried to move, but my arms felt like dead weight. The pain was overwhelming. I saw the bus roof and the broken window high above. The adrenaline faded, leaving me with a deep sense of exhaustion and pain.

As I struggled to free my arms, I inadvertently rolled off the bus. I hit the ground hard, my body crumpling into a heap. The impact is jarring, and I couldn't move.

The air filled with eerie screams again. My vision grew blurry as people with yellow eyes approached me. My strength was nearly gone. I was unable to move, my body protesting with every attempt.

Just as the creatures drew near, the roar of an engine cut through the chaos. The figures looked toward the sound. I couldn't turn my head properly, but a vehicle sped into view. It slammed into the creatures, sending one body flying over the car while another is crushed underneath.

A woman stepped out of the car. Through my fading vision, I recognized her face. It was Diane. Relief flooded through me, but it was short-lived as everything faded to black. I slipped into the comforting darkness of unconsciousness, hoping that Diane's arrival signified a turning point in this relentless nightmare.

CHAPTER 13

"Hey!"

The shake and voice seeped through the fog of my unconsciousness, distant yet insistent. The darkness was oppressive, and the voice, though familiar, seemed to come from another world. I tried to focus but found it nearly impossible.

"Hey! It's time to wake up now. Hey, Jack!"

The voice growled louder, more urgent. My body twitched at the sound of tapping on my shoulder.

"Wake up now, Jack!"

Panic gripped me. Was I back in that dark, tormenting hole? The voice ripped me from unconsciousness.

"Hey! Wake up! Jack! Jack! Jack! Jack!"

The incessant calling became deafening, piercing through the haze. Suddenly, a jolt of searing pain spread across my body. My eyes opened, blurry at first. Moving lights danced across my vision.

As my sight cleared, I saw a woman standing over me. I tried to move my arms but found them restrained. Chains? My heart raced with terror.

"Huh?" I attempted to react but only knocked the tray she was holding away. It clattered to the floor, spilling its contents. I tried to sit up, but the pain in my arms is unbearable. I looked down; both my arms were encased in cast.

"Where am I? What is this? Who are you? What's going on?"

The woman, trying to calm me, looked exasperated.

"Whoa! Calm down! Hey, hey! Calm down. Calm the hell down!"

"What are you doing to me? Where am I?"

"I'm not doing anything to you." She glanced down at the mess on the floor with frustration. "Oh shit! Ugh!" She sat on the bed next to me, her demeanor softening despite her irritation.

"What happened to me?" I asked, my voice cracking with confusion and fear.

"Okay, I know it surprised you, and I'm sorry for waking you up like that. They rescued you and brought you here to an old military base. You had serious injuries, two broken arms and multiple concussions. You've been unconscious for a couple of days now. It also surprised me when I saw you here because we thought you were dead."

As my eyes focused more clearly, recognition dawned. Her face became clearer with each passing second.

"Diane!" I tried to reach out, but my broken arms reminded me of my limitations. Diane giggled as I winced in pain.

"Yes! I'm glad you remember me! That means your head is still working well. I'm so glad you survived. Here, I'll give you a hug instead." She pulled me into a gentle embrace. Her familiar scent was comforting, almost overpowering. She lingered in the embrace, her hands caressing my back.

"Yeah, two men attacked me. Both had glowing yellow eyes. They seemed much stronger than normal men. I killed one and pushed the other out of a window. We fell on top of a bus. The last thing I remember was people coming after me with those same yellow eyes. A car hit a few of them. Are they dead? And you were there!"

My memories flooded back, sharp and vivid. Diane's face was a beacon of familiarity in the chaos.

"Yes, I found you there. You were lucky I was out on patrol in that area." She tapped my shoulder, her touch lingering. "Diane, I have so many questions."

She smiled playfully, her hand brushing against my cheek. "Well, one at a time, and I'll try to answer to the best of my knowledge."

"So, this place? How long has it been around?"

"It's been two years since we were torn apart... two years, Jack. The world you knew is barely recognizable anymore." She glanced away, her eyes distant as if recalling horrors she couldn't fully put into words. "That demon... it's everywhere now. It took everything."

She took a deep breath and looked back at me, her voice shaking but filled with urgency.

"The United States... most of it... it's gone. Not just the people, but the land itself. The demon possesses entire towns, turning the people into its puppets, and it corrupts the ground beneath their feet. Cities that once thrived, like New York, Los Angeles, even small towns you wouldn't think twice about... all of them have become wastelands. Barron, decayed, stripped of life."

She paused, tears glistened in her eyes but refused to fall.

"Entire regions are nothing but ash and dust. People tried to fight it, but it... it was like fighting the wind. It slipped through their fingers, spread faster than anyone could keep up with."

She clenched her fists, her voice lowering to a whisper.

"There's nowhere left to run. Most of us... we hid underground. Those who are still out there... they're either dead or worse—possessed. It's like their minds are trapped, screaming inside their own bodies, unable to break free."

She exhaled heavily, her voice breaking.

"I don't even know how many of us are left. But it's not many. Most days, we can't even hear anything outside except the wind howling through the dead trees... but we know the demon's still there, waiting. Unfortunately, he has been very successful so far. He killed three people within the year prior to us joining this base and two more survivors yesterday while on a food run. Our supplies are running low, and we have a couple of elderly people here who won't survive much longer in these conditions."

"So, you and Anne got here a year ago? Is Anne still, you know, alive? Did I really time travel?" My questions came out in a jumble.

Diane raised her hands, palms out, as if trying to physically slow the flood of information. "Whoa, hold up. I said one at a time." A teasing laugh slipped out, though her slightly uneven breath betrayed her struggle to process everything. She tucked a loose strand of hair behind her ear, the movement quick and almost absent-minded. "Well, apparently," she began, her tone light but laced with an underlying tension, "from what my sister and I could gather, that flashing light in the white room didn't just teleport us to a new location. Our limited studies show that it also teleported us into the future."

"Holy shit! The future? Are we? I mean, have we? Huh, how?" My confusion and excitement intertwined.

"So, we are just going to disregard the one-question thing now?" Diane chuckled. "We don't know how. But I can tell you we are about two years in the future."

"Wow, really? Damn. This is so crazy. I can't believe it." My head spun with the implications.

"Well, you better because this is happening. Oh, and my sister is not dead. She is alive." Diane finished picking up the food and water from the floor. I realized it was just basic supplies. "Sorry about the mess. I thought it was something else."

"Oh, that's fine. At least now we know your brain is working." Diane's smile was flirtatious, and I found myself surprised by her look. I missed her more than I realized.

Diane shifted slightly, looking around the bunker as if to remind herself of how much had changed. She stared at me. "After the third trial began, everything shifted. We were scattered, lost in moments that weren't our own. Those of us who survived landed here... years before you did." She sighed deeply, her fingers idly tracing a scar on the table. "It was chaos when we arrived. No one knew where—or 'when'—we were. This place… this bunker was deserted. It must've been abandoned before everything fell apart. But it had food, weapons, supplies... it became our home."

Her tone turned grim.

"The first survivors who found this place set up rules—strict ones. We had to. With the demon out there and no way to know who might be possessed... we couldn't take chances. We scouted for others, anyone the Queen had sent through time, anyone who landed in this new hell. We found some... but not many."

She looked at me with a hard expression.

"We've been collecting survivors for over a year now." She paused meaningfully. "You... you're the last one, Jack. The last piece of whatever twisted game the Queen is playing."

Her voice lowers to a whisper, filled with frustration and confusion.

"Why us? Why pull us out of time just to fight for survival in a world that's already dead? I don't know. None of us do. But we've had no choice but to keep going. If we don't fight... we die."

"The Queen told me it was to make sure we couldn't team up and work together all at once."

Diane looked at me, amused. "Really? That's happening anyway, though."

I laughed, glancing at my arms. "Yeah, I don't know. So, how long do I have to keep these cast on?"

"About ten to twelve weeks. It all depends on how well they heal. They had to do emergency surgery when you arrived. From what I was told, it was pretty nasty." Diane leaned in closer, her face inched from mine, her breath warm on my skin.

"Oh wow, that's not good. Well, I've learned not to tackle anyone out of windows, especially when the building is way too high off the ground!"

"Haha yeah, that would be a good idea not to." Diane's hand rests on my chest, her fingers tracing gentle patterns. "I've missed you, Jack. It's been so hard without you. Every day, I wondered if you were alive."

"How is the training going?" I smirked, trying to lighten the mood. "It can't be too hard—I killed one with a pen."

"Oh wow! You don't sound like the one who got injured." Diane's laughter was warm and genuine. "Well, you know what? I killed one with just my eyes." She winked seductively, her hand sliding up to my neck. The touch was electric, and my heart skipped a beat. I'm both charmed and flustered.

"Haha yeah, I could see that happening." I shifted, and a sharp pain shot through my side, making me wince.

"Ouch." I reached for the pain, but my hand faltered. Diane's touch is there before I can even move, her fingers gently pressing against the spot.

"Hey! I just told you you were seriously injured. You must be careful. Don't make any sudden movements."

"Yeah." I looked at Diane, her closeness intoxicating. Concern filled her eyes, and the warmth of her hand on my skin sends mixed signals through my mind.

"Wait, how did my clothes get changed?"

"They were going to assign someone to take care of you. I volunteered." Diane's voice softened with a mixture of professionalism and personal care. "Since we knew each other well, I figured it might help when you woke up, and I was right." Her eyes held a glimmer of satisfaction and tenderness. "Once I had you in my care, I had to clean you up because you stank so badly. Most of the dried blood wasn't yours, thankfully. I threw out your dirty clothes and changed you."

I blushed, feeling exposed. "You didn't see anything, did you?"

"Oh! I made sure to look!" Diane giggled mischievously, her hand resting on my thigh. The boldness of her touch sends a jolt through me, and my eyes widen in shock.

"I meant not to look." I tried to regain my composure.

"What?" Diane asked, still laughing. "Oh, come on! You're acting like a girl!" She inched closer, her lips almost brushed mine.

"Ha, wow! I've never been accused of acting like a girl. Should I flip my hair back?" I mockingly tossed my hair, trying to deflect the intensity of the moment.

"Ha! Yep, it suits you. Why still worry about that when you were almost dying?" Diane's touch became more deliberate, her fingers lingering on my skin with a softness that is both soothing and electrifying.

"I—I don't know. It's just that I've never been so helpless before. And you're an attractive woman. It's intimidating." My voice was barely a whisper, my heart pounding in my chest.

"Just don't worry about me. It was my job, and my pleasure." Diane's tone shifted from playful to earnest. "Besides, after everything we've been through, I know we have a special connection now." She leaned in, pressing her forehead against mine. Her breath mingles with mine, and I can feel the warmth of her closeness.

I nodded, feeling a warmth in my chest. "Yeah, we do have a special connection. It's just been so long, and everything felt so different now."

Diane's fingers gently traced the line of my jaw. "Different, yes, but in some ways, it feels like no time has passed at all." Her eyes searched for mine, a mix of longing and relief. "I've been desperate to see you, Jack. Every day without you felt like a lifetime."

Her touch sent shivers down my spine, her presence both familiar and intoxicating. "I've missed you too, Diane. More than I can say."

She leaned in even closer, her lips brushing against my ear as she whispered, "Then don't say it. Show me."

I swallowed hard, my heart racing. Diane's boldness was intoxicating, her touch setting my skin on fire. Despite the pain and confusion, I leaned into her, drawn by the undeniable chemistry between us.

"You'll never lose me," she whispered, her lips almost touching mine. The world seemed to fade away, leaving just the two of us in a cocoon of shared emotion. But Tiffany's face flashed in my head, and I turned my head away, shattering the moment.

"I'm sorry, Diane. I'm not ready," I said, frustration clear in my voice. The guilt of not being able to fully commit to this moment weighed heavily on me.

Diane looked down, her shoulders trembling slightly. She bit her lip, trying to hold back the flood of emotions she had kept buried for so long.

"For you... it was just hours." She looked up at me, her eyes filled with longing and hurt. "For me... it was a year. An entire year of thinking you were dead, of waking up every day wondering if you'd been possessed by the demon... or worse, killed."

Her voice cracked, and she stood up, pacing a few steps before stopping. She moved with agitation; her face a mask of pain. "I waited, Jack. Every day I hoped you'd walk through those doors. But as time went on... My hope began to fade away. I tried to be strong for the others, tried to convince them we'd all make it through this... but inside... I felt empty."

She turned to face me, tears now falling freely down her cheeks. "I spent nights just... sitting here. Thinking about you. About what we had, what we lost. Every second felt like an eternity. And there were days... days when I almost wished the demon would just come for me. At least then... I wouldn't have to feel this anymore."

She walked toward me, hands trembling as she reached out to touch my face. Her touch was tender but filled with an ache that mirrored my own. "But now you're here... and I don't know what to do. I don't know how to let go of the fear... the pain. I've spent so long without you that I don't even know if... if I can let myself believe this is real."

I grabbed her hand gently, my voice soft but full of determination. "I'm here now, Diane. And I'm not going anywhere. I promise you."

Diane broke down, leaning into me, her voice muffled against my chest. "Don't leave me again. Please... I can't take it anymore. I thought I lost you for good."

I wrapped my arms around her tightly, holding her as if afraid she might slip away again. My heart ached with the depth of my feelings for her. "I'm not leaving you. Never again."

We stayed like that, locked in each other's arms, the weight of our shared suffering slowly lifting as we found solace in our reunion. The world outside may be a wasteland, but here, at this moment, we had each other—and that's all that mattered.

"Thanks, by the way," I said as she pulled away, trying to ease the lingering tension.

"You're welcome," Diane replied, a small, bittersweet smile on her lips. She started cleaning up the mess, her movements steady but still tinged with the emotions of the moment. She stood with the tray in hand. "I have to go now. I need to get more food and water. But I hope you won't waste it next time." Diane walked away, her hips swaying with each step. I couldn't help but watch her, feeling a mix of gratitude and something deeper, something that seemed to stir beneath the surface of everything we had just shared.

She glanced back, catching me staring. A devilish smile spread across her face.

"And you two are tough survivors!" Diane said, looking down at my exposed crotch before winking at me seductively.

I looked down, realizing what she meant. I tried to cover myself with my hands but winced as I forgot my arms were in cast. Diane's laughter filled the room, mixing with my embarrassed shout.

"Ah, yeah, thanks," I mumbled, feeling my face flush. Diane was already out the door, leaving me alone with my thoughts.

When Diane left, I remained alone in the sterile, dimly lit room. The silence that followed felt oppressive, amplifying the turmoil inside me. I tried to process everything she told me, but the weight of it all was almost too much to bear. The comforting familiarity of Diane, contrasted with the stark reality of my situation, made my emotions surge uncontrollably.

"How did everything get so messed up?" I whispered to myself, the confusion mingling with a deep sense of loss. I stared at the ceiling, trying to steady my breathing, but the pain in my side and the throbbing in my head only made it harder.

I tried to find some solace in Diane's words about the bunker and the future. "Two years ahead... in the future..." The idea still felt surreal. "Is this real? How do I even process this?"

A sudden burst of tears surprised me. The reality of my mother's death was overwhelming. I hadn't fully allowed myself to grieve, to face the finality of it all. Her sacrifice, the choice she made to protect everyone else, echoed in my mind like a haunting melody I couldn't escape.

"Mom... why did you have to..." My voice cracked, and the tears flowed more freely. With my good arm, I clutched the blanket to ground myself. If only I had been stronger. I should have done something. "I could have." I stopped, knowing there was no point in second-guessing. The guilt and self-blame only deepened my sorrow.

The room seemed to close in on me, the weight of everything pressing down. The walls were silent witnesses to my grief, my pain, my longing. And during it all, the memory of Diane's touch, her warmth, her unwavering presence, was the only thing that kept me from breaking completely.

The door creaked open, and Diane stepped in, carrying a fresh tray of food. Her face was a picture of resolve and tenderness, a stark contrast to the exhaustion that marked my own.

"I thought you might be hungry," she said softly, placing the tray on the bedside table. Her eyes met mine with a warmth that immediately made me feel a little less alone.

"Thanks," I said, trying to muster a small smile. "I didn't expect you to go through so much trouble."

Diane shrugged lightly as she arranged the food. "It's no trouble. You need to eat. And... well, I needed to be here with you. Especially after..."

The weight of unspoken emotions filled the room as her voice trailed off for a moment. "After...?" I prompted gently.

Diane looked down at the food, her expression softening. "After everything that happened. Losing your mom, fighting demons, the chaos. It's been a lot, Jack. And seeing you like this..."

In a barely audible whisper, I said, "I know. I never imagined it would be like this. I keep thinking about her, and..."

Diane sat down next to me, her hand resting gently on mine. "You did everything you could. She made a choice to protect everyone, and you honored her memory by fighting on, by being here."

With a lump in my throat, I looked at her. "I just... I keep replaying things in my mind. What if I'd acted differently? What if I'd been faster or braver?"

"Stop," Diane said firmly, though her voice was soothing. "You can't change the past. What matters is that you're here now. We're all here to support each other. And right now, that means you need to focus on healing."

I nodded, feeling the sincerity in her words. "It's hard to let go of the guilt, though. I felt like I should have been stronger."

Diane's gaze softened, and she took my hand in both of hers. "You're stronger than you know. But right now, you need to focus on getting better. You can't carry the weight of everything on your own."

She stood up and helped me with the food. "Here, let me help you," she said, gently lifting a spoonful of soup toward my mouth. "It's not much, but it'll help."

I hesitated for a moment, feeling self-conscious. "You don't have to—"

"I want to," Diane interrupted, her tone firm but kind. "You need to eat, and I want to be here for you. Besides, it's not every day I get to take care of you like this."

She fed me slowly, each bite a small comfort amidst the chaos of my thoughts. As she moved from one dish to the next, we continued to talk, her presence a balm to my troubled mind.

"You know," Diane said softly, her eyes meeting mine as she offered a forkful of mashed potatoes, "your mom would be proud of you. She'd see how much you've grown, how you've handled everything with such courage."

As I swallowed, my emotions welled up again. "I hope so. I just wish I could have made her last moments easier."

Diane's hand gently brushed against my cheek. "You did your best. And sometimes, that's all we can do. She knew you loved her. That's what matters."

The sincerity in her voice made me feel a little less burdened. Diane continued to feed me, her touch and words a soothing presence. The intimacy of the moment, her closeness, and the care she showed all worked together to make me feel more at ease.

As Diane placed the last bit of food back on the tray, she looked at me with a soft, almost fragile smile. "How are you feeling now?"

"Better," I admitted, a genuine smile breaking through the haze of my sorrow. "Thank you, Diane. For everything. For being here, for understanding."

Her eyes, glistening with a mix of relief and something deeper, locked onto mine. "I'm always here for you, Jack. No matter what."

Her words, though comforting, were a bittersweet reminder of the harsh reality we faced. I looked at her, seeing the depth of care in her eyes—a look I hadn't realized how much I missed. "Diane, thank you. I don't know what I would have done without you. You saved my life."

"You'd have done the same for me," she replied with a soft smile, her voice steady despite the raw emotion in her eyes. "We're a team, remember? And besides, it wasn't just me. We all work together to protect each other."

I tried to laugh, but it came out as a sob. "It's just—" I swallowed hard, "—I never imagined things would end up like this. I thought I could make a difference, but it feels like everything is falling apart."

Diane's hand tightened reassuringly on my arm, her touch warm and firm. "You did make a difference. You fought bravely, even when it seemed hopeless. That's something to be proud of. And as for the future, we're all going to have to adjust. But we'll get through it. You're strong, Jack. You've proven that already."

I could see she truly believed in me. The sincerity in her voice and the warmth of her presence made me feel less alone. Her eyes were pools of unwavering support, their depth reflecting the long hours she'd spent worrying, hoping, and waiting.

"I wish I could be as strong as you," I admitted quietly.

"You are," Diane said firmly, her voice a soothing balm. "Maybe you don't see it now, but you are. And I believe in you. We all do."

As she stood up to leave, picking up the tray, I felt a pang of reluctance. "Diane, wait. Could you... could you stay a little longer? I know it's probably a lot to ask, but I don't want to be alone right now."

She looked back at me, her eyes softening with an emotion that seemed almost palpable. "Of course. I'll stay with you as long as you need. We'll get through this together."

Diane set the tray back down and lay next to me, her head resting on my chest, her arm draped around my stomach. Her warmth was like a shield against the cold reality outside. We lay in silence, the occasional sound from outside the room punctuating the quiet. Her presence was a gentle reminder that, despite everything, I wasn't alone in this fight.

Breaking the silence, Diane spoke softly, "You know, I've thought about this moment for so long. Wondered what I'd say to you when I finally saw you again."

I turned my head slightly to look at her, our faces just inched apart. "What did you imagine?"

"I imagined telling you how much I missed you," she said, her voice trembling slightly, her eyes shimmering with unshed tears. "How every day without you felt like an eternity. And how I promised myself that if I ever got the chance, I'd never let you go again."

Her words cut through the fog of my grief, reaching a place deep within me. The pain and longing in her voice were as real as the warmth of her body pressed against mine. "Diane, I... I don't know what to say."

"You don't have to say anything," she whispered, leaning in closer, her breath warm against my skin. "Just know that I'm here for you, always."

The tension between us was palpable, an electric current that seemed to pull us together. Despite my reservations, I felt an overwhelming need to be close to her, to let her in. Her nearness was a balm to my wounded soul, and I could feel her heart beating steadily against my chest, a reassuring rhythm amidst the chaos.

"Diane, I don't know how to move forward from here," I admitted, my voice shaking with raw emotion. "But having you here... it means everything to me."

She smiled softly, her fingers gently brushing a stray tear from my cheek, her touch both tender and electrifying. "One step at a time, Jack."

In that moment, the world outside our small, dimly lit room seemed to dissolve, leaving just the two of us in our cocoon of emotion. I leaned into her touch, finding strength in her presence. Her eyes locked onto mine with a fierce, unwavering intensity, her gaze conveying a depth of feeling that words could scarcely capture. "I'm not going anywhere."

Diane kissed my cheek, her lips lingering with a warmth that spoke of all the moments she had missed. As she rubbed my chest, her touch was both soothing and intimate. The soft sounds of our hearts beating, our breathing, our hands connecting, our fingers intertwining, and her leg draping over mine filled the silence that followed.

The quiet intimacy of the moment enveloped us, each touch and glance affirming the bond we shared. As we lay there, the weight of the world outside seemed to dissipate, leaving us in a peaceful cocoon of shared warmth and connection. Sleep crept in, pulling us into its gentle embrace. We remained there, silently taking in the moment, the closeness between us a profound balm for the turmoil inside.

The door to my room burst open with surprising force, abruptly shattering our quick nap. Anne stormed in, her face alight with infectious excitement. "Jack! You're awake!" she exclaimed, her voice brimming with joy.

Both Diane and I reacted sharply. Diane's face flashed with concern while I jerked involuntarily, sending a jolt of pain through my broken arms. I winced and cried out, "Ouch! Damn it!" The sudden movement exacerbates my pain, making me grimace. Diane remains steadfastly by my side, her eyes filled with worry.

"Anne, what the hell!" Diane's voice was a mix of annoyance and frustration as she quickly rubbed me reassuringly, her gaze darting between me and Anne. "Can't you see he's in pain?"

Anne's enthusiasm faltered momentarily, her eyes widening with concern. "Oh no, Jack! I'm so sorry. I didn't mean to hurt you." She moved to the side of the bed, not occupied by Diane, her previous excitement replaced with genuine worry.

"It's okay, Anne," I said through gritted teeth. "Just surprised me, that's all." I shift uncomfortably, trying to ease the pain in my arms.

Diane, still hovering protectively by my side, cast a disapproving look at Anne. "You could have been more careful. He's not exactly in the best shape right now."

Anne perched on the edge of the bed, her expression shifting from concern to intrigue. "So, how are you feeling, Jack? Diane's been talking about your brave fight."

I glanced at Diane, who seemed to be fighting back a grin. "Yeah, I had quite the ordeal. I don't remember much, but Diane filled me in."

Anne's gaze flicked to Diane's position beside me, her lips curving into a teasing smile. "Looks like you two have become quite the pair."

Diane tilted her head, a smirk tugging at her mouth. "Oh, have we? Maybe you should give us a little space, Anne."

Anne arched a brow, clearly reveling in the playful exchange. "Careful, Diane. I might just have to demonstrate some of these jiu-jitsu moves I've been working on."

Diane let out a soft laugh, the corners of her mouth twitching with amusement. "Sure, Anne, because we all know this is really about impressing Jack."

Anne laughed, nudging Diane playfully, her hand lingering on my arm. "Maybe. But I'm really looking forward to catching up with you, Jack."

Diane, her patience wearing thin, gives Anne a pointed look. "You're not trying to steal him away from me, are you?"

Anne raised her hands in mock surrender, her eyes sparkled with mischief. "I promise I won't steal him. I may just enjoy his company though," she added with a playful smirk, leaning in closer.

Diane's eyes flashed with a mix of annoyance and mischief. "Oh, is that so? Well, if you're going to be like that..." Diane pretended to reach into my pants, her gesture bold and provocative.

Anne's eyes widened, and she stood up quickly, her cheeks flushed. "Okay, okay, point taken!" She gives me a teasing smile, leaning in to blow me a playful kiss. "Take care, Jack. And remember, if you need anything, just let me know."

As Anne headed toward the door, Diane's expression hardened, a mix of frustration and protectiveness in her eyes. Her shoulders slumped as she sighed heavily, clearly exasperated by Anne's antics. She muttered under her breath, "Ugh, she's insufferable sometimes. Always needs to be the center of attention. It's like she can't be satisfied unless she's getting a rise out of everyone."

I managed a small, uncertain smile, unsure how to navigate the charged atmosphere between the two sisters.

"Are you going to take your hand out or should I start paying rent?"

Diane, pretending not to hear me, gave my member a squeeze. "Oh, I'm not sure what you're talking about."

Diane's frustration fades, her breath warms against my neck. She kissed it lightly, her lips lingering with a gentle warmth that sent a flutter of excitement through me. The intimacy of the moment gets me aroused as Diane's hand gets a surprise. She squealed in delight before giggling as she finally released me.

As Diane stood up to leave, I watched her walk away, the warmth of her presence lingering. The room felt less daunting now, as I now had a new problem which I'd have to suffer through. I forced myself to get my mind off of her and the feel of her warm hand.

CHAPTER 14

As the days of my recovery dragged on, the monotony of being confined to bed starkly contrasted with the chaos that had preceded it. Diane became my unwavering companion, her presence a soothing balm amid my physical discomfort and emotional turmoil.

"Good morning, Jack," Diane greeted me each day with a bright smile as she entered the room. Her cheerful voice and warm touch provided comfort in the sterile environment of the bunker. She'd lay beside me, her head resting on my chest, her arm around my waist, and her leg draped over mine. This routine, though simple, became a comforting constant.

The room, once cold and impersonal, transformed into a space of intimacy. Diane's presence brought a new warmth, and our days together included watching movies or reading, which helped distract us from the ongoing discomfort. Her stack of books, magazines, and the occasional movie night became highlights of my recovery.

Our bond grew deeper. Diane's late-night conversations and her unwavering support through tougher moments made the days feel more bearable.

One quiet afternoon, Diane helped me take an awkward piss. "Okay, Jack," she said with a chuckle, "let's get this over with." She grabbed my penis with her warm hands. "Just think of it as another part of the recovery process."

It was extremely difficult not to get excited, but I managed. Barely.

Acting embarrassed, I mumbled, "I still can't believe this is happening."

Diane's demeanor was casual, aiming to ease my discomfort. "It's all part of the healing process. We've become quite close, and this is just another way to help you get better. Plus, it felt nice. Hmmm."

Shit. Puke. Demons. Beasts. Ugly Mrs. Dishrag' from high school. Just anything for me to not make this situation more embarrassing than it already is. Please, God!

Her nonchalant attitude and light-hearted chatter about bunker gossip, such as Anne's latest workout regimen, helped distract me. Diane's humor was a relief amidst the awkwardness.

However, Anne's frequent visits added a layer of tension. Her playful teasing, though meant to be light-hearted, often carried an undercurrent of jealousy. Her vibrant energy marked her visit. "Jack, you won't believe what I've been working on!" she'd announce, her enthusiasm palpable. Her energetic presence provided a welcome distraction from my recovery routine.

One day, Anne entered with a set of weights. "Guess what I've got for us?" she teased, setting them down with a flourish.

I raised an eyebrow. "What's this about?"

Anne struggled to contain her excitement. "I've been working on new exercises. Thought it'd be fun for us to train together once you're up and about."

Diane, sitting next to me, raised an eyebrow. "And what's this new technique of yours?"

Anne's excitement turned to irritation. "It's about making a recovery dynamic, not just techniques."

Diane snickered. "Or maybe you're just looking for another way to show off."

Anne's eyes narrowed. "Maybe I want to make things interesting. Jack could use some motivation."

Leaning in closer, Anne whispered, "Ready for some training sessions, Jack? I promise it'll be both challenging and fun."

Diane intervened, her patience wearing thin. "Anne, Jack's recovery is the priority, not your training fantasies."

Anne's frustration was obvious, but she masked it with a grin. "When you're ready, Jack, I'm dragging you to the training room."

Diane placed a reassuring hand on my shoulder. "We'll take it one step at a time, Jack. No rush."

Anne's playful demeanor faltered, but she quickly recovered. "All right, I'll let you two have your space. But remember, Jack, I'm here to get you back into shape."

As Anne left, Diane's eyes followed her with a mix of irritation and concern. I offered a weak smile, navigating the tension between the sisters. Diane's steady presence and Anne's antics became the highlights of my days. Diane's routine of helping me with personal tasks became more comfortable.

Despite the ongoing confinement in the bunker, I eagerly expected stepping back into the world, knowing that Diane's support and Anne's energetic presence would always be a part of my journey.

When I could finally walk, Diane accompanied me as I walked around the bunker. Each step was tentative, my legs still shaky from weeks of disuse, but Diane's presence was reassuring. She guided me gently, making sure I didn't overexert myself.

"Take it easy, Jack. You've been through a lot," Diane said, her voice a soothing balm to my anxiety.

We started our tour with the basics. Diane led me down the main corridor, pointing out key areas along the way. "This is the mess hall," she said, opening a door to reveal a large room filled with long tables and benches. The smell of cooking food lingered in the air, and a few people were still lingering over their meals, chatting and laughing.

"It's where we all gather for meals and meetings," Diane explained. "You'll get to know everyone here pretty quickly."

Next, she took me to the training room. Upon stepping inside, I immediately felt a rush of nostalgia. Various exercise equipment, sparring mats, and training dummies filled the room. The air was thick with the scent of sweat and effort.

"Impressive setup," I remarked.

"We take our training seriously," Diane said with a grin. "You'll be back in here soon enough."

As we walked through the bunker, I finally got to meet everyone. People stopped what they were doing to greet me, their faces lighting up with recognition.

"Jack! It's great to finally meet you," one resident said, extending a hand. "We've all heard about your victories in the tournament."

I shook hands, exchanging pleasantries, but each mention of my past victories brought a pang of frustration. "Thanks," I said, forcing a smile. "I'm just trying to get back on my feet."

"We believe in you, Jack," another person said. "You've done the impossible before."

As kind as their words were, the constant reminders of my broken arms were hard to bear. The injuries were a stark contrast to the image they had of me—a champion, invincible.

"How did you defeat those two demons?" someone asked, eyes wide with curiosity.

I took a deep breath, trying to push past the discomfort. "It was a tough fight," I said. "I was just lucky."

Diane noticed my unease and gently steered the conversation away. "Jack's still recovering," she said, giving me a sympathetic look. "Let's give him some time."

We continued our tour, and I couldn't help but feel a mix of emotions. The admiration from the others was overwhelming, and while I appreciated their support, the constant reminders of my injuries were a bitter pill to swallow.

As Diane and I walked back to my room, she halted and turned to me with a playful smile. "Hey, before we go to your room, why don't I show you mine? It's not far, and we could hang out for a bit."

"Sure, I'd like that," I replied, curious about her space.

We made our way down the corridors of the bunker until we reached her door. She pushed it open, revealing a small but cozy space filled with personal touches. Posters adorned the walls, and there were a few books stacked neatly on a makeshift shelf.

"Welcome to my humble abode," Diane said with a beam, motioning for me to sit on her bed. "It's not much, but it's home."

I sat down, feeling the softness of the mattress beneath me. "It's nice, Diane. It really feels like you."

She sat down beside me, our knees almost touching. "So, what do you think?"

"I think it's perfect," I replied, looking around. "I could see your personality everywhere."

She chuckled. "Yeah, I like to keep a few reminders of the outside world. Helps me stay grounded."

There was a comfortable silence as we both took in the moment. Diane's room had a warmth to it that made me feel at ease, even in the midst of the chaos outside.

"So," she began, breaking the silence, "how are you really feeling, Jack? And I don't mean just physically."

I sighed, leaning back against the wall. "It's been tough. Every time someone mentions those demons, I can't help but think about everything that happened."

Diane reached out and placed her hand on mine, her touch warm and reassuring. "You're a fighter, Jack. You've been through so much, and you're still here. That says a lot about your strength."

I looked into her eyes, feeling a surge of gratitude. "Thank you."

She smiled, a hint of a blush creeping up her cheeks. "And you'll always have me, Jack. No matter what." She shifted closer, her eyes glinting with mischief. "Hey, do you remember the day we first met? Getting chased by that beast?"

I laughed, the memory flooding back. "How could I forget? That was insane."

Diane's mouth twitched in amusement. "And that old factory where we hid? You stood lookout for me so I could pee. You were such a gentleman."

I grinned, shaking my head. "Well, I couldn't let you get caught with your pants down, could I?"

Diane's evil grin said it all, "But you did, Jack." Her bold question caught me off guard. "Do you remember what color my panties were?"

Without thinking, I answered, "White, with flowers."

"Oh, yeah I forgot about the flowers." She pushes my shoulder playfully, "Perv."

We both laugh. "Then it started raining, and we were soaked to the bone. Anne teased us so much when we got back."

I chuckled, remembering Anne's smirk. "Yeah, she did. She always finds a way to tease us."

Diane's eyes softened. "And then we shared those moments with your mom around the fire."

"She meant everything to me," I said. "I'm just glad you and Anne were there to help."

Diane's hand lingered on mine, her touch gentle but firm. "We always have each other's backs, Jack."

Her gaze grew more intense, and she leaned in closer. "Do you remember later when I sat in your lap?"

I felt my cheeks heat up at the memory. "Yeah, I remember. It was... an interesting night."

Diane's fingers traced lightly over my arm, sending shivers down my spine. "Interesting is one way to put it. You were so shy back then."

"I didn't want to make things awkward," I admitted, my heart racing at her touch.

She looked amused, her hand moving to my chest. "Well, we're not shy anymore, are we?"

I swallowed hard, the room suddenly feeling much smaller. "No, we're not."

Diane's eyes sparkled with mischief as she leaned in even closer, her breath warm against my ear. "You know, I've always wondered what it would be like if we didn't have to hold back."

Her words sent a jolt of electricity through me. "Diane..."

She pulled back slightly, her expression both playful and serious. "Relax, Jack. I'm just teasing... unless you don't want me to stop."

I took a deep breath, trying to steady myself. "You really know how to keep things interesting, don't you?"

She grinned, her hand slipping down to rest on my thigh. "Life's too short to be boring. And besides, it's fun to see you flustered."

We sat there for a moment, the tension between us palpable. I couldn't deny the attraction I felt for Diane, but there was a part of me that was still cautious.

"Diane," I began, choosing my words carefully, "I really care about you. More than I can put into words."

She softened, her teasing demeanor giving way to genuine warmth. "I care about you too, Jack. And I want you to know that you can always count on me, no matter what."

I smiled, feeling a sense of peace settle over me. "Thank you, Diane. That means a lot."

Diane glanced at the clock on the wall. "Wow, it's getting late. We should probably head back to your room so you can get some rest."

I nodded, not wanting the moment to end but knowing she was right. "Yeah, you're probably right."

As we stood up, Diane leaned in and gave me a quick kiss on the cheek. "Thanks for spending time with me, Jack. I really enjoyed it."

I lifted the corners of my mouth, feeling a flutter in my chest. "Me too, Diane. Let's do this again sometime."

With that, we left her room and headed back to mine. The walk back was quiet but comfortable, our earlier conversation still lingering in the air.

When we finally reached my room, Diane helped me settle into bed. "Get some rest, Jack. Tomorrow's a new day."

"Thanks, Diane," I said, feeling a warmth spread through me. Instead of leaving, Diane lingered, her eyes searched mine. "Do you need anything else before I go?"

I hesitated for a moment, then shook my head. "No, I'm okay. Just... thanks for everything, Diane."

She gave me a warm look, brushing a strand of hair away from my face. "That's what friends are for, right?"

I nodded, feeling a lump form in my throat. "Right. Friends."

Diane's eyes sparkled with something deeper, but she didn't push it. Instead, she laid down next to me in her usual position. "Mind if I stay here for a bit? Just to make sure you're okay?"

I shook my head. "I don't mind at all."

We sat in comfortable silence for a while, the only sound being the soft hum of the bunker. Diane reached out and took my hand, her fingers warm and reassuring around mine.

She leaned in and kissed my cheek, her lips lingering for a moment longer than necessary. "Goodnight, Jack. Sweet dreams." Giving me one last smile before heading to her room. As I lay there, the events of the day replaying in my mind, I couldn't help but feel lucky.

The next day, Anne convinced me to train with her. I stood in the training room, clad in workout gear, feeling a mix of anticipation and unease. Anne, clearly delighted with her victory, approached me with a mischievous grin. "I knew you'd be up for this," she said, her hand sliding up my arm and lingering on my chest.

She let her hand rest there, her fingers tracing circles over my shirt. "You're looking good, Jack. Strong. Ready to take on anything." Her voice dropped a notch, taking on a sultry tone as she leaned closer, pressing herself against me.

"Anne..." I started, uncomfortable with the closeness, but she cut me off by placing a finger on my lips.

"Shh," she whispered, her eyes locked on mine. "Let's not talk. Just feel." Her hand moved lower, rubbing against my chest with a boldness that left no doubt about her intentions.

I tried to step back, but she moved with me, keeping the proximity tight. "You know, Jack," she purred, "training isn't just about physical strength. It's about... connection. Don't you feel it?"

Her other hand slipped around to the back of my neck, pulling me closer until her lips were just inched from mine. The tension in the room was thick, and I was struggling to keep things from going further. Anne's boldness had crossed into territory I wasn't comfortable with, and it was clear she wasn't taking no for an answer.

Just then, the door to the training room swung open, and Diane walked in. Her eyes immediately took in the scene—Anne pressed against me, her hands inappropriately roaming over my chest, her intentions unmistakable.

Anne froze, her expression shifting from predatory to defensive in an instant. She straightened up but didn't step away from me. Instead, she turned to Diane with a sneer. "Oh, great. Here comes the fun police," she spat, her voice dripping with sarcasm.

Diane's expression remained calm, though there was a flash of something dangerous in her eyes. "I was just checking to see how Jack's training was going," she said evenly, her gaze never leaving Anne. "But it seemed like things got a little out of hand."

Anne's face darkened with anger. She muttered something under her breath in Tagalog, the words sharp and venomous. I couldn't understand what she said, but the tone made it clear it wasn't anything polite. With a last glare at Diane, she stepped back from me, her hands finally falling away from my body.

"Bahala ka na," Anne snapped at Diane before storming out of the room, her footsteps echoing down the hall.

I stood there, awkward, as Diane approached me. She looked me over, her eyes softening as she saw the discomfort on my face. "Are you okay?" she asked, her voice gentle.

"Yeah," I nodded, still processing what had just happened. "That was... unexpected."

Diane sighed, her expression a mix of frustration and concern. "Anne's been really pushing her limits lately. But don't let her get to you, Jack. You know where you stand."

I nodded again, grateful for her steady presence. "Thanks, Diane. I appreciate it."

She gave me a small smile, reaching out to squeeze my hand. "Let's just focus on what really matters."

The incident left a sour taste in my mouth, and Anne's inappropriate behavior had crossed a line.

As days went by, Anne's focus shifted away from her previous antics. The frustration she felt was clear in the way she carried herself—less playful, more withdrawn. Her plan to get closer to me hadn't worked out as she'd hoped. Despite the lingering tension, the bond between Diane and me continued to grow stronger. Diane's support, her unwavering presence, and the quiet understanding between us became the foundation of my recovery.

CHAPTER 15

The days swiftly turned into weeks, and Diane's unwavering support became the bedrock of my recovery. Each day, as I ventured further around the bunker and met more survivors, Diane's presence was a constant source of comfort. One late night, as Diane and I cleaned up after dinner in the kitchen, I struggled with a dish. Diane noticed my discomfort and gently took the dish from my hands.

"Thanks, babe," I blurted out. "Oh, I meant... Diane!"

Diane's eyes sparkled with amusement. "Okay, hon."

As we worked side by side, Anne entered the kitchen with a mischievous glint in her eyes. Her presence was both enticing and unsettling. She wrapped her arms around me, pulling me into a long, tight hug. I tensed, my heart pounding with a mix of surprise and discomfort. Before I could react, she leaned closely, her breath warm against my ear.

"If you need any help, you know where my room is," she whispered, her lips brushing my ear in a teasing kiss.

Diane's face turned a deep shade of red. Her anger was palpable as she stormed over, grabbing my arm and dragging me out of the kitchen.

"Putang ina mo, Anne! What the hell do you think you're doing?" Diane's voice was trembling with fury, her eyes blazing.

I tried to defuse the situation. "It's okay, Diane. I can handle Anne."

Diane's frustrated voice softened. "You don't get it, Jack. It's not just about handling Anne. It's about respect. She crossed a line tonight."

The next morning, Anne's behavior continued to escalate. At breakfast, she leaned in closer than necessary, her hand brushed against my thigh with an unsettling intimacy. Her flirtations were blatant, and I struggled to maintain my composure.

Anne suggested a walk around the bunker and challenged me to a game of pool. Her eyes sparkled with mischief as she won effortlessly, her smile a mixture of triumph and flirtation.

"Looked like you're cleaning my room for the next week," she said, her tone teasing, but her eyes held a deeper meaning.

Later, Anne invited me to her training session. As she showed jiu-jitsu moves, her movements were fluid and confident. She used every opportunity to flirt, her comments laden with double entendres. Each touch, each glance, made me feel increasingly conflicted. I could see Diane's hurt in her eyes, and it tore at me.

When Diane returned from training, her eyes were stormy as she saw Anne's arm draped possessively around mine. Diane smiled forcefully; her voice filled with pain.

"Did you enjoy spending time with her?" she asked, her words barely concealing her hurt.

I hesitated, searching for the right words. "Anne is fun to be around."

Diane's face flushed, her voice rising with a mix of anger and sadness. "Seemed like more than just fun to me."

"I care about you, Diane. Anne is just… Anne," I said, trying to reassure her, though the words felt hollow.

Diane's eyes welled with unshed tears. "You need to figure out what you really want. I can't keep doing this."

Later that evening, Diane's words replayed in my head like a broken record: "You need to figure out what you really want." Her tone, filled with hurt and frustration, cut deeper than I cared to admit. I sat alone in the common area, staring blankly at the wall as the weight of her ultimatum settled over me.

What did I really want? The answer should have been simple: Diane. It had always been Diane. But Anne had a way of complicating everything. Her charm, her boldness, the way she seemed to see through me—it all pulled at parts of me I didn't fully understand. And yet… part of me was angry at myself for letting it get this far. If I truly cared for Diane, why hadn't I shut Anne down sooner? Why had I allowed her flirtations to fester?

The silence of the common area pressed in around me, amplifying my thoughts until they were deafening. I needed clarity, but instead, I felt like I was sinking deeper into quicksand with every passing second.

Movement in the hallway caught my attention, and I glanced up to see Anne walking toward her room. She paused when she noticed me, her expression unreadable. For a brief moment, our eyes met, and something unspoken passed between us—an invitation, a challenge, or perhaps just an acknowledgment of the storm we were both caught in.

Before I could stop myself, I stood and followed her.

I didn't know where I was going until I found myself standing outside Anne's room. A part of me told me to walk away, to turn back and find Diane, but another part—the part that sought answers, that wanted closure—pushed me to knock.

Anne opened the door almost immediately, her expression softening when she saw me. "Jack," she said, stepping aside to let me in. "I didn't think you'd come."

The faint scent of her perfume filled the room, wrapping around me as I stepped inside. The atmosphere was heavy, charged with unspoken tension. Anne's gaze was intense, her usual playful demeanor replaced by something more vulnerable.

"Anne," I began, but she cut me off, closing the door behind me.

"Before you say anything, just listen," she said, her voice trembling slightly. "I know I've been… forward. And I know you're torn. But I need you to know how I felt."

She stepped closer, searching for my reaction. "I care about you, Jack. More than you realize. And I think you feel the same way, even if you're too scared to admit it."

Her words stirred something inside me, but before I could respond, she leaned in and pressed her lips to mine. The kiss was desperate, pleading, but it only filled me with a surge of anger and guilt. I pushed her back firmly, my voice sharp.

"Anne, enough!" I shouted. "This has to stop. I came here to tell you that I want to be with Diane."

Her eyes welled with tears, her vulnerability breaking through her confident exterior. "Please, Jack," she whispered. "I'm sorry. I didn't mean to make things worse."

I shook my head, stepping toward the door. "It's too late, Anne," I said, my voice softening. "This isn't right. I need to go."

As I turned to leave, Anne's voice stopped me. "She's lucky, you know," she said, her tone laced with both sadness and sincerity. "I just wanted to be the one who could make you happy."

Her words hung in the air, heavy with finality. I didn't respond. I left without another word, the sound of the door closing behind me echoing in my ears. The weight of everything—the tension, the heartbreak, the confusion—pressed heavily on my shoulders as I walked away.

For the first time, though, I felt clarity. I cared for Diane. No, it was more than that—I wanted to be with her. And it was time I stopped letting anything, or anyone, get in the way of that.

As I walked down the hall, the memory of Anne's kiss still lingered, a bitter reminder of how tangled things had become. I knew I had to talk to Diane, to explain everything. She deserved to know, and I wanted her to understand that it was her I wanted, no one else. But guilt gnawed at me—why had I let things get this far?

When I reached Diane's room, I knocked, my stomach a twisted knot of apprehension. The door opened, and she looked up at me, her gaze sharp, instantly sensing something was wrong.

"What's going on, Jack?" she asked, concern mixed with frustration.

I swallowed, taking a deep breath. "I went to Anne's room to confront her," I began, feeling the weight of the confession pressing on me.

Diane's eyes narrowed, her expression darkening. "And?"

"She… she kissed me," I admitted, my voice wavering. "I didn't kiss her back, Diane. I stopped it right away. I told her no. I even yelled at her."

Her face flushed with anger, her jaw clenched, and I could see the hurt bubbling beneath her fury. "So, she just kissed you out of nowhere, and you just stood there?" Her voice was sharp, edged with jealousy and pain.

"No, Diane, I didn't just stand there! I—" I started, trying to explain, but she cut me off, her emotions spilling over.

"I knew it," she spat, her voice cold, wounded. "I knew I was just a placeholder to you. Someone to keep you company until someone 'better' came along. Well, now you have Anne, so why are you even here?"

Her words hit me like a slap, sharper than any physical blow. "Diane, that's not true. I went there to tell her I wanted you, to end this whole mess. I want you, Diane. Anne—she's just—"

"Just what, Jack?" she snapped, her eyes blazing. "A distraction? Another 'mistake'? You say you want me, but then you let her flirt with you, get close to you—enough that she felt like she could kiss you! Do you even realize what that does to me?" Her voice cracked, raw emotion spilling over. "You know how complicated things are between us. And yet you keep letting her in, letting her pull you into these… games."

"I didn't mean for it to happen," I said, desperation creeping into my tone. "Diane, please… you have to believe me. I never wanted her. I just wanted to set things straight, to make it clear to her that it's you I want."

She shook her head, looking away, her hands clenched at her sides. "You may have told her that, but why did you put yourself in that position in the first place, Jack?" Her voice was quieter, trembling with emotion. "If you truly wanted me, you wouldn't have let her get this close. You should have shut it down long ago."

Desperate to bridge the growing chasm between us, I reached out, lightly touching her shoulder, hoping to calm her. But she reacted instinctively, her hand flying up, grabbing my arm with surprising strength. Before I could register her movement, she twisted, throwing me to the floor in one swift motion. Pain flared in my injured arm, but it was the shock of her reaction that hit harder.

Diane stood over me, her breath ragged, fists clenched as she struggled to contain her emotions. "Jack, you need to leave," she said, her voice low, almost breaking.

I stared up at her, a mix of hurt and understanding filling me as I realized the depth of the pain I'd caused. Slowly, I got to my feet, my arm throbbing. I opened the door, only to find a small crowd of onlookers in the hallway, their faces filled with curiosity and concern. The weight of their gazes only added to my shame.

I turned back to Diane one last time, but her eyes were cold, distant. She didn't say a word, didn't soften. I nodded, accepting her silence, and walked away, feeling the weight of her anger and hurt pressing down on me like a boulder.

As I made my way down the hall, I felt like I was carrying the weight of both sisters' emotions, their love, their rivalry, their jealousy. Each step felt heavier, and the looks from everyone around me only deepened my sense of failure. What had I done? How could I fix this?

The answer seemed distant, obscured by the chaos I'd stirred. And for the first time, I didn't know if I could make it right.

Two days later, I woke up to a knock on my door, more urgent than gentle. When I opened it, Anne stood there, holding a tray of food. She wore a simple sleeveless sundress, and her expression was softer than usual, tinged with hesitation and determination.

"Good morning, Jack," she said with an uncertain smile as she stepped into the room without waiting for an invitation. "I made your favorite today."

I blinked, caught off guard by her gesture. "Anne… I'm not sure this is a good idea."

She glanced at me, her smile faltering slightly. "You have to eat, Jack. And I figured… maybe we could talk."

She set the tray down on my bed, taking a seat beside it. The air between us felt heavy with unspoken words. I sighed, trying to keep my frustration in check. "Anne, I appreciate this, but I'm really not in the mood for company right now."

Anne's lips pressed together as she looked down at her hands. "I know you're hurting," she said quietly. "I just thought maybe… I could help. I hate seeing you like this."

Her vulnerability caught me off guard. For a moment, I didn't know how to respond. But then she glanced up at me, and I saw something deeper in her eyes—care, maybe even love. It made my stomach churn with guilt.

"Anne…" I started, my voice softening, but she cut me off.

"I know I've been forward, and I know things are complicated," she said, her voice trembling slightly. "But I care about you, Jack. More than I should, probably. And I just… I wish you'd see that we could be good together."

Her words hung in the air, and I felt the weight of them pressing down on me. She wasn't being manipulative or demanding—just honest. But that honesty still felt suffocating. "Anne, I'm sorry. I can't… I can't do this with you."

Her shoulders sagged, and she looked away, her hands tightening into fists on her lap. "You don't have to say it, Jack. I got it. I've pushed too hard."

I reached out, my hand hovering over hers before pulling back. "Anne, I didn't mean to hurt you. I just—"

She stood abruptly, cutting me off. Her eyes shimmered with unshed tears, and she gave me a wobbly smile. "It's okay. You don't need to explain. I'll leave you alone."

Her voice cracked on the last word, and before I could say anything else, she turned and walked quickly to the door. Her hand lingered on the handle for a moment as though she wanted to say more, but she didn't. Instead, she opened the door and stepped out, shutting it softly behind her.

The quiet that followed felt deafening. I sank onto the edge of the bed, staring at the tray of food she'd left behind. My chest tightened as I replayed her words, her expression, the tears she'd tried so hard to hide. Anne wasn't a villain—just someone caught in a web of emotions as messy as my own.

But her feelings didn't change mine. Diane's face flashed through my thoughts—her anger, her frustration, the way she had thrown me out of her room two days ago. I had tried to talk to her, to explain, but she wouldn't listen. She was hurt, and I couldn't blame her. But now, with Anne's vulnerability lingering in my mind, I realized just how deeply I was caught between them.

I stood and began pacing the room, the walls closing in around me. I needed to fix this; to make Diane understand how much she meant to me. But how could I reach her when she wouldn't even look at me?

The thought pressed down on my chest, each breath feeling heavier as I stood frozen in front of the door, my hand hovering just above the handle. My fingers trembled, not from fear but from the sheer gravity of what I needed to say, of what I needed to make her understand. My heart pounded against my ribs; each beat a reminder of what I stood to lose if I didn't act now. I couldn't let doubt keep me here, stuck in this paralyzing in-between. Diane wasn't just important—she was everything. The thought of her slipping further gnawed at me, a relentless ache deep in my gut. I swallowed hard, the lump in my throat making it difficult to breathe, let alone think. No matter the cost, I had to step through that door and prove to her what I couldn't seem to put into words. She had to see it—she had to feel it.

CHAPTER 16

The blaring alarm jolted me awake, slicing through the haze of sleep. I blinked against the harsh light streaming through the small window of my bunk, my stiff body protesting every movement as I struggled to get out of bed. The usual buzz of activity outside was muted, replaced by hurried footsteps and muffled voices.

Throwing on my clothes, I headed toward the briefing room, the tension in the air thickening with every step. Inside, Diane and Anne stood among other teammates, focused on a hastily scrawled message on the whiteboard:

Mission: Rescue Team Trapped at Old School Building.

Anne turned when I entered, her expression softening with relief. "Jack, you're here." Her voice carried a touch of warmth, though there was still an underlying intensity I couldn't ignore.

Diane glanced at me briefly but said nothing, her silence weighted with the unresolved tension between us. I forced myself to focus on the mission briefing, determined not to let personal matters cloud my judgment.

Anne lingered near me, offering quiet reassurance as we prepared to move out. Her support was genuine, yet her proximity felt both comforting and complicated. Diane kept her distance, her sharp focus on the mission a stark contrast to Anne's subtle concern for me. The room buzzed with activity as we quickly received a briefing. The team prepared the vehicles and urged everyone to move out immediately. I joined the team, the urgency of the situation overriding the personal turmoil I felt. I pushed Diane's silence and Anne's strange, almost possessive behavior toward me to the back of my mind.

We moved quickly, our convoy of vehicles racing toward the old school building. The road was bumpy, and the air was tense with anticipation. Suddenly, the convoy encountered an ambush as we approached the school. Fiery blasts destroyed the vehicles in front of us as explosions erupted around us.

The shockwave threw me off balance, and I hit the ground hard. Bleeding from a cut on my forehead, I struggled to get up. The chaos was overwhelming; smoke billowed through the air, and flames danced around the wreckage.

As I scrambled to my feet, I saw that the remaining vehicles were in ruins or had become rendered useless. Those who weren't injured or killed had already left on foot, leaving the rest of us stranded. Diane and Anne were nowhere to be seen; their departure had been swift and unnoticed amidst the pandemonium.

Desperate and disoriented, I stumbled toward a vehicle that appeared to still be operational. With a frantic effort, I started it up. The engine roared to life, and I quickly took the wheel, driving through the smoke and debris. The truck jostled over the rough terrain, each bump and shake a reminder of the urgency of the mission.

As I drove off, my mind was a whirlwind of thoughts—concern for my teammates, a desire to catch up with Diane, and the need to make sense of the chaos. I pushed forward, determined to reach the school and ensure the safety of those who needed it most.

The road stretched before me, the old school building emerging as a dark silhouette against the morning light. The area around the building was swarming with demonic activity, a chaotic and menacing dance of shadows and twisted forms. My heart pounded as I drove closer, knowing that time was running out and that every second counted.

I gritted my teeth, fighting off the wave of panic threatening to overwhelm me. The building completely barred its windows and doors, leaving no visible way in. My desperation grew as I scanned the area, searching for any entrance.

"There's no other choice," I muttered to myself, my voice barely audible over the roar of the truck's engine. I steered the vehicle toward the front of the building, my hands trembling with urgency. Two demons stood guard in front of the heavy, barred doors. Their yellow eyes glowed with an eerie intensity, their forms menacing and unyielding.

As I approached, my pulse quickened. The building seemed to mock me with its impregnable facade. I took a deep breath, bracing myself for the collision. "Here goes nothing," I whispered, the words barely escaping my lips as I slammed the accelerator.

The impact was brutal. The truck lurched forward with a bone-jarring force, crashing into the doors with a deafening explosion of wood and metal. Debris exploded outward, sending splinters and blood into the air. The truck shuddered violently, its front end embedding itself into the wreckage, the force of the impact knocking me against the seat.

Dazed but driven by sheer determination, I shook off the disorientation. Smoke billowed from the hood, mixing with the dust and debris that filled the air. The acrid smell of burning oil was suffocating, and the crackle of flames on the truck's hood added to the chaos.

I pushed open the truck door with a desperate heave, stumbling out into the wreckage. My eyes watered from the smoke and dust, making it nearly impossible to see more than a few inches in front of me. I choked on the heavy air, each breath labored and filled with the stench of destruction.

I forged ahead, forcing myself through the dark, debris-strewn corridor that led into the building. Every step was a struggle as I navigated the dense haze of dust and smoke. My heart raced with a mix of fear and determination. The distant sounds of demonic growls and muffled cries from inside the building spurred me forward.

I stumbled over debris, my movements fueled by sheer willpower. The building seemed endless, its dark, foreboding halls stretching out before me. I could feel the weight of every second ticking away, the urgency of finding Diane and the others pressing down on me with each step.

I pushed through the choking dust and oppressive darkness, my hands brushing against the cold, rough walls for guidance. The chaos and danger of the situation intensified with every moment, but my resolve remained unshaken. I was determined to overcome whatever obstacles lay ahead, driven by a single thought: to reunite with Diane and save the team.

The building loomed around me, its oppressive darkness swallowing the light from outside. I pressed on through the wreckage, my desperation guiding me deeper into the heart of the old school, ready to face whatever awaited me in the shadows.

The thick smoke swirled around me as I moved cautiously through the darkened hallway. My heart raced with each step, adrenaline surging through my veins. Broken furniture and scattered debris created ominous silhouettes in the gloom.

A shadowy figure emerged from the haze—possessed, with eyes glowing a sickly yellow and a gun in his hand.

"Hold it right there!" he snarled, his voice a guttural growl.

I didn't hesitate. With a burst of adrenaline, I lunged forward, tackling him and twisting the gun out of his grasp. The weapon discharged with a thunderous blast; the bullet searing past my face. I barely dodged the deadly projectile.

The possessed man staggered, his gun slipping from his fingers. Seizing the opportunity, I landed a solid punch to his face. He dropped to the floor, dazed but not out. His rage intensified as he scrambled to his feet, fists swung wildly.

Without a second thought, I struck him again, this time targeting his throat. He staggered back, blood trickling from his mouth, before collapsing with a final groan.

Determined, I pressed on. The sounds of a fierce battle guided me to a doorway. I froze at the sight that greeted me: Diane, battered but fiercely engaged in combat. Despite her injuries and a bandaged shoulder, Diane skillfully dispatched demons in combat. My heart leaped at the sight—Diane was here.

I charged into the fray, kicking a demon away with enough force to send it sprawling. Diane glanced over, her eyes wide with a mix of surprise and frustration.

"Jack?" she exclaimed, her voice strained.

"Yeah," I called back, throwing a knife past her to take down a demon approaching from behind. Diane's expression showed guarded relief, but she remained silent.

We fought side by side, the synchronization between us almost instinctive. Despite the tension between us, we moved as a unit. Every punch, every kick was precise, and together we cut through the demonic horde with lethal efficiency.

When the last demon fell, Diane and I stood amidst the wreckage, our breaths coming in ragged gasps. The silence that followed was heavy, laden with the aftermath of our intense battle. Diane didn't acknowledge me; she merely turned and walked ahead, her back stiff and her pace brisk.

I wiped sweat from my brow, trying to keep my emotions in check. The sting of her rejection was sharp, but I forced myself to stay focused. I knew we had to find the others and get out, but Diane's silence weighed heavily on me. Every step I took was a reminder of the chasm between us, but my resolve remained unshaken.

As we continued through the darkened corridors, Diane led the way with a determined stride. Her silence was deafening, but I kept my gaze fixed forward, determined to push through the personal pain for the sake of the mission.

We made our way down the hall. The noise from the auditorium grew louder, a chaotic symphony of violence and conflict. As we approached, the clamor of battle intensified.

Entering the auditorium, the scene was a violent maelstrom. Most of our team clashed with demons, the room a battleground of frantic shouts, gunfire, and bodies.

"Where's the commander?" I shouted, but the chaos swallowed my words.

Diane's gaze darted around, her face a mask of determination and anger. She seemed to be focused entirely on the fight, avoiding eye contact with me. Her movements were sharp and precise, her fury driving her strikes.

A possessed individual with a knife lunged at me. Reacting on instinct, I grabbed his wrist and twisted, forcing him to stab himself. He screamed in agony, blood spraying around the room.

Another possessed person with a shotgun aimed at Diane. I quickly used the flailing man as a shield. The shotgun fired, the blast taking out the possessed man's head and splattering blood across the room, some hitting Diane. She didn't flinch; her focus still locked on her target.

"Where's the commander?" I yelled again, but the clamor of battle drowned out my voice.

As we fought our way through the crowd, a possessed person took aim at me. I grabbed the gun and pushed it away just as it fired, the bullet narrowly missing my nose. Another possessed person charged from my left, the bullet striking him in the head and dropping him to the floor.

Diane, her eyes fierce and unyielding, threw a punch that sent one demon sprawling. Her face showed resolve, but she didn't direct it at me. She fought with a ferocity that matched her frustration.

Two possessed individuals sprinted toward the exit. Before I could act, a new attacker emerged from the side. Diane quickly dispatched him, but the door was locked by the time I reached it.

Diane's eyes widened as she recognized a familiar face among the possessed. "That's Lynn!" Her voice was a mix of sorrow and fury. Lynn, now possessed, aimed a gun at Diane. She pulled the trigger, but only a click echoed—the gun was empty.

"Damn!" Diane cursed, grabbing the gun from Lynn's hand. In a swift, fluid motion, she threw it at a possessed attacker, hitting him square in the forehead and sending him crashing into a piano.

Lynn's gaze shifted to surprise, giving Diane a brief opening. Diane lunged at her, but Lynn moved with supernatural speed. She blocked Diane's punches, then delivered a brutal headbutt that broke Diane's nose. Blood spurted out as Lynn kicked Diane's leg out from under her, sending her crashing to the floor.

Diane, face twisted with pain, quickly scrambled to her feet. Despite the injury, her eyes burned with fierce determination. She charged at Lynn with renewed strength, striking her with a series of devastating blows. With a final, powerful push, Diane knocked Lynn unconscious.

"We need to move, now!" I urged, reaching out to pull Diane toward the exit.

But Diane yanked her arm away, her expression a mix of anger and pain. "I'm not going anywhere with you!" she snapped, her voice sharp and filled with frustration.

I looked at her, hurt and confused, but I knew we had to keep moving. "Diane, we don't have time for this. We need to get out of here!"

Diane kept her gaze focused ahead, with her jaw set. She didn't acknowledge my plea and continued fighting her way through the crowd of demons. Her anger was palpable, but there was no room for personal issues in the middle of a battle.

As we pushed forward, I followed closely, determined to protect her and ensure we both made it out alive. The auditorium, now eerily quiet, was finally clear. Our team regrouped outside, and we burst through the doors, leaving chaos behind.

Diane's anger was still clear, but there was no chance to address it now. We had to focus on the mission, our personal issues would have to be resolved later. For now, survival was the priority.

We entered the gym, a scene of unrelenting chaos. The sounds of battle filled the room: people shouting, gunfire, and the clash of bodies. Diane and I quickly scanned the area, our eyes locking on Anne, who was fending off a group of possessed individuals with impressive skill.

"There she is!" Diane shouted, pointing toward Anne. Anne was fighting fiercely, her movements precise and deadly.

Without a word, Diane charged forward, not bothering to wait for me. I followed, determined to reach Anne. Diane ducked under a swipe from a demon and delivered a swift kick, sending it sprawling. I blocked a punch from another demon and countered with an elbow to its jaw, knocking it out.

Anne saw us coming and her eyes lit up with relief. "I'm glad you made it!" she shouted over the din of battle. Her gaze lingered on me with an intensity that made me uncomfortable.

"Let's finish this!" I responded, raising my weapon and stepping up to fight alongside her.

As we fought, Diane continued to push ahead, engaging demons with a ferocity that spoke of her deep-seated frustration. She was clearly intent on helping the rest of our team and ignored both Anne and me, her anger driving her movements. Her eyes never once turned back to check on us, focusing instead on clearing a path through the gym to assist our other teammates.

We had to fend off the demons in the immediate area. With enthusiasm, she struck aggressively and almost recklessly. I fought beside her, but I found myself divided between the battle and Diane's cold distance.

Finally, the last demon fell, and the gym fell into a tense silence. Exhausted but victorious, the remaining members of our team gathered around. Diane's earlier fury had turned into a determined focus on finding and aiding other teammates, leaving Anne and me to our own devices.

"We need to find the commander," I said, trying to make sense of the situation. Diane didn't acknowledge my words, her focus was already on helping others.

Blood-streaked Diane's face, her expression grim but resolute. She did not spare a glance toward Anne or me. Her focus was solely on her mission, and she moved swiftly to assist our other teammates.

Anne gave me a hopeful glance, but I avoided her eyes, focusing on our objective. The personal issues between Diane, Anne, and me were clear, but we had to push through them for the sake of our survival.

With Diane helping our teammates and Anne's attention still fixed on me, the tensions between us simmered. I could sense Diane's frustration and her unwillingness to acknowledge either Anne or me. We moved forward, our personal conflicts adding another layer of complexity to the already dire situation.

Despite our fractured unity, we moved as one with renewed resolve. The surviving team followed closely, their faces set in a mix of determination and fear. We all knew there was no extraction team; I was the backup, the only chance they had of getting out alive.

"Stay close and stay alert," I instructed, my voice steady despite the weight of everything going on around us.

Diane moved ahead with purpose, her movements precise as she scanned every corner, not sparing a glance in my direction. Anne, a few steps behind me, matched my pace, her focus entirely on the mission at hand.

We approached a large set of double doors, the faded sign above them reading "Administration Office." I motioned for everyone to stop, then pushed the doors open, revealing a darkened room filled with overturned desks and scattered papers. The air was thick with the smell of decay and something far more sinister.

"Search the room," I whispered. "We need to find any clues about the commander's whereabouts."

Without a word, Diane immediately set to work, her movements efficient as she rifled through the room. Anne followed suit, her eyes flashing over the disarray, though her gaze occasionally flicked in my direction as if assessing my reaction.

"Over here!" Anne called out, breaking the tense silence. She held up a crumpled map, its edges worn and torn.

The team gathered around her, studying the map. It showed the layout of the school, with several areas marked in red. They designated one mark as the "Safe Room."

"This has to be it," Diane said briskly, her finger tracing the path on the map. She didn't hesitate or look at me, her focus entirely on the mission. "The commander must be there."

"Let's move," I said, folding the map and slipping it into my pocket. "Stay sharp and watch each other's backs."

We pressed on, tension growing with each step. Every shadow seemed to hide a threat, every sound a potential danger. As we turned a corner, a sudden burst of gunfire erupted. The team dove for cover, returning fire as best they could. I peeked around the corner, spotting a group of possessed individuals blocking our path.

"Keep them pinned down!" I yelled, firing my weapon to provide cover.

Diane moved with deadly precision, her bullets hitting their marks with unerring accuracy. Anne was right behind her, seamlessly joining the fray. The team followed, and soon our enemies' bodies littered the hallway.

We moved forward, adrenaline surging. The map led us to a heavily fortified door, its surface scarred by countless battles.

"This is it," I said quietly, more to myself than anyone else. "The commander's inside."

I stepped forward and pounded on the door. "Commander! It's Jack! We're here to get you out!"

A tense silence followed, then the sound of heavy bolts sliding open. The door creaked, revealing the weary face of the commander. Relief washed over him as he saw us, though his eyes quickly assessed the strained dynamic.

"Jack, Diane, Anne," he greeted, his voice hoarse. "I'm glad you're here. But we don't have much time—I've located the group that's been captured. They're being held in the basement level, near the boiler room. I came down here to retrieve the blueprints and gather intel, but the demons cut me off before I could make my move."

"Then let's finish this," I said, helping him out of the room.

We retraced our steps through the school, the commander now part of our formation. As we moved, the urgency grew. The sounds of demons were closing in, their presence an ever-looming threat.

The commander led us to a heavy, reinforced door. "This is the entrance to the basement level. Beyond this, it's a straight shot to the boiler room, but it won't be easy. They'll be waiting for us."

I readied my weapon, the weight of the mission pressing down on me. Diane was already at the door, poised to breach it without hesitation. "Let's get them out of there," she said, her voice firm.

With that, we pushed through the door, ready to face whatever lay ahead to save the captured people.

The moment we breached the door, the stench of rot and decay hit us like a wall. The air was thick and oppressive, the darkness that seemed to cling to your skin. We were in the basement now, the heart of the school's underbelly, and the sounds of the demons echoed through the narrow, twisting hallways.

The commander took the lead, his flashlight cutting through the darkness as he guided us. "The boiler room is just ahead," he whispered, his voice barely audible over the distant growls and hisses. "They've fortified it, so expect heavy resistance."

Diane remained at the front, her shoulders tense but her movements steady. She hadn't said a word to me since we regrouped, her focus solely on the mission. I could feel the weight of her silence, but now wasn't the time to confront it. We had a job to do.

Anne was right behind me, close enough that I could feel the warmth of her presence. Despite the situation, she had this intense energy about her, a drive that was hard to ignore. It was something I both admired and resented, especially given the tangled mess of emotions that had formed between us.

We reached another set of doors, these heavy and reinforced, just as the commander had warned. "This is it," he said, his voice low but firm. "We get in, take out the demons, and get the captives out. No one gets left behind."

Diane nodded, her eyes already scanning the door for weak points. She signaled for two of the team members to get ready with the breaching charges. I caught her eye for just a moment, but she glanced away, focusing on the task at hand.

We set the charges, and we all took cover as the blast ripped through the silence. The door flew open, and a hail of gunfire and guttural roars hit us immediately. The demons were waiting, just as the commander had predicted.

"Go, go, go!" I shouted, pushing forward as the team unleashed everything we had. Bullets, flashbangs, and the occasional blast of energy from Anne's weapon. It was chaos, pure and simple, as we fought our way into the boiler room.

The demons were relentless, their yellow eyes glowing with a malevolent intensity. They moved with unnatural speed and strength, but we fought back with everything we had. Diane was a blur of motion, taking down demons with precise, lethal efficiency. She didn't slow down, didn't hesitate, even as the bodies started piling up around us.

Anne fought with a kind of reckless abandonment, her strikes hard and fast, almost as if she was trying to prove something. Every now and then, she glanced my way, a look of determination in her eyes that I couldn't quite place.

We pushed deeper into the room, and that's when I saw them—the captives. In a corner, I saw them huddled together, bound and gagged, their eyes wide with fear. My heart pounded in my chest as I fought my way toward them. The thought of getting them out of this nightmare drove me forward.

"Cover me!" I shouted, motioning for the others to keep the demons at bay as I reached the captives. I quickly began cutting their bonds, working as fast as I could.

"Thank you," one of them gasped as I freed them, their voice trembling with relief.

"Don't thank me yet," I replied, my focus still on the task. "We're not out of here."

As I worked, I noticed something out of the corner of my eye—movement, fast and erratic, coming straight for me. I barely had time to react as a demon lunged at me, its claws outstretched, its eyes burning with an inhuman rage.

I braced myself for the impact, but before it could reach me, Diane was there, her blade slicing through the air. The demon fell at her feet, its body twitching as it let out one final, guttural hiss.

"Watch your back, Jack," Diane said, her voice cold as she turned and moved on, not waiting for a response.

I didn't have time to process her words. The fight was far from over. I finished untying the last of the captives, then turned to the commander. "We're ready to move," I said, helping the newly freed prisoners to their feet.

"Let's get them out of here," he replied, his voice tight with urgency.

The team formed a protective circle around the captives as we began our retreat, fighting off any demons that dared get too close. The basement was a maze of narrow hallways and blind corners, every step we took filled with the tension of knowing that danger could lurk around the next turn.

Anne was close by, her breathing heavy but steady as we pushed forward. I could feel her eyes on me every so often, but I couldn't afford to be distracted. Diane, meanwhile, was up ahead, leading the way with a kind of icy determination that was hard to reconcile with the woman I once knew.

We reached the stairs, and that's when the real trouble began. The demons had regrouped, blocking our exit with their twisted, snarling bodies. It was clear they would not let us leave without a fight.

"Hold the line!" I shouted, raising my weapon. "We're getting out of here, no matter what!"

The team opened fire, their weapons blazing as they fought to clear a path. It was a brutal, desperate fight, the kind where every second counted. I could feel the fatigue setting in, but I couldn't let it slow me down.

Diane was right there in the thick of it, her movements sharp and precise as she cut through the demons with ruthless efficiency. She never looked back, never hesitated, even as the bodies started piling up around her.

Anne was fighting just as fiercely, her strikes quick and deadly. But there was something different about the way she moved, a kind of reckless intensity that made me uneasy. She was pushing herself harder than I'd ever seen, almost as if she had something to prove.

Finally, after what felt like an eternity, we broke through the demon's ranks. The stairs were clear, and we didn't waste any time. We quickly guided the captives up the steps, their faces pale with fear and exhaustion.

We reached the main floor, the cold, stale air of the basement giving way to the slightly less oppressive atmosphere of the school's hallways. But we weren't safe yet. The demons were still on our heels, and we needed to get out of the building before they could regroup.

"Keep moving!" I shouted, leading the way. "We're almost there!"

Diane was already ahead of me, her pace relentless as she guided the captives toward the exit. Anne was right behind me, her presence a constant reminder of the unresolved tension between us.

The front doors of the school loomed ahead, our final obstacle before freedom. We burst through them, spilling out into the night air, the cool breeze a welcome relief after the suffocating heat of the basement.

The demons didn't follow. They lingered at the threshold of the school, their yellow eyes glowing with frustration as we made our escape.

We didn't stop until we were a safe distance from the building, the adrenaline finally wore off. The captives collapsed onto the ground, their breaths coming in ragged gasps as they realized they were finally free.

"We did it," the commander said, his voice a mix of exhaustion and relief. "We got them out."

I nodded, my eyes scanning the group. I nodded, scanning the group and accounting for everyone.

Diane was already walking away, her steps quick as she headed toward the perimeter where the rest of the team was regrouping. I watched her go, the weight of everything that had happened pressing down on me.

Anne stood beside me, her expression unreadable. She said nothing, just watched as Diane disappeared into the darkness. The silence between us was heavy, filled with things left unsaid.

"We should check in with the others," Anne finally said, her voice soft.

"Yeah," I replied, though my thoughts were elsewhere.

As we walked toward the perimeter, the tension between us lingered, unspoken but ever-present. The mission was over, but the real battle—the one between us—had only just begun.

Sixteen of our comrades had fallen, their sacrifices etched into our memories, haunting us as we made our way back to the bunker. The survivors, bruised and battered, walked in somber silence. The battle against the demon had taken its toll on everyone, yet the fire in our hearts still burned. This wasn't over—far from it.

The bunker, once our sanctuary, loomed ahead like a fortress in the night. Its familiar walls, though cold and unyielding, offered a brief reprieve from the horrors we had just faced.

"Get some rest," The commander instructed the team, his voice firm but laced with a rare gentleness. "We'll debrief in the morning."

Diane worked quickly, helping tend to the injured while avoiding me entirely. Anne, on the other hand, hovered close by, her presence a steady reminder of the emotional weight we carried.

"Jack," Anne said softly, catching me alone for a moment. Her eyes held a mixture of gratitude and something deeper. "You did well today. You saved lives."

I nodded, exhaustion pulling at me. "It wasn't just me. Everyone did their part."

Her gaze lingered, her expression tender. "Still, you've been through so much lately. You deserve some credit."

Anne hesitated, then stepped closer. Before I could react, she hugged me tightly, her arms warm and reassuring. "I'm glad you're okay," she whispered, her voice trembling slightly.

The gesture was kind, but I couldn't ignore the flicker of unease it brought. As I gently pulled back, I met her eyes, offering a faint smile. "Thanks, Anne. I mean it. But I need to check on the others."

She nodded, stepping aside with a small, understanding smile. "Of course. Just… don't forget to take care of yourself too, okay?"

Before I could retreat to my quarters, the commander called out to me. "Jack, a word?"

I nodded, following him to his office. The day had started with hope, but it seemed like everything was unraveling. As we walked, I couldn't help but feel like things were only going to get worse from here.

Inside the commander's office, the strong cigarette smell invaded my nose. The commander settled behind his desk, his face a grim mask of authority. I stood before him, not knowing what to say.

"Sit down, Jack," he instructed, motioning to a chair.

The commander stared at me as I sat down. "The conflict between you, Diane, and Anne has escalated beyond acceptable levels."

"I know," I said, my voice heavy with regret. "I'm trying to handle it."

"I need results, Jack. Not empty promises."

I opened my mouth to respond, but he cut me off. "I understand the situation is complex, but this cannot continue. The safety and efficiency of our missions will be compromised. I've had enough."

I shifted uncomfortably in my seat. "What do you want me to do?"

The commander leaned forward, his gaze sharp. "I've decided that you and Diane will be mandated to go on patrol together tomorrow morning."

My eyes widened. "But, sir, Diane is going to be furious. She—"

"I don't care," the commander interrupted, his voice brooking no argument. "You need to resolve this situation, Jack. The tension between you and Diane is affecting the entire team, and it's my responsibility to ensure that we operate effectively. If you can't work this out on your own, I'm going to make sure you have no choice but to confront it."

I tried to argue, but the commander's stern expression clarified that he wasn't interested in excuses. "You're mandated to work things out with Diane during this patrol. It's not up for discussion."

I stared at him, feeling a mix of frustration and helplessness. "I understand, sir," I said, though it was clear I was far from happy about the situation.

The commander nodded, his expression softening slightly. "Good. I trust you'll handle it. Dismissed."

I stood up, feeling the weight of the commander's words press heavily on me. As I left the office, I couldn't help but feel a pang of anxiety about the upcoming patrol. The mess hall incident was just the beginning, and now I had to face Diane and try to mend things under the worst possible circumstances.

Later that night, the survivors gathered outside the bunker under a somber, overcast sky, a fitting reflection of our mood. The air was thick with grief as we assembled to honor those we had lost. Diane stood apart, her demeanor stiff and distant, her eyes fixed on the ground. The commander stood at the forefront, his presence commanding respect and solemnity.

"I hate these things," I muttered, the weight of my father's funeral still fresh in my mind.

Anne, standing close, her gaze lingering on me, replied softly, "I know, Jack. It's never easy." Her touch on my arm was tentative, but charged, reflecting her lingering attachment.

The ceremony began with heavy silence. The commander, with a voice that resonated with authority and sorrow, began reading the names of the deceased. Each name felt like a piercing reminder of the lost lives. Diane's expression remained impassive, her gaze never leaving the ground, while Anne's eyes flickered between me and the commander.

"I still can't believe they're really gone," Diane murmured to herself, her voice barely audible over the quiet of the crowd.

I didn't respond, my focus on the ceremony. The eulogies were heartfelt and filled with admiration for the bravery of our fallen friends. The commander's words were moving, underscoring the sacrifices made, and the void left behind.

As the ceremony concluded, the survivors dispersed, each lost in their own thoughts. Diane continued to avoid me, her anger and sorrow clear. Anne's gaze lingered on me, filled with an uncomfortable intensity.

Throughout, the commander remained a steadfast figure, but he had settled his words to me before the ceremony. As the crowd thinned, I caught Anne's gaze again. Her attention was unsettling, and I could sense the unspoken tension between us.

I turned to head inside the bunker, needing to process the ceremony and the complex emotions it stirred. The commander's leadership and the ceremony's gravity had not eased the burden of our fractured relationships or the challenges ahead.

CHAPTER 17

Diane was already in the training room, her gear fastened with precise, jerky movements that spoke volumes about her mood. Her face was a mask of anger and hurt, eyes narrowed, and jaw clenched. When I stepped in, she didn't even spare me a glance.

"Let's get this over with," she snapped, her voice icier than I'd ever heard it. She snapped, her voice icier than I'd ever heard it, the words edged with venom, making it clear she wanted nothing more than to be rid of me.

I tried to reach out. "Diane, I—"

But the door slammed shut behind her, the sound reverberating through the empty corridor and echoing my sense of rejection. Frustrated, I fumbled with my gear, the clatter of metal against metal heightening my already frayed nerves. I stumbled through the narrow corridors, the weight of my gear feeling like a burden too heavy to bear. Each step felt like an assault, the sharp pain in my head a constant reminder of the chaos that had unfolded. The darkness of the corridor mirrored the darkness within me, both thick with unresolved emotions.

Why should she be the only one hurting? I didn't ask for Anne's kiss. My anger grew, fueled by a sense of unfairness and helplessness. If Diane wants to be angry, then damn it, so will I!

As I reached the entrance, the heavy steel door groaned open, revealing the night-clad forest beyond. The chill of the night air seemed to seep into my bones, heightening my sense of isolation. Diane was already moving, her form a shadow against the dense darkness of the trees. Her movements were brisk and mechanical, every step deliberate in its distance from me.

She threw a disdainful glance over her shoulder, her eyes cold and empty, and muttered, "Stay close."

Despite being quiet, her voice had a sharp edge that penetrated me. I gripped my weapon with white-knuckled intensity, the cold metal a stark contrast to the heat of my frustration. My head throbbed with every beat of my heart, a relentless reminder of the emotional turmoil that gripped me.

Diane forged ahead, her pace quick and determined. I followed, trying to ignore the ache in my heart and the simmering anger that threatened to boil over. The forest seemed to close in around us, its oppressive darkness a reflection of the chasm that had opened up between us. Each step was heavy with unspoken words and unresolved feelings, the silence between us a chasm as vast and impenetrable as the night itself.

Then, someone or something emitted a piercing shriek, and before I could react, we realized we were surrounded. Yellow eyes glowed in the darkness, demonic figures emerging from the shadows. There were at least twenty of them, their snarls and growls echoing in the night.

"Come on, fuckers!" Diane shouted, her voice a mixture of fury and determination as she raised her weapon.

My heart pumped with adrenaline, my blood boiling with anger. The demons lunged, and the chaos of the fight began. Diane moved with practiced precision, her attacks fierce and relentless. I stayed at Diane's place. Every duck, every hit matched hers. But then I fended off one demon, but another knocked me to the ground.

"Jack, get up!" Diane's voice was a frustrated shout.

I quickly got to my feet, frustration was in my voice. "Worry about yourself!"

The demons were relentless, their attacks brutal. I swung my weapon, hitting one, and quickly dodged another attack from the side. I took that one out as well.

I screamed, my anger building. Diane was fighting off three demons at once, her movements a blur of aggression. Even though she was knocking them out, more kept surrounding her. Our blind fury was putting us both in greater danger. We were losing. I could feel it. My mind wasn't in this fight, and our inability to work together was sealing our fate.

"Diane, behind you!" I shouted.

Diane spun, barely dodging a lethal strike. She glanced at me, her eyes full of anger. "Shut the fuck up!" she yelled, struggling to maintain control.

In a moment of clarity, I lunged forward, using my body to shield Diane from an incoming attack. The demon's claws dug into my side, but I didn't care. We had to survive this. "Fuck you, too!" I screamed out in retaliation.

Diane seized the opening, her attacks growing more ferocious. Fueled by adrenaline and pain, I fought with everything I had left. But despite our efforts, Diane was eventually overwhelmed. My rage was at its boiling point as I beat the hell out of the demons. The sudden chaos gave me a brief respite. I threw my last knife at one demon surrounding Diane, but my anger caused me to miss. Instead, the knife hit Diane in the shoulder.

"You fucking idiot!" Diane screamed in agony. "Can't you do anything right?"

The demons seized the opportunity and beat her mercilessly. As I went to help her, a bullet struck my arm. Diane, barely hanging on, frantically pulled out her gun and shot aimlessly until all three demons fell. Finally, the last demon fell, its body dissolving into the ground. I made my way to her, my gunshot wound throbbing painfully, and helped Diane up. She was a bloody mess.

"Jack… you're a fucking shit for brains," she said, her voice breaking with a mixture of pain and anger, tears of frustration in her eyes.

Before I could respond, Diane's fist connected with my jaw, sending me sprawling to the ground. The shock of the blow left me dazed, my vision swimming.

"What the hell were you thinking?" Diane's voice trembled with rage. "You almost got us both killed out there, you asshole!"

I got up quickly, bleeding from my arm. "What the fuck? You shot me, you crazy bitch!"

"Yeah? You deserved it for stabbing me! You were a liability!" She turned away, her fists clenched in frustration. "We can't go on like this, Jack."

"The same can be said about you, Diane."

The walk back to the bunker was a silent, painful journey. Both of us are bleeding from our bodies. Each step seemed to deepen the rift between us, a constant reminder of our failure to work together.

When we finally approached the bunker, Diane and I marched straight to the commander's office, our steps heavy with unresolved tension. Diane's face displayed a grim mask of determination, and she moved with each movement tight with suppressed anger. I followed closely behind, my fury simmering like a pot on the verge of boiling over.

Diane stormed into the commander's office without bothering to knock, her frustration palpable. "Commander, we need to talk. Now!" she barked, her voice sharp and unyielding, cutting through the stillness of the room.

The commander looked up, his stern demeanor momentarily softening as he took in our disheveled and bloodied appearances. Blood smeared Diane's shoulder, and my arm dripped with it, leaving a trail of dark red stains on the floor. His concern was clear, though he struggled to mask his surprise. "What happened out there?"

Before either of us could respond, we erupted simultaneously, our voices clashing in a chaotic symphony of blame and frustration. Diane's accusations and my defenses tangled in a frantic rush, each of us shouting over the other. The room reverberated with the discord of our arguments, a cacophony of anger and betrayal.

"Enough!" The commander's voice cut through our tumult with commanding authority. "One at a time. Diane, you first."

Diane's chest heaved with every breath as she fought to control her rage. Her face was flushed, her anger almost palpable. "Commander, Jack is a liability. He almost got us killed tonight! He's so wrapped up in his own problems that he can't focus on anything else. He even threw a knife at me—"

The commander's eyebrows shot up at the mention of the knife, his gaze shifting to me with increasing concern. "Jack, your side?"

I clenched my jaw, the pain from my injuries merging with the sting of Diane's accusations. "Commander, Diane's out of control. Her anger made her reckless. She threw herself into the fight without any strategy, and she even shot me!"

The commander's face darkened, his frustration clear as he rubbed his temples, the weight of our failures settled heavily on him. "You both have serious issues to address. This kind of behavior is unacceptable."

Diane's glare was searing, her eyes blazing with a mix of resentment and pain. "I was trying to protect us, but Jack kept getting in the way. He's a danger to everyone, including himself!"

"Danger?" I shot back, my voice rising in indignation. "You're the one who can't control her emotions! Your rage almost got us both killed."

The commander slammed his hand on the desk with a force that made us flinch. "Enough! Your inability to work together has jeopardized the mission again and put everyone at risk. Jack, I'm sorry, but I'm removing you as leader effective immediately. You saved us at the school, but this ongoing drama between you three has been a constant letdown."

Diane yelled, her voice rising into a storm of curses and objections. The commander's expression hardened, his patience wearing thin. The shouting match grew heated, but the commander, resolute, finally shouted over them both, "You're both suspended from patrols, food runs, and rescue missions until further noticed. You will be confined to the bunker and required to report to therapy sessions immediately."

The shock of his decree hit us like a tidal wave, leaving us stunned and speechless. We both tried to object, our voices wavering under the weight of his decision, but our protests were futile. The realization of our predicament settled in, and we reluctantly nodded, the gravity of the situation sinking deep into our bones.

"Dismissed," the commander said, his voice tinged with weary authority as he turned back to his paperwork. "And make sure you head straight to the infirmary. No more incidents, or else. Understood?"

"Yes, sir," we muttered in unison, our voices subdued and resigned as we turned to leave.

As we exited the office, the silence between us was oppressive, each step back to the infirmary heavy with the weight of our mutual failure. The corridors of the bunker felt colder, their walls closing in on the stark reality of our situation. Diane walked ahead, her posture rigid and her expression a mask of stubbornness and hurt. I trailed behind, feeling the sting of both physical and emotional wounds, the harsh reality of our circumstances pressing down on me like an unrelenting storm.

As Diane and I walked down the corridor toward the infirmary, our footsteps echoed in the tense silence. The argument from earlier still hung between us, unresolved and heavy. I could feel Diane's frustration radiating off her, but neither of us spoke.

Anne appeared ahead; her usual confident demeanor tempered by the late hour. She smiled as she approached, though her steps were slower, more tentative than usual.

"Well, look who's here," Anne teased, her tone lacking its usual sharp edge. "How are you two holding up?"

Diane's jaw tightened; her irritation barely contained. "Anne," she said, her voice firm but weary, "this isn't the time."

Anne's smile faltered slightly, but she held her ground. Her gaze flicked to me, softening. "Jack, I just wanted to check in. Make sure you're okay after everything."

I nodded, appreciating the sentiment but wary of the tension simmering between the two sisters. "Thanks, Anne. I'm fine. Really."

She hesitated, her expression conflicted. "That's good. I just… I care about you, Jack. I hope you know that." Her voice was quiet, earnest.

Diane's eyes darkened, her frustration bubbling to the surface. "Anne, can we not do this right now?"

Anne glanced at her sister, then back at me. "I'm sorry. I didn't mean to cause trouble." She stepped back, her hands raised slightly in a gesture of peace. "I'll see you both later."

Her retreat was uncharacteristic, but it left the tension between Diane and me simmering. As we continued to the infirmary, Diane's silence was deafening, her emotions clearly bubbling just beneath the surface.

In the infirmary, Diane and I sat across from each other, the silence thick and oppressive. The soft hum of the fluorescent lights was the only sound breaking the heavy stillness. Despite the treatment of our physical wounds, the emotional divide between Diane and me remained raw and unhealed.

I occupied one of the narrow beds, my posture rigid with weariness. Diane sat on the opposite bed, her eyes fixed on the floor, her shoulders tense. The air seemed to press down on us, the weight of our argument and the strain of the night palpable in the silence.

Our gazes occasionally met, but neither of us spoke. Exhaustion and frustration etched my face, while Diane's eyes portrayed a mix of anger, pain, and regret. The silence between us was almost suffocating, a testament to the depth of our conflict and the difficulty of bridging the emotional gap.

Every so often, I would catch Diane's eye, and she would look away, her expression reflecting the tumult of emotions she was struggling to process. I softened my gaze, showing a hint of vulnerability and quietly pleading for understanding. Diane pressed her lips into a thin line, her face masking conflicted emotions.

As the minutes ticked by, the silence shifted from a barrier to a space where we could confront our shared pain. Diane's eyes flickered with the weight of our earlier confrontation, and my expression mirrored a slow, hesitant recognition of the hurt we'd caused each other. There was an unspoken apology in my gaze, a silent acknowledgment of the mistakes and the longing for reconciliation.

Diane's shoulders sagged slightly as she took a deep breath, her gaze meeting mine with a hint of acceptance. Her hardened expression softened, and I caught a glimmer of the caring and connection that she had buried beneath the anger. My own eyes reflected a similar sentiment—a quiet, tentative hope for healing.

The silence between us no longer felt like a chasm but a fragile bridge, connecting us through the shared experience of pain and the slow process of understanding. Our eyes continued to communicate, each glance a testament to our struggle and our desire to move past the conflict.

Eventually, Diane's gaze softened further, revealing a sliver of the care she still felt despite the turmoil. My eyes mirrored this, a quiet acknowledgment of our shared pain and the possibility of finding a way forward, even if it was uncertain and fraught with challenges.

After leaving the infirmary, Diane and I walked down the dimly lit corridor, the silence heavy with unspoken thoughts. Each step seemed to echo the weight of our recent arguments and the struggle to rebuild what had fractured.

We approached the point where our paths diverged. I glanced over at Diane, and for a moment, our eyes locked. In that brief, silent exchange, there was a shared understanding—a recognition of the emotional battle we had endured and the tentative steps toward reconciliation.

Diane's eyes conveyed a mixture of resolve and fatigue, reflecting the emotional toll of the night. My gaze mirrored her sentiment, a blend of regret and hope. Without a word, we turned and walked toward our respective rooms, the silence between us a delicate thread of connection in the wake of our turbulent day.

Later that evening, I sat on the edge of my bed, the day's events replaying in my mind. The knock at my door was soft, hesitant. When I opened it, Anne stood there, a tray of food balanced in her hands.

"Hey," she said, her voice quiet. "I thought you might need something to eat. Long day, huh?"

I nodded, stepping aside to let her in. She placed the tray on the table, her movements careful, almost nervous.

"I know you're tired," she said, glancing at me. "I just… I wanted to make sure you were okay. After everything."

Her sincerity caught me off guard. "Thanks, Anne. That's… thoughtful of you."

She hesitated, then sat down across from me. "Jack, I know things are complicated right now. Between you, me, and Diane. But I want you to know, whatever happens, I'm here for you. Always."

Her words were genuine, lacking the intensity that often made me wary. I nodded, appreciating her effort. "I know. And I appreciate it. But I need to figure things out—with Diane. It's not fair to anyone otherwise."

Anne's smile was small, bittersweet. "I get it. Just… don't forget you're not alone, okay?"

As she stood to leave, she paused at the door, her hand resting on the frame. "Goodnight, Jack."

"Goodnight, Anne," I replied, the weight of the day pressing down on me once again.

Alone, I ate in silence, each bite a bitter reminder of the isolation I felt. The anger and frustration still simmered beneath the surface, mingling with the exhaustion from the day's events. As I finished my meal, the darkness in the room seemed to press in tighter, reflecting the emotional weight of the night.

CHAPTER 18

The next day, I found myself lost in a fog of regret, trying to make sense of everything that was going on between Anne and Diane. Their sibling rivalry had escalated to dangerous levels. Their heated exchange in the mess hall yesterday left a bad taste in my mouth.

Interrupting my thoughts, Tim burst into my room, his face flushed with excitement.

"Jack! You've got to see this!" he exclaimed, barely containing his enthusiasm. "There's a fight going on in the training room! Diane attacked Anne! It's insane!"

Curiosity and concern overrode my hesitation, and I followed Tim down the corridor. A crowd had gathered outside the training room, their murmurs growing louder as we approached.

The door swung open, revealing the chaos inside. Equipment lay scattered across the floor, and in the center of the room, Diane and Anne were locked in an intense battle. Diane, wielding a wooden staff, moved with fierce determination. Anne, with her fluid jiu-jitsu skills, dodged and countered with precision.

I pushed through the crowd, desperate to get closer. The clash of wood against flesh and the sound of labored breaths filled the room. Their argument was loud, cutting through the chaos.

"Why are you doing this, Anne?" Diane shouted; her voice raw. "What the hell were you thinking? Kissing Jack? You crossed the line!"

Anne's expression twisted with a mix of frustration and sadness. "I wasn't thinking, okay? I just—" She ducked under Diane's swing, her words faltering before she continued. "I've spent so much time being second to you, Diane. I thought… maybe this time, it could be different."

Diane's movements grew sharper, her frustration fueling her attacks. "This isn't about being second! Jack isn't some prize to be fought over!"

Anne sidestepped another swing, her eyes brimming with unshed tears. "I know that! But I… I care about him. I didn't mean for things to get like this."

Their words hit harder than their blows, but neither seemed ready to back down. My heart pounded as I stepped closer, raising my voice above the fray. "Stop it! Both of you! This isn't the way to handle this!"

The room's tension thickened as they both paused momentarily, catching their breath. Anne glanced at me, her expression softening, but Diane's fierce determination didn't waver.

"Stay out of this, Jack," Diane snapped, her grip tightening on the staff.

Before I could say anything, Anne took a step back, her breathing heavy but her voice steady. "Diane, I don't want to fight you. I'm tired of this—tired of feeling like I'm always the one who's wrong."

Diane scoffed, her eyes narrowing. "Then stop acting like I'm your enemy. You're tearing us apart. And for what? To prove something?"

Anne looked away, her jaw tightening. "No. I just... I wanted to matter."

The rawness in her voice stilled the room for a moment, but it didn't stop the fight. Diane advanced again, her movements calculated and relentless. Anne defended herself with precision, blocking each strike, but I could see the exhaustion in both of them.

I moved closer, hoping to intervene physically, but as I stepped behind Diane, Anne launched a spinning kick aimed at her sister. Diane ducked, and the blow struck me squarely in the head. Pain exploded through my skull, and the world tilted as I stumbled back.

"Jack!" Diane's scream echoed as I collapsed to the floor. Everything went dark.

When I came to, I was on the floor, my head throbbing and the room spinning. Diane was kneeling beside me, her face pale with worry. "Jack, stay with me," she said, her voice firm but laced with concern.

Anne was sprawled on the floor a few feet away, unconscious. The commander had arrived, barking orders to the bystanders.

"Diane!" he bellowed, his voice sharp. "What the hell happened here?"

Diane didn't even glance at him, her focus entirely on me. "Fuck off, commander," she muttered under her breath, her tone defiant as she carefully helped me to my feet.

"You're out of line," he growled, his eyes narrowing, but Diane ignored him, flipping him off without breaking stride as she guided me toward the infirmary.

The silence between Diane and me was heavy, punctuated only by my labored breathing and the occasional murmurs of onlookers. Diane's grip on my arm was firm, steadying me as we walked. Her jaw was tight, her eyes forward, but I could sense the storm of emotions brewing beneath her composed exterior.

Once we reached the infirmary, Diane finally spoke, her voice quieter now. "I'm sorry, Jack. For… everything."

Her gaze met mine briefly, and in that fleeting moment, I saw the weight of her regret. Before I could respond, she turned and left, her footsteps fading down the hall.

Left alone, I sank onto the infirmary bed, the pain in my head throbbing in time with the lingering chaos of the day's events. The echoes of their argument, their raw emotions, and Anne's accidental blow played on a loop in my mind.

As I stared at the ceiling, one thought rose above the noise: something had to change. This rivalry wasn't just tearing them apart—it was dragging all of us down.

The following day, the atmosphere in the bunker remained charged with tension. The commander, visibly stressed and stern, had taken decisive action. Diane and Anne were both confined to their rooms for the week, with their meals delivered by the staff to ensure they remained isolated and could cool off.

I was still recovering from the bruises Anne had inflicted during the fight. My arm was throbbing, and every movement reminded me of the pain. Despite not being fully healed, I volunteered to deliver Diane's meals. I saw it as a chance to make amends and hopefully bridge the gap between us.

As I made my way to Diane's room, the hallways seemed unusually quiet. The silence was a stark reminder of the unrest that had taken over the bunker. I knocked softly on Diane's door before entering with her meal. Diane sat on her bed, her eyes still reflecting the exhaustion and frustration from the previous day's events.

"Hey, Diane," I said, trying to keep my voice calm and neutral.

Diane looked up from where she sat, her expression a mix of weariness and lingering anger. "Jack," she acknowledged, her tone guarded.

I set the tray down on a small table beside her bed. "I brought you some food. Thought you might want a break from the same old routine."

Diane took a deep breath and nodded, though she didn't immediately reach for the meal. "Thanks," she said, her voice barely above a whisper. "I didn't expect you to come by."

"I figured it was the least I could do," I replied, trying to keep the conversation light. "After everything that happened, I wanted to check in and see how you're doing."

Diane looked at me with a mix of emotions. "I'm… okay, I guess. It's just hard to deal with all this mess and trying to make sense of everything. I didn't expect things to get so out of hand."

I nodded, understanding her frustration. "Neither did I. I'm sorry about what happened. I should have handled things differently. And for what it's worth, I wish we could just move past this."

Diane sighed, her gaze dropping to the food on the tray. "I know. I've been trying to process everything. It's just... difficult. Anne and I have always had our issues, but this was something else entirely."

I leaned against the wall, trying to find the right words. "Look, Diane, I don't know how to fix things right away. But I want to try. I don't want this to come between us more than it already has."

Diane finally picked up the food, taking a few bites, as she seemed to consider my words. "Thanks for coming by, Jack. It means something, even if I don't know how to deal with all this yet."

We sat in silence for a few moments, the weight of the situation hanging heavy between us. Although I wanted to offer more comfort, I also recognized the importance of giving space and time for healing.

As I left her room, I couldn't help but feel a glimmer of hope. Though the path to mending our relationships was still uncertain, I was determined to put in the effort, no matter how long it took.

Over the next two days, the conversations between Diane and me shifted. Diane, initially guarded and distant, started engaging in small talk during my visits. It was subtle, but noticeable. Her questions about my healing progress and casual comments on the food became more frequent.

One day, as I handed her another meal, Diane looked up with a faint, almost tentative smile. "How's your arm doing today?" she asked, her voice carrying a softer edge than before.

"It's getting better," I replied, managing a small smile in return. "Still sore, but I'm managing. Thanks for asking."

Diane nodded; her expression thoughtful. "That's good to hear. I've been worried about you. And I have to say, the staff's cooking isn't half bad."

I chuckled, a bit of the tension easing from my shoulders. "Glad you think so. They've been putting a bit of effort into making sure the meals are decent, given the circumstances."

Another day, Diane seemed more engaged. As I entered with her meal, she looked up with a more relaxed demeanor. "Jack, have you tried the apple pie they made yesterday? It was actually pretty good."

"I missed it," I admitted. "But I'll have to keep an eye out for it. Thanks for the tip."

Diane smiled faintly, and for a moment, the walls between us felt a little less imposing. "You should. It's worth it. I've had worse during my time here."

Our interactions, while still somewhat formal, were becoming less tense. Diane's softening tone and willingness to chat showed she was slowly processing everything and had moved past some of the anger she had felt.

While we weren't back to normal, these small steps were encouraging. I could sense that Diane was working through her emotions and that our attempts at communication were making a difference. The progress was slow, but it was a start.

By the third and fourth days, the nature of our conversations had evolved. Diane opened up more, sharing her feelings and frustrations with me. Each visit felt more like a genuine attempt at communication rather than just delivering a meal.

On the third day, as I handed her a tray, Diane looked up with a sigh. "Jack, I've been thinking a lot about what happened. It's been really tough for me."

I set the tray down and took a seat, giving her my full attention. "I can imagine. Things have been pretty chaotic. What's been on your mind?"

Diane hesitated, then whispered. "It's just... all this anger. I feel like I'm constantly on edge. Seeing Anne and everything that happened between us, it made me question a lot of things. I've been pushing people away, including you."

I nodded, trying to offer a comforting presence. "I understand. It's been hard on all of us. But you don't have to go through this alone. We can talk about it if you want."

She looked at me with a mix of gratitude and vulnerability. "Jack, I am grateful for that. I just... didn't know how to handle everything. I felt betrayed, and I let it all out in the worst possible way."

The next day, our conversation delved even deeper. As I entered with her meal, Diane was waiting with a contemplative expression.

"Jack, I've been thinking about how things have changed," she began. "I feel like I've let my anger control me. I didn't mean for things to get so out of hand, and I regret it."

"I know, I think we all have regrets about how things played out. But talking about it and trying to understand each other is a good step forward."

Diane nodded, her gaze steady. "I want to make things right. I know it's not going to be easy, but I want to try. It has become clear to me that shutting everyone out and fighting was not the solution."

I smiled slightly, relieved by her words. "It's a start. We'll work through this together. I'm here to help however I can."

Diane's expression softened, and she managed a small smile. "Thank you, Jack. It means a lot to me."

Our conversations, once fraught with tension, were transforming into something more meaningful. Diane was allowing herself to be vulnerable, and I was doing my best to offer support and understanding. The path to healing was still uncertain, but these moments of honest dialogue were helping to mend the rift between us.

On the fifth day, I arrived at Diane's room with her meal, but this time there was a noticeable shift in her demeanor. She greeted me with a more open expression, as if the weight of our recent tensions was lifting. As I handed her the tray, I saw her eyes soften, and she motioned for me to sit.

After a few moments of silence, Diane finally broke it, her voice tinged with nostalgia. "Jack, you know, life was so different back in the Philippines. After our parents died, Anne and I had to rely on each other more than ever." She looked down, her fingers fidgeting with the edge of her plate. "Our parents were everything to us. They were our rock. Losing them was like having the ground pulled out from under us."

Her eyes became distant, as though she was recalling a time long past. "We had each other, and for a while, that was enough. We were each other's comfort and strength. The dreams we had, the plans we made—they were our way of coping. But as we grew older, that strength became a battleground. It was no longer about survival; it was about who could achieve more, who could stand out. Our sibling rivalry escalated, and it started to drive us apart."

Pain and resignation filled Diane's gaze. "The competition became fierce. It was no longer just about who was better at school or who was more popular. It became personal. When Anne began focusing on Jack, it felt like yet another contest—one I was destined to lose."

I listened, my heart heavy with the weight of her words. Diane's face reflected deep regret and frustration. "The kiss, it wasn't just a betrayal. It felt like everything I had worked for, everything I believed in, was thrown back in my face. It made me question everything about our relationship."

Diane's voice grew more intense as she recounted the fight. "When I fought Anne, it was like a release of all the pent-up frustration and anger I had been holding back. I wasn't just fighting her; I was fighting everything that had been wrong between us for years. I let my rage control me, and it went too far."

Her eyes met mine, and there was a flicker of vulnerability that struck me deeply. "I'm sorry for what happened," she said softly. "I'm sorry for letting my anger get the best of me and for also hurting you. I don't want things to stay this way. I want us to move forward and rebuild what we had."

The sincerity in Diane's voice was like a balm to the wounds of our recent conflicts. I took a deep breath, ready to share my story. "I understand more than you might think," I began. "My past isn't easy either."

I paused, gathering my thoughts. "My father, Jack, was murdered when I was young. He was everything to me—strong, protective, and full of life. His death left a huge void in my life. My mother, Marishka, tried to keep things together, but things went from bad to worse. She met Kyle, my stepfather, and it seemed like a fresh start. But Kyle was abusive. He made our lives miserable, and my mother was too afraid to stand up to him. I witnessed the violence firsthand, and it left scars that didn't just disappear."

Diane listened intently, her eyes reflecting empathy. "It's hard to move past that kind of pain," I continued. "I think I've been holding onto a lot of anger and hurt, just like you. And I saw now that it was affecting my relationships with others."

I took another breath, feeling a mix of relief and sadness. "Anne's actions, as wrong as they were, reminded me of how much unresolved anger I have. It's a lot to work through, but hearing your story helps me understand that we're both dealing with a lot."

Diane nodded, her expression softening. "We've both had a rough time, Jack. But talking about it, sharing these things—it's a start. We've got a lot of healing to do, but if we can keep having these conversations, maybe we can start mending what's broken."

The room was quiet, but the silence felt more like a calm after the storm. Diane's openness and the shared understanding between us made me hopeful. Despite not being fully healed yet, we considered this conversation a crucial step toward rebuilding our relationship and moving beyond the pain that had plagued us.

CHAPTER 19

On days six and seven, Diane's mood noticeably brightened. She seemed more relaxed, and her playful side emerged. The atmosphere between us shifted from tense to warm, surprisingly.

As I entered her room on the sixth day, Diane greeted me with a genuine smile. "Here's our daily dose of gourmet dining!" she said in a teasing tone.

I set the tray down with a grin. "I'm thinking of adding a tip jar for my services. You never know when a good meal might come in handy."

Diane laughed, a sound that felt like a breath of fresh air. "Well, if I had to pay, I'd be broke by now. You're too generous."

I chuckled. "Just don't expect me to sing for you. My talents are strictly in the culinary arts."

Diane raised an eyebrow playfully. "Oh, so you're not a secret Broadway star? That's disappointing."

"Sorry to let you down," I replied with a wink. "Maybe next time."

Over the next two days, our conversations grew more personal. Diane began sharing stories from her past with a wistful tone. One day, she recalled a childhood memory with a nostalgic smile. "When Anne and I were kids, we used to put on these ridiculous fashion shows in our backyard. We'd raid our mother's closet and use old bed sheets. One time, I ended up wearing a curtain as a cape, and Anne was dressed in a quilt. The neighbors probably thought we were crazy, but it was so much fun." I laughed, picturing the scene. "That sounds like a blast. Did you ever get caught?"

"Only by our little brother," Diane said with a grin. "He'd join in and demand ice cream to keep quiet. We couldn't have him blabbing to our parents."

As Diane's laughter faded, I found myself intrigued by her story. "You mentioned a little brother—what was he like? I didn't know you had a sibling other than Anne."

Diane's expression shifted from playful to contemplative. "Yeah, we had a little brother named Marco. He was a couple of years younger than us. Always full of energy and mischief. He had this knack for getting into trouble, but he was also incredibly sweet."

I leaned in, curious. "What happened to him? Did he stay in the Philippines with you and Anne?"

Diane's eyes grew distant for a moment, her smile fading. "After our parents died, Marco was taken in by some distant relatives. It was a tough decision, but it was the best option for him. He needed stability, and we couldn't provide that on our own."

I could see the pain in her eyes, and I reached out, touching her arm gently. "Is he still alive? Do you keep in touch?"

Diane nodded slowly. "Yeah, he's alive. He's grown up and has a family of his own now. We don't talk as often as I'd like, but I do get updates from time to time. It's hard being so far apart, especially with everything that's happened."

Sadness tinged her voice, and I could sense the weight of her memories. "I can imagine. It must have been difficult to be separated like that." Diane sighed, nodding. "It was. Marco was a big part of our lives, and losing him like that was another blow. But Anne and I tried to stay strong for each other. We had to, for his sake."

I sat quietly, absorbing her words. The depth of Diane's past and the struggles she faced added a new layer of understanding to our interactions. "I'm really sorry, Diane. It sounds like you've been through a lot."

Diane offered a faint smile. "We all have our battles. Sometimes it helps to talk about them, though. It makes them a little easier to bear."

I nodded in agreement. "I get that. My past has been rough, too. Losing my father was a tremendous blow, and my stepfather didn't make things any easier."

Diane's eyes widened slightly. "What happened with your stepfather?"

As Diane's curiosity about my past grew, I struggled to decide how much to share. But the weight of my experiences felt too heavy to keep hidden, and Diane's openness made me feel safe enough to open up.

I took a deep breath, my mind drifting back to painful memories. "My stepfather, Kyle, was... well, he was an abusive drunk. He came into our lives after my father died, and things went downhill pretty quickly. He was volatile and had a temper that could explode over the smallest things."

Diane's expression softened with empathy as she listened. "That sounds really hard."

I nodded, trying to keep my voice steady. "It was. He made life miserable for us. My mother started isolating herself from friends and family because of his behavior. We moved far away from everyone we knew, and that made everything worse. It felt like we were trapped."

Diane's eyes widened slightly. "That must have been so isolating."

"It was," I agreed. "Things got even worse when my mother got pregnant again. Kyle... he lost it when he found out. I remember that day vividly. He started beating her, and I tried to protect her, but I was only eight. There wasn't much I could do."

Diane's face showed a mix of horror and sympathy. "Oh my God, Jack. I'm so sorry."

I continued, my voice trembling. "In the middle of the attack, Kyle grabbed a knife. He was threatening my mother, and she jumped in front of me to protect me. She ended up taking the knife in her back. I still remember calling 911, trying to keep it together while the operator talked me through what to do."

Tears welled up in my eyes as I relived the traumatic moment. "We went to the hospital, but she lost the baby. And then... Kyle just vanished. No one knows where he went. He's been missing since then."

A mix of sadness and shock filled Diane's eyes. "That's... so tragic. I can't even imagine going through something like that."

"It was a nightmare. I had to grow up fast after that. My mom was left trying to heal physically and emotionally, and I had to take on a lot more responsibility."

Diane reached out, placing a comforting hand on my shoulder. "Jack, you've been through so much. It's incredible that you've managed to stay strong through all of this."

I offered a small, grateful smile. "Thanks, Diane. Talking about it helps a bit. It's good to share these things, especially with someone who understands what it's like to deal with loss and hardship."

After sharing my harrowing past with Diane, I took a moment to gather my thoughts before continuing. I knew there was more I needed to say, especially about how my life had unfolded since those dark days.

"As I got older, I realized I needed to get away from the constant reminders of that painful time. I moved out and tried to build a life for myself, but things were never easy. My mom was left to deal with everything on her own. I felt guilty for leaving her, but I had to find my path."

Diane listened intently, her gaze steady and compassionate. "I can understand that. Sometimes, you have to find your own way to heal."

I nodded. "Exactly. And for a while, things seemed to be looking up. I was even dating someone named Tiffany. She was a bright spot in my life, someone who brought joy and a sense of normalcy. We were together for a couple of years, and I thought things might finally be turning around for me."

Diane leaned forward, interested. "What happened with Tiffany?"

I took a deep breath, my expression turning somber. "Tiffany and I were close. She knew about my past, and she was incredibly supportive. she died during the tournament we're in right now."

Diane's eyes widened in concern. "What do you mean? How?"

"She was shot just before I met you on Beast Island," I continued, my voice heavy with emotion. "I had to deal with that beast right after I got the news. I was still reeling from the loss, trying to process it while fighting for survival."

Diane's face reflected shock and sadness. "I had no idea. It must have been incredibly difficult to face something like that while dealing with everything else."

"It was," I admitted. "The timing was brutal. It felt like I was fighting two battles at once—one against the beast and one against the grief I was still carrying. It's been a struggle to keep going, especially with the way time travel messes with everything. For me, it's been like the loss happened just yesterday."

Diane reached out, placing a comforting hand on my shoulder. "Jack, I can't even begin to imagine what you've been through. But I want you to know that I'm here for you. I know things have been tough, and I'm sorry if I haven't been the most understanding."

I looked at her, grateful for her support. "Thank you, Diane. Your understanding means a lot to me. It's been a rough journey, but having someone to talk to helps more than you know."

We shared a quiet moment, the weight of our pasts creating a bond that was both painful and healing. Diane's presence was a reminder that even during our struggles, there was still room for empathy and connection.

As I brought Diane her breakfast on the seventh day, she greeted me with a mischievous glint in her eyes. "Jack, if you keep showing up with food, I might start expecting breakfast in bed."

I grinned, playing along. "I'm not sure I'm equipped for that level of service. But if you keep asking, I might have to start a breakfast delivery service."

"Deal," Diane said with a laugh. "But only if you promise to bring fresh fruit next time."

" Fresh fruit, huh?" I chuckled. "I'll see what I can do. You're pushing your luck here."

As we settled into our routine, Diane's tone was lighter and her laughter more frequent. The stories she shared about her past grew more detailed, and I found myself drawn into her memories.

"There was this one time," Diane began with a nostalgic smile, "when Anne and I decided to build a treehouse. We were so determined, but we had no idea what we were doing. We used old planks we found in the shed and some rope. It looked like a death trap, but we were so proud of it."

I laughed, picturing the makeshift treehouse. "Did it hold up?"

"Barely," Diane said with a grin. "One day, our little brother decided to climb up. He got halfway and then the whole thing started swaying. He was screaming his head off, and Anne and I were trying not to laugh while we scrambled to get him down."

I shook my head, amused. "Sounds like a classic sibling adventure. Did you ever manage to make it safe?"

"Nope," Diane said, shaking her head. "It eventually fell apart, and we had to get creative with excuses. Our parents weren't too happy, but they laughed it off once they saw how proud we were of our 'masterpiece.'"

Inspired, I shared one of my childhood stories. "You know, I had a similar adventure with my mom. When I was around six, she and I decided to build a fort out of blankets and chairs. It was the most elaborate setup you could imagine. We had an entire city in there, complete with a kitchen and a bedroom."

Diane raised an eyebrow. "That sounds impressive! Did it survive long?"

"Well," I said, laughing, "it lasted until my stepfather came home. He wasn't exactly the patient type. He came in, looked at our 'fort,' and said, 'You're both going to have to clean this up.' My mom tried to argue, but he was in a bad mood. We spent the entire afternoon taking it down."

Diane giggled, shaking her head. "I bet that was a mess. Your mom sounds like she was a lot of fun, though."

"She was," I said, a touch of sadness in my voice. "She had a great sense of humor, and she tried to make life as enjoyable as she could, even with everything going on."

As I finished sharing my childhood story, Diane's eyes sparkled with a mix of amusement and curiosity. "All right, Jack, if you're gonna spill your secrets, I suppose I should too. But don't expect me to make it easy for you."

I raised an eyebrow. "Oh? What kind of secrets are we talking about here?"

Diane leaned back, a playful grin spreading across her face. "Well, since you asked, here's one: I used to be the queen of embarrassing myself in front of my crushes. You know those moments when you try to look cool but end up tripping over your own feet? That was me. Anne would always laugh and tease me, and I'd turn bright red."

I laughed. "That's pretty relatable. I think everyone's had their fair share of embarrassing moments."

Diane smirked. "Oh, but it gets better. One time, I was so determined to impress this guy I liked that I decided to cook him dinner. I had this grand idea of making an elaborate meal, but I accidentally set the kitchen on fire. My mom was not impressed, and the guy never showed up. I'm pretty sure he thought I was trying to burn down his future."

"Wow," I said, chuckling. "That's quite the disaster. Did you ever live it down?"

"Not really," Diane admitted, laughing. "Anne never lets me forget it. She's got this collection of stories about my culinary disasters that she loves to pull out at the worst possible times."

I grinned. "Sounds like Anne's got a treasure trove of embarrassing stories on you. I guess I should be careful about sharing too much, or I might end up as the next subject of her teasing."

Diane's eyes sparkled with mischief. "Oh, don't worry. I've got some dirt on Anne too, but I'm not sharing all of it. A little mystery keeps things interesting; don't you think?"

I nodded, enjoying the playful banter. "Definitely. And it's nice to see you opening up a bit. I felt like we're starting to really understand each other."

Diane's smile softened, and she looked at me with a mixture of warmth and sincerity. "Yeah, I guess we are. And despite everything, I'm glad we're talking. It's made this whole situation a lot better."

"All right, Diane, if you're going to spill your embarrassing secrets, I suppose I should share a few of mine. Fair warning, they're not pretty."

Diane raised an eyebrow, a smirk on her face. "Oh, this I gotta hear. Let's see what you've got."

I leaned back, trying to look nonchalant. "So, when I was a kid, I had an obsession with this superhero costume. I had this ridiculous cape that I thought made me invincible. One day, I tested my powers by climbing up on the roof of our house and jumping off, convinced I could fly. Spoiler alert: I couldn't."

Diane's eyes widened in mock horror. "You jumped off the roof? What happened?"

"I ended up in the bushes," I said, grinning sheepishly. "My mom found me with twigs and leaves stuck all over me. She wasn't exactly thrilled, and my superhero career ended that day."

Diane burst out laughing. "Oh man, that's gold. I can't believe you actually thought you could fly. And here I thought my kitchen fire was bad."

I chuckled. "Yeah, it was quite a spectacular failure."

Diane wiped a tear from her eye, still giggling. "All right, your turn to top this. I've got another one for you. I once tried to impress my friends by cooking a fancy dinner, but I accidentally used salt instead of sugar in the dessert. Let's just say it wasn't the sweet surprise they were expecting."

I laughed. "That's pretty brutal. Imagine thinking you're getting a sweet treat and getting a mouthful of salt instead. That's dedication to the prank."

Diane grinned. "It gets better. The worst part was that I had to face them all the next day. They still tease me about it."

I shook my head, enjoying the exchange.

Diane leaned in with a mischievous glint in her eye. "All right, Jack, my turn again. When I was in high school, I was on the track team, and we had this huge relay race. I was supposed to be the anchor leg, but I got so nervous that I accidentally ran the wrong way. Instead of finishing the race, I ended up running straight into the stands. My teammates were mortified, and I was the laughingstock of the team for weeks."

I laughed, shaking my head. "Running into the stands? That's priceless. I'm guessing you didn't make it to the next race?"

"Nope," Diane said with a grin. "I was benched after that. But it made for some pretty funny stories at parties."

"All right, your turn to laugh at me again," I said. "I once tried to impress a girl by baking her a homemade pie. I was so proud of it until I realized I forgot to put sugar in it. She took one bite and tried to be polite, but I could see the horror on her face. The pie ended up in the trash, and I never heard from her again."

Diane burst into laughter. "That's brutal! A sugarless pie? That's next level. What did you say when she tried it?"

"I just tried to play it cool," I said with a chuckle. "Told her I was experimenting with new recipes. She didn't seem to buy it."

Diane wiped a tear from her eye. "Man, you've got some great stories. All right, here's another one from my side. Once, in an attempt to impress my friends at a sleepover, I did a dramatic reading of my favorite book. I got so into it that I started acting out the scenes. I knocked over a lamp and ended up with a concussion when I hit my head on the bedside table."

I gasped, grinning. "You were acting out a book? That's both impressive and dangerous. Did you at least get an excellent review from your friends?"

"They still tease me about it," Diane said, laughing. "But they also made sure to put my head in a bucket of ice for a while. It was a memorable night."

I shook my head, laughing. "All right, I'll give you one more. In college, I tried to join a salsa dance class to impress someone. Turned out, I have two left feet and absolutely no rhythm. I ended up stepping on everyone's toes and got a nickname that stuck—'The Human Hazard.'"

Diane's laughter was infectious. "'The Human Hazard'? That's amazing. I bet you were the star of the class in your own way."

"Yeah, the star of stepping on people's toes," I said with a grin. "I'm just glad I didn't injure anyone seriously."

Diane's eyes sparkled with amusement. "Well, Jack, I've got to hand it to you. You're a pretty good sport about all this."

"And you're not so bad yourself," I said. "Trading embarrassing stories like this is definitely better than our usual serious talks."

We both laughed, enjoying the light-hearted exchange. Our shared moments of vulnerability and humor helped to strengthen our bond, clarifying that despite our challenges, we could find joy and connection in our interactions.

As my visit ended and I prepared to leave, Diane's eyes met mine with a mixture of warmth and sadness. We shared a hug that seemed to stretch on forever, both of us reluctant to let go. The comfort of her embrace was a welcome solace, a reminder of the closeness we had once shared.

I could smell the faint hint of her perfume mixed with the subtle scent of her skin. It was oddly comforting, evoking a sense of familiarity and safety that I had missed. Diane took a deep breath, her face buried in my neck

"You miss my scent as well?" I asked softly, trying to lighten the moment.

Diane remained silent, but then I felt her shoulders tremble. I could hear the faint sound of her crying, her tears soaking into my shirt. I held her tighter, offering what comfort I could, letting her emotions flow freely. We stood there for a while, wrapped in each other's arms, neither of us speaking as Diane let her tears fall.

The weight of the moment hung heavy, but it was also cathartic. Diane's sobs gradually softened, her breaths becoming more even. I let her cry it out, understanding that this moment of vulnerability was a significant step in our healing process.

As Diane pulled back slightly, her eyes were still moist but held a touch of warmth. "Thank you, Jack," she said quietly. "I've needed this."

Then, with a sudden shift in tone, she looked up at me with a flirty smile. "Yes, I did miss your scent," she said playfully, her eyes twinkling with mischief.

I raised an eyebrow, a smile creeping onto my face. "Oh, really? I guess I'll have to make sure to keep up with my fragrance then."

Diane laughed, her mood visibly lightening. "Definitely. You never know when you'll need to be on standby for a scent check."

Our playful banter felt like a refreshing change, a sign that we were finding our way back to the easy rapport we once had. As we prepared to part ways, we felt a mix of comfort and lightheartedness, which gave us hope for the days ahead.

As we reached the door, Diane's fingers lingered on mine. Her touch was warm, and for a moment, neither of us wanted to let go. Her eyes met mine with a mix of warmth and hesitation.

"Goodbye for now," she said softly, her voice almost a whisper.

I nodded, gently pulling my hands away. "See you tomorrow, Diane."

She gave me one last lingering smile before I stepped out. The door closed softly behind me, and I walked away, feeling a mix of relief and anticipation for our next meeting.

As the evening sun cast a warm glow over the bunker, I brought Diane a comforting dinner of steak and potatoes. The rich aroma of the meal filled her room, contrasting with the more basic fare she had been eating all week. Diane's face lit up when she saw the food.

"Wow, Jack, you've outdone yourself tonight," she said, her eyes twinkling with anticipation. "Steak and potatoes? I felt like I'm at a fancy restaurant."

I set the tray down with a smile. "Well, I thought you deserved a treat. How's the week been treating you?"

Diane settled into a more comfortable position on her bed, savoring the first bite of the steak. "It's been a rollercoaster. Being cooped up has been tough, but knowing I could count on you to bring me food and listen has made it a lot better."

While watching her enjoy the meal, I pulled up a chair and felt a warmth inside. "I'm glad to hear that. I've missed our time together."

Diane grinned and leaned forward, playfully teasing, "I'll bet you've missed my company as much as I've missed yours."

"Absolutely," I replied with a smirk. "I wouldn't trade our dinner conversations for anything. Even if you do tease me relentlessly."

Diane laughed, a sound that felt like a balm. "Guilty as charged. But you're not so innocent yourself, you know. You've got some pretty embarrassing stories too."

"Oh, do I?" I raised an eyebrow, playing along. "Let's hear yours first."

Diane leaned back with a mischievous smile. "All right, here's one. When I was about ten, I tried to impress some kids at school by showing off my 'cool' dance moved. I ended up tripping over my own feet and face-planting in front of everyone. My siblings still tease me about it."

king my head. "That's fantastic. All right, my end. When I was younger, my mom r me in a school talent show. She signed me up act, but I could barely pull off a simple card trick. performance, I accidentally made the entire deck scatter everywhere. The audience laughed so hard nearly fell out of their seats."

Diane burst into laughter. "That's priceless! I bet you were mortified."

"Oh, you have no idea," I said, grinning. "But hey, we all have our moments. It's what makes us human."

As our conversation continued, Diane's stories grew more personal. She shared memories of her family, her voice tinged with nostalgia. "I miss those simpler times. When Anne and I used to sneak into the kitchen at night to raid the fridge. We'd make these elaborate midnight feasts and get in trouble for leaving a mess."

I smiled, feeling a deep connection as she spoke. "Sounds like you had some great times. It's nice to hear those stories."

Diane's eyes softened, and she looked at me with a mix of affection and gratitude. "Thank you, Jack. For being here, for listening, and for understanding."

Our conversation moved to the next day's plans. Diane's excitement about leaving her room was palpable. "I can't wait to get out of here," she said, her voice full of enthusiasm. "We have so much catching up to do. Maybe we could start with a sparring session?"

"I'm looking forward to it," I replied, smiling. "And don't worry, we'll figure out how to handle Anne if she tried to come near us. I don't want to see her either."

Diane's smile faltered slightly. "I appreciate that. I'
ready to deal with her yet."

Our evening concluded with another long, drawn-out l
Diane nestled into my arms, her head resting on my shoulc
I could feel her warmth, her heartbeat against my chest. Sl
took a deep breath, inhaling my scent as a playful reminder o
our inside joke.

"You really do miss my scent, don't you?" I teased gently.

Diane didn't answer right away. Instead, her tears
dampened my neck. Her embrace tightened as she let her
emotions flow. "I've needed this," she whispered, her voice
trembling. "It's been so hard."

I held her close, letting her cry it out, offering silent
support. The moment felt healing, the weight of past tensions
dissolved with each shared breath.

Eventually, Diane pulled back slightly, her eyes red but
her soft and genuine smile. "Yes, I did miss your scent," she
said with a flirty smile, her tone lightening despite the
emotion.

I smiled, trying to mask my own lingering sadness. "Glad
to hear it. I missed you too."

Reluctantly, I pulled away, but Diane clung to me, her
arms wrapped around me tightly. "Noo, don't go..." she
whined playfully, her voice muffled against my chest.

"I have to," I whispered, though my heart ached at the
thought of leaving. "But I'll be back tomorrow."

Diane sighed dramatically, but finally released me. She
walked me to the door, her hand lingering on mine. Before I
left, she leaned in and planted a tender kiss on my cheek.

"Goodnight, Jack," she said with a smile that held a
promise of more to come.

"Goodnight, Diane," I replied, my heart full. As I stepped out of the room, I felt a mix of longing and hope, eager for the next day and what it would bring.

CHAPTER 20

The week sped by, and Diane was finally free from her confinement. Her release brought a mix of relief and hesitation. Though she was no longer confined to her room, she remained cautious, still navigating her feelings and attempting to steer clear of Anne. As a result, our interactions had become less frequent.

When Diane appeared, her presence was a welcomed breath of fresh air. Despite her efforts to avoid Anne, the tension still lingered in the background, but it was Anne's reduced visibility that allowed Diane to breathe more easily. We treasured our moments together more than ever.

One evening, as Diane and I shared a quiet dinner in the mess hall, the warmth between us was palpable. Diane's laughter rang through the room, a sound that had become increasingly rare but was now more cherished.

"You know," Diane said, leaning in with a teasing smile, "I think I've become a pro at avoiding Anne. Maybe I should offer lessons."

I laughed, shaking my head. "If you do, I'm signing up for the advanced course."

Diane's eyes sparkled with mischief. "I'll add that to my resume. Expert at dodging conflict and creating excuses to hang out with Jack."

"Sounds like a promising career move," I teased. "But I think you're already a master at the art of both."

Our conversations continued with a blend of light-hearted teasing and deeper reflections. Diane spoke of adjusting to life outside her room, finding comfort in the small victories of daily life. Her stories and laughter were easing the remaining tensions between us.

One afternoon, as we took a walk outside, the air was crisp and invigorating. Diane was more relaxed, her demeanor open and at ease. "I've missed this," she said, stretching her arms out to embrace the open space. "Being outside, feeling like a normal person again."

I smiled, enjoying the simple pleasure of her company. "It's good to see you back to your old self. The bunker wasn't the same without your energy."

Diane shot me a playful look. "And you weren't too bad yourself. I had to put up with your terrible jokes and endless teasing."

"Hey, those jokes are a valuable service," I said, grinning. "They're like therapy."

Diane laughed, her eyes crinkling at the corners. "Well, if they're therapy, then I must be on the road to recovery."

As the day ended, we punctuated our moments together with the same lingering hugs that had become our ritual. We filled each embrace with unspoken words, a blend of comfort and affection. Diane's hugs were longer, more heartfelt, and our inside jokes continued to be a source of shared amusement.

The connection between us was undeniable. Despite the challenges and the lingering tension with Anne, Diane and I found solace in each other's company. Our flirtatious gestures and lingering touches spoke volumes, bridging the gap left by the week's separation.

One evening, as we said our goodbyes, Diane pulled me into a warm hug. "I guess we're back to our old routine," she said, her voice a mixture of playfulness and sincerity.

"Seemed like it," I replied, holding her close. "I've missed this."

Diane smiled against my shoulder. "Me too. It's good to have things feel a bit normal again."

As we finally pulled away, Diane's eyes met mine with a soft, lingering gaze. "Goodnight, Jack."

"Goodnight, Diane," I said, feeling the warmth of our connection. "See you soon."

With that, we parted ways, both of us carrying the comfort and affection of our shared moments into the evening. Despite the complexities of our situation, the bond between us remained a bright spot, offering hope and a promise of better days ahead.

One night, driven by determination, I trained a bit, hoping to regain some semblance of normalcy.

I carefully lifted a wooden staff and attempted to perform a kata. My arms were better, and it felt good. I was about to really get into it when Diane entered the training room. Her concern was obvious as she saw me.

"Hey, there you are. You weren't at our usual spot, so I got worried. Are you all right?" she asked softly, approaching me.

I looked up, my face flushed with effort. "Yeah, just trying to get back into shape."

Diane walked over without hesitation. "Let me help you with that."

Her willingness took me by surprise as she stepped close, placing her hands over mine on the staff. Her touch was warm and soothing.

"Are you sure about this?" I asked, trying to hide my nervousness.

Diane's voice was gentle and reassuring. "Yes."

Together, we guided the staff through the kata. Diane's hands were firm and supportive, helping me keep balance and follow the movements. As we practiced, I could feel the tension in my arms easing with each coordinated motion. Her closeness was both comforting and confusing, and I found it difficult to focus solely on the kata.

"How are you holding up?" Diane asked, her voice close to my ear as we moved together.

"I'm getting there," I replied, focusing on the kata. "It's just frustrating not being at my best."

"You're doing great," Diane said, her touch steady and reassuring.

I felt soothed by her presence, but I could sense that she still kept her feelings guarded. Diane's warmth was clear in her lingering touches. With her, I felt like I was at home.

"I've missed this," Diane said after a moment of silence. "Training with you, spending time together. It feels… normal."

I nodded, trying to keep my focus on the kata. "I've missed this more than you realize."

Diane's eyes met mine with a sincere gaze. "We've been through a lot, and it's all been worth it, being able to stand here with you."

Her words carried a lot of weight.

As we finished the kata, Diane's hands lingered on my hands, holding the staff for a moment before she stepped back. "You did well today," she said, her smile warm but her tone reserved.

"Thanks, Diane," I said, returning her smile. "You're the best."

Diane nodded, her smile consuming me. "Hey, any chance I get to sniff you is always good."

I chuckled, feeling a mixture of amusement and affection. "You know, I'm starting to think you have a thing for my scent."

"Maybe I do," she teased, her eyes twinkling with playful mischief. "But seriously, Jack, you're doing great."

Feeling a renewed sense of determination. "Thanks for being here."

Diane's smile softened. "Anytime, Jack."

As Diane walked me to the door, I felt her hand give a playful squeeze to my ass. I looked at her, a mix of surprise and amusement on my face. Her smile was mischievous, her eyes twinkling with a mix of affection and humor.

"Guess you're not just here for the training," I said, raising an eyebrow.

Diane's grin widened. "I just wanted to remind you that I'm here for you, in more ways than one."

I chuckled, shaking my head. "Well, I appreciate that."

She smiled teasingly. We both started giggling as we walked toward our spot we unofficially claimed in the common room.

"Remember when we first found this spot?" Diane asked, her tone light and nostalgic as we settled into our corner.

I nodded, leaning back against the wall. "Yeah, it was one of those rare quiet days. We just claimed it as ours."

Diane laughed. "And we've defended it fiercely ever since. It's our little haven."

I smiled, feeling a sense of warmth and contentment. "Yeah, it is."

We sat there in comfortable silence for a moment, the camaraderie and connection between us palpable. We spent the rest of the day hanging out there. Diane's teasing and the shared history made everything feel a bit more normal, a bit more hopeful.

A few days later, the common room buzzed with activity as people milled about, some eating and others resting. Diane and I sat comfortably in our spot, watching an action movie on a used laptop free to everyone in the room. We sat down on our favorite beanbag chair, it was red, worn down, and stretched enough to fit both of us. The familiar scent of old leather and popcorn filled the air as we settled in, sharing a big bowl of popcorn.

Diane's laughter mingled with mine as we exchanged quips about the movie's over-the-top scary scenes. Her head rested lightly on my shoulder, and I could feel the warmth of her body pressed against mine. It was a moment of peace and normalcy that felt almost surreal in our chaotic world.

"This is nice," Diane murmured, her eyes never leaving the screen.

"Yeah, it really is," I replied, feeling a sense of contentment wash over me.

We continued watching, our hands occasionally brushing as we reached for popcorn at the same time. Each touch sent a small jolt through me, a reminder of how much I cherished those quiet moments with her. Diane's presence was a balm to my frayed nerves, her laughter a soothing melody in the background.

As the movie reached an intense scene, Diane leaned closer, her breath warm against my neck. "You know, I've missed this," she said softly. "Just being with you like this."

I smiled, turning slightly to look at her. "I've missed it too. More than you know."

Our eyes met, and for a moment, everything else faded away. It was just the two of us, sharing a connection that felt unbreakable. Diane's fingers gently intertwined with mine, her touch both comforting and exhilarating.

Before we could say more, a loud shout shattered the calm.

"His eyes! They're yellow!" a panicked voice yelled.

Everyone turned to see a man, eyes glowing with an eerie yellow light. Fear rippled through the room as people backed away.

"Get back! He's possessed by the demon!" I stood up quickly, alarmed, my heart pounding.

Diane grabbed a nearby staff and moved to stand beside me. "We need to contain him before it spreads."

The possessed man lunged toward us with a feral growl. I braced myself for a fight, ready to face him head-on. As he charged, I ducked under his first swing and landed a solid punch to his gut, making him stagger.

Diane stepped in, her stance determined. "Let's take him down!" she called out, her voice steady.

We fought together, our movements synchronized from countless training sessions. Diane swung the staff at his legs, aiming to destabilize him. He grabbed the staff, yanking it out of her hands and tossing it aside. Diane didn't hesitate; she threw a punch at his jaw, her knuckles connecting with a sickening thud. The man staggered but quickly recovered, lunging at Diane again.

I saw the danger and rushed in, landing a kick to his side, but a second demon appeared from behind us, catching me off guard. The second demon tackled me to the ground, and I struggled to break free.

"Jack!" Diane shouted; her eyes wide with concern as she fought off the first possessed man.

Anne arrived at the mess hall just in time, her sudden entrance catching everyone by surprise. Without a word, she dove into the fray, tackling the second demon and bringing him to the ground with a forceful impact. Her movements were precise, a testament to her rigorous training as she grappled with the demon, her powerful blows weakening him under her relentless assault.

The chaos of the fight seemed to pause momentarily as Anne took control, and I watched in awe as Diane, regaining her composure, grabbed the discarded staff and joined Anne. Their combined effort quickly turned the tide, and soon the demon was subdued.

The residual energy of the fight filled the room, now settling into a tense silence. Anne and Diane stood there, catching their breath. The strain of the battle etched their faces, and their bodies trembled slightly from adrenaline and relief.

The silence between them was heavy, charged with unspoken words. Their eyes met, and in that brief, intense moment, they communicated everything they couldn't say aloud. Their connection, despite the tension and distance of the past, was palpable. The bond between them, forged in years of shared experiences and trials, was undeniable.

Tears welled up in Diane's eyes as she looked at Anne. She had always been the strong one, but the weight of the night's events and the emotional reunion broke through her facade. Her tears fell freely, a testament to the pain and relief she felt.

Anne's own eyes mirrored Diane's, filled with a deep, aching sorrow. Her tears flowed, mingling with Diane's as their emotional dam finally gave way.

Without a word, they moved toward each other, their steps synchronized in their desperate need for reconnection. When they embraced, it was as if they were piecing together a part of themselves that had been missing. Their hug was intense and emotional, a silent acknowledgment of all they had been through and the bond that had endured despite everything.

Diane buried her face in Anne's shoulder, her sobs shaking her body as Anne held her close. Anne's hands stroked Diane's back, offering and seeking comfort in equal measure.

"I've missed you so much," Diane said through her sobs, her voice breaking with each word.

"Me too," Anne whispered, her voice trembling. "I'm so sorry, Diane. For everything."

Their embrace tightened, their tears mingling as they held on, grounding each other in a moment of profound connection. The warmth of their hug, the familiarity of their touch, was a balm for their wounded hearts. The rift between them mended, each sob and tear a step toward healing.

After what felt like an eternity, they slowly pulled back, their faces still wet with tears but softened by tentative smiles. They looked into each other's eyes, finding in them the reflection of their shared pain and enduring love. The moment was a pure, unfiltered connection, a bridge over the chasm of their past misunderstandings.

As they finally let go, the room seemed to release a collective breath. The immediate danger had passed, and the tension eased, replaced by a renewed sense of understanding between the sisters.

Diane and I settled into a beanbag chair, leaning into each other for comfort. Diane's eyes, still red from crying, met Anne's across the room. There was a silent understanding between them, acknowledging that while their relationship was healing, there was still work to be done.

Diane's hand found mine, squeezing gently. It was a reassurance that, despite the chaos and pain, things would eventually be all right. The immediate threat was over, but we knew there was more to be done to protect everyone in the bunker and prevent further dangers.

Later that night, The commander gathered everyone together in the common room to discuss the situation. The flickering light of a single lantern cast shadows on the walls, creating an atmosphere of both urgency and solidarity as we brainstormed ways to strengthen our defenses.

"We need to find out how he got possessed," Anne said, her tone serious and determined. The weight of responsibility hung heavy in her voice. "And we need to make sure it doesn't happen to anyone else."

Diane nodded, her voice steady and authoritative. "Agreed. We should increase patrols and set up a rotation to watch for any signs of possession."

I added, "We also need to educate everyone on how to spot the early signs and what to do if they suspect someone is possessed."

The discussion continued late into the night, with everyone contributing ideas and strategies. Despite the fear and uncertainty, there was a newfound sense of solidarity and purpose. We were no longer just surviving; we were fighting back. The meeting soon wrapped up, and exhausted, we all retired to our rooms for the night. Diane and I did our nightly ritual hug that always lingered purposely, a silent promise of protection and affection.

In the following days, the bunker became a hive of activity as we implemented our new plans. Patrols were more frequent, and everyone was on high alert for any signs of possession. The sense of community and determination was palpable, and it felt like we were finally taking control of our fate.

Anne approached me with a determined look in her eyes. She had been avoiding me since the fight in the mess hall, but now it seemed she was ready to talk.

"Jack, can we talk?" she asked, her voice softer than usual, carrying a hint of vulnerability.

I nodded, gesturing for her to sit down. "Of course, Anne. Let's talk."

She took a deep breath, looking genuinely remorseful. "I'm really sorry for everything. My emotions got the best of me and I ended up hurting you and Diane. I never wanted to cause so much pain."

Her words hung heavy in the air, and I could see the sincerity in her eyes. It softened my heart. "I know, Anne. We've all been under a lot of stress. It's been a rough time for everyone."

Anne's eyes filled with tears, and she reached out to take my hand. Her grip was firm, yet tender. "I just want you to know that I'm happy being friends with you. I got petty and let my emotions get the best of me, but I want to make things right."

I hugged her back, feeling a sense of relief. "Anne, we all make mistakes. What's important is that we learn from them and move forward. I appreciate your honesty."

She hugged me tightly, the warmth of her embrace a stark contrast to the coldness of the bunker. "Thank you, Jack. I promise I'll do better."

As she pulled back, there was a newfound determination in her eyes. The tension between us eased, replaced by a tentative but genuine friendship. We both knew that the road ahead would be challenging, but we were ready to face it together.

As Anne walked away, Diane approached, having witnessed our exchange. She smiled softly, her eyes reflecting a mixture of relief and gratitude. "That was a big step," she said, slipping her hand into mine.

"Yeah," I agreed, squeezing her hand. "It feels like we're finally starting to heal."

Diane nodded, leaning her head on my shoulder. "We've got a long way to go, but we'll get there."

In that moment, surrounded by the dim glow of the lantern and the quiet murmur of the bunker, I felt a renewed sense of hope. Despite the darkness that had threatened to consume us, we had pushed through, to find light in each other. And with that, I knew we could face whatever came next.

After a few weeks, our little community in the bunker found a new rhythm. We replaced the chaos that had once consumed us with a quieter, more cooperative atmosphere. People were more supportive of each other, their actions reflective of the shared experiences that bound them together. The tensions that had once run high eased, making room for a newfound sense of unity and hope.

Anne became a visitor again, though her presence was less frequent than before. She still brought me the latest gossip and updates, injecting moments of levity into our days. Her approach, however, was now more respectful and thoughtful. She had taken to heart the need for a more considerate approach to our strained relationships.

Diane returned to being by my side throughout the day. Her presence was a constant source of comfort and strength. Our bond, once strained, healed, strengthened by the time we spent together. We resumed our training with renewed vigor. Each session in the training room was more than just a physical workout; it was a reaffirmation of our trust and understanding. Diane pushed me to regain my strength and skills, her encouragement unwavering.

One night, after another particularly vivid nightmare, I woke to find Diane already by my bed. Her presence was a calming balm to my frazzled nerves.

"Hey, it's okay," she said softly, her fingers brushing a damp lock of hair from my forehead. Her touch lingered for a moment, as though she was willing me to find peace.

I took a deep breath, struggling to steady myself. "Thanks, Diane. I don't know what I'd do without you."

She tilted her head slightly, her expression softening into something unreadable but deeply reassuring. "You don't have to go through this alone, Jack. I'm always here for you."

Her words were like a soothing balm to my aching heart, yet I couldn't stop the lump that formed in my throat. I managed a whisper, raw and honest. "I know. And I appreciate it more than you can imagine."

She started gently wiping down my body, her movements tender and deliberate. Each touch felt purposeful, as though she were not just helping me but reminding me that I wasn't broken. I couldn't help but marvel at her patience, the way she cared without hesitation. It was in these quiet, intimate moments that our connection deepened. The past wounds between us were gradually healing, and with each passing day, our bond grew stronger. Diane and I were becoming one, our shared experiences and quiet moments weaving a tapestry of trust and affection.

The next morning, as we walked to the common room together, Diane's thoughtful expression returned. She seemed lost in her own thoughts, her silence weighing heavily on the air. When she finally spoke, her voice was measured. "Jack, do you ever think about what's next? For us, I mean."

Her words landed with a weight I hadn't expected. I stopped walking and turned to her, studying her for a moment. There was something vulnerable about the way she stood, as though the question had cost her more than she wanted to admit. "I do," I said, my tone steady despite the knot forming in my chest. "I think about it a lot. And I know that whatever comes next, we've got this."

Diane's gaze lingered on me, a flicker of uncertainty crossing her face before it settled into quiet determination. "I hope so. I really do."

We sat down in our favorite spot on a worn-out beanbag in the common room. The soft glow of a lantern cast a warm light over us, creating a cozy and intimate atmosphere. Diane turned to me, a playful quirk tugging at her lips. I couldn't help but mimic her, the tension between us easing into something softer.

As the beanbag molded around us, we leaned into each other, the flickering light playing over her features. I noticed how the shadows danced along her jawline, the way her breath seemed to catch when she spoke. "Jack," she said softly, her voice carrying an undercurrent of emotion, "I want you to know that I'm proud of you."

Her words touched something deep inside me, a place I hadn't let anyone see for a long time. "I couldn't have done it without you, Diane. You've been my rock through all of this."

Her lips parted as though she wanted to say more, but instead, she leaned in slightly, her expression tender. "We're in this together, Jack. Always."

I pulled her closer, my arm instinctively wrapping around her waist. "Always," I echoed, the word feeling like a promise I was desperate to keep.

In that moment, everything felt right. The world outside might have been falling apart, but here, in our little corner of the bunker, we had each other. And that was enough to keep us going.

Feeling a surge of emotion, I leaned in, hesitating just for a moment as doubt flickered in my mind. What if this changed everything? But the way Diane looked at me, the way her lips curved ever so slightly as though she were waiting, pushed the doubt aside. I closed the distance between us, our lips meeting in a tentative kiss.

It was awkward at first, our inexperience showing in the way our movements faltered. Diane pulled away slightly, her cheeks tinged with color, her gaze searching mine. "Jack..."

But before she could say more, I gently placed my hand on her cheek, the warmth of her skin grounding me. She mirrored the gesture, her fingers brushing against my jaw. For a second, we simply looked at each other, as though the moment itself was holding its breath. Then, as if drawn by an unseen force, she kissed me back.

This time, the kiss lingered, deepening as we found a rhythm. The world outside seemed to dissolve, leaving only the quiet hum of our connection. Her hands slid up to rest on my shoulders, her touch both grounding and electrifying. I felt her melt against me, the lines between us blurring as we lost ourselves in each other.

We eventually parted, breathless, our foreheads resting together. The room was silent except for the sound of our breathing, and for a moment, I felt like the ground beneath me had steadied.

After a while, we settled back into the beanbag, deciding to watch our favorite scary movie, Scream. The familiar scenes played out on the screen, and though we had seen it countless times, it felt different now. We stayed up late into the night, the movie serving as a comforting backdrop to our newfound connection.

As the credits rolled, Diane leaned her head on my shoulder. "This feels like a new chapter, doesn't it?"

I nodded, squeezing her hand. "It does. And I'm glad we're writing it together."

We stayed there, wrapped in each other's warmth, feeling the promise of what was to come. The night might have been dark, but the future felt a little brighter with Diane by my side.

CHAPTER 21

The training room's dim light seemed almost too gentle, casting long shadows that played across the floor and walls, hiding the full force of the tension building between us. Diane and I sat on the edge of the mats, catching our breath after a grueling session. Our sweat-slicked bodies felt the lingering heat of exertion, and the closeness of our proximity was almost too much to bear. Diane's arm brushed mine—a casual gesture, but it sent a spark of electricity through me, making my pulse quicken.

I glanced sideways, taking in the sight of her damp hair clinging to her forehead, cheeks flushed with the exertion of our workout. Her lips, slightly parted as she panted, seemed almost to beckon me closer. The room felt charged, thick with the unspoken, as her voice cut through the heavy silence. "Jack," she murmured, the sound low and tinged with an intimacy that made my heart pound. "Do you ever think we're pushing ourselves too hard?"

Her question lingered, heavy with implications that I could feel even if she didn't voice them. I swallowed, trying to steady the thudding in my chest as the warmth of her skin pressed against mine. "We can't afford not to be prepared," I replied, my voice strained.

Diane's fingers traced a path along the back of my hand, each touch igniting a trail of fire. "But I'm talking about us, Jack. Not just the training."

I hesitated, the intensity of her gaze making my resolve waver. The tension between us was palpable, a pressure that had been building for too long. "Yeah," I admitted, my voice rough. "It's overwhelming."

Her hand tightened on mine, and I could feel the heat radiating from her touch, fueling a blaze that I struggled to contain. "So why are we holding back?" Her eyes locked onto mine, filled with a desire that mirrored my own and made it hard to deny the truth of our feelings.

"I'm not ready," I said, perhaps too sharply. I saw the flicker of hurt in her eyes, a pang of guilt hitting me. "It's not that I don't feel it. I do. It's just... everything's so complicated."

She pulled away slightly, the absence of her warmth a stark reminder of the tension between us. "I get it, Jack. But it's hard to be this close and not want more."

The frustration in her voice mirrored my own, and as we stood to resume training, our movements became almost mechanical, driven by an undercurrent of unresolved tension. Each strike, each dodge, brought us dangerously close, the proximity of our bodies making it almost impossible to focus.

Diane lunged at me, and our chests collided, her softness pressing against my hard frame. Her breath was hot against my neck, making my pulse race. "Careful," she whispered, her lips brushing my ear, sending a shiver down my spine. "I'm already excited."

The sensation made my brain turn to mush, and I stammered, "I'm sorry."

Diane giggled, a sound both teasing and maddening. "Sorry for what?"

Her fingers trailed down my leg, the touch maddeningly gentle and sensual. "You're good at this, Jack. But maybe there's something else we could be good at together."

Her gaze met mine, a challenge and an invitation all rolled into one. My resolve faltered as her words washed over me, making it harder to hold back. "I want to, Diane. But I need more time."

Disappointment flashed in her eyes, but she nodded, her understanding apparent. "I don't want to push you into something you're not ready for. But it's hard not to feel this way. It's driving me crazy."

The frustration in her voice echoed my own, and I took her hand, gripping it. "I felt it too. But I don't want to risk what we have. Not yet."

We resumed our training, the air still charged with tension, each touch and glance loaded with unspoken desire. As we grappled, our bodies pressed together, the sensation was almost too much to handle. Her hand brushed my chest, lingering longer than necessary, and the heat between us was undeniable.

"Jack," she breathed, her lips tantalizingly close to mine. "This is getting hard to ignore."

"I know," I whispered, my voice thick with emotion. "But—"

Her hand slid to my abdomen, her fingers brushing my skin, making my resolve crumble. "What are you afraid of, Jack?" she asked, her voice soft yet insistent.

"I'm afraid of ruining everything," I admitted, the words coming out raw. "Of losing you."

"You won't lose me," she said firmly, her tone leaving no room for doubt. "But I can't keep pretending there's nothing between us. It's killing me."

Her words cut deep, striking a chord within me. I knew she was right, but fear still held me back. "Diane, I... I need time. Please."

She sighed, her breath warm against my cheek as she leaned in close. "I understand. But don't make me wait too long, Jack. Life's too short."

Her lips brushed my cheek, a fleeting touch that left me aching for more. "I promise I won't."

At that moment, the world seemed to narrow down to just the two of us, our breaths mingling in the small space between us. Her hands roamed further, her touch urgent and tender, making it almost impossible to maintain my composure.

Before I could act on the overwhelming desire that surged between us, an alarm blared, shattering the moment. We quickly separated, our faces flushed, our breaths ragged. The intensity of our feelings remained, the promise of what could linger in the air, waiting for the right moment to break through.

In the days following our conversation, the tension between Diane and me continued to build. The bunker's atmosphere seemed to crackle with it, an electric charge that was impossible to ignore. Anne's teasing comments didn't help, only heightened the emotional and physical strain between us.

One evening, as the sun dipped below the horizon and cast long shadows in the mess hall, Anne sidled up to Diane and me, her eyes twinkling with mischief. "So, how's the chemistry experiment going? Any breakthroughs?"

Diane shot her sister a sharp look. "Anne, not now."

Anne's grin widened. "Oh, come on. It's all anyone talks about. The way you two look at each other—it's like watching a soap opera in real life."

My face flushed, and I tried to brush off the comment. "We're just focused on our training."

Anne raised an eyebrow, clearly unconvinced. "Sure, Jack. And I'm the Queen of England. It's obvious there's something more. But hey, don't worry, I'm here to offer moral support. Just keep it PG around me."

As Anne walked away, Diane's cheeks burned with embarrassment, and I felt a pang of frustration. The growing attraction between us was becoming a public spectacle, and it was driving me to the edge.

Later that night, alone in my bunk, I wrestled with my thoughts. Diane's touch, her scent, the way her eyes sparkled—it was all-consuming. I knew I needed to address the escalating tension between us, but it was hard to find the right words.

The next morning, I found Diane in the training room, stretching and preparing for another session. Her presence was a balm to my restless mind, but it also ignited the unresolved tension between us. I approached her, my heart pounding. "Diane, we need to talk."

She looked up, her expression was serious. "I know."

We sat down on the edge of the mats, the air between us heavy with unspoken words. "Diane, I can't deny what's happening between us. It's intense, and I'm struggling to ignore it," I said, my voice rough.

Diane's eyes softened, and she reached out to take my hand. "Jack, I felt the same way. It's been building for a while now."

I squeezed her hand gently. "But I can't keep pretending it's not there. We need to figure this out together."

She nodded, a tear slipping down her cheek. I wiped it away with my thumb, feeling the weight of her emotions. Diane leaned into me, resting her head on my shoulder. I wrapped my arms around her, holding her close, the warmth of her body grounding me even as it heightened the intensity of my feelings.

As we stood up, the world outside the bunker seemed to vanish. We sparred with renewed intensity, our movements synchronized, almost as if we were dancing rather than training. Each touch, each brush of our bodies, carried a charged meaning, making it increasingly difficult to ignore the attraction between us.

Anne watched from the sidelines, a knowing smile on her lips. "You two are something else," she called out with a hint of teasing in her voice. "I've never seen such... enthusiastic sparring."

Diane shot her with a pleading look. "Anne, please."

Anne laughed, clearly enjoying the spectacle. "Oh, come on. It's obvious there's more going on here than just training. Just don't make me a witness to anything... more intense."

The teasing only added to the growing pressure between Diane and me. Each accidental touch, each lingering glance, was like fuel on a fire, making it harder to keep our feelings in check.

During one particularly intense moment, Diane stumbled, and I instinctively reached out to catch her. Our bodies collided, and we froze, faces inched apart. Her breath was hot against my lips, and I could feel her heartbeat racing.

Anne's voice broke the spell. "I'll leave you two lovebirds alone," she said with a wink, heading toward the door. "Just try not to kill each other."

Diane and I both laughed, the tension easing slightly. "Thanks, Anne," I said, grateful for the distraction.

Once Anne had left, Diane looked at me,. "Jack, this... whatever this is, it's getting harder to control."

I nodded, feeling the same struggle. "I know. It's like every time we're together, it's electric."

She sighed, her hand brushed against my arm. "We need to figure out what we want and what we're willing to risk."

I took her hand in mine, feeling the warmth of her touch. "We'll get through this, Diane. We just need to be honest with each other."

Diane smiled, her eyes filled with a mix of emotions. "You're right. Let's take it one step at a time."

As we resumed our sparring, we tempered the intensity with a new understanding. Each movement was deliberate, a silent promise to face whatever came our way together. The rest of the session blurred into a mix of focused training and subtle touches; our connection undeniable.

When the session ended, sweat-soaked and breathless, I knew we had made a significant step toward something deeper. As we left the training room, Anne caught up with us, her grin knowing.

"So, how was the... session?" she asked with a teasing lilt.

Diane rolled her eyes but couldn't suppress a small smile. "Productive, as always."

Anne laughed, linking her arm with Diane's. "Good to hear. Just remember, I'm rooting for you two."

I watched them, feeling a sense of warmth and belonging. Despite the tension and the challenges ahead, it felt like we were moving closer to something real, something that was worth every bit of the struggle.

The next day, the harsh, artificial light of the training room cut through the early evening shadows, bathing everything in a stark glow. The mingled scents of sweat and determination hung heavy in the air. My clothes clung to my body, drenched from the grueling session, and I could feel every ache in my muscles as I wiped the sweat from my brow with a towel. Across from me, Diane was catching her breath, her chest rising and falling as she rolled her shoulders to ease the tension.

"You really know how to push someone to their limit," I said, my voice hoarse but full of admiration.

Diane smirked, the corner of her mouth quirking up in a way that made my exhaustion seem less significant. "It's what we need," she said, her voice firm despite her heavy breathing. "We've got to be ready for anything. Especially with everything on the line." Her gaze lingered on me, and for a moment, the hardness in her expression softened, something unspoken passing between us.

I stepped closer, demonstrating a new move I'd just mastered. "Watch this," I said, moving slowly to show her the details. She followed my lead, our bodies moving in perfect sync, and each touch, each brush of skin, seemed to hum with energy.

As I adjusted her stance, my arm brushed against hers. The contact sent an unexpected jolt through me, and I could feel it reflected in her as well. Diane's eyes locked with mine, and suddenly, the intensity of our training session shifted into something deeper.

Then, in a moment of clumsiness, I lost my balance and stumbled into her. We both went down, and I landed awkwardly on top of her. My heart raced as I realized how close our faces were, our breaths mingling in the confined space between us.

"Sorry," I murmured, barely above a whisper, my voice thick with the tension I was trying to ignore. My gaze dropped to her lips, so close and so tempting.

Diane's hand rose to the back of my neck, her fingers trembling just slightly. "No need to apologize," she said, her voice low and sultry. Her eyes held mine, filled with something that looked like both longing and affection.

Time seemed to stop as she pulled me closer. Our lips met in a kiss that was tentative at first, but the pent-up emotions between us quickly ignited into something fierce and passionate. Her hands slid over my back, pulling me closer, and I responded instinctively, my own hands moving to explore the curves of her body with reverence.

The kiss deepened, and the world outside faded into nothingness. Diane's fingers tangled in my hair, pulling me closer still, and my hands found their way to her waist, gripping her like she might disappear if I let go. The heat between us was overwhelming, our breaths coming faster as the kiss grew more frantic.

Diane's soft gasps against my lips drove me wild as her fingers traced down my chest. "We've waited so long for this," she whispered, her voice filled with a mix of desire and relief.

"I know," I murmured, pressing my lips to her neck, kissing and nipping at her skin. "We needed this."

The training room transformed into our own private world. Every touch, every kiss, felt like it was erasing the barriers we'd held onto for so long. My hands roamed over her back, pulling her closer, and she responded with equal intensity.

But just as the moment reached its peak, the door burst open with a loud clang. I froze, my heart lurching in my chest as I turned to see Diane's twin sister, Anne, striding in with a few of her friends.

"Whoa," Anne said, her voice dripping with mischief. "Looks like we interrupted something." Her friends giggled behind her, their wide-eyed stares making my face burn with embarrassment. Diane quickly pushed me off and scrambled to her feet, her face flushed. "Anne, seriously?" she snapped, her irritation barely masking her embarrassment.

Anne, with a mischievous grin, sauntered closer. "So, Diane, how's Jack as a kisser?" she asked, her tone both teasing and provocative.

Diane's cheeks turned a deeper shade of red. "Anne, that's not funny," she said firmly, trying to regain her composure. "Get out of here before I really lose my patience."

Anne laughed, holding up her hands in mock surrender. "All right, all right. I'm just messing with you." She turned and walked out, her laughter echoing down the hall.

Once the door shut behind Anne, Diane and I exchanged a look, a mix of relief and lingering tension in our eyes. Diane let out a nervous laugh, brushing a strand of hair from her face.

"Well, that was unexpected," I said, attempting to lighten the mood.

"Yeah," Diane agreed, still chuckling. "But we should probably get cleaned up and figure out what to do next."

We made our way back to our rooms, the air between us still charged with the unresolved emotions from the training room.

After Diane and I separated, the moment still lingering in the air, I stumbled back to my room. The intensity of what had just happened was almost overwhelming. My mind buzzed with confusion, and my body still hummed with the aftereffects of our passionate encounter.

Once inside my room, I stared at the wall for a moment, trying to steady my racing heart. My thoughts were a tangled mess, and I could still feel the warmth of Diane's touch and the intensity of her kiss. The frustration and need for clarity were almost palpable.

"I need a cold shower," I muttered, my voice carrying a mix of desperation and determination. I stripped off my sweat-soaked clothes, tossing them aside, and headed for the bathroom.

The bathroom was a stark contrast to the heat of the training room—cold, clinical, and filled with the hum of the overhead light. I turned on the faucet and adjusted the water to its coldest setting. The rush of cold water hit the tiles with a sharp, almost brutal force. I stepped under the stream, shivering as the icy droplets pelted my skin.

The cold was shockingly invigorating, a sharp contrast to the warmth that had enveloped us just moments before. It was both a physical and mental reset. The chill of the water slicing through the haze of desire and confusion that had clouded my thoughts. I could feel the water running over my shoulders and down my back, the biting cold making me gasp and shiver. Each droplet felt like a tiny jolt of clarity, pulling me back to reality.

I let the water continue to cascade over me, its relentless coldness helping to ground me. As the seconds ticked by, the initial shock of the cold subsided, and I slowly regained some semblance of calm. The water smoothed out the rough edges of my emotions, though the intensity of what had happened between Diane and me still lingered at the edges of my mind.

Eventually, I stepped out of the shower, the chill of the water giving way to the warmth of the bathroom air. I wrapped a towel around myself, sitting on the edge of my bed, the steam still clinging to my skin. My mind buzzed with the chaotic emotions from earlier. The sudden buzz of my phone broke the silence. It was Diane:

"Hey, can we talk? I think we need to sort things out. Meet me in my room?"

My heart skipped a beat. Even though it was late, I knew this conversation couldn't wait. I quickly dressed in a fresh shirt and sweatpants, the urgency in Diane's message pulled me from my thoughts and headed out of my room.

When I knocked on Diane's door, she opened it almost instantly. Her damp hair and soft robe, fresh from a shower, made my heart race. She stepped aside; her gaze was full of nervous hope, and I followed her into the dimly lit room.

The warm glow of a bedside lamp cast soft shadows, adding a cozy but intimate feel to the space. Diane gestured for me to sit on the edge of her bed. I sat down, the weight of our earlier conversation pressing heavily on me. Diane took a seat beside me, the tension between us almost palpable.

"I'm really sorry about earlier," Diane began, her voice soft yet earnest. "I did not intend to rush things. I just... I felt so strongly about us, and I guess I wanted to make sure you felt the same way."

Her words cut through the fog of my thoughts, and I met her gaze, torn between affection and confusion. "Diane, I do feel something. There's no denying it. But everything's been so overwhelming lately. I'm trying to make sense of it all."

Diane reached out and took my hand, her touch warm and comforting. "I understand. I just wanted you to know that I'm here, and I'm willing to take things at your pace. I don't want to rush you or make you feel pressured."

Her sincerity melted some of my anxiety. "I appreciate that. It means a lot. It's just... we've been through so much, and I'm afraid of making a mistake."

Diane's eyes locked with mine, a mix of longing and understanding shining through. "Sometimes, Jack, taking a chance is worth the risk. I believe we have something special here, and I don't want to lose that."

The space between us crackled with unspoken emotions. I leaned in slowly, and our lips met in a tentative kiss. It began gently, but soon ignited into a fervent embrace. Diane's arms encircled my neck, pulling me closer, while my hands roamed over her face, exploring the softness of her skin. As the kiss deepened, it became an intense fusion of warmth and urgency. My hands couldn't resist slipping into her robe, squeezing her tits with bold new intensity.

When we finally pulled apart, both of us were breathless. Diane's hair was tousled, her robe slightly open, and her cheeks were flushed. She looked at me with wide eyes, a mix of affection and surprise evident, and her lips were slightly swollen from our passionate kiss.

"Ang halik na iyon ay sobrang init. Parang nagliyab ang buong katawan ko," she murmured in Tagalog, her voice trembling with the intensity of the moment.

She met my eyes with a shy smile, translating softly. "That kiss was so intense. It felt like my whole body was on fire."

Diane's laughter, light and almost musical, filled the room as she glanced at the tent in my sweatpants. "I think I might need to take another shower now," she said, her voice teasing. "And it's not just because I'm a mess. You really have a way of making things... memorable."

I chuckled, feeling a rush of warmth at her playful comment. "I think I might need a cold shower too," I said, trying to lighten the mood.

Diane's gaze continued to stare at my tent as she took in my disheveled state, her laughter bubbling with mischief. "Well, at least we know it's not just me feeling the aftereffects," she teased. "But seriously, Jack, I'm glad we talked. And… I'm glad we shared that."

Her playful energy was infectious as she watched me adjust myself, her eyes twinkling with amusement. She walked me to the door; her robe more open, exposing her left tit, a playful glint in her eyes. Leaning in for one last, soft kiss on the cheek, her hand squeezing my bulge over my pants, making the moment even more charged.

In a low, teasing moan, she whispered, "Payback."

Before I could react, Diane bounced back with a giggle. "Good night, Jack."

"Good night, Diane," I replied softly, giving her one last look before adjusting myself once more and stepping into the hallway. All I could think about was that cold shower as I ran back to my room.

CHAPTER 22

A few nights later, Diane and I found ourselves on the roof of the bunker, where a small crack in the ceiling revealed a slice of the night sky. The stars sparkled brightly, their distant light breaking through the darkness, casting a soft, ethereal glow over us. The roof, usually a place of practical escape, felt like a sanctuary tonight.

We huddled close together on the cold, uneven surface of the roof. The chill in the air was sharp against our skin, but the proximity of our bodies offered a soothing warmth. The contrast between the biting cold and the heat of our shared space created a cocoon that felt both intimate and comforting.

"I used to love stargazing," I said, my voice low and filled with nostalgia as I traced the constellations above. "It's been so long since I've seen the sky like this."

"It's beautiful," Diane murmured, her voice soft and reflective. She lay back slightly, her head resting against the roof. "It's like a reminder that there's more out there, beyond all of this." She glanced over at me, her eyes shimmering with a mix of longing and peace.

The silence that followed differed from the usual tension that had hung between us. Tonight, we experienced a rare pause, a moment where we could set aside the weight of everything else. The cool night air felt like a gentle embrace, the stars a quiet witness to our private conversation.

"Diane," I began, my voice slightly shaky with vulnerability. I turned to face her fully, the weight of my feelings pressing against my chest. "There's something I've been meaning to tell you."

Her gaze was steady, her expression open and curious. "What is it, Jack?"

I took a deep breath, trying to steady the storm of emotions inside me. "You've been there for me through so much. This is the closest I've ever felt to anyone. I think... I think I'm in love with you."

Diane's eyes widened in surprise, then softened with a profound warmth. Her lips parted as if to speak, but no words came. Instead, she reached out, her hand finding mine in the darkness. Her touch was gentle, but it sent a rush of electricity through me, grounding me at the moment.

"Jack..." Her voice trembled slightly, the emotion in her tone unmistakable. "I've been scared to admit it, too. But being with you... it makes everything bearable. I felt like we're connected in a way I've never felt before. I think... I think I love you, too." Diane said in a playful way, teasing the way I said it.

The intensity of her confession mirrored my own feelings, creating a bridge between us that felt both fragile and unbreakable. We leaned in closer, the space between us narrowing until our faces were just inched apart. The stars above seemed to blink more brightly, as if reflecting our newfound closeness.

When our lips met, the kiss was a tender exploration, full of the tenderness and longing we had both kept at bay. Diane's lips were soft and warm, and as the kiss deepened, our breaths mingled in the cool night air. Each touch, each caress, was a silent declaration of our mutual desire and affection.

As the kiss grew more passionate, our bodies pressed together, seeking comfort and reassurance. Diane's hands tangled in my hair, pulling me closer, while my arms wrapped around her, holding her against me with a fierce tenderness. The night seemed to wrap around us, a protective shroud that shielded our intimacy from the world outside.

When we finally separated, our breaths became uneven, and our faces flushed with a mix of heat and emotion. We lay back together, our fingers intertwined, our bodies still close. The stars above felt silent, approving audience to our newfound connection.

We stayed on the roof, wrapped in each other's presence and the serene beauty of the night. The cool air brushed against our skin, but it felt refreshing rather than cold, as if the universe itself was celebrating our bond. The world outside felt distant and irrelevant, eclipsed by the profound sense of connection and love we had found in each other's arms.

Later that night, in my bedroom, I got ready for a shower. I let the hot water soothe my muscles and wash away the remnants of the day's training. As I stepped out and wrapped a towel around my waist, Diane entered the bathroom.

She walked in without a towel, her confidence palpable. Her eyes locked onto mine as she leaned against the doorway, her expression bold and playful. "You know," she began, her voice low and teasing, "I've been thinking about that moment back in the training room."

I met her gaze, my heart racing. "Yeah? What about it?"

Diane's eyes sparkled with mischief as she slowly traced her fingers along her collarbone. "Well, we've been building up a lot of tension. And I think we both know what we want."

I let the towel drop, my gaze shifting to her as I took a step forward. The atmosphere was thick with anticipation, every touch and glance magnified by the intensity of the moment.

As Diane moved closer, the warmth between us was undeniable. The space between us vanished, and our bodies brushed together with a heightened intensity. Our hearts raced in unison, and the need to express our feelings became overwhelming. Words fell away, irrelevant in the face of the deep connection we shared.

We fell into each other's arms, our embrace fierce yet tender. The vulnerability of the moment revealed our raw emotions. Diane's eyes locked onto mine, filled with a mixture of longing and trust. The heat between us was almost tangible, driving us to respond with an urgency that spoke to our shared desires and fears.

Diane's moans, soft and unguarded, echoed the depth of our bond. Each touch, each caress, was a testament to our unspoken understanding. The bed became a mess of tangled sheets, a silent witness to the fervor of our connection. We communicated through our actions, letting our feelings unfold without the need for words.

Our shared experience was intense and consuming. We were acutely aware of each other's presence, the way our bodies moved together, and the way our breaths came in quick shared gasps. The world outside seemed to fade away, leaving just the two of us in our own universe of closeness and passion.

When the moment finally passed, we lay tangled together, both physically and emotionally spent. Our bodies, still intertwined, barely moved as we drifted into sleep. Our breathing filled the room with soft sounds, a quiet testament to the depth of our bond. We found comfort in each other's presence, knowing that, despite everything, we had each other. The world outside was distant and irrelevant as we rested, wrapped in the warmth of our shared connection.

The next day, Diane and I were busy transforming my room into a shared space. As we rearranged furniture and unpacked boxes, Anne popped in to help, her usual teasing adding a layer of levity to our task.

Anne carried a box into the room, her eyes twinkling with mischief. "So, I guess the training room will now be strictly for, well, training?" she teased, her tone light but clearly hinting at the recently charged atmosphere between Diane and me.

Diane, her cheeks flushing slightly, laughed. "Yeah, you caught us. Our bed is now our personal training room," she said with a playful smirk. Her eyes met mine, and a shared understanding passed between us—a promise of passionate nights ahead.

Anne grinned, clearly enjoying the banter. "Just make sure you don't overdo it. I'd rather not have to listen to your 'training' exploits from anyone else." She gave Diane a knowing look before giving her a hug. "Congratulations, you two. I'm really happy for you."

Diane embraced Anne warmly, her gratitude clear in her smile. "Thanks, Anne. And don't worry, we'll keep the details to ourselves."

With a final playful glance, Anne left us alone in the room. As the door clicked shut behind her, Diane and I exchanged a look filled with relief and affection. The room, now filled with our belongings, felt like a symbol of our shared future.

We settled onto the bed, the soft, cool sheets beneath us. Diane lay beside me, her hand resting on my chest. We both looked around, taking in the sight of our new living space, the product of our combined lives. It was a far cry from the sterile, impersonal bunkers we'd grown accustomed to.

"Can you believe we're finally here?" Diane's voice was soft, her eyes reflecting a mix of awe and contentment.

I shook my head slightly, a smile tugging at my lips. "No, it feels almost surreal. All the moments leading up to this... the tension, the waiting—it was worth it. I'm glad we're finally together like this."

Diane's fingers traced light patterns on my chest, her touch sending shivers through me. "It feels like a dream, but it's real. Every time we almost gave in to our desires during training, it just made everything more intense, more meaningful."

I nodded, the memories of our passionate moments bringing a smile to my face. "Exactly. It was like every touch; every glance was building up to something greater. And when we finally gave in, it was... perfect."

Diane's eyes met mine, her expression softening with affection. "I think all that waiting made our connection even stronger. We didn't rush into anything; we let our feelings grow naturally. And now, here we are."

I brushed a strand of hair away from her face, my heart swelling with emotion. "I'm grateful for every moment we shared, even the ones that were difficult. They brought us to this place, where we can be honest and open with each other."

Diane's gaze was tender, her voice barely above a whisper. "I've never felt this close to anyone before. Being with you makes everything seem more bearable. It's like we're creating our own little world together."

The intimacy of the moment was palpable, a blend of relief and excitement. We shared a kiss, a gentle and tender connection that spoke of our deepening bond. It was a kiss that conveyed both the passion we had been holding back and the love that had blossomed between us.

As we pulled away, Diane rested her head on my shoulder, her breathing steady and content. "I'm really looking forward to our future," she said, her voice filled with warmth. "To all the moments we'll share, the good and the bad."

I wrapped my arms around her, holding her close. "Me too. I'm ready for whatever comes next, as long as we're together."

We lay there for a while, wrapped in each other's embrace, the world outside our room fading into insignificance. The quiet of the room contrasted starkly with the earlier tension, but a comforting sense of togetherness filled it. The stars outside, visible through the small crack in the roof, seemed to shine just for us, a silent testament to our love and the future we were building together.

Eventually, we drifted into a comfortable silence, our hands entwined, and the promise of what lay ahead filling the space between us. The night was peaceful, and as we lay there, it felt like we had finally found a place where we truly belonged—together.

Later that night, the room was dimly lit by a small lamp, casting soft, flickering shadows across the walls. I jolted awake, my heart racing and sweat slick on my forehead. The nightmare had been vivid, too real, dragging me from sleep with its relentless grip. Diane, who had been sleeping beside me, stirred at my sudden movement and immediately noticed my distress.

"Jack, what's wrong?" Her concerned voice broke through the remnants of my dream as she asked, "Jack, what's wrong?"

I sat up abruptly, running a shaky hand through my damp hair. "Just a nightmare. My father... I keep seeing his eyes. It's like he's staring right at me."

Diane, sensing my turmoil, swiftly moved closer, her arms wrapping around me with a comforting warmth. Her touch was soothing, grounding me in the present moment. "You're safe here, Jack. I'm here with you." Her embrace enveloped me, her warmth a refuge from the haunting memories.

I leaned into her, letting the tension in my muscles slowly dissolve. "Thank you, Diane. I don't know what I'd do without you."

"You'll never have to find out," she replied softly, her voice steady and reassuring. "I'm not going anywhere."

With practiced care, Diane helped me clean up, offering a clean pair of boxers and gently helping me change. Her tender touch and the soft rustling of fabric felt oddly comforting, a contrast to the distress I felt. Once I was settled, she slipped back into bed beside me, her presence a balm for my frayed nerves.

We lay back down, our bodies pressed close, and I found solace in her warmth. The rhythm of her breathing calmed me, and my heart rate gradually slowed. The nightmare's grip on me loosened, replaced by the peace of Diane's steady presence.

But sleep did not come easily again. With a sudden jolt, I woke up, my chest still constricted from the lasting impact of the nightmare. I glanced over at Diane, relieved to see she was still sleeping peacefully, undisturbed by my restless movements. I slipped out of bed quietly and moved to my desk, hoping to escape the heavy weight of my thoughts.

Sitting down, I opened the top drawer and pulled out a photograph. In a moment of happier times, the image captured my parents. The photograph had aged; the edges were faded, and there were wrinkles and creases from years of handling. I traced the outlines of their faces with my eyes, the familiar pang of loss intensifying as memories flooded back.

The memory of that day—my father lying on the ground, his blood spreading out in a dark pool—gripped me fiercely. I was frozen in that closet, helpless, unable to move or make a difference. The sense of failure, of not being able to save him, weighed heavily on me. The vision of my mother sacrificing herself to destroy the beast followed closely, a painful reminder of my inability to save either of them.

The anguish was suffocating, a reminder of all that I had lost and the helplessness that had defined those moments. I sat there, staring at the photograph, the silent weight of the past pressing down on my shoulders. The memories were harsh, relentless, and unforgiving. I felt trapped between the haunting past and the uncertain future.

Despite the room's quietness, I found little comfort as I attempted to compose myself. The photograph in my hand felt like a lifeline, a tangible link to the family I had lost and the pain that had shaped my journey. The weight of my regrets and the burden of my memories seemed almost too much to bear.

After a long moment of reflection, I carefully put the photograph back in the drawer and closed it, taking a deep breath to steady myself. In order to move forward despite the shadows that clung to me, I needed to confront these ghosts. I made my way back to bed, careful not to wake Diane, and lay down beside her. I turned to face her, letting the comforting reality of her presence anchor me once again.

I gently reached out to hold her, drawing strength from her warmth and closeness. Her breathing was steady, her presence a soothing balm to my troubled mind. As I closed my eyes, I clung to the hope that, despite the pain and loss, there was still a future to build—one where Diane and I could face the challenges ahead together.

The next day in the bunker's training room. It's early morning, and the room is quiet. Diane and I face each other on the training mat, ready to spar.

"Ready to lose, Diane?" I grinned.

"You wish. Let's see what you've got," she laughed.

We circled each other, exchanging playful banter as we spar. Our movements were fluid, each countering the other's attacks with ease.

"You've been practicing. I'm impressed," I said.

"I have an excellent teacher," she replied.

I lunged, but Diane sidestepped, playfully tapping my shoulder. "Gotcha!"

I laughed, catching her hand and pulling her close. "Not so fast."

We paused, breathless and laughing, the playful tension between us turning into something more.

"You're getting better every day, Jack," she said.

"It's all thanks to you," I replied.

We shared a tender moment, our foreheads touching, before continuing our sparring with renewed energy.

Diane and I sat together in the common area, talking about our hopes and dreams. We talk quietly while others go about their routines nearby.

"Have you ever thought about what you'll do once this is all over? If we defeat the demons?" I asked.

"All the time. I want to find a place where we can rebuild and start fresh. Maybe even a garden," Diane said.

I smiled, picturing the life she described. "That sounds perfect. I'd like that too. A place where we can live without fear."

"We'll make it happen, Jack. We just have to keep fighting, keep surviving," she said.

I took her hand, squeezing it gently. "And we will."

We share a kiss, our love and hope for the future, giving us strength to face the challenges ahead.

CHAPTER 23

Two weeks after Diane moved into my room, we found ourselves in the debriefing room for a meeting. The atmosphere was focused but relaxed; Diane and I were clearly at ease with each other, and Anne's presence felt more natural. We'd been getting back to a sense of normalcy.

The commander stood at the front of the room; his expression was serious. "Jack, we've reviewed your recent performance. Given your leadership and recovery, we're promoting you to team leader once more."

The team applauded, and Diane's smile was warm, while Anne offered a nod of approval. I felt a renewed sense of pride and responsibility.

Our next mission was to check out a report of a captive being held in an abandoned house nearby. The intel was solid, and we needed to act quickly. We gathered our gear and set out.

As we approached the house, a sense of unease settled over us. The building loomed in the twilight, its broken windows and overgrown vines giving it an ominous appearance. We moved cautiously, aware of the potential dangers.

Out of nowhere, demon-possessed individuals ambushed us. They emerged from the shadows, their yellow eyes glinting menacingly. The battle erupted violently, and our team was quickly overpowered.

"Diane! Stay with me!" I shouted, trying to keep her in view as we fought side by side. Her movements were fierce and determined, but the onslaught was relentless.

Despite our best efforts, the team fell one by one. Anne, despite her tenacity, was clearly struggling. The situation became desperate.

Seeing Diane engaged in a fierce struggle and realizing we were outnumbered; I made a swift decision. I took a deep breath, broke through the front door of the house, and charged inside. Eerie silence filled the dim interior, only disturbed by distant cries and muffled noises.

"Focus, Jack. You have to save them," I murmured to myself, navigating the dark, creaking rooms. The silence inside felt suffocating as I followed the sounds of distress, driven by the urgent need to rescue the captive.

Outside, the chaos continued, but I had no choice but to press on, determined to complete the mission and save whoever was held captive.

I moved through the house, every creak of the floorboards echoing with an eerie sense of foreboding. My breath came in steady, measured gasps as I remained vigilant. The first possessed burst from a darkened doorway, its eyes glowing a menacing yellow. It lunged at me with a guttural snarl. I dodged the attack, rolling to the side, and grabbed a nearby mop. As the possessed regained its balance and turned to face me, I swung the head of the mop into its head, sending it crashing into the wall. Dazed, it slumps to the floor. With a swift, brutal motion, I drove the broken end of the mop into the guy's throat, killing him.

"One down," I muttered, pushing forward, my heart pounding in my chest. I advanced deeper into the house, the air growing colder with each step. Two more possessed appear, emerging from the shadows. They charge at me simultaneously, their strength clear in their uncoordinated yet relentless attacks. I snatched a wooden chair from the nearby dining room. As they swung wildly, I used the chair to block their blows. The chair shatters under their ferocity, but I use the splintered remains to my advantage. I jab a sharp piece of wood into the throat of the first possessed, watching as it collapses, gasping.

The second one grabbed me from behind, attempting a chokehold. I slammed my head backward, the satisfying crunch of breaking bones signaling the end of the choke. I twisted around, grabbing a broken chair leg from the floor, and drove it into his midsection. He crumpled, and I finished him with a vicious swing of the chair leg to his head.

Moving through the hallway, I found another possessed at the top of the stairs. It charged with a frenzied roar. I ducked under its swing and grabbed a metal candlestick from a nearby table. With a quick swing, I smashed it into the possessed's knee, hearing a sickening crack. As the creature fell, I didn't hesitate. I pressed the candlestick against its throat, applying pressure until its struggles ceased.

Ascending the stairs, the next challenge awaited. Two more possessed block my path, their eyes glowing with a malevolent light. One wielded a metal pipe, swinging it wildly. I ducked, rolled to avoid the attack, and grabbed a nearby vase. I threw the vase at his head, shattering it and leaving him dazed.

Turning, I met the second possessed who attempted to tackle me. I sidestepped, grabbing him and using his momentum to slam him into the wall. He collapsed, and I didn't give him a chance to rise. I grabbed a large, heavy picture frame from the wall and drove it down onto his head, breaking his neck. The other possessed guy got up and shook his head clear. Reaching for an unplugged lamp on the stand next to me I swung it as hard as I could and hit his head with enough force to take him off of his path. He crashed through a big television screen head-first. That wasn't not enough. I got behind him and wrapped the cord around his neck. We struggled for a bit until he lumped down. Fuck this shit. I need to end this already.

I reached the bedroom door, but another possessed burst through, seizing me by the throat with surprising strength. I gasped for air, clawing at its hand. With a desperate effort, I brought my knee up into its groin, eliciting a howl of pain. As it doubled over, I grabbed him and threw him into the window next to me. Glass shattered everywhere as I waited for him to get up. Nothing. He's just positioned there on his knees, head in the window. What the fuck? I moved closer and immediately saw it. His head somehow squeezed through the steel security bars. Fuck, it was messy. Blood and skin were everywhere. His skull broke in many places. Sucks to be him.

Inside the bedroom, two more possessed stood between me and the captive. They charged at me with a coordinated assault. I ducked under the first guy's swing, grabbing another but heavier lamp from the bedside table. I swung it with all my strength, smashing it into the side of the first possessed, sending it crashing into the second. Both staggered, providing me with the opening I needed. I seized a metal rod from the floor and delivered a brutal winging kick to one, sending it crashing into the wall.

The other recovered and charged, but I blocked his wild swings with the rod. Swinging the metal rod to deliver precise, brutal strikes to its head and torso. Blood sprayed as he finally collapsed, and I jabbed the rod into his skull. The first guy was already up and about to attack as I dodged his swing. He took a big knife out from his side and waved it in front of me.

"You shouldn't play with sharp objects, fuck nuts."

"Huh?" The guy barely had enough time to spit that out when I grabbed his knife wielding arm, breaking it, making him stab himself in the face. I wiped the blood that splashed on my face.

Breathing heavily, covered in blood and sweat, I approached the captive. My body aches with exhaustion and pain, but relief floods through me. A young woman bound and gagged, her eyes wide with fear. Quickly, I untied her restraints and helped her to her feet. Her trembling hands gripped mine as we made our way back downstairs, navigating the dark, eerie silence punctuated by distant, desperate cries.

"It's okay. You're safe now," I reassured her.

As we reached the bottom of the stairs, more possessed individuals emerged from the shadows. They moved with an unnatural, jerky rhythm. I smashed one of the possessed figures into a mirror head-first. The blood splattered around me. I quickly picked up a thick piece of mirror and stabbed the guy in the eye as he turned around.

"Watch out!" The woman's urgent shout alerted me. I barely had time to react as another possessed figure lunged at me with a screwdriver. I sidestepped and quickly shifted the screwdriver into his neck as he fell forward with momentum. The figure crumpled, but not before leaving a trail of crimson in its wake.

Bursting through the front door, I saw Diane and the others fighting valiantly against the possessed. Relief washed over me briefly, but confusion quickly overshadowed me as the young woman we had saved stopped in her tracks. Her eyes turned an eerie yellow, and her chilling laugh echoed through the night.

"Oh Jack, my hero," she hissed, her voice now a grotesque mockery of humanity. "Thanks for finally meeting with me. Our last meeting didn't end well, as you know falling onto a bus wasn't how it was supposed to go."

"Well, things don't always go as planned, but I did enjoy it."

"Fuck you, Jack!" Its voice was more demonic now. "You will die here tonight along with all these other humans!"

"Everyone, get back!" I shouted, but it was too late. The woman raised her hands, and everyone, including Diane, froze. Their eyes turned yellow, their bodies becoming puppets of the demon's control.

"Fuck me!"

"With pleasure, Jack!"

"That's a nope from me."

I grabbed a metal pipe from the debris and charged at the demon, my heart pounding with fierce determination. "Let them go!" I roared.

The demon, now fully revealed, mocked me with a malevolent grin. "You'll have to make me."

"Make you? Isn't that the plan? How old are you? Like two in demon years?"

The demon just yelled at me as it charged. The fight was a savage, unrelenting clash. Its movements were unnaturally fast, and every swung of my weapon barely fazed it. It taunted me, using my friends as human shields, forcing me to be cautious with every strike.

Diane was zombie-like under the demon's spell. As she lunged at me, I swiftly took her big knife. I punched her on the side of her head, knocking her out. She'll be fine, I think.

My quick reflexes allowed me to stab the demon in its chest as I ducked another swing. That just pissed it off more as the knife handle broke off. It grabbed my hair and threw me back. Good thing I learned to tuck my head as I rolled backward before standing again.

"Well, fuck I guess my haircut isn't a hit with some people," I taunted.

The demon hurled a broken piece of furniture at me, and I was too slow to dodge. The impact sent me crashing into a wall, my vision going black momentarily. Pain exploded through my body as I struggled to get up, my side throbbing with a deep, aching agony. Why couldn't a radioactive spider bite me?

I struggled to rise, feeling the sharp reminder of the damage inflicted with each labored inhale. I struggled to rise, blood dripping from my wounds. It was then that I saw him— the commander. He emerged from the shadows, his eyes glowing yellow, his face twisted in a cruel parody of the mentor I respected.

"Jack," the commander's voice took on a chilling edge, distorting his usual authoritative tone. "You didn't really think you'd make it through without facing me, did you?"

My heart sank. The commander had been a mentor, someone who had guided me through countless battles and had promoted me with the belief that I could lead. It hurt to see him like this, possessed and twisted into something monstrous.

"I don't want to do this," I said, my voice breaking. "But I know if it were the other way around..."

The commander lunged at me with brutal ferocity. I barely had time to react, raising the metal pipe to deflect his blows. His strength was overwhelming, every strike fucking hurt. I fought back with everything I had, even sticking the pipe into his leg.

Our battle was violent and chaotic. The commander's attacks were relentless, and each hit left me more battered and bruised. He was skilled, his movements precise and deadly. Despite the pain, I fought on, driven by the need to end the demon's reign of terror.

With a swift, powerful blow, the commander's knife slashed across my chest, the blade cutting deep. I gasped in pain as I fell back a few feet. A mix of anger and sorrow, the agony of fighting someone I had admired and learned from fuels me. Ugh, I can't even hulk out.

"Why can't you just fight me yourself?" I shouted at the demon, watching with amusement.

"It's fun watching you fight your friends." The demon laughed.

With a final, desperate surge of strength, I tackled the commander into the side of the car. The impact sent a bone-shaking jolt through my entire body, but I didn't care. The door dents inward, the glass window splintering with a sharp crack, showering us with shards. He let out a low grunt; the air punched from his lungs, but he wasn't done. Not by a long shot.

Blood dripped from my brow, my vision swam as I blinked to clear it. His fists came out of nowhere—a blur of violence. One slammed into my ribs, and I heard the crack before I felt it. White-hot pain shot through my side, but it only made me angrier. I roared through the pain and slammed my forehead into his face. His nose exploded in a gush of blood, but instead of going down, he snarled, eyes wild, and threw me off with a feral growl.

We stagger apart, gasping for breath. My chest heaved, each inhale was like shards of glass in my lungs. Blood from his broken nose struck across his face, mingling with sweat and grime. I could feel the adrenaline coursing through me, pushing me forward despite the screaming agony in my muscles. Every inch of my body begs me to stop, to give in— but I couldn't. I wouldn't.

"You're dead, Shaw," the commander spat, his voice hoarse and filled with venom.

"Not before you," I rasped back, wiping the blood from my mouth. My hand comes away sticky, my lips split and swollen.

He lunged first, his movements wild, desperate. His fist caught me across the temple, and my head snapped back, stars exploding in my vision. I stumbled, barely able to stay upright. Pain radiates through my skull, but I wouldn't give him the satisfaction of seeing me fall. I threw a punch, reckless and fueled by rage, but he blocked it, landing another blow to my ribs. I felt something give—a deep crack that reverberated through my chest, and I gasped, nearly buckling under the force of it.

I could barely breathe, but I lashed out again, grabbing his arm and twisting it viciously. The commander howls in pain, and I slammed my fist into his gut. He doubled over, coughing and sputtering, but he's still not going down. He drives his shoulder into my chest, ramming me into the car with a thud that rattles my bones. I felt the cold metal dig into my back, bruising me down to my core, but I pushed him back with every ounce of strength I had left.

This was a brutal, filthy brawl—no grace, no strategy. Just blood and violence.

We traded blows like animals, both of us exhausted, both of us bleeding. His knuckles split open as he slammed another punch into my face. My vision turned black, and I staggered back, my breath coming in ragged, painful gasps. My burned, each breath harder than the last.

And then I saw the pipe sticking out of his thigh, the same pipe I jammed there earlier. It's still there, blood pouring from around it. He's limping, each step slower, each swing weaker.

I charged, fueled by nothing but fury and desperation. I tackled him again, sending us both crashing to the ground. The impact knocked the wind from us, but I was the one on top now. I hammered him with my fists, over and over, not caring where I hit as long as I hit something. His jaw, his temple, his chest—I wanted to break every bone, make him feel every ounce of pain he's inflicted.

He spat blood at me, his eyes blazing with hatred, but I didn't stop. I couldn't stop. I grabbed the pipe, my fingers slicked with blood, and yanked it free. The sound of it tearing out of his flesh is sickening, a wet, awful noise that makes my stomach churn. The commander screams, his body convulsing in agony as blood gushes from the wound.

I raised the pipe high, my arms trembling, my breath coming in ragged sobs. His eyes locked with mine, filled with rage and desperation.

"Shaw, you son of a—"

I didn't let him finish. "You don't get to talk anymore," I growl through clenched teeth. Then I swung.

The pipe came down hard, slamming into his skull with a nauseating crack. The force of it reverberated up my arms, but I didn't stop. I brought it down again, and again. His head jerked with each blow, blood splattering across the pavement, across my arms, and across my face. His skull caved in with the third strike, a sickening crunch as bone gave way to the relentless assault. The commander twitched once, then went still, his body slumping beneath me.

I dropped the pipe, my hands shaking, covered in blood. It clattered to the ground; the sound lost in the roar of my breathing. I felt overwhelmed, as if someone had run me through a grinder, leaving my entire body broken, bruised, and exhausted. The pain was all-consuming, but it didn't matter.

It was over. He was dead.

I sat back on my heels, staring down at the commander's lifeless body. Blood pooled around him, thick and dark, staining the asphalt. His blood, my blood, covered my hands. There was no telling whose blood was whose anymore. All I knew was that the demon got what it wanted. Bastard.

My legs buckled beneath me, the ground rising to meet me as the weight of what I'd done pressed down like an unbearable force. My breath hitched, shallow and ragged, each gasp clawing at my throat. My hands, trembling and bloodstained, hung limply at my sides. A hollow ache spread through my chest, tightening with every fleeting memory of the commander—the way he had led us, fought alongside us, the respect he'd earned without ever asking for it. The realization twisted in my gut, sharp and unrelenting. I hadn't just killed a man—I'd extinguished a light, someone who had fought for survival just as fiercely as I had.

I gripped the earth beneath me, the rough texture grounding me in the suffocating tide of grief and guilt. My throat burned with the scream I couldn't release, my vision blurred as the edges of the world closed in. He deserved better—better than this, better than me.

Standing up, I turned back to face the demon. This fucking ends now!

"Is that the best you got?" I spat out as blood followed. "Looked like your plans keep failing. Maybe that's your power?"

The demon seemed more annoyed now. Good. More possessed survivors come at me.

I braced myself as the first possessed survivor charges, their movements jerky and unnatural. They threw a wild punch, but I ducked under it and slammed my fist into their knee with a sickening crack. Their leg buckles, the bone snapping like a twig, and they collapse with a howl of pain. Another comes at me from the side, faster this time. I twisted around, grabbing their arm and yanking it hard, dislocating their shoulder with a gruesome pop before delivering a sharp elbow to their face. Blood spurts from their nose as they crumble to the ground, unconscious.

The third and fourth came at me simultaneously, their eyes glowing that sickly yellow. One swung a crowbar, but I sidestepped it, driving a brutal kick into their shin, shattering the bone. They screamed as they fell. The other went for a tackle, but I grabbed them by the throat mid-lunge, slamming them down with a thud. Before they could react, I stomped down hard on their arm, snapping it at the elbow. The fifth one rushed me, faster than the others, but I was ready. I sidestepped, grabbing their leg and twisting sharply. There was a sickening crunch as their ankle breaks, sending them sprawling to the ground, writhing in agony.

I stood there, panting, my body battered but still holding on. The demon, no longer hiding behind the others, steps forward, its black, soulless eyes locking onto mine. "Finally," I muttered, wiping the blood from my mouth. The air between us crackled with tension, the ultimate confrontation looming.

"Just you and me now." The demon grinned, a sinister, inhuman smile spreading across its face.

"So does this mean we're dating now?"

The demon raised its hand, and my body felt numb. Shit, he was possessing me.

The air was thick with a damp, oppressive fog as I rose to my feet. My body felt sluggish, like I was wading through tar. Everything around me was hazy, shifting in and out of focus, but the realization hit hard—I was inside my mind, and the demon was here with me. The bastard had found its way into my head. The ground beneath me was wet, sticky, and cold. It smelled of decay, of rot. I laughed bitterly, trying to keep the panic from clawing at me.

"Hey, if you're not going to pay rent, I need you to get out!" I shouted into the nothingness.

A voice, smooth and oily, echoed from everywhere and nowhere. "Your mind is weak, Jack. This is my playground now."

I turned sharply, trying to pinpoint the direction, but the world spun, distorted, and bent. The fog thickened, and then the demon stepped out from it, towering over me, its form twisted, shifting. It was no longer a singular figure but a grotesque amalgamation of all the people it's ever possessed—the commander, Tiffany, even faces I don't recognize, all merging and morphing together. Their voices mingled in my ears, whispering doubts, fears, things I buried deep. I could feel it trying to pull me apart from the inside.

I stepped back, instinctively, but the ground stretched beneath me like quicksand, dragging me down. "No. This is my mind!" I shouted, trying to steady myself. But the demon only laughed, the sound vibrating through my skull.

"You've never had control, Jack. You've always been at my mercy. Every fear, every regret—it's all here, festering, and I'm going to rip it all apart. Piece by piece."

Suddenly, the world shifted violently, and I stood in my childhood home. The walls warped and towered over me, oppressively. My father's lifeless body lay at my feet, the blood fresh as if it happened just now. I dropped to my knees, overwhelmed by the sight, the memories crashed into me like waves. The smell of iron filled my nose, and the guilt—god, the guilt—was suffocating.

"You couldn't save him," the demon whispered, appearing beside me, its breath cold against my neck. "You've never been strong enough."

I clenched my fists, shaking. It was trying to break me, to drown me in my own nightmares. But I couldn't let it. I have to out-think it. "This isn't real," I muttered, forcing myself to look away from the body. "None of this is real."

"But it feels real, doesn't it?" the demon hissed, and suddenly, the demon reappeared as Tiffany. She was bruised, bloodied, just like the last time I saw her alive. "You couldn't save me either, Jack. You let me die."

The sight of her brought me to my knees again. Her face— her eyes accusing, filled with pain, I couldn't escape. The last time I saw her alive was etched into my mind forever, and now the demon was using it to tear me apart. My breath caught in my throat, and tears blurred my vision. "I tried... I tried so hard, Tiffany," I whispered, my voice breaking. "I didn't want to lose you."

"But you did," she snapped, stepping closer. "Just like you'll lose everyone else you care about."

The weight of it all—the guilt, the helplessness, the overwhelming despair—it threatened to consume me. I could feel the demon's grip tightening on my mind, its laughter echoing in the dark corners of my consciousness. I was on the edge of giving in, of letting it take control completely. Maybe I was too weak. Maybe I didn't deserve to keep fighting.

But then I heard it. "Jack!" Diane's voice, strong and sharp, cut through the fog like a beacon. I turned, desperate to find her, but the scene shifted again. The alley fades, the blood vanishes, and I'm back in the dark, only now... now it's worse.

Kyle stepped out from the shadows, dragging my mother with him. She gasped for air, clawing at his hand, her eyes wide with terror. Every muscle in my body tensed. Not her. Not again. I lunged at them, but my legs wouldn't move. I was stuck watching my worst nightmare play out in front of me.

Kyle sneered, tightening his grip on her throat. "This is your fault, Jack," he growled. "You were never strong enough to stop me. Never strong enough to protect her."

I shook, fury and fear raging inside me. "Let her go!" I shouted, straining against the invisible chains holding me back. But my voice wavers, thick with doubt, the demon feeding off my fear. My chest tightened as I watched her slip further from my grasp, Kyle's laugh sliced through me like a blade. I was losing again.

Just as I felt myself sinking deeper into the abyss, Diane charged forward. She didn't hesitate, tackling Kyle to the ground, her fists flying in a blur. Her rage, her strength was everything I wished I had in that moment. I should have been fighting, but I couldn't move. I was trapped in my mind, paralyzed by the demon's influence. Diane pounded Kyle into the ground, the sound of bone crunching beneath her knuckles, but it wasn't enough. Kyle wouldn't stay down.

"Jack, snap out of it!" she screamed, and something inside me jolts awake.

I closed my eyes, forcing myself to focus. This wasn't real. I had to break free, but the demon's hold was strong. I could feel it coiling around my mind, whispering that I'd never be enough. That I'd always lose the people I love. My mother's dying gasps echoed in my ears, Kyle's cruel laughter reverberated through my skull.

But then Diane's voice cut through chaos again, grounding me. "Jack, you're stronger than this! Fight!"

Searching for the strength I buried so long ago, I gritted my teeth, pushing past fear and doubt, digging deep. I am stronger. I have to be. For her, my mom, and everyone else I have lost. The fog around me flickered, and I latched onto that spark, pushing back against the demon's suffocating grip.

"No," I growled, standing taller. "You don't control me."

The world crumbles around me, the oppressive fog lifting as I regain my footing. The demon screeches, its form shifting again. But I don't care. I imagine a weapon—a sword—appearing in my hand, and it materializes instantly, its blade sharp and gleaming. I grip it tightly, feeling the weight of it, and charge at the demon. It screeches, trying to shift the world back, to drag me down into the darkness again, but I won't let it. Not this time.

I swung the sword, and it sliced through the demon's form like smoke. The creature lets out a howl, its body unraveling, its grip on my mind loosening. I kept swinging, again and again, until only shadow remained, fading into the air.

The world around me solidified. I was back in control.

I stood there, breathing hard, the sword dissolving from my hand as I looked around. The demon was gone. I'd won. I took back my mind.

The battle wasn't over, though, as the demon's form was now a monstrous amalgamation of consumed souls. It was no longer just a shadow or a trick of the mind, it was a grotesque reality, every inch of its being pulsating with dark, malevolent energy. The surrounding air was thick and charged, crackling with the remnants of absorbed life forces.

With a roar, the demon unleashed its newfound power. The survivors the demon had drained were left as empty husks; their bodies lifeless on the ground. Their screams echoed in my ears, mingling with the demon's taunting laughter. It was as if the world itself had turned against me; the environment shifting and warping under the demon's influence. Twisting grotesquely, the walls of the space around us buckled and bent as if in pain. The floor cracked and heaved, threatening to swallow me whole.

I picked up a heavy metal rod from the debris, my hands slick with sweat and blood. Swinging it with all my might, I aimed for the demon's core. The metal connected, but instead of piercing through, the demon's form seemed to absorb the blow, its dark energy swirling around the impact. It retaliated with a ferocity that left me scrambling. Debris flew—chunks of concrete, shards of glass—all propelled with inhuman force. I ducked and rolled, narrowly avoiding a jagged piece of metal that embedded itself into the wall behind me.

The battleground was chaotic. As if alive and distorted, the walls pulsed and undulated under the demon's command, despite once being solid and secure. The floor buckled, sending tremors through the ground that threatened to knock me off balance. I had to stay on my feet, but each step was a struggle against the shifting terrain. The demon hurled flames from its outstretched hand; the fire scorching the air and forcing me to dive for cover.

I grabbed another piece of heavy metal, using it to shield myself from the flames. My muscles screamed with exhaustion, my body covered in cuts and bruises from the demon's relentless attacks. Every time I thought I was gaining the upper hand, the demon's power surged, and I was back on the defensive. It clawed at me with its dark, twisted limbs, each swipe tearing through the air with a force that left deep gashes in the walls and my flesh.

The demon's strength seemed boundless, but I refused to give in. I cornered it against a wall, its form writhing and distorting with dark energy. I lunged forward, grabbing a large piece of metal from the rubble and using it to pin the demon in place. It thrashed violently, its roars of anger reverberating through the space, shaking the very foundation. The metal rod bent under the strain as the demon fought against its restraints, but I held firm, every muscle in my body straining with the effort.

Blows landed with sickening thuds as I continued to assault the demon. Each strike felt like it was draining the last of my strength. The demon's retaliatory attacks were brutal, using every piece of debris and energy at its disposal. It lashed out with its claws, each swipe creating explosive bursts of energy that sent me crashing into the walls. My body was a canvas of pain, each movement a struggle against the overwhelming force of the demon's power.

Despite the agony and exhaustion, I found a well of resolve deep within me. I refused to let this end in failure. The thoughts of Diane and the lives at stake pushed me to continue. I gritted my teeth, pushing through the pain as I swung the metal rod with renewed determination. The demon's form was a blur of dark energy and shifting shadows, but I kept pressing on, every strike fueled by a desperate need to end this nightmare.

With a final, explosive effort, I brought the metal rod crashing down. The demon's form convulsed violently, its dark energy flaring wildly as it struggled against my relentless assault. I could feel the pressure building, the demon's power buckling under the force of my attacks. The environment seemed to pulse everywhere with the impact, the walls and floor shaking violently.

In one final, climactic burst, the demon's form shattered. Dark energy exploded outward, filling the room with a blinding light. Abruptly, the demon's roar was cut off, and an eerie silence descended upon the air. I collapsed to the ground, my body shaking uncontrollably.

The fight is now over, with the demon gone. I had finally reclaimed my mind, but my body is broken. The weight of the battle lifted slightly with every breath, leaving me with a profound sense of exhaustion and relief. As the dust settled and now quiet, I lay there, spent and battered, knowing that I had faced my darkest fears and emerged victorious.

As the demon perished, the yellow light in my friend's eyes faded. They collapsed, exhausted but free from its control, except for the poor souls it had drained from them. After our brutal struggle, we felt the weight of the aftermath as debris scattered across the battlefield. I fell to my knees, panting heavily and drenched in blood. The weight of the fight hit me all at once, making my limbs feel like lead.

Diane crawled over to me, her face etched with deep worry and concern. Her breath came in ragged gasps as she reached out to touch my shoulder. "Jack, are you okay?" she asked, her voice trembling with fear and relief.

"I'm fine," I said, offering her a weak smile despite the exhaustion. "We did it. It's over."

The pain from the deep gash in my chest was almost unbearable. Blood flowed freely, soaking through my clothes and painting the floor beneath me. Each breath I took was ragged and labored, making it hard to focus on anything other than the searing pain.

Diane's face was a mix of fear and determination as she kneeled beside me. "Jack, you're losing a lot of blood," she said urgently, her voice trembling. "We need to get you back to the bunker—now!"

Anne, who had been fighting valiantly beside us, rushed over, her face a mask of worry. "Jack, stay with us," she said, her voice strained but resolute. "We've got to get you out of here."

Diane and Anne carefully lifted me onto a makeshift stretcher with their help. Anne's hands shook as she supported my head, her concern clear. The medics arrived quickly, assessing my condition with grim efficiency.

"We need to move," one medic said, his tone urgent. "He's in critical condition."

Diane and Anne loaded the stretcher into one of our vehicles, stabilizing me as much as possible. Diane held my hand tightly, her eyes never leaving me. Anne, though visibly shaken, worked to keep the situation under control.

The drive to the bunker was a blur of pain and urgency. Every bump and jolt in the vehicle sent waves of agony through my chest. Diane's presence was a steadying force, her hand gripping mine as Anne sat across from us, her face a mix of anguish and determination.

"Hang in there, Jack," Diane whispered, her voice trembling with fear. "We're almost there. Just a little longer."

Anne, sitting next to Diane, tried to offer words of encouragement, though her voice was strained. "We're almost at the bunker. You're going to be okay."

The bunker gates loomed ahead, and the vehicle sped up. The medics quickly wheeled me inside, the urgency of the situation clear in their swift movements. Diane and Anne followed closely; their faces etched with worry.

In the hallway leading to the infirmary, Anne looked back at me with a desperate expression. "We're here, Jack," she said, her voice barely a whisper. "Just hold on."

Inside the infirmary, the medics went to work immediately. They cut away my blood-soaked clothes, their hands moving with practiced precision. Diane stepped back, her face pale with concern, while Anne nervously paced outside the treatment area.

Minutes felt like hours as the medics fought to control the bleeding and close the wound. I could see Diane's eyes fixed on me through the small window of the treatment room, while Anne's anxious pacing and worried glances revealed her distress.

Finally, the head medic approached Diane and Anne, offering a glimmer of reassurance. "He's stable for now," he said. "We've managed to control the bleeding and close the wound. He'll need rest and monitoring, but he's made it through."

Anne's shoulders sagged with relief; her eyes moist as she looked back at me. Diane's expression softened as she took Anne's hand, both of them finding solace in the medic's words. The enormity of the battle and its toll on us all was settling in.

As I lay in the infirmary, the soft beeping of medical equipment and the murmurs of the staff were a distant backdrop to my pain and fatigue. Diane's and Anne's presence was a comforting anchor, and their support was the only thing keeping me tethered to consciousness.

The next day, we gathered for another funeral. The somber, overcast sky mirrored the heaviness in my heart. I was still grappling with the physical and emotional aftermath of the brutal battle. My body was a patchwork of bruises and cuts, the most painful being the deep gash across my chest, crudely stitched and aching with every breath. My movements were slow and labored, and each step seemed to carry the weight of the world.

Diane, ever my pillar of strength, was at my side. Her eyes were red from the previous day's tears, but her determination to support me never wavered. She gently guided me through the crowd, her hand gripping mine with a firm yet comforting hold. The pain in my chest flared with every step, but Diane's presence was a soothing balm, her quiet encouragement helping me to navigate the sea of mourners.

The ceremony began with a solemnity that matched the overcast sky. As the names of the fallen were read aloud, I could barely contain the surge of grief that washed over me. Each name was a reminder of the lives lost, including the commander's—a man I respected and, in a twisted sense, admired despite our troubled relationship.

I struggled to stay upright as the eulogies were delivered. With the commander's death weighing heavily on me, the guilt of having killed him to save others gnawed relentlessly at my conscience. The pain of my injuries was nothing compared to the emotional toll of taking a life, especially someone who had once guided and taught me. The agony of knowing that my actions had led to his demise was almost unbearable.

Diane's hand was a lifeline, her touch grounding me in the present as I fought to keep my composure. She adjusted my stance when I swayed, her concern clear in the gentle way she guided me to sit down when I grew too weak to stand. Her eyes held a mix of sadness and determination, reflecting the shared pain and resilience we faced together.

Anne was present too, her support unwavering. Despite her own grief, she stayed close, her presence a comforting reminder of the bond we all shared. She stood beside us, her quiet strength adding to the collective resolve of those gathered.

The eulogies were heartfelt, each one a tribute to the bravery and sacrifice of those we had lost. Diane's shoulders shook with silent sobs, and I could see the strain on her face as she tried to maintain her own composure while helping me. Her eyes met mine occasionally, conveying a mixture of empathy and unspoken love.

As the ceremony drew to a close, Diane helped me to my feet, her touch gentle but firm. The weight of my injuries and losing the commander made every step a struggle. Anne stayed close, her presence a comforting reminder I wasn't alone in this.

Diane guided me toward the podium, a determined look on her face. "Hold on, I have something to give you." I felt awkward under the spotlight, my discomfort clear as I stood there, the crowd's eyes on me. Diane let go of my hand briefly, her steps hurried as she went to fetch something.

Anne stood nearby, her expression a mix of support and sadness. She had been with us through so much, and her silent presence was a reassurance.

Diane returned, carrying a plaque. She approached the microphone, her voice clear but trembling with emotion. "Jack Shaw, I know this is long overdue, but I've been trying to find the right moment to do this." As she revealed the plaque, my breath caught. The sight of my mother's face on the plaque made tears well up in my eyes.

Diane continued, her voice choked with emotion, "I present to you this plaque in honor of your courageous mother, Marishka Shaw, for her resilience, determination, and sacrifice to save not only us survivors but her most beloved gift, her son."

The plaque bearing my mother's name and picture was overwhelming. It was a tangible tribute to her bravery and sacrifice. I struggled to hold back tears, feeling an intense wave of gratitude and love. Diane's gesture was deeply meaningful, connecting me to my mother's memory profoundly.

The crowd erupted with applause, and emotion consumed me. Tears streamed down my face as Diane embraced me, her support unwavering. The plaque felt like a bridge to my mother's memory, a way to honor her legacy amidst the pain.

As I composed myself, I walked to the front and placed my mother's plaque alongside the photographs of everyone else we had lost, including the commander. The commander's loss was heavy, as he had been both a mentor and a leader. I imagined his stern face among the others, a reminder of his sacrifice and the bond we had shared.

Taking a deep breath, I stepped up to the microphone for one last message. My voice was steady, though the emotion was clear. "I want to thank everyone for their support today. My mother, Marishka Shaw, was a hero, and I'm honored to celebrate her alongside all the brave souls we've lost. The commander, too, was a guiding force in our lives, and his sacrifice will be remembered with the deepest respect. They fought with incredible courage, and their sacrifices will never be forgotten. We carry their memory forward in our hearts, and we continue to fight for the future they believed in. Thank you."

With that, I stepped down from the podium and rejoined the crowd, my heart was heavy but full. Diane took my hand, her support a steady presence, while Anne stood beside us, her presence a comforting reminder of the strength we had found in each other. As we mingled with the survivors, the collective grief was palpable, but so was the strength we drew from each other. The ceremony had been a powerful reminder of our shared resilience and the enduring spirit of those we had lost.

Later, lying in bed, Diane and I spoke about the future. The solemn atmosphere lingered, and my injuries from the fight with the commander and the demon made every movement painful.

"We need to take some time for ourselves," Diane said, her voice firm but tender. "We've fought so hard, and with the demon gone, who knows when we'll get another chance to just... live a little."

I nodded, the exhaustion and pain from my injuries weighing heavily on me. "You're right. We need this break. We deserve it. But... it's hard to shake the feeling that everyone I care about keeps disappearing."

Diane's gaze softened as she looked at me. "Jack, I want us to leave the bunker. To find a place where we can just be us, without the constant threat hanging over our heads."

I took her hand, squeezing it gently despite the pain. My voice trembled with emotion. "Before all of this... before the commander died... I had talked to him about taking the money from the safe downstairs. He gave us permission."

Diane's eyes widened in concern. "How much money are we talking about?"

"There's easily one hundred thousand, maybe more. Nobody's been willing to count it all," I replied, struggling to keep my voice steady. "But it's not just about the money. But... I can't stop thinking about everyone who's died. My father, my mother, Tiffany, and now the commander... I feel like I'm cursed. Everyone I care about dies. It's like I'm meant to be alone."

Diane's expression was full of empathy. She squeezed my hand tighter. "Jack, you're not cursed. You're carrying the weight of so much loss, and it's natural to feel this way. But you have to remember that you're not alone. We've faced these challenges together, and we will face them together."

Tears welled up in my eyes as I looked at her. "What if I'm the reason they're gone? What if I could have done something differently?"

Diane shook her head, her voice filled with compassion. "It's normal to question yourself, but you did what you had to do. The circumstances were beyond our control. The people you've lost were heroes in their own ways, and their sacrifices mean something. We have to honor their memories by not by being consumed by guilt."

I nodded, feeling the weight of her words sink in. "You're right. We need to make sure we're prepared. Extra gas, supplies, everything we need. We'll drive until we find life, until we find our new beginning."

Diane leaned in, her lips brushing against mine in a tender kiss. "I believe in us, Jack. We can do this. And we'll face everything together, no matter what."

As we lay there, wrapped in each other's arms, I felt a sense of peace settled over us. The future was uncertain, but with Diane by my side, I knew we could face anything. This was the start of a new chapter; one filled with hope and the promise of a better tomorrow.

CHAPTER 24

The trip was long and arduous, sometimes even boring. The desolate landscape stretched out before us, a grim reminder of the world we had left behind. Empty, abandoned buildings, gas stations, and houses littered our path. We had to stop twice to fill up with gas, using all our reserves. Each time we stopped, the weight of uncertainty bore down on us.

"Do you think we'll ever find something out here?" Diane asked during one of our stops, her voice tinged with doubt.

I sighed, staring out at the barren horizon. "I don't know, Diane. But we can't give up now. We have to keep going."

As we continued our journey, hope waned. The endless stretch of wasteland seemed to mock our efforts. As we trudged along, the silence between us grew heavy. Diane finally broke it. "Jack, what if we're just chasing ghosts? What if there's nothing left?"

I glanced at her, seeing the exhaustion in her eyes. "We're not chasing ghosts, Diane. We're searching for a future. For something better than this." My voice cracked, betraying my own doubts.

She shook her head, tears welling up. "I'm so tired, Jack. Tired of running, tired of fighting. When does it end?"

I pulled her into a tight embrace, feeling her shoulders shake with silent sobs. "I don't know when it ends. But as long as we're together, we have a chance. We can't lose sight of that."

She clung to me, her fingers digging into my back. "I don't know how much longer I can do this."

I pulled back slightly, looking into her eyes. "We'll find a place, Diane. We have to believe that. We have to keep moving even when it feels impossible."

She nodded, wiping her tears away. "Okay. But promise me, Jack, if it ever gets too much… we stop. We find a way to live, even if it's not what we imagined."

"I promise," I said, my voice firm despite the uncertainty gnawing at my insides. "We'll find a way. Together."

We continued our journey, each step forward, a minor victory in the vast wasteland that tested our resolve daily. As the sun dipped below the horizon, casting long shadows across the barren land, the weight of our conversation hung heavily between us. Despite the demons being gone, we still faced the ever-present threat of bandits, a danger that nearly cost us everything.

We had stopped at an old gas station to scavenge supplies. The place was eerily silent, with only the wind howling through the broken windows. Inside, I was busy rummaging through the store's remnants when Diane's scream cut through the quiet. I bolted outside to find her surrounded by rough-looking men, their eyes glinting with malice.

"Back off!" I shouted, drawing my weapon. The bandits laughed, closing in on us.

"You've got some guts, boy," the leader sneered. "But guts won't save you."

They spread out, encircling us. Diane and I moved into a defensive stance, but the odds were against us. The leader lunged at me with a rusted knife. I blocked the attack with my forearm; the blade grazing my skin and leaving a painful cut. Diane grabbed a metal pipe and swung it at one bandit, but another grabbed her from behind, pinning her arms.

I fought fiercely, using my training to deliver precise blows. I disarmed the leader, twisting his wrist until the knife fell to the ground. But for every bandit I took down, another seemed to appear. A heavy blow to my head sent me sprawling, my vision swimming. I saw Diane struggling; her face a mask of fear and determination. Summoning every ounce of strength, I pushed myself up and charged at her attackers, tackling one and pounding him with desperate fists.

Diane broke free, grabbing the fallen bandit's knife and slashing at her remaining attacker. We fought back-to-back, driven by adrenaline and sheer willpower. Eventually, we pushed them back, but the battle had left us battered. I suffered a slash on my side, and Diane's arm hung limply, dislocated. We stumbled to our vehicle, the reality of our vulnerability sinking in.

"Jack," Diane whispered, her voice trembling, "we can't keep going like this."

"I know," I said, pain and frustration etched on my face. "We need to find somewhere safe. Soon."

The bandit attack was a harsh reminder that even with the demons gone, the world was still fraught with danger. Our journey had taken a toll, leaving us vulnerable to every threat in the wasteland. But as we drove away from the gas station, a silent determination took hold. We would survive. We would find a way. Together.

Once we were a safe distance away, I pulled the car behind a large, crumbling barn. Exhaustion and pain from the adrenaline wore off, making every movement a struggle. We needed to tend to our injuries before moving on.

I rummaged through our makeshift first-aid kit, pulling out bandages, antiseptic, and a splint. "Let's get you fixed up first," I said, looking at Diane's dislocated arm.

Diane nodded, biting her lip to stifle a groan as she sat on an old wooden crate. I kneeled beside her, my fingers trembling slightly as I prepared to reset her shoulder. "This is going to hurt," I warned.

"Just do it," she whispered, closing her eyes.

I took a deep breath and, with a swift motion, pushed her shoulder back into place. Diane let out a sharp cry, her face contorting with pain. Tears sprang to her eyes, but she quickly blinked them away. "It's okay," she said,. "I'm okay."

I wrapped her shoulder with the splint, securing it in place. "Try not to move it too much," I advised, gently patting her hand.

"Your turn," Diane said, her voice steadier now. She took the antiseptic and bandages from me, carefully cleaning the gash on my side. The wound was deep, but not life-threatening. She worked quickly, her hands steady despite her own pain.

"You're good at this," I commented, my voice tight with pain as she stitched the wound.

"Had to learn," she replied, focusing on her task. "You don't survive this long without picking up a few skills."

After bandaging my wound, I leaned against the barn wall, catching my breath. "We can't keep taking risks like that," I said. "We need to be more careful."

"I know," Diane agreed softly. "But what choice do we have? We can't stay in one place for too long. It's not safe."

I nodded, looking out at the darkening sky. "We'll rest here for a bit, then move on. Hopefully, we can find somewhere safer soon."

We sat in silence for a while, the reality of our situation sinking in. Despite the pain and exhaustion, we had each other. And that was something.

As the night grew colder, we huddled together for warmth, our resolve hardening with each passing moment. We would survive. We would find a way. Together.

The first light of dawn was still hours away when I stirred from a fitful sleep. A faint noise outside pricked my ears. I nudged Diane awake, signaling for silence. We both listened intently as the rustling outside grew louder.

I peered through a crack in the barn wall and saw shadowy figures rummaging through our car. The bandits had found us.

"We have to go," I whispered urgently.

Diane nodded, wincing as she moved her injured arm. We gathered our belongings as quietly as possible. I slipped my knife into my belt and signaled for Diane to follow me through the back exit of the barn, hoping to avoid direct confrontation.

As we slipped into the early morning gloom, someone shouted loudly from behind, alerting us we had been spotted. The bandits gave chase, their footsteps pounding behind us. We ran, pushing through the pain and exhaustion.

"Head for the trees!" I shouted, pointing to a nearby grove.

We sprinted toward the grove, the bandits closing in. I threw a makeshift Molotov cocktail behind us, creating a temporary barrier with the flames.

We reached the trees, diving into the underbrush. I grabbed Diane's hand, pulling her through the dense foliage. The sounds of the bandits grew fainter as the darkness and trees provided cover.

After what felt like an eternity, we finally slowed down, collapsing against a large tree to catch our breath. My side throbbed painfully, and Diane's arm hung limp, but we were alive.

"We need to keep moving," Diane said, her voice strained. "They'll search the area."

I nodded, wiping sweat and dirt from my brow. "We'll find a new hiding spot. We can't let them catch us."

We continued through the forest, each step a painful reminder of our injuries. But the danger reignited our determination. Our survival came after facing demons. We had faced bandits and escaped. We would keep going, no matter what.

As dawn broke, we found a small clearing with a stream. Exhausted, we drank deeply and washed our wounds. The cold water was a reminder that we were still alive, still fighting.

"We'll find a place, Diane," I said firmly. "We'll find somewhere safe."

Diane looked at me, hope mingling with the pain in her eyes. "I hope so," she said.

"I know it," I agreed.

We sat by the stream, gathering our strength before setting off again. We kept walking, no longer caring about direction. Just as despair set in, we saw it—a massive wall stretching up to the sky.

"What is that?" Diane's voice trembled with awe.

"I don't know," I replied, barely above a whisper. "But we're going to find out."

We approached the massive gate, its size suggesting it could withstand anything. My heart pounded as I explored. To my surprise, I found an unlocked door. The creaking sound of the door as we slipped inside was almost deafening in the silence.

Inside, the atmosphere was stifling, broken only by the occasional drip of water. The air smelled of damp concrete and old machinery. We moved cautiously through the compound, our footsteps echoing ominously.

I found a power box and flipped the switch. The lights flickered on, revealing a sprawling, fortified compound filled with empty buildings and storage facilities. The contrast to the wasteland outside was overwhelming.

"Jack, look at this place," Diane said, awe in her voice.

"I can't believe it," I replied, emotion filling my voice. "This might be exactly what we need."

We continued exploring, and I found a control panel with a large button. Beside it was an old, rusty car. I pressed the button, and the gate slowly opened, revealing a promising landscape.

"Diane, come on! The gate's open!" I shouted with excitement.

Diane hurried to me and found the car keys. She tried starting the engine, and with a few attempts, the engine roared to life.

"It's working! Let's get out of here!" I grinned, my eyes gleaming with relief.

We drove through the gate, the world outside transforming into vibrant green fields and tall trees swaying in the breeze. The sun beamed down on us, a stark contrast to the dusty sky we'd left behind.

The sense of relief that washed over me as I took in the lush, vibrant scenery was overwhelming. Diane's voice trembled with awe beside me. "This is incredible. It's like a dream."

I dipped my head, a wave of emotions surging through me—hope intertwining with disbelief, creating a lump in my throat. "It's hard to believe," I murmured, my voice thick. "But it feels like a second chance, doesn't it?"

As we drove further, the bustling village appeared, alive with activity. The scene was almost surreal people going about their daily lives, chatting, working, and laughing. Diane's eyes were wide, taking in the vibrant colors and the comforting sounds of normal life.

"Look at them," she said softly, her voice choked with emotion. "They're living like nothing ever happened."

I pulled the car over to the side of the road, letting the sight sink in. "We need to be careful," I cautioned. "We don't know how they'll react to strangers."

We stepped out of the car and made our way toward the village, our steps cautious but filled with cautious optimism. The village was a stark contrast to the wasteland we had traversed. The buildings in the village were well-kept, the gardens were in full bloom, and the air carried the fresh scent of grass and flowers.

As we walked down the main street, curious glances from the villagers greeted us. Some smiled warmly, while others watched with a mixture of suspicion and curiosity. The lively atmosphere was almost overwhelming, a far cry from the isolation we had endured.

Diane took my hand, squeezing it gently. "I can't believe we're here," she said, her voice trembling with a mix of relief and joy. "We actually made it."

I looked at her, my eyes softening with gratitude. "Yeah, we did. And it's beautiful."

We continued exploring, discovering a small market with fresh produce, a bakery with the irresistible aroma of bread, and a cozy inn that seemed to offer a much-needed place to rest. The village felt like a sanctuary, a place where we could finally find some semblance of normalcy and safety.

As the day turned to evening, we found a quiet spot in the village square. We sat on a bench, the sunset painting the sky in hues of orange and pink. The warmth of the scene was a soothing balm for our weary souls.

"We're going to build a new life here," I whispered, my voice filled with determination. "We'll make it our home."

Diane leaned against me, her head resting on my shoulder. "Together," she whispered, her voice filled with hope.

I nodded, wrapping my arm around her. "Together."

The surrounding village was a promise of a new beginning, a place where we could leave our past behind and start anew. As the stars twinkled in the night sky, Diane and I felt a renewed sense of purpose and belonging.

Luckily, I had the foresight to keep the money in the bag I carried. We stayed at the local inn, which looked quaint and inviting. The inn's exterior was charming, with flower boxes hanging from the windows and a cozy porch with rocking chairs.

As we approached the inn, the warm glow from inside spilled out into the cool evening air, creating a welcoming ambiance. Diane took a deep breath, savoring the comforting smell of wood smoke and fresh linens. The sight of the inn's sign, with its hand-painted letters, filled her with a sense of relief and hope.

I pushed open the heavy wooden door, and a wave of warmth and the soft hum of conversation greeted us. The interior was cozy, with a large fireplace crackling at one end and comfortable armchairs arranged around it. Rustic décor adorned the walls, and the soft light from hanging lamps cast a gentle glow over the room.

"Good evening!" the innkeeper, an older woman with a kind smile, called from behind the counter. "How can I help you?"

I stepped forward, my face breaking into a weary but genuine smile. "We'd like a room for the night, please."

"Certainly," the innkeeper replied, her eyes twinkling with warmth. She retrieved a ledger and wrote. "We have a few rooms available. Would you prefer one with a view of the garden or the street?"

Diane looked at me, her eyes reflecting her exhaustion and relief. "The garden, please," she said softly.

The innkeeper nodded and handed me a key. "Room 5, on the second floor. Breakfast is served from 7 to 9 in the morning. If you need anything else, just let me know."

"Thank you," I said, taking the key and giving the innkeeper a grateful nod.

We made our way up the staircase, each step echoing softly in the quiet hallway. As we reached room 5, I unlocked the door and pushed it open. The room was warm and inviting, with a large bed covered in a soft quilt, a window overlooking a blooming garden, and a small table with two chairs.

Diane sank onto the edge of the bed, her eyes closing in relief. "I can't believe we're finally here," she said, her voice filled with wonder. "An actual bed."

I set down our bag and unpacked our belongings. One thing I pulled out was the money I had carefully kept. "I know," I said, my voice filled with quiet satisfaction. "It feels like a dream."

Diane's eyes suddenly lit up with excitement. "Oh my God, Jack, we finally have a chance to shower!" she exclaimed.

I looked at her, my fatigue momentarily forgotten. "You're right. I didn't even think about that. A hot shower sounds amazing."

Diane wasted no time hurrying to the bathroom and turning on the taps. The sound of water filling the tub was music to our ears. The bathroom was modest but clean, with a small shower stall and a large, fluffy towel neatly hung on the rack. Steam filled the room as the water heated up.

"Come on, Jack," Diane called, her tone inviting and eager. "Let's make the most of this."

I followed her into the bathroom, where Diane was already stepping into the shower. She looked back with a playful smile. "Join me?"

With a chuckle, I stepped into the shower alongside her. The hot water cascaded over us, the steam enveloping us in a warm, soothing embrace. Diane let out a contented sigh as the heat melted away the tension from our bodies.

We took turns rinsing off the water, washing away the grime of our journey. Diane reached for the soap and began lathering it in her hands. She gently scrubbed my back, her touch tender and affectionate. "I can't believe how good this feels," she murmured, her voice barely audible over the sound of the water.

I closed my eyes, savoring the sensation. "It's incredible. I never knew a shower could feel so rejuvenating."

I took the soap from Diane's hands and washed her back in return. My movements were slow and deliberate, easing the weariness from her muscles. "You've been amazing throughout all this."

Diane's heartwarming smile reflected the sentiment in her eyes. "We've both been through so much," she replied, her voice filled with emotion. "I'm just glad we're here now."

We took our time, allowing the hot water and soap to cleanse not only our bodies but also our spirits. As we rinsed off, Diane reached for a shampoo bottle and began massaging it into my hair, her fingers working through the tangles with gentle care.

My eyes fluttered open, and I looked at her with a mix of gratitude and affection. "I think this is the best part of the day," I said.

Diane smiled; her face illuminated by the warm glow of the bathroom light. "It really is. It feels like we're washing away all the problems from our past, starting fresh."

I nodded, my expression mirroring her sentiment. "Here's to new beginnings," I said, pulling her into a warm embrace under the shower's cascade.

As we stood there, the steam swirling around us, the weight of our journey seemed to lift. The soothing rhythm of the water and the warmth of our shared moment brought a sense of peace and renewal. It was a rare chance to reconnect and relax, a simple pleasure that reminded us of our resilience and the hope that lay ahead.

Eventually, we stepped out of the shower, our bodies refreshed, and our spirits lifted.

As Diane wrapped herself in a fluffy towel and moved to the window, I followed her, feeling a sense of calm I hadn't experienced in a long time. The moonlight cast a silver glow over the garden, illuminating the flowers and neatly trimmed grass. Diane stood there, lost in the serene beauty of the scene.

"It's beautiful," she whispered, her voice soft with awe. "It's like a different world."

I joined her at the window, wrapping my arm around her shoulders. The warmth of her body against mine was comforting. "We made it," I said, my voice filled with emotion. "We finally found a place where we can rest."

We stood in silence, savoring the tranquility of the moment. The soft hum of the inn's activity below and the gentle rustling of the leaves in the garden created a soothing backdrop. For a moment, it felt like the world outside had faded away, leaving only this peaceful sanctuary.

After a long day, our stomachs had reminded us of how hungry we were. We'd headed downstairs for dinner, drawn by the irresistible lure of a warm meal. The inn's dining area was a welcoming space, with the rich aroma of home-cooked food filling the air. We noticed a few patrons scattered about, enjoying their meals and conversations, which created a stark contrast to the desolate world we had left behind.

We took a seat at a corner table, our eyes scanning the menu with eager anticipation. Relief colored Diane's voice as she spoke, "We haven't had a proper meal in days. I don't even know where to start."

I nodded, my gaze fixed on the menu. "Let's just order everything that looked good. We've earned it."

Our choices were an indulgent feast of hearty stews, freshly baked bread, roasted meats, and crisp vegetables. The waitress, a young woman with a knowing smile, took our order with a hint of amusement. "You two must be starving. I'll bring out a little bit of everything."

When the food arrived, it was more than we could have hoped for. Plates piled high with steaming; delicious dishes filled our table. Diane's eyes widened with delight as she dug into the roast beef, while I savored the rich, flavorful stew. We ate with an almost frantic hunger, our conversations punctuated by contented sighs and appreciative murmurs.

"This is amazing," Diane said between bites. "I never thought I'd enjoy a meal so much."

I grinned, feeling a deep sense of satisfaction. "I know. It's like a taste of normalcy we've been missing." After our feast, we returned to our room, feeling pleasantly full and at ease. As we prepared for bed, Diane's excitement turned to reflection. "Can you believe we're finally here?" she asked softly, pulling back the covers. "It feels like a dream."

I sat on the edge of the bed, my expression thoughtful. "It does. We've come so far. We should start planning for our future."

Diane's eyes brightened with hope. "I was thinking about looking into houses in the morning, after breakfast. It would be nice to finally have a place to call our own."

A hopeful smile spread across my face. "That sounds perfect. We can start fresh and make it our home."

But our conversation took a more serious turn. Diane's brow furrowed slightly as she voiced her concern. "I've been thinking about the Queen. We haven't heard anything since the demon was defeated. It feels strange. It was always something we had to worry about."

My expression turned serious as well. "Yeah, it's unsettling. We should stay alert. The Queen might be plotting something, or maybe it's just a lull before another storm."

The room fell quiet as we both contemplated the possibility of being thrust back into danger. Our hopes for a peaceful life clashed with the lingering fear of another threat.

"We've fought so hard to get here," Diane said softly, her voice filled with uncertainty. "But what if this is just a temporary reprieve? What if danger is lurking, waiting to strike again?"

I took her hand, my grip firm and reassuring. "We've faced so much already. We'll face whatever comes next, too. But for now, let's enjoy this peace. We deserve it."

Diane looked into my eyes, searching for solace. "You're right. We have to hold on to our hope. Maybe this is our chance to finally live the life we've always wanted."

I nodded, my gaze steady. "Exactly. We'll stay vigilant, but we'll also embrace the good we've found. We can't let fear overshadow our happiness."

As we lay down to sleep, the weight of our past struggles seemed to lift, if only for a moment. The promise of a new beginning and the comfort of our surroundings provided a much-needed respite. With hope battling against the fear of what might come, we closed our eyes, determined to cherish our newfound peace while preparing for whatever challenges lay ahead.

The next morning, the sun streamed through the inn's windows, promising a new beginning. We enjoyed a hearty breakfast in the cozy dining area, savoring every bite of the delicious food. With full stomachs and hopeful hearts, we set off to meet the realtor.

Diane sat at the kitchen table; the phone pressed to her ear as she listened to the ringing on the other end. The sun was setting outside, casting a warm glow through the windows of our new house. It was a serene moment, a sharp contrast to the world we had left behind.

Finally, the ringing stopped, and Anne's voice came through, filled with surprise and a hint of anxiety. "Diane? Is everything okay?"

Relief and joy filled Diane's smile. "Yes, Anne, everything's more than okay. I wanted to share some incredible news with you… Jack and I… we made it. We found a way out of that hellhole. We found civilization, Anne. A real, living world beyond the wasteland."

Anne's breath caught on the other end, and Diane could almost see her sister's disbelief. "You… you found civilization? How? Where?"

"It wasn't easy," Diane began, her voice steady but tinged with emotion. "After we left the bunker, we crossed a desolate wasteland. There were bandits everywhere, people driven mad by survival. We had to fight, and sometimes, we had to run. It was terrifying, Anne. Every moment felt like it could be our last."

Anne was silent, absorbing every word. Diane knew her sister was imagining the horrors they had faced.

"We kept going," Diane continued, her voice trembling slightly as she remembered. "We didn't know if there was anything out there, but we couldn't stop. And then… we found it. A wall, stretching as far as we could see in every direction. We thought it was the end."

Diane paused, letting the gravity of the moment sink in. "But there was a big overhead door, large enough for a vehicle. We managed to open it, and Anne, what we saw on the other side was like stepping into another world. We left the door open, just in case."

Anne's voice shook with emotion. "You… you left the door open? So, others could follow?"

"Yes," Diane replied, pride in her voice. "We wanted to make sure anyone who made it that far could get through. We found a city, Anne. A real city, full of life. People living their lives like nothing ever happened."

Diane's eyes filled with tears as she thought about how far they had come. "We bought a house here, Anne. It's beautiful. Jack and I… we're finally happy. We're finally safe."

On the other end of the line, Anne was silent, her emotions palpable. When she spoke again, her voice was thick with tears. "Diane… I can't believe it. You really did it. You found a way out."

"We did," Diane whispered. "And you can too. You and the others… you can come here. There's room for all of us."

In the background, Diane could hear the excitement of the other survivors, their disbelief turning into hope.

"You have to tell us where to go," Anne said, urgency in her voice. "We'll leave as soon as we can. We need this, Diane. We need to find you."

"I'll tell you everything," Diane promised. "It won't be easy, but if we made it, I know you can too. Follow the path, find the wall, and come through the door. We'll be waiting."

Anne's voice was determined, the fear replaced by hope. "We'll find you, Diane. We'll all find you. And then we can be together again, like we always talked about."

"Yes," Diane said, her heart swelling. "We'll be together again. And this time, we'll really be free."

After hanging up, Diane turned to Jack, who had been listening from the doorway.

"They're coming."

Jack nodded, pulling her into his arms. "They'll make it. They're strong, just like us."

Diane rested her head against his chest, letting the weight of their journey lift. "We're going to be okay, Jack. All of us."

He kissed the top of her head, holding her close. "Yes, we are."

Months later, Anne and a small group of survivors from the bunker finally arrived. As they pulled up in front of our house, there was a moment of disbelief—a collective pause as they took in the home's sight, where we had found refuge.

Anne stepped out of the car; her eyes wide with wonder. "This… this is amazing," she whispered, almost afraid to believe it was real.

Jack and I came down the steps to greet her. We embraced, the relief and happiness almost overwhelming. It had been so long since we'd seen each other, and the contrast between our past struggles and this moment of peace was striking.

"It's not just amazing, Anne," I said, pulling back to look her in the eyes. "It's real. We made it."

Anne smiled through tears, hugging me again. "I can't believe it. I really can't. And the others—they're on their way too. They'll be here soon."

One by one, more survivors arrived, each with the same stunned expression as they took in their new surroundings. They had lived in fear for so long that accepting their newfound safety was almost too good to be true. But as they settled in, the reality sank in—they had found a place where they could start over.

Our house became the central point of reunion, a place where old friends reconnected and shared their stories. For the first time in years, we could laugh, relax, and plan for the future without the constant threat of danger hanging over us.

Anne and the others settled in the city, just a few miles away from us. The city was bustling and full of life, a perfect contrast to the quiet serenity of our countryside home. It was close enough for frequent visits, yet far enough for everyone to build their own lives.

CHAPTER 25

Two days after I proposed to Diane, I stood at the entrance of a dinosaur-themed amusement park. The choice for our first actual date post-engagement was unconventional, but I was eager to make it memorable. Excitement and nervousness bubbled within me as I took in the park's vibrant atmosphere.

The park was on a beach, with a picturesque bridge stretching across a tranquil lake. The sound of children laughing and waves gently crashing against the shore filled the air, mingling with the scent of saltwater and sunscreen. As I crossed the bridge toward the outdoor restaurant, I marveled at the park rides visible in the distance and the serene lake adding a tranquil touch to the setting. I arrived early, hoping to explore the park before meeting Diane.

A guide appeared to show me around, which struck me as unusual for an amusement park, but I shrugged off my unease. The park was a fascinating mix of kiddie rides and colossal roller coasters, each more intriguing than the last. One ride caught my attention: a massive ship roller coaster that dove underwater into caves before bursting back up onto the surface. It was thrilling to watch.

While wandering, I stumbled upon lifelike dinosaur statues, including my favorite, the Tyrannosaurus Rex. I couldn't resist getting close and touching the rough texture of its skin. I couldn't resist getting close and touching the rough texture of its skin because it felt so real.

When I finally headed back to the restaurant, Diane was already there, looking stunning in her jean shorts and bikini top. The engagement ring on her finger sparkled in the sunlight, completing her radiant appearance. But she seemed upset.

"Where did you go?" she asked, her voice tinged with frustration. Her Filipina accent was more pronounced when she was upset.

"I'm sorry, when I showed up, you weren't here yet," I explained, feeling a pang of guilt. "I decided to check out the park. That guide—" I pointed toward the guide who had helped me earlier, I realized he was nowhere to be seen. I scanned the area, puzzled, but he had vanished.

Diane sighed, her shoulders relaxing slightly. "It's okay. I had to use the bathroom anyway," she said, pulling me from my thoughts. I looked at her, her beauty entranced, our eyes meeting. "Are you okay?" She giggled, snapping me back to reality.

"Oh, yeah, of course," I replied, sitting down at the table. "I'm sorry if I made you worry. I just wanted to make sure everything was perfect for us today."

Diane's frustration melted away into a shy smile. "I was excited and a bit nervous myself."

"I promise, I won't leave you alone like that again," I said, reaching for her hand. "So, what do you think of the park? Pretty cool, right?"

"Yeah, it's amazing! I saw some rides on the way in," she said, her eyes lighting up. "Did you see that huge rollercoaster? It looks terrifying!"

"I did! It's incredible. I even touched one of the dinosaur statues. It felt so real," I shared enthusiastically.

"Really? I'd love to see that," Diane replied, her excitement growing. "But first, let's enjoy our meal."

As we waited for the server, I recounted everything I had seen in the park, trying to convince her to explore it with me.

"Maybe later, honey," she replied with a smile.

We enjoyed our meal, chatting and laughing as we ate. The restaurant offered a stunning view of the ocean, with waves gently lapping against the shore. Despite the earlier tension, we found ourselves lost in each other's company.

"So, have you thought more about wedding plans?" Diane asked, her tone light but curious.

"A bit," I admitted. "I was thinking maybe we could have it somewhere like this. Outdoors, with a beautiful view."

"That sounds wonderful," Diane said, squeezing my hand. "But I want to make sure it's a place that means something to both of us."

"Absolutely," I agreed. "We'll find the perfect spot together."

After finishing our meal, I stood up and extended my hand to Diane. "Ready to explore the park?"

"Lead the way," she said, taking my hand with a grin.

As we walked through the park, the earlier tension melted away. We laughed, took pictures with the dinosaur statues, and even braved the massive ship rollercoaster together. The thrill of the ride and the joy of being with Diane made the day unforgettable.

Just as we were finishing up, a series of televisions around the park suddenly flickered to life. The screens came alive with the image of the Queen, her chilling laugh echoing through the area.

"Thank you for enduring everything so far," she said, her voice dripping with mockery. "I've enjoyed watching you try to live a normal life. Congratulations, Jack, for defeating the demon. You've truly been the MVP of these Trials."

Diane and I exchanged horrified glances as the Queen's words sank in. The realization hit us like a punch to the gut. Everything we had experienced, everything we thought was real, had been a fabrication—a cruel trick.

The Queen's smile widened as she continued, her voice a sinister purr, "And here I was, worried you might disappoint me. But you've proven yourself worthy of my attention. You're my top pick, Jack. I always knew you had potential."

Her tone shifted to a flirtatious lilt. "You know, there's something irresistibly fascinating about you. Most participants are so... predictable. But you, Jack, you've got that special spark. I think you and I are going to have quite the adventure together. Who knows? If you play your cards right, you might even earn a special place by my side."

Jack's face darkened, his frustration boiling over. "Enough of your twisted Trials! What's going to happen to us?"

The Queen's eyes gleamed with delight as she leaned closer to the screen, her voice dripping with mock sympathy. "Oh, Jack, you're my centerpiece. But I must say, Diane here—she's becoming a bit of a liability. I do hope she doesn't slow you down too much. It would be such a shame if she met an unfortunate end soon. But then, she's only a minor inconvenience compared to the grand spectacle ahead."

Diane's eyes flashed with indignation. "How dare you! I'm not some obstacle to be eliminated. We're in this together, and you won't get away with this!"

The Queen's laughter was manic and triumphant. "Oh, Diane, always so fierce. But you see, it's all part of the entertainment. Watch as the true nature of this Trial unfolds. And remember, Jack, you're always welcome to join me in making it even more... intriguing."

At that moment, the sound of screaming and crashing near the rides grew louder. The park's fade of safety shattered. We turned to see a real triceratops rampaging through the area, its destructive path revealing the truth behind the supposed amusement.

Our smiles faded completely as we grasped the full extent of the Queen's deception. What we believed was a happy and normal life was, in reality, just an intricate illusion. The realization was abrupt and devastating. We had never escaped; we were still ensnared in the Queen's hellish trap.

We both stood up, rushing to get a closer look. The screams and chaos were horrifying. Another dinosaur emerged from the area the triceratops had fallen into. This one looked like a Tyrannosaurus Rex, but with longer arms. It climbed over the wall, snatching people from the ride and devouring them.

"Jack, what do we do?" Diane's voice trembled, gripping my hand tightly.

"We need to get out of here," I replied, my heart pounding with fear and adrenaline.

As scared as we were, we found ourselves frozen, watching the nightmare unfold. In a rampage, the T-Rex tore the metal ride apart, causing it to screech and groan and sending sparks flying. The creature's massive tail swung wildly, smashing structures and sending debris crashing into the water below. The air filled with the deafening roars of the beast and the desperate screams of people trying to escape.

"Dammit, this contest will never end," I muttered, feeling the weight of the nightmare bearing down on us once more.

"Jack, we have to move. Now!" Diane urged, snapping me out of my trance.

Grabbing her hand, we ran, weaving through the panicked crowd. The ground shook beneath us as the T-Rex continued its rampage. We dodged falling debris and leaped over overturned tables and chairs, the chaotic scene around us blurring into a cacophony of destruction and terror.

"We need to find shelter," Diane said, her voice steady despite the fear in her eyes.

"Over there!" I pointed to a small building that looked sturdy enough to provide some protection. We made our way toward it, pushing against the tide of fleeing park-goers.

Just as we reached the building, a piece of debris flew past us, narrowly missing Diane. I pulled her close, shielding her with my body as we stumbled inside.

Catching our breath, we looked around the dimly lit room. It was some sort of storage area, filled with supplies and equipment. The walls vibrated with each roar and crash from outside.

"What do we do now?" Diane asked, her voice barely above a whisper.

"We wait here until it's safe to move," I replied, trying to sound confident. "We'll figure out a way to survive this. We always do."

Holding each other tightly, we braced ourselves for the horrors to come. The ride lifted out of the water, revealing the long mechanism that moved the ship and part of the track. A T-Rex ripped a massive chunk off, hurling it toward the storage building. The top collapsed onto the roof with a thunderous crash, and I grabbed Diane's hand, pulling her out just before the building fell in on itself. The ground shook, and the air filled with dust and splintered wood.

"Run!" I shouted, guiding Diane away from the collapsing structure. We stumbled over debris, coughing as the dust choked our lungs.

"The bridge! It's gone!" Diane pointed out, her voice rising in panic.

I looked toward where the bridge once stood, now a twisted wreck of metal and wood, offering no clear path to safety. The lake shimmered ominously in the distance, the only thing between us and potential safety on the other side.

"Jack, what do we do?" Diane's eyes were wide with fear, her grip on my hand tightening.

I scanned our surroundings, desperately searching for any escape route. "We have to find another way across the lake," I said, trying to keep my voice steady. "Look for anything that floats—boats, rafts, anything."

We sprinted along the edge of the lake, the sounds of destruction behind us fueling our urgency. Amidst the chaos, we spotted a small dock with a few rowboats tied up.

"There!" I pointed, leading Diane toward the dock. The T-Rex's roars echoed behind us, closer than ever.

Desperately, we jumped onto the small boats and debris floating nearby. The first two boats had no keys, our feet slipped on the wet surfaces. Debris rained down around us, and I could hear the terrified cries of people still trapped.

"Keep moving!" I shouted, urgency lacing my voice.

We hopped from one piece of wreckage to another; each jump a desperate bid for survival. The water churned with debris and bodies, and the stench of smoke and blood filled the air. We were nearly across the lake when I started moving faster than Diane, my heart pounding in my chest. She slipped, her scream piercing the chaos. I grabbed her from behind, lifting her with me as I leaped from one unstable platform to the next.

"Jack, don't let go!" she cried, clutching my arm.

"I won't. We're almost there!" I assured her, my grip tightening.

As we stood on an unstable piece of the restaurant's roof, we looked back. People screamed in terror as the T-Rex devoured them, while it continued to tear the place apart. My heart ached for them, but I couldn't do anything. I spotted two big propane tanks just before the T-Rex smashed into them.

"Diane, jump!" I yelled, pulling her into the water as the explosion erupted. The shockwave hit us with a force that felt like being punched by a giant. We narrowly escaped the flames, swimming desperately to the opposite shore.

The water was cold and murky, filled with debris that made every stroke a struggle. My muscles burned, but the thought of Diane kept me going. As we reached the shore, dragging ourselves onto the sand, coughing and gasping for air, the terror lingered. The area was full of people, fallen into chaos. I noticed Diane's bikini top was missing and quickly pulled her close, her bare chest pressed against me, trying to shield her from prying eyes.

"Hey, what are you doing?" Diane yelled, her voice trembling.

"Your top is missing," I explained, moving us back into the water. She clutched my arms, her nails digging into my skin as she realized the situation.

"Thank you," she whispered, her voice breaking. Her head rested against me, her body shivering with a mix of cold and fear.

"Stay here, I'll get a towel," I said, my voice shaky but determined.

"I'm not going anywhere with my lack of clothing," she smirked weakly, trying to lighten the mood.

"You look amazing, but let's save the show for a safer time," I joked, trying to keep the mood light despite the surrounding chaos.

She laughed softly. "You're such a dork."

I smiled back, wading out of the water. My hands trembled as I grabbed a towel from the beach and wrapped it around her, even though it got wet almost immediately.

"Thanks again," she said, her playful smile not reaching her eyes this time.

"You're welcome," I replied, forcing a grin. "And not to sound like a pervert, but they look good," I added mischievously, trying to lift her spirits, and make her forget all the bad for just a moment.

She blushed and giggled. "Such a perv," she teased before kissing me, her lips soft and warm against mine.

"Whoa! What was that for?" I asked, breathless.

"I don't know. I felt like it," she smirked, her eyes sparkling for a moment.

"My favorite kisses are the no-reason kind," I said, kissing her again. She shivered, her body trembling against mine.

"I'm getting cold. I need something warm, away from here," she said, her teeth chattering slightly.

"Okay, let's find you a shirt," I suggested as we left the water.

I found a shirt lying on a bench and gave it to her. "Thank you, babe," she said, grabbing the shirt and heading to the bathroom.

Fun time was over, and we needed to get out of there. "Hurry up, I don't want to be here when those dinosaurs get here."

Diane's laugh turned serious. "Yes, sir," she said sarcastically, while saluting me. Even in all this madness, she still got me to laugh.

A guy wearing a hat stared at her walking by, then at me. I just nodded my head and sat on the sand, looking at the wreckage across the lake. Waiting impatiently, while people ran by in panic.

As Diane returned, now wearing the shirt, she looked at me with determination. "We need to find a way out of here, Jack. This place isn't safe."

I nodded. "I know. We need to find some transportation and get as far from here as possible."

She grabbed my hand, pulling me up. "Let's go. We can't stay here."

We started moving again, weaving through the panicked crowd. The sounds of chaos behind us pushed us forward. The memory of the dinosaurs and the destruction they caused fueled our determination to survive.

"Remember that time we got lost in the woods, and you insisted you knew the way?" Diane asked, trying to lighten the mood as we hurried through the chaos.

I chuckled, even as we dodged frantic people. "Hey, I did know the way. Eventually."

"You had us wandering for hours!" she laughed, the sound a beacon of normalcy amid the madness.

"Yeah, but it was worth it, wasn't it?" I said, squeezing her hand. "We found that beautiful waterfall."

"That we did," she agreed, smiling. "You always know how to find something good in the worst situations."

Suddenly, I realized Diane was no longer holding my hand. Panic surged through me as I looked around, frantically pushing past people. Anxiety gripped me, thinking back to earlier moments. She was here one second, gone the next. I called out her name, but it was useless.

"Diane! Diane!" I shouted, pushing through the crowd, my heart pounding in my chest. I couldn't lose her, not now.

CHAPTER 26

Hours passed as I searched for her, my mind racing with fear and dread. Every scream and roar from the distance only heightened my urgency. I ran through the park, scanning every face, every corner, hoping to find her.

I reached a quieter area, exhausted and desperate. My mind was a whirlwind of fear and anger. How could I have let this happen? She depended on me, and I failed her. Tears mixed with the dirt and sweat on my face as I fell to my knees. I pounded the ground, frustration boiling over. I think back to earlier. Where did the guides go? During the destruction, I didn't see them. My guide seemed familiar, and then it hit me. Kyle! I got up, looking around, but the guy who was staring at Diane was gone. It was the same guy—the guide was Kyle!

My heart raced again, the realization crashing down on me. This nightmare wasn't over. It'd never be over. I ran to the men's bathroom, scanning the area frantically. Damn, nobody was there.

I get pissed and rushed out, sprinting toward the women's bathroom. My heart pounded as I burst through the door. Nothing. Fuck!

Why did he care so much about Diane? Memories of the abuse I endured flashed through my mind—Kyle stabbing my mom, the pain he caused. I was so angry I couldn't think straight. I wandered aimlessly around the beach, not knowing what to do.

Time was running out, but I didn't know where Diane could be now. Tears blurred my vision as I whispered, "I'm sorry, babe. I'm so sorry you're caught in this mess. I'll find you; I swear to God!"

I screamed her name again, my voice raw with emotion, but there was no response. My mind raced with thoughts of what Kyle might do to her. The fear and anger threatened to consume me, but I couldn't give up. Diane needed me, and I would find her, no matter what it took. After a frantic search, I spotted a building with a surveillance camera pointing toward the beach parking lot. If there was any chance of finding out what happened to Diane or who took her, this might be it. I raced toward the building, adrenaline fueling my every step.

I took the stairs to the top floor; I found the place eerily empty. Computers and monitors clutter the room, but there was no sign of people. The monitors were on, displaying the beach parking lot, but the images looped endlessly. Confused, I approached the screens, trying to make sense of it all.

As I focused on the footage, my heart sank. I saw Diane being grabbed by several men and forced into a familiar white van. The van speeds away, and my stomach churns as I spotted Kyle among them. The sight of him made my blood boil. I kept watching, hoping for any clue that might help, but the footage just kept repeating.

I heard a voice behind me, startling me. I spun around and swung but missed. The man was too far away.

"I had to," he repeated, his voice filled with anguish.

"What are you talking about? What's going on? Why is this on repeat?" I demanded, grabbing the man and slamming him against the wall.

"I had to do it. She made me do it," he sobbed, tears streaming down his face.

"Who made you do it?" I pressed, feeling a surge of frustration.

"The Queen. She made me. She did something to me." His cries grew louder, his words increasingly jumbled.

"The Queen? Who is the Queen?" I asked urgently, but before he could respond, his eyes glazed over and his head made a sickening click. He collapsed to the ground, lifeless.

Dammit! I needed to alert Anne. I dialed her number, my voice trembling as I paced the room.

"Anne, it's Jack. Something happened to Diane. We were attacked by dinosaurs, but we managed to escape."

Anne's voice came through, panic-stricken. "Jack, there's chaos everywhere!" The background noise was deafening—roars, screams, and crashes. "Where's Diane?"

"She was abducted. I saw the footage—Kyle and some other people took her. I can't believe this," I said with desperation.

Anne's shock is palpable. "What? Oh, my God! Where are you? I'll meet you to help look."

"No, the city's too big. If you can, just search where you are. I'll handle it from here."

"The city is huge, and crawling with T-rexes!"

"Just be careful," I said, my voice softer, more pleading.

"Jack," she said, her voice wavering, "we're going to find her. Just stay safe, okay?"

"You too," I replied before hanging up.

I stepped outside, immediately confronting the ongoing chaos. The sound of a T-Rex roaring nearby made my blood run cold. I sprinted toward the street, dodging debris and panicked people. The massive creature burst through the trees, its jaws snapping at anything in its path.

I barely dodged a car; it was flung aside like a toy. My heart pounded as I ran down an alleyway, the T-Rex hot on my heels. Every step sent tremors through the ground, the monster's roar deafening. I glanced back, the sight of its gaping maw pushing me to run faster.

Up ahead, I saw a narrow passage between two buildings. It was a tight squeeze, but it might slow down the T-Rex. With a burst of speed, I dove into the gap, scraping my sides against the rough brick. The T-Rex slammed into the buildings, roaring in frustration, its head too large to fit through the passage.

I kept running until I burst out onto another street, gasping for breath. I needed to find Diane, and I needed to survive. The city was in chaos, but I would not let it defeat me. Not now, not ever.

With the T-Rex momentarily stuck, I took a deep breath and continued my search, my determination burning brighter than ever.

I raced through the city streets, my heart pounding in my chest like a war drum. The city had descended into utter chaos—cars screeched and crashed, people screamed and ran in all directions, and the ground shook with the thunderous steps of the rampaging T-rexes. Every passing moment felt like an eternity as I desperately searched for any trace of Diane.

"Diane!" I shouted, my voice hoarse from yelling, but the surrounding cacophony swallowed my cries. I had no idea where to start, but I couldn't stop. I wouldn't stop. The weight of the situation pressed down on me, a relentless burden threatening to crush my spirit, but I forced myself to stay focused. I will find her. I have to.

A deafening roar shook the air, and I spun around to see a T-Rex charging down the street, its massive tail smashing through streetlights and storefronts like they were made of paper. My breath caught in my throat as I dove behind a parked car, barely avoiding the beast's stomping feet. The ground quaked with each step it took, the sheer power of its presence making the car rattle and sway.

I peeked out from my hiding spot, my eyes scanning the area frantically. People ran in every direction, their faces masks of terror and desperation. The T-Rex continued its rampage, its jaws snapping at anything that moved. I had to move, but the beast's erratic path made it nearly impossible to predict.

Spotting a gap in the chaos, I bolted from my hiding spot, sprinting down a side street. My lungs burned with effort, but I couldn't afford to slow down. Not with Diane out there, somewhere, needing me. The thought of her in danger fueled my determination, pushing me to run faster, harder.

As I turned a corner, I saw a group of people huddled together, their faces pale and wide-eyed. A T-Rex roared in the distance, and they scattered, some tripping and falling in haste. One woman looked at me, her eyes filled with a pleading desperation that mirrored my own.

"Have you seen a woman—dark hair, about this tall?" I shouted, holding my hand to indicate Diane's height. The woman shook her head, tears streaming down her face, before she turned and ran. My heart sank, but I couldn't let it slow me down. I had to keep moving.

I weaved through the streets, dodging debris and narrowly avoiding a car that swerved wildly before crashing into a storefront. The air was thick with smoke and the acrid smell of burning rubber. My eyes stung, but I forced myself to stay focused. Every second counted.

Suddenly, another T-Rex barreled into view, its eyes wild and filled with a primal rage. It roared, a deafening sound that seemed to shake the very air. My heart skipped a beat as I dove into an alleyway, pressing myself against the rough brick wall. The beast's massive foot slammed down just inched from where I stood, the impact sending tremors through my body.

I held my breath, my muscles tense and ready to move at a moment's noticed. The T-Rex's head swung in my direction, its nostrils flaring as it sniffed the air. For a terrifying moment, I thought it had caught my scent, but then it turned away, distracted by the movement of people in the distance.

Seizing the opportunity, I sprinted down the alley, my mind racing. I had to find a safe place to regroup, to figure out my next move.

Eventually, I made my way to a quieter area of the city where there was no immediate danger. Mentally and physically drained, I sought refuge and sustenance at a nearby restaurant. It was bustling with evening diners, the sounds of clinking cutlery and muted conversations a stark contrast to the chaos outside.

I burst in, scanning the room. When I burst in, the room fell silent and everyone looked at me with startled expressions, recognizing my disheveled and wild-eyed appearance. Ignoring the stares, I made my way to the counter.

"I need help," I said, my voice urgent and strained. The manager, a middle-aged man with a kind face, stepped forward.

"What happened? Are you all right?" he asked, concern etched in his features.

"I'm looking for someone—my fiancée. She was taken by some men. Please, have you seen anyone being forced into a white van?" My words tumbled out in a desperate rush.

The manager shook his head slowly. "I'm sorry, but I haven't seen anything like that. Maybe you should rest for a bit, get something to eat. You look like you've been through hell."

I nodded, my exhaustion catching up with me. "Thank you," I murmured, taking a seat at the counter.

As I waited for the food, I couldn't shake the image of Diane being dragged away. My heart pounded as I spotted Diane at a corner table, bruised and bloody. A thug stood over her, gun in hand, while another guy sat across from her. My eyes locked onto Diane, and fury filled my voice.

"Diane! What have they done to you?"

The thug smirked, pressing the gun against Diane's temple. "Stay back, pal. You don't want her to get hurt, well, anymore, do you?" Tears streamed down Diane's face as she looked back at me.

"Jack, don't... He'll kill you. Just go."

I stepped forward, every muscle tensed. "I'm not letting you take her. Not again. You hear me, pal? This ends now."

Thug number two got up and moved toward me, a malicious grin on his face. "You shouldn't have shown up, Shaw. You're in way over your head."

I head-butted him, making him drop in a heap on the floor. I grabbed a steak knife from a nearby table, facing Thug number one with resolve.

"Put the gun down and step away from her!"

Thug number one sneered, eyes glinting with malevolence. "You really brought a knife to a gunfight?" He lunged, trying to overpower me. I sidestepped his lunge, my training kicking in. The restaurant patrons screamed and scattered, tables overturning in chaos. Thug number two tried to recover, lunging at me again, but I was quicker and sent a roundhouse kick that sent him crashing into a table.

Thug number one swung the gun, trying to pistol-whip me, but I ducked and countered with a swift punch to the gut. He staggered back, raising the gun again. I grabbed his wrist, twisting it. The gun went off, shattering a window and causing more panic. I quickly stabbed Thug number one in the head, breaking off the fight. Breathing heavily, I stood over him, looking over as Kyle walked out of the bathroom. Our eyes locked. I grabbed Diane's hand..

"Diane, we need to go. Now!"

We hurried outside, the urgency of our situation crystal clear. As I planned our escape, a police car pulled up, its sirens blaring. The officer, Riley, jumped out, drawing his taser.

"Stay where you are!" he shouted.

In a split second, I pushed Diane out of the way just as Riley fired. The taser prongs hit me, and my body convulsed with electric shocks. I collapsed to the ground, muscles seizing.

As I writhed on the ground, struggling against the electric pain, Riley radioed in.

"Officer Riley to dispatch."

"Whatcha got for us, Mike?"

"Yeah, I found someone who fits the description at the restaurant. He seemed pretty beaten up. I'm going to give him a lift to the hospital."

I saw Kyle sneaking out the door and grabbing Diane. Mustering all my strength, I pulled the taser prongs out and lunged at Riley, knocking his radio from his hand. He stumbled, trying to regain control, but I was faster. I grabbed his baton and swung it, connecting with his side. He grunted in pain, dropping to one knee.

Suddenly, two more officers rushed in, drawn by the commotion. One tackled me to the ground while the other tried to cuff me. I fought with everything I had, adrenaline surging through my veins. I elbowed one officer in the face, sending him reeling, but the other pinned me down, twisting my arm behind my back.

Kyle took advantage of the chaos, dragging Diane toward the van. She screamed, kicking and struggling, but he was too strong.

"Jack!" Diane's voice was full of fear.

I roared in anger, breaking free from the officer's grip for a moment. I swung wildly, connecting with his jaw and sending him sprawling. But Riley recovered, pulling his gun.

"Freeze!"

Ignoring the command, I charged at him. Riley fired, but I ducked and tackled him to the ground. We wrestled for control of the gun; the weapon discharging wildly and shattering the restaurant's windows.

Kyle was almost at the van with Diane. My heart pounded as I knew I had only seconds. I wrenched the gun from Riley's hand and pistol-whipped him, knocking him out cold.

I scrambled to my feet, but it was too late. Kyle had Diane in the van, driving away in desperation.

"Diane!" I screamed, sprinting toward the van. I stood in the middle of the street, gasping for breath, my mind racing.

Officer Riley staggered out; gun drawn. He aimed it at me with shaking hands.

"You're under arrest. Don't make this worse."

Ignoring his command, I kept my eyes on the retreating van, fury and desperation boiling within me. "My fiancé just got abducted! please! It's not me you're after!"

For a moment, Riley hesitated, seeing the raw desperation in my eyes. But then he snapped the cuffs on my wrists, pushing me toward the police car. "Get in the car!"

The door slammed shut, cutting off my cries. Riley started the car, turning it around and heading toward the hospital. I tried to talk sense into him, but I was incoherent and manic. Riley was in no mood and wouldn't listen, especially with how busy his night had been dealing with dinosaur calls.

"Look, officer, listen to me," I pleaded. "This guy named Kyle got my fiancé, and he's taken her. You can't just ignore this!"

Riley shot me an irritated glance in the rearview mirror. "You think I have time for this? You know what my night's been like? T-rexes rampaging through the city, people getting trampled, and now I have to babysit you."

The radio crackled again. "Riley, what's your status?"

Riley snapped back into the radio. "I'm heading to the hospital."

The city outside was a scene of utter chaos. People abandoned cars in the streets, emergency vehicles sped by with sirens blaring, and the distant roars of T-rexes echoed through the night. People were running in every direction, in fear. Fires burned in some buildings, sending plumes of smoke into the sky, and the air was thick with the acrid smell of burning rubber and fear.

"Officer, please," I begged, leaning forward as far as the cuffs would allow. "You have to help me. Her life depends on it!"

Riley slammed his hand on the steering wheel in frustration. "Do you not get it? I've got bigger problems than your girlfriend right now. The whole city is falling apart!"

Suddenly, dispatch was alerting Riley to another call related to a T-Rex attack. "I'm already busy, have Jefferson take this one," Riley barked into the radio.

Our ride to the hospital took a few minutes. The tension in the car is heavy.

"Dammit," Riley muttered under his breath. "You always find a way to make things worse. You think I enjoy this? Hauling your ass around while the city burns?"

"Officer, I know it sounds crazy," I insisted. "But you have to trust me. This guy is dangerous, and he's got Diane. We need to stop him before it's too late."

Riley shook his head, his knuckles white on the steering wheel. "I don't have time for your wild stories. My job is to get you to the hospital and then back on patrol. End of discussion."

As we approached the hospital, the chaos of the city seemed to intensify. Emergency vehicles were everywhere, their lights flashing as they sped to various scenes of destruction. My adrenaline was fading, replaced by the gnawing pain and exhaustion from the day's events. I was struggling to stay conscious, my vision blurring and my thoughts becoming disjointed.

"I can't do anything in this condition," I muttered to myself, despair seeping into my voice. I couldn't help but recall a moment from the past—my friend's girlfriend had overdosed, and he had to stab her in the leg with an epinephrine injector to save her. She had nearly jumped out of her skin from the shock.

Riley pulled into the hospital entrance, and I saw an ambulance pull up, obviously gearing up to head to another attack site. With a flicker of determination, I realized this might be my only chance. As Riley opened the car door to pull me out, I summoned every ounce of energy I had left. Kicking the door with all my might, I caught Riley off balance. He stumbled backward, and I seized the opportunity to bolt from the car, my hands still cuffed behind me.

"Stop! Don't make this worse!" Riley yelled, his voice filled with frustration and urgency.

I sprinted through the hospital parking lot, weaving between cars and emergency personnel. My lungs burned, my heart pounded, and my body was on the brink of collapse. I knew I had only moments before more officers would join the pursuit. I broke my cuffs off, then spotted an ambulance with one door ajar. Desperation drove me toward it.

As the ambulance doors swung open, two paramedics sitting inside noticed me.

"Hey! What are you doing?" one paramedic shouted, moving toward me.

I waited for the paramedic to stick his head out of the back and slammed one of the doors shut, hitting him hard. He flew backward, knocked out cold. The other paramedic ran at me, but I grabbed him and smashed his head against the side of the ambulance. The force broke his nose, and he crumpled to the ground, screaming and clutching his face.

Rummaging through the supplies on the wall, I found a box labeled:

FOR EMERGENCIES ONLY!

"Now's a good time as any," I muttered, trying to joke through my pain. I opened the box, took out the Epinephrine auto-injector, and glanced at the instructions. I quickly grew impatient and ripped off the safety cap. As I was about to swing my arm down to my thigh, Officer Riley appeared at the back of the ambulance, his pistol pointed directly at me.

"Freeze, asshole! It's all over with!"

Riley's voice was authoritative. I hid the needle behind me as my resolve was stronger.

"Now I want you to come on out of there nice and quiet!" Riley demanded.

I jumped out of the ambulance, hands still raised. Riley's face showed his irritation.

"Now put your fucking hands up!" he ordered.

I stood motionless, defiant. Riley's frustration boiled over. "Now!"

When I didn't move, Riley waved his hand in front of my face. "Hey dumbass, you ever hear of these amazing things we call hands?"

Riley's annoyance grew as he realized I wasn't responding. He muttered to himself, "Why do I always get stuck with these kinds of people?" He waved his hand again, clearly thinking I was just a nut job.

In a split second, I grabbed Riley's hand and slammed it into his face. He staggered back, bleeding from his nose. Seizing the moment, I thrust the injector into my thigh with all my remaining strength.

An instant rush surged through my body, revitalizing me. I felt invincible, the pain and fatigue melting away. I pulled out the needle and threw it on the ground. Riley, recovering quickly, aimed his gun at me.

"Hands in the air! Now!" he shouted.

"Okay, okay," I said, slowly raising my hands.

"Now put them behind your head!" Riley demanded.

I complied, moving my hands behind my head. Riley walked closer; his gun still trained on me. As he reached for my handcuffs, I acted swiftly. Grabbing his hand holding the gun, I twisted his elbow violently, breaking it and making him drop the weapon. With a spin kick, I sent Riley crashing to the ground.

Just then, a group of paramedics rushed out of the hospital, their faces etched with urgency, but before they could reach me, a T-Rex roared nearby. The beast's enormous body crashed through the hospital, sending debris and wreckage flying. As it took each step, the ground shook, and its roar echoed through the city streets.

"Not now," I muttered, frustration seeping into my voice. I grabbed Officer Riley's keys from the ground and stole his car. The engine roared to life, and I sped away, the T-Rex's roar fading into the distance but leaving a lingering tremor in the air.

CHAPTER 27

Relief was short-lived. A police car screeched out in front of me, forcing me to swerve hard left. I barreled down a narrow, one-lane street, realizing too late that I was heading in the wrong direction. The siren of the pursuing cop car blared behind me, its lights flashing through my rearview mirror. As I glanced back, I saw the same cop car that had made me turn, now closing in, and another one appearing in my side mirror.

A jolt from hitting a bump caused the glove compartment to fly open, revealing a .40mm handgun. I snatched it up and slowed just enough to aim. The cop car directly behind me and another one on my left were now closing in. I pointed the gun at the rear tire of the closest cop car.

BANG! The bullet struck the tire, causing the car to swerve uncontrollably. I floored the accelerator, narrowly avoiding the out-of-control vehicle. It veered sharply left, rolling onto its side with a violent crash. The second cop car, unable to stop in time, plowed straight into the overturned vehicle, smashing into it head-on.

I was now completely cut off by a new cop car that had pulled directly in front of me. With no room to maneuver, I slammed on the brakes, tires screeching as I skidded to a halt. The officer's voice crackled through the speaker of the parked cop car.

"Step out of the vehicle with your hands up!"

I stayed still, trying to figure out my next move. The officer got out of his car, gun drawn, aiming directly at me. As I was about to act, a car flew through the air in my peripheral vision. The officer barely leaped aside as the airborne car crashed into the police car's windshield, instantly knocking out the officer inside.

Using the chaos to my advantage, I backed up a few feet and then gunned the engine, maneuvering around the wreckage. I skidded past a row of parked cars, setting off their alarms with a cacophony of blaring sounds.

Before I could make any headway, a massive explosion erupted behind me. I glanced back to see the result of the two cop cars exploding, which triggered a chain reaction. Flames and debris were spewing everywhere, and I could see the surrounding cars catching fire. With my car now burning, I dove out, rolling on the ground to extinguish the flames.

Leaping up, I sprinted toward a nearby police motorcycle. I yanked the officer off and quickly mounted the bike. With a roar of the engine, I sped away, the burning wreckage and chaos of the city quickly receding behind me.

As I maneuvered through the streets, the roar of the T-Rex grew louder again. Looking over my shoulder, I saw the beast charging through the city, its massive frame crashing through buildings and sending debris scattering. The T-Rex's roar was a constant reminder of the peril closing in. It was now pursuing me with a ferocity that matched my desperation.

I pushed the motorcycle to its limits, swerving around obstacles and darting through narrow gaps. The T-Rex's footsteps were thunderous, and its roars seemed to get closer with every second. I knew I had to keep moving, or I'd become just another part of its destructive path.

The city was a maelstrom of chaos as I maneuvered the motorcycle through the debris-strewn streets. The ground shook with each thunderous step of the T-Rex, its enormous jaws snapping dangerously close behind me. Sirens blared from all directions, and police cars were closing in, their lights flashing in a disorienting strobe.

Ahead, another T-Rex's colossal foot came crashing down on a car, sending a rain of metal and glass into the street. I swerved violently to avoid the debris, narrowly missing a panicked pedestrian who darted out of the way. The streets were a minefield of wreckage and terrified civilians.

Desperation surged through me as I sped into a narrow alley. The walls were so close that the pursuing police car scraped along them, slowing down but still not giving up. I burst out of the alley onto the main road, taking a quick glance over my shoulder. The T-Rex was still relentless, its massive jaws snapping open and shut with an unnerving rhythm.

I pulled out my phone with shaking hands, barely dialing Anne's number. The roar of the T-Rex filled my ears as I tried to focus. The conversation was urgent, and my voice was strained.

"Anne, I found Diane, but she was taken again. I had to escape police custody and now I'm being chased by a T-Rex! I need help, fast!"

Anne's voice crackled through the phone, a mix of panic and determination. "Jack, hold on! What's your location? I'm coming for you. Just stay on the line!"

I glanced back, seeing the T-Rex's jaws closing in. "I'm near the old mill—"

The phone line was abruptly cut as the T-Rex roared again, its breath hot and acrid. I could feel the vibrations of its footsteps through the ground as it stomped closer.

The urgency in Anne's voice was clear as she responded, "I'm on my way, just hold on! Don't get caught by that thing!"

I took a deep breath and hung up, turning my full attention back to the chase. The motorcycle roared beneath me, its engine screaming as I pushed it to its limits. The T-Rex's massive jaws snapped just inches from my back, and I could hear the crunching of debris beneath its feet.

I weaved through traffic and debris, desperately trying to stay ahead. The city was in a state of pandemonium, and every second counted as I fought to keep the T-Rex and the police at bay. I glanced over my shoulder, seeing the T-Rex's massive jaws snapping perilously close. My heart raced as I spotted an overturned bus creating a makeshift ramp. Desperation spurred me forward. With a roar of the motorcycle's engine, I aimed for the ramp, launching myself into the air.

The T-Rex's roar intensified as it lunged after me. Time seemed to slow as I twisted the handlebars, aiming straight for the gaping maw of the beast. The motorcycle hurtled toward the T-Rex, and with a deafening explosion, the impact caused its body to collapse, blocking the road in a grotesque pile of debris.

The shockwave from the explosion sent me tumbling through the air. I hit the ground hard, pain radiating through my body as I rolled to a stop. The fallen T-Rex caused police cars to crash into it, creating a massive pileup of twisted metal and mangled vehicles.

As I struggled to my feet, police officers quickly surrounded me. "Freeze!" one shouted, but I was already in motion. Pivoting on my heel, I delivered a powerful roundhouse kick that sent the first officer sprawling.

Another officer lunged at me. I grabbed his outstretched arm, twisted it, and flipped him over my shoulder. Two more officers tried to tackle me at once. I sidestepped one and used a palm strike to the other's chest, knocking the wind out of him.

The first officer recovered, and swung a baton at me. I caught it mid-swing, disarmed him, and used it to trip another officer who was rushing in. More officers joined the fray, but I had honed my martial arts skills to a razor's edge. I blocked punches and kicks with fluid movements, countering with precise and devastating strikes. I used one officer's momentum to throw him into a group of his colleagues, creating a chaotic pile of bodies.

Amidst the chaos, another T-Rex appeared, its massive feet crushing cars as it roared in fury. The situation was spiraling out of control when Anne's car screeched into view.

She slammed on the brakes; her face set in a determined grimace. The door flew open, and she shouted, "Get in! We need to go, now!"

I sprinted toward the car, dodging a flurry of police officers and the looming threat of the new T-Rex. Anne's car sped away, leaving the mayhem behind as we raced through the streets. The T-Rex's thunderous footsteps shook the ground behind us, its roar echoing through the city as it pursued.

Anne floored the gas pedal, weaving through traffic with precision. The city streets blurred around us, and the T-Rex's massive form loomed ever closer in the rearview mirror. We sped through intersections, narrowly avoiding collisions with other vehicles.

Ahead, Anne spotted a bridge stretching across a river. Desperation marked her decision as she sped up toward it, hoping the structure might provide a means to lose the relentless beast. The bridge loomed closer, its support beams casting long shadows over the road.

As we approached, the T-Rex lunged forward, its massive jaws snapping dangerously close. Anne swerved sharply to avoid the jaws, and the T-Rex's weight collided with the side of the bridge. The impact caused a violent tremor, and the bridge began to shudder and crack under the strain.

"Hang on!" Anne shouted as she pushed the car faster. The bridge creaked ominously, and debris rained down around us. We sped across the collapsing structure, the ground falling away beneath us as chunks of concrete and metal crashed into the river below.

The T-Rex roared in frustration as it struggled to free itself from the crumbling bridge. Its massive body, now partially submerged, flailed as the bridge gave way completely. The dinosaur's roars turned to gurgles as it slowly drowned, the bridge's remains sinking into the river with a massive splash.

Anne maneuvered the car to a safe distance, finally bringing us to a halt on solid ground. We looked back at the scene of destruction—the bridge now a twisted wreckage in the water and the T-Rex disappearing beneath the waves.

Breathing heavily, Anne glanced at me. "We made it. For now."

I nodded, the adrenaline was still coursing through my veins. "Thanks. We need to keep moving. Diane's still out there."

Anne's eyes were resolute. "I've been able to locate her sister's whereabouts using satellite information."

"Isn't that illegal?" I asked, still trying to wrap my mind around the situation.

Anne's look made it clear that my priorities were misplaced. "Do you want to save her or not?"

I hesitated, torn between the legality of the situation and the urgency of finding Diane. "Fine, let's just get to her."

Anne nodded and shifted into gear. The car roared back to life, and we set off, the city's chaos slowly receding behind us. As we drove, the tension in the car was palpable. We both knew the risks and the stakes, but right now, finding Diane was the only thing that mattered.

The road ahead was clear for now, but the urgency of the situation kept our pace swift and our focus sharp. Anne fixed her eyes on the GPS, tracking the location as we sped toward our destination.

We arrived at the cave entrance, the dark and eerie atmosphere only heightened by the oppressive silence. The air was thick with the smell of damp earth and mold. Anne and I exchanged a determined nod, knowing what was at stake, before rushing into the darkness.

Navigating the cave's twisting passages, our footsteps echoed ominously off the damp stone walls. The flickering light from our flashlights cast long, eerie shadows, making the cave seem almost alive. I could feel the weight of the darkness pressing in, and every sound felt magnified.

"Jack, we need to find her fast," Anne said, her voice steady but laced with urgency.

"I know," I replied, my breath coming in short, ragged gasps. "I can't lose Diane. Not again."

Anne's face was a mask of determination. "We will find her. She's my sister. I won't let anything happen to her."

As I glanced over at her, I couldn't help but note the raw emotion in her eyes. "I don't know what I'd do if anything happened to her. I—"

Before I could finish, the ground beneath us gave way without warning. One moment, we were on solid ground; the next, we were falling through a hidden pit.

As we tumbled through the darkness, Anne's voice cut through the chaos. "Jack! Hang on!"

I reached out in the blackness, my flashlight tumbling from my grip. The fall seemed endless, a rush of disorientation and panic. Just as the world went completely black, Anne's voice echoed one last time, filled with the same fierce determination.

"We're getting her back, Jack. We have to."

The ground slammed into us with a jarring impact, and everything went silent.

CHAPTER 28

I jolted awake, the cold metal chair digging into my back. The dimly lit underground chamber felt suffocating, the air was thick with the stench of sweat and fear. Flickering torchlight danced across the walls, revealing the sinister figures of Kyle's thugs, their eyes gleaming with malice.

In front of me, Kyle paced back and forth, a smirk curling his lips. His voice was sharp and cruel. "Welcome to the end of the line, Jack. Did you really think you could just waltz in here and take her back? After everything?"

I strained against my restraints, muscles bulging as I tried to break free. My voice was low, trembling with barely suppressed rage. "Kyle, you're going to pay for this. For everything."

Kyle's smirk deepened, and he leaned in close, his voice a venomous whisper. "Pay? Oh, Jack, I've been paying for years. But not in the way you think. You've been blind to the truth all along."

Confusion flickered in my eyes. Before I could speak, Kyle's attention shifted to Diane, who two of his thugs held captive nearby. He grabbed her roughly, forcing her closer, his hand wrapping around her throat in a twisted mockery of an embrace.

"Look at her, Jack," Kyle sneered, his grip on Diane tightening. "She's mine now. Just like everything else I've taken from you."

Diane struggled, her eyes wide with terror. "Let me go!" she cried, her voice trembling with fear and fury. "You're a monster, Kyle!"

Kyle's eyes narrowed, a cruel smile playing on his lips. "A monster? Maybe. But I'm the monster who's been in your life all along, Jack. I'm the one who took your father from you."

My world stopped. The air seemed to disappear, leaving me gasping for breath. "What… what did you just say?" My voice was a whisper, disbelief and horror crashing over me.

Kyle's smile twisted into something darker, more sinister. "That's right. I killed your father, Jack. It was me. I put a bullet in his head and left him to die. And then, to twist the knife even deeper, I married your mother. She never suspected a thing, poor Marishka. She thought I was her savior, but I was the devil in disguise."

My chest tightened, my heart pounding with a mixture of rage and agony. Memories of my father, the man who had been my hero, flooded my mind. The warmth, the laughter—all of it was now shattered by the man standing before me.

"You… you bastard!" My voice cracked with fury, tears of rage and pain welling up in my eyes. My body trembled with the force of my emotions. "You took everything from me!"

Kyle's grip on Diane tightened as he forced her closer, his lips brushing her ear in a sickeningly intimate gesture. "And now, I'm taking her too, Jack. Just like I took your father. Just like I took your mother."

Diane's eyes filled with tears, but there was defiance in them—no submission. With a sudden burst of strength, she lashed out, scratching Kyle's face with her nails, drawing blood.

Kyle recoiled, his face contorting with anger as he touched the bleeding wound. "You little—!" He snarled, and before anyone could react, he pulled a gun from his belt and pressed it against Diane's head.

"Diane, no!" My scream was raw, ripped from the depths of my soul. The sight of the gun pressed against Diane's temple was more than I could bear. My heart shattered, rage boiling over, blinding me to everything but the need to tear Kyle apart.

Kyle's eyes glittered with twisted satisfaction as he forced Diane to face me, keeping the gun trained on her. "You see, Jack? You're powerless. Just like you were when I killed your father."

Diane, shaking but resolute, looked into my eyes. "Jack… I'm so sorry," she whispered, tears streaming down her face. "I love you."

My heart wrenched, a silent scream tearing through my mind. I found myself trapped, unable to reach her, to protect her from the monster who had haunted our lives.

Kyle's smirk deepened as he kept the gun on Diane, his other hand gripping her arm like a vise. "Say goodbye, Jack."

But at that moment, Diane acted. Using the split second of distraction, she twisted in Kyle's grip, her knee slamming into his groin with all her strength. Kyle grunted in pain, his grip loosening just enough for Diane to wrench herself free.

She darted toward me, but Kyle recovered quickly, his face twisted with fury. He raised the gun, aiming it at Diane's back, but before he could pull the trigger, I, fueled by pure adrenaline, snapped the restraints holding me.

With a roar, I launched myself at Kyle, tackling him to the ground. The gun skittered across the floor, out of reach, as we grappled in a brutal struggle. Kyle fought with the strength of a madman, but my fury made me unstoppable. I rained down blows on Kyle, each one fueled by years of pain, anger, and the need for justice.

As I raised my fist for a final, crushing blow, Kyle sneered, blood dripping from his split lip. "You'll never escape, Jack. Not alive, anyway."

Before I could react, Kyle slammed his fist into a hidden switch on the floor. The ground beneath us gave way, revealing a pit filled with sharp, jagged spikes. I barely leaped aside, but Kyle wasn't so lucky—his leg caught on the edge, and he screamed as the spikes tore into him. Kyle got up and ran deeper into the cave.

Breathless and battered, I scrambled to my feet, grabbing Diane and pulling her into my arms. "Are you okay?" I whispered, my voice thick with emotion.

Diane nodded, her face pale but determined. "I'm okay. We need to get out of here."

Anne, who had freed herself amidst the chaos, joined us, her eyes wide with a mixture of fear and resolve. "Kyle's set up booby traps all over this place. We have to be careful."

We carefully navigated around the pit, but the next obstacle came quickly hidden tripwires that, when triggered, sent a barrage of arrows shooting from the walls. I barely pulled Anne and Diane out of the way in time, the arrows whizzing past us and embedding themselves in the stone.

Breathless, we continued onward, our movements cautious, every step a potential trap. The deeper we went, the more treacherous the path became—swinging blades, collapsing ceilings, and walls that closed in with crushing force.

But Diane, Anne, and I moved with a single-minded determination. Every trap was a reminder of Kyle's twisted mind, his desire to see us suffer. But we pressed on, driven by the need to escape, to survive.

Finally, the end was near, and I could feel it in my bones. This was the moment of truth. Refusing to let Kyle take anything more from me, I protected not only Diane but also my future. This time, I would win.

We reached an enormous cavern where Kyle was attempting to escape with Diane through a hidden exit. It was filled with stalactites and stalagmites, creating a labyrinth of stone. I was breathless but resolute, my voice echoing off the cavern walls.

"Kyle! This is your last chance. Let her go!"

Kyle turned to face us, a crazed look in his eyes, his face twisted with hatred and desperation. "You just don't know when to quit, do you, Jack?" He pressed a button on a remote control, triggering a massive explosion within the cave. Rocks and dust flew everywhere as the ground shook beneath us.

Anne and I dove for cover, shielding ourselves from the onslaught of debris and falling rocks. We struggled to regain our footing amidst the chaos. The explosion blew open the side of the cave wall, leaving it wide open to the outside.

Coughing with a strained voice, I said, "Anne, Diane… Where's Diane?"

Anne, frantically searching, her voice filled with urgency, replied, "I don't know, Jack! Keep looking!" We heard a faint cough amidst the rubble. We rushed over and started clearing the debris, our hearts pounding with fear and determination.

My voice cracked with relief. "Diane! Hang on, we're getting you out!" We uncovered Diane, her leg trapped under a heavy boulder. We quickly lifted it off, revealing her injured leg.

Diane grimaced in pain. "I... I can't walk."

Anne's supportive voice tries to reassure Diane, "It's okay, Diane. We'll get you out of here." As I scanned the cave, I spotted Kyle stirring in the distance, clutching his bat, while the distant roar of a T-Rex echoes through the cavern. My eyes narrowed as I locked onto Kyle.

"Anne, help Diane. Get her out of here. I'll deal with Kyle."

Anne nodded, determination in her eyes. "Be careful, Jack."

She helped Diane limp toward the cave entrance, supporting her weight as they navigated through the rubble and chaos. I picked up a piece of wood, ready to confront Kyle in a final, brutal showdown amidst the crumbling cave.

I stepped forward. "Kyle..."

Kyle grinned wickedly, brandishing his bat. "Jack, you never learn, do you? You're no match for me."

I tightened my grip on the wood. "Maybe when I was a kid, but now... We'll see about that."

We circled each other, the tension thick in the air. Kyle swung his bat with lethal precision, aiming for my head.

"Your mother was weak, just like you," Kyle mocked me. I dodged his swing and retaliated with a swift strike.

"Shut your mouth!"

We clashed with ferocity, each blow echoing through the cave. I ducked and weaved, evading Kyle's attacks while delivering punishing blows of my own. Kyle grunted with effort.

"You can't stop me, Jack. I'm invincible!"

Gritting my teeth, I replied, "Not today, asshole."

My rage fueled my strikes, each one driven by years of pent-up anger and determination to protect those I loved. Kyle backed off momentarily, catching his breath.

"You're a fool if you think you can defeat me."

I advance relentlessly. "You almost took everything from me. I won't let you disappear again!"

Kyle swung wildly, desperation creeping into his movements as I countered with precision and strength. He lunged forward in a last-ditch effort.

"Die, Jack!"

I sidestepped, seizing the opportunity. With a swift motion, I disarmed Kyle, sending the bat clattering to the ground. I towered over him, my voice was low and menacing. "It's over."

"Never!" Kyle quickly threw dirt in my eyes. Blinded, I tried to get the dirt out. He tackled me to the ground, knocking the air from my lungs. Kyle grabbed an axe nearby and stood over me, his voice shaking with fury. "Now it's over."

The ground trembled violently. The cave shook as the roar of a T-Rex echoed through the chamber. Kyle turned his attention toward the noise, his eyes widening in disbelief.

"No..." The T-Rex burst into view at the cave entrance, its massive jaws snapping shut around Kyle in a swift, brutal motion. Kyle screamed in terror, his voice drowned out by the creature's roar. Blood sprayed across the cavern walls as the T-Rex thrashed its head, crushing Kyle's body in its powerful jaws before tossing him aside like a rag doll.

I got on my feet as the crazed dinosaur set its sights and teeth on me. It stood between me and the hole in the wall. The T-Rex lunged at me, I rolled and grabbed the ax. The T-Rex attacks again. I sidestepped and swung the ax as hard as I could into the side of its jaw. I ran as fast as I could to get outside. Emerging from the cave, my heart raced as I stood on the rugged mountainside, the ground trembling beneath me as the colossal predator pursued me.

"I can't let that thing catch me..."

The path ahead wound steeply upward, flanked by jagged rocks and dense foliage. My muscles ached with exhaustion, but fear pushed me onward as the T-Rex's thunderous footsteps echoed behind me. The sound of crashing waves grew louder as I ascended. The path narrowed, leaving me with little room to maneuver.

As I rounded a sharp bend, the path ends at a sheer drop-off. I skidded to a halt, teetering on the edge as the vast expanse of ocean.

"I need to find higher ground..."

The T-Rex's enraged roar shook the ground, its massive form looming ever closer. I spotted a narrow ledge along the cliff face, offering a precarious route away from the predator's reach. With adrenaline coursing through my veins, I stepped onto the narrow ledge, each movement calculated to maintain balance. The wind gusted, threatening to knock me off course and into the churning sea below.

Rocks dislodged from the cliff face as the T-Rex charged forward, its primal instincts driving it onward. My heart pounded, every nerve on edge as I navigated the treacherous path. Gritting my teeth, I had to stay focused.

"Just a little farther..."

The ledge twisted and turned, testing my agility and nerve. I pressed forward, determination fueling every step as I evaded the T-Rex's snapping jaws by mere inches. As I neared the end of the ledge, I faced a daunting gap leading to a small outcrop of rock beyond the T-Rex's reach. With a burst of adrenaline, I leaped across the divide, landing with a stumble but keeping my footing.

I scrambled to safety, my heart pounding with relief as the T-Rex roared in frustration below, unable to follow me onto the narrow outcrop. Breathing heavily, I caught my breath.

"Made it..."

I took a moment to gather myself, knowing I'd bought precious time but that the danger wasn't over yet. I looked out over the expansive ocean; the horizon stretched infinitely before me. In the distance, I spotted a rugged coastline dotted with small islands and crashing waves.

The path back to the cave entrance lay ahead, winding steeply through the rocky mountainside. I knew I had to find my way back quickly, before the T-Rex did and before any harm came to my loved ones. With renewed determination, I retraced my steps along the treacherous path. Every muscle in my body ached from exhaustion, but fear for Diane and Anne fueled my urgency.

As I navigated the rugged terrain, debris from the T-Rex's earlier rampage littered the path, a stark reminder of the creature's destructive power. The distant sounds of the T-Rex's movements grow louder, its thunderous footsteps reverberating through the canyon. I quickened my pace, my mind focused on reaching the cave entrance before it was too late.

Finally, I rounded the last bend and spotted the cave entrance ahead. The air inside was thick with dust and echoes of past chaos.

I moved cautiously, scanning my surroundings for any sign of the T-Rex or my loved ones. The cave was eerily quiet now, a stark contrast to the earlier chaos. Suddenly, I heard faint voices echoing from deep within the cave. Recognizing Anne's urgent tone, I picked up my pace, following the sound of their voices.

As I rounded a corner, I spotted Anne and Diane huddled together in a small alcove, safe but visibly shaken. Relief flooded me as I rushed to their side. I knelt beside them, my voice filled with relief.

"Diane, Anne, are you okay?"

Anne nodded, tears in her eyes. "Jack, we thought..."

Diane winced in pain. "Kyle... he..."

She clutched her injured leg as I hugged her. I helped Diane to her feet, my mind raced with a plan to protect them from the T-Rex's wrath. My voice was firm as I scanned the cave entrance.

"We have to get out of here. The T-Rex is still out there, and it's not safe."

Together, we carefully make our way toward the cave entrance, navigating the debris and remnants of our earlier ordeal. As we reached the mouth of the cave, the ground shook once more. The T-Rex's colossal form looms in the distance, its primal roars echoing through the canyon. My eyes narrowed again, but my determination blazes.

"We can't let it terrorize this place any longer. I'll lure it away while you two find a way to safety."

Anne grabbed my arm, her voice urgent. "Jack, no! It's too dangerous!"

Despite her injured leg, Diane hands me a makeshift bomb hastily assembled from supplies found within the cave. Her voice was urgent.

"Jack, take this. It's not much, but it might buy you some time. It's crude but an effective device, rigged with a timer and enough explosives to cause significant distraction and damage."

"What? How?..." I had so many questions.

"Just take it, dammit!" She shoved it in my chest. With no choice, I nod gratefully.

"I'll make sure this counts." I inspected the bomb quickly, ensuring it was secure and ready for use. I knew its potential to divert the T-Rex's attention away from Diane and Anne, giving them a chance to escape. With a deep breath, I turned to face the T-Rex, its massive form closing in with each thunderous step. I gripped the bomb tightly, adrenaline coursing through his veins. "Get out of here. I'll buy you time," I said to Diane and Anne.

"Jack, please be careful..." Diane said with worry. I stepped closer to her, and we kissed quickly. I then smiled reassuringly.

"I'll see you both soon. Now go." Diane and Anne exchanged worried glances. They scrambled away from the cave entrance, navigating the rocky terrain with Diane's injured leg, slowing their progress.

I stumbled through the dark, humid cave, the air thick with the scent of damp earth and moss. The heavy, thunderous footsteps of the Tyrannosaurus Rex echoed off the jagged walls. Each roar from the beast reverberated through the cavern, shaking loose stones from the ceiling and making the ground tremble beneath my feet. I tightened my grip on the makeshift bomb I had hastily crafted from scavenged materials. It was a crude device, but it was my only hope.

The narrow passageways twisted and turned, the flickering light from my torch casting eerie shadows. My breath came in ragged gasps as I rounded a corner and found myself in a vast, open chamber. The T-Rex's massive silhouette blocked the only exit, its eyes glinting with primal fury. Saliva dripped from its gaping jaws as it let out a deafening roar, shaking the very foundation of the cave.

I scanned the chamber quickly, my mind racing. Stalagmites and stalactites dotted the cavern, offering potential cover. I knew I had to time this perfectly. As the T-Rex lowered its head and charged, I sprinted to the side, narrowly avoiding the creature's massive foot as it slammed down where I had stood moments before. Rolling to my feet, I grabbed a loose rock from the ground. With all my strength, I hurled the rock at the cavern wall opposite the beast.

The sound echoed through the chamber, momentarily distracting the T-Rex. The beast turned its head toward the noise, giving me the precious seconds I needed. I dashed behind a cluster of stalagmites, pressing my back against the cool, damp stone. The bomb felt heavy and ominous in my hands. I had one shot, and it had to count.

The T-Rex's nostrils flared as it caught my scent again. It swung its massive head around, its eyes locking on me. My heart skipped a beat. I activated the timer on the bomb, my fingers trembling as I counted down from five. The beast roared and charged again, its jaws wide open, rows of razor-sharp teeth gleaming in the dim light.

"Three... two... one," I whispered under my breath.

At the last possible second, I threw the bomb with all my strength, aiming for the open maw of the beast. The T-Rex instinctively snapped at the projectile, swallowing it whole. I dove for cover behind a large boulder, covering my head with my arms.

The explosion was deafening. Flames and shrapnel erupted from the T-Rex's throat, and the beast let out a final, terrible roar of pain and fury before collapsing to the ground. The force of the blast shook the cavern, and I felt the ground heaving beneath me. Chunks of rock rained down from the ceiling, and the walls began to crack and crumble.

There was no time to celebrate. The explosion had destabilized the entire cave. I scrambled to my feet, adrenaline coursing through my veins. I sprinted toward the exit, my lungs burning with exertion. Dust and debris filled the air, making it hard to see and breathe. The light from the cave entrance was a beacon of hope in the chaos, guiding me forward.

As I ran, I dodged falling rocks and leaped over fissures, opening up in the ground. A massive boulder crashed down behind me, barely missing me by inches. My legs ached, but I pushed on, driven by sheer willpower. I could see the mouth of the cave getting closer, the light growing brighter.

With one final, desperate burst of energy, I dove through the cave entrance just as the entire structure behind me collapsed. I tumbled onto the ground outside, rolling to a stop in the dirt. I lay there, gasping for breath, my body trembling with exhaustion and relief. The roar of the collapsing cave slowly faded, replaced by the sound of the wind rustling through the trees.

Sitting up, I dusted myself off and looked back at the sealed entrance. I did it. I defeated the T-Rex and survived. The makeshift bomb had worked, and I had escaped the cave's collapse by a hair's breadth. Breathing heavily, relief washing over me.

"It's over..." I stand, adrenaline still coursing through his veins. I instinctively survey the scene.

"It's finally over..." The air was thick with smoke and the scent of charred earth. Debris from the explosion littered the landscape, testament to the fierce battle that unfolded moments ago. Diane and Anne emerged cautiously from behind Anne's car. As they approached me, they wore expressions of relief and gratitude. Diane limped slightly; her voice filled with emotion.

"Jack, you did it... You saved us." Hugging me tightly, tears in her eyes.

"I thought I lost you..." I embraced Diane. Despite our injuries and exhaustion, we found solace in their reunion. Diane leaned on me for support. I placed a hand on her shoulder. My concern is apparent.

"Are you okay?" Diane managed to make a weary smile.

"Yes, thankfully." As we stood together, the distant sounds of approaching sirens echo through the canyon. My heart sank at the realization that their ordeal wasn't over yet.

"We need to get out of here. The police are coming." Anne's voice was urgent as she started her car. Diane and I both got in the back seat. Anne drove off as the police rushed past us. Catching her breath, Diane's voice was determined.

Diane leaned into my side, her trust in me clear as she wrapped her arms around me. "I never want to let you go."

I turned my face to her with a gentle smile. My hand reached for hers, fingers intertwining once more in a silent promise of solidarity and affection.

"You won't have to. I'm here."

We shared a brief, tender kiss in the backseat, our bond deepened by the trials we'd overcome together. The rising sun cast a warm glow over the landscape, a peaceful contrast to the chaos we'd endured.

CHAPTER 29

Two and a half weeks later, the sun shone softly through the stained-glass windows of the church, casting a warm glow over us. Today was the day we would get married. Unsure of our future and when that bitch, the Queen, would return, we decided to fast-track things. That way, if we ended up dead, we'd at least die as husband and wife.

I stood nervously at the altar, my heart pounding in my chest. The only witnesses to our union were Diane's twin sister, Anne, the priest, and the two of us. The absence of friends and family was a stark reminder of all we had lost, but we had each other, and that was enough to keep us going.

The music began—a soft, melodious tune that filled the church with a sense of hope. Diane appeared at the end of the aisle, her twin sister walking beside her. Diane's gown, an intricate design of lace and silk, glimmered softly in the light. She looked like a vision out of a dream, her face a mixture of joy and nerves.

As Diane approached, I could see the tears forming in her eyes, reflecting the weight of our past and the hopeful future we were about to embrace. Anne gave her a reassuring squeeze before stepping aside, leaving Diane to walk the final steps alone. Our eyes met, and in that moment, all the hardships and fears of the past seemed to dissolve.

I reached out to take Diane's hands, feeling the warmth and strength in her grip. "You look absolutely perfect," I whispered, my voice choked with emotion.

Diane's smile widened, and she squeezed my hands. "And you," she said, her voice trembling with happiness, "look like my forever."

The priest began the ceremony, speaking about the sanctity of marriage and the journey we were embarking on together. As we exchanged our vows, the weight of our promises felt like a sacred bond.

"I vow to stand by you in every trial and triumph, to love you fiercely and unconditionally," I said, my voice steady despite the lump in my throat.

"And I vow to cherish every moment with you, to love you beyond all measure, and to face whatever comes our way," Diane responded, her eyes shining with sincerity.

As the priest asked if anyone had any objections, the air in the church suddenly grew heavy, charged with an eerie stillness that made the hair on the back of my neck stand up. Just as he was about to pronounce us husband and wife, the wind outside howled fiercely, rattling the windows.

Then, without warning, a deafening roar erupted, shaking the church violently. The walls trembled as if they were being torn apart by an invisible hand.

"What the hell is that?" Diane shouted, gripping my arm as the floor beneath us vibrated with terrifying force.

A thunderous crash echoed above us, and suddenly, the roof tore away with a horrifying screech. A tornado—a massive, swirling funnel—ripped through the sky, descending upon the church with unrelenting fury.

"Get down!" I yelled, pulling Diane to the floor as debris rained down around us. Anne screamed as the wind howled like a beast, sucking the air from the room.

The stained-glass windows exploded, sending sharp shards flying through the air. The tornado's sheer force ripped pews from the floor and tore the altar to pieces, the wind pulling us toward its deadly vortex.

"Anne!" Diane cried, reaching out as her sister was nearly swept away by the force of the storm. I grabbed onto Diane's hand with all my strength, trying to hold us both steadily as the church crumbled around us.

But it was no use.

The tornado's pull grew stronger, lifting us off the ground. I felt Diane's hand slip from mine as we were yanked into the air, spinning helplessly. The last thing I saw before the darkness overtook me was Diane and Anne being swept into swirling chaos.

When I opened my eyes, everything was blindingly white. I blinked several times, trying to adjust to the brightness. The last thing I remembered was the tornado...the church being torn apart...and then nothing.

I sat up slowly, my body aching as if I'd been through a war. Diane lay beside me, unconscious but breathing. On her other side, Anne stirred, groaning as she rubbed her head.

We were no longer in the church—or anywhere familiar, for that matter. The room was stark white, its surfaces gleaming and sterile, as if we had been dropped into some kind of surreal, endless void. No doors. No windows. Just white everywhere.

"Where...where are we?" Diane's voice was groggy as she sat up, glancing around in confusion.

"I don't know," I muttered, my heart racing as I scanned the room for any sign of an exit or explanation. But there was nothing.

Anne groaned again, sitting up and staring at the walls. "What...what happened?"

I shook my head. "The tornado...it came out of nowhere. It tore the church apart. And now we're...here."

Diane reached for my hand, her grip tight with fear. "This has to be her doing," she whispered, her eyes wide. "The Queen."

I nodded, my stomach twisting with dread. We had thought we could escape her reach, even if just for a moment, but it seemed the Queen wasn't done with us yet.

We were trapped once again, in some strange, otherworldly place—and there was no telling what would happen next.

The TV on the wall flickered to life, and the familiar face of the Queen appeared. An aura of sinister delight overshadowed her unsettlingly attractive presence. Her eyes sparkled with a cruel amusement that made my skin crawl.

"Ah, how delightful to see you again," the Queen said, her voice dripping with mock sweetness. "I must apologize for the interruption. I hope you weren't too attached to that wedding ceremony. It was quite a dramatic end, wasn't it? The building collapsing, the priest...well, let's just say he didn't make it. But I must admit, the show was spectacular."

Diane's face turned from shock to fury. "You ruined our wedding! You killed the priest! How could you—"

The Queen cut her off with a twisted smile. "Oh, I've enjoyed every moment of the Jack and Diane show. Your attempts at normalcy, your fleeting happiness—such entertainment! But you can't live a normal life anymore. Not with what's coming next."

Her smile widened, her eyes gleaming with sadistic pleasure. "Congratulations on making it to the fifth Trial. Quite an accomplishment, considering the odds. Only the three of you remain."

Diane's face hardened into a mask of defiant anger. "What's next? What are you going to do to us now?"

The Queen's smile grew broader. "You'll be boarding a plane to the location where your next Trial will begin. I'm sure you'll find it... quite revealing. It's designed to test every ounce of your resolve."

Anne's eyes blazed with raw defiance, her voice trembling with barely contained fury. "You think this is just some kind of sick joke? We're not your puppets!"

"Oh, far from it," the Queen said with chilling calmness, savoring every word. "The fifth Trial will push you beyond anything you've ever imagined. I've pulled out all the stops to make sure it's unforgettable."

Anne's voice was a fierce snarl. "We're not letting you control us anymore. We're done with your twisted games!"

The Queen's gaze was unyielding, her tone dripping with malevolent satisfaction. "You may try to resist, but remember, the rules are set. Your defiance only makes the Trial more exhilarating for me."

Diane's voice cut through the tension, firm and raw with emotion. "What's the point of all this? What are you hoping to achieve?"

"The point," the Queen replied, her voice laced with derision, "is to see how far you're willing to go. To witness the ultimate test of will and survival. The grand spectacle of your desperation and endurance."

Anne's eyes were blazing with anger, her hands clenched into fists. "We're not afraid of you. We're not playing along with your sick fantasies."

The Queen's laughter rang out, cold and mocking, reverberating through the room. "Oh, I do enjoy a bit of resistance. It adds such a delightful twist to the Trials. The more you fight, the more entertaining this becomes."

As the screen went dark, a heavy silence descended. The weight of the Queen's taunting and the grim reality of our situation pressed down on us. Diane's eyes were wide with a mixture of fear and resolve, while Anne's expression was one of fierce determination.

I declared with a strained yet resolute voice, "We must maintain our focus." "We've faced horrors before, and we've survived. We can't give up now."

Diane nodded; her face etched with the intensity of her emotions. "We've come this far. We have to keep fighting. We can't let her win."

Anne's anger was palpable, but her unyielding determination matched it. "Let's show her that we're not just here for her amusement. We're here to fight, to survive, and to defeat her once and for all."

As we braced ourselves for the next phase of the Tournament, the gravity of the Queen's twisted game weighed heavily on us, but our resolve to escape and survive remained unshaken.

They herded us onto a massive passenger jet, and the sheer size of it seemed absurd given the small number of us. The plush interiors, the overabundance of seats, all felt like mocking excess.

"This doesn't make sense," I whispered to Diane as we scanned the plane. "Why such a big plane for just a few people?"

Diane squeezed my hand reassuringly, her eyes scanning the surroundings. "Whatever the reason, we need to stay alert. There's definitely something off about this."

As we were being ushered to our seats, the plane's engines roared to life, sending vibrations rattling through us. With a close watch, the henchmen, imposing and menacing, bound us to the chairs. The straps were tight, and the discomfort was immediate. Mocking our predicament, the plane's enormity was overwhelming. The Queen made her entrance, a vision of dark allure amidst the sterile luxury.

Her footsteps echoed down the aisle, and her presence was magnetic, drawing every eye to her. She wore a form-fitting outfit that accentuated her predatory grace. Her eyes sparkled with malevolent amusement as she approached us.

"Well, isn't this a charming setup?" she cooed, her voice smooth and taunting. She glanced at each of us, her gaze lingering a bit too long. "You must be thrilled to be here. How does it feel to be the center of my attention?"

Anne glared at her, her face contorted with a mix of anger and revulsion. "We're not interested in your games. Just let us go."

The Queen's smile widened, a hint of cruelty in her eyes. She leaned closer to Anne, her breath warm against her face. "Oh, but where's the fun in that? You see, I have a taste for drama, and you're all so delightful to watch."

She moved on to Diane, her touch almost sensual as she lightly brushed Diane's shoulder. "And you, dear. So brave and beautiful. Tell me, how does it feel to be so vulnerable?"

Diane flinched at the touch, her eyes darting away. "Stop it. Just stop."

The Queen's laughter was low and chilling. She then turned to me, her gaze lingering on my face with a predatory interest. "And you, Jack. How does it feel to be caught in my web? Do you find my company... enticing?"

Her eyes roamed over me, and she leaned in closer, her lips brushing my ear as she whispered, "I do enjoy seeing how each of you reacts under pressure. It's such an... intimate experience."

She stepped back, her gaze sweeping over all three of us. Her eyes sparkled with sadistic pleasure as she took in our discomfort. "You know, I've always found that fear and desire are quite close companions. Don't you agree?"

Anne's face was flushed with anger. "You think this is a game? We're not your toys!"

The Queen's expression was one of mock sympathy, her voice dripping with condescension. "Oh, but of course it's a game. And you're all such eager players. I simply can't resist."

She strutted down the aisle, her movements calculated and graceful. As she walked past Diane again, she leaned in, her hand trailing lightly across Diane's arm. "I can't wait to see how you all fare in the next round. Will you succumb to your fears? Or will you find a way to survive?"

Her words were laced with a perverse pleasure, each touch and glance meant to unsettle us further. The Queen's flirtation was anything but innocent; it was a deliberate act of psychological torment designed to unnerve us.

The Queen made herself comfortable in the seat next to Anne, her presence oppressive. She settled in with a calculated grace; her gaze never leaving Anne's face. Anne's discomfort was palpable; she shifted uneasily in her seat, trying to avoid the Queen's penetrating stare.

The Queen's voice was smooth and seductive as she spoke, her words dripping with dark amusement. "Isn't this just a delightful setup? I must say, I do enjoy watching the three of you squirm."

Anne tried to ignore her, focusing on the floor or the window, but the Queen's proximity made that impossible. "You must feel so special, Anne. You're the focal point of my attention right now."

Anne's jaw clenched; her face flushed with frustration. "Just leave me alone."

The Queen leaned closer, her voice a low purr. "Oh, come now. We're all friends here. I simply want to get to know you better. After all, we're in this together for the time being."

Anne flinched as the Queen's hand brushed against her arm, the touch both intimate and invasive. "You know," the Queen continued, her tone turning more conspiratorial, "There's something fascinating about watching people like you struggle. It's a dance of sorts, don't you think?"

Anne was very uncomfortable as she shifted in her seat, trying to create some distance. "I'm not dancing for you," she snapped.

The Queen's smile widened, a glint of cruel satisfaction in her eyes. "Oh, but you are. Whether you realize it or not, you're part of my performance. And you're doing so well."

She turned her attention to Diane and me, her gaze lingering with unsettling interest. "And you two. Such a lovely couple. Tell me, how do you feel about being so close to each other, yet so far from safety?"

I met her gaze with as much defiance as I could muster. "We're not interested in your games."

The Queen's laughter was a soft, mocking sound. "Ah, but you are. Whether you like it or not, you're all part of this grand spectacle." She continued to chatter, her voice a constant drone of unsettling commentary.

The Queen's voice took on a darker, more ominous tone as she turned her attention back to Diane and me. The plane's interior seemed to grow colder, the tension mounting with every word she spoke.

"Diane," she said, her voice silky and threatening, "I must give you a little warning. In this final round of the tournament, there can be only one winner. One survivor. One person who will walk away from this ordeal."

Diane's eyes widened in alarm, her grip tightening on my hand. "What are you saying?"

The Queen's gaze shifted to me, her smile widening. "If you and Jack manage to survive until the end, you'll be faced with a rather... unpleasant choice. You'll have to fight each other to the death. Only one of you will be left standing."

Diane's face went pale, her breathing quickening. "No... that's not possible."

The Queen's eyes gleamed with malevolent satisfaction. "Oh, but it is. It's the ultimate test of survival. You see, the drama of it all is simply irresistible."

Her attention then shifted to Anne, who had been trying to avoid the Queen's gaze. The Queen leaned in close, her hand brushing Anne's shoulder with an unsettling intimacy. "And Anne, my dear, you're not exempt from this little rule. If it comes down to it, you too will be part of this grim spectacle."

The Queen leaned in even more, her other hand slowly drifting across the back of Anne's seat. The movement was subtle, but unmistakable. Anne tensed as the Queen's fingers slowly, unsettlingly, slid down to rest on Anne's chest. Anne's eyes widened in horror, her body stiffening in reaction. "Stop it," she said, her voice cracking with a mixture of fear and anger.

The Queen's smile only widened. "Oh, but I do enjoy seeing you squirm. If Diane and Jack are forced to confront each other, you'll have to face the same harsh reality. You see, there's no escaping this."

Anne glared at her, her voice trembling with anger. "You're insane."

The Queen's laugh was a cruel, tinkling sound. "Perhaps. But it's all part of the fun. The true challenge lies in how you all handle this reality."

The Queen's smile was sickly sweet as she leaned closer, her hand lingering with a deliberate, invasive touch.

"Oh, Anne, you're such a fascinating creature," she purred, her voice dripping with mockery. "I'm merely appreciating the finer details."

Anne's face flushed with a mix of anger and humiliation. She tried to push the Queen's hand away, but the Queen's grip was insistent.

"Get your hands off me!" Anne shouted, her voice rising in desperation.

The Queen's gaze remained fixed on Anne, her eyes dancing with cruel delight.

"Such fire," she said, her tone a blend of amusement and menace. "It only makes this game more interesting."

Diane and I exchanged helpless glances, our concern for Anne palpable. The Queen's behavior was a stark reminder of the twisted nature of the tournament and the extent to which she would go to exert her control and instill fear.

The Queen's smile only widened. "Oh, but I do enjoy seeing you squirm." finally withdrawing, she continued to watch Anne with a predatory glint in her eyes. Anne's chest heaved with shallow breaths, her anger barely contained.

The plane continued its journey, the oppressive atmosphere inside growing heavier with each passing moment. Diane and I exchanged worried glances, our minds racing with the implications of the Queen's twisted revelations. The fear of what lay ahead hung heavily over us, compounded by the Queen's cruel game and her relentless, invasive presence

CHAPTER 30

Hours dragged on as she maintained her relentless stream of conversation, her words a mix of taunts, dark humor, and cruel observations. The plane's interior seemed to close in around us, the Queen's voice echoing in our ears as we waited for whatever lay ahead.

As the plane began its descent, the captain's voice crackled over the intercom, announcing their imminent arrival. The sound momentarily distracted the Queen, who looked away, her attention diverted by the flight announcement.

Anne seized the opportunity. Her eyes, still burning with anger and resolve, darted around the cabin. With a swift movement, she pulled out a concealed blade she'd hidden. In one fluid motion, she sliced through the ropes binding her to the seat. Her training and quick reflexes took over as she sprang into action.

Anne leaped from her seat, her body a blur of motion. With precision honed by countless hours of practice, she executed a flawless jiu-jitsu maneuver, disarming the henchman who had been keeping watch. He barely had time to react before she had him on the ground, immobilized and gasping for breath.

The second henchman, surprised by Anne's sudden assault, fumbled with his weapon. Anne moved like a force of nature, her movements calculated and swift. She took him down with a well-placed kick to the chest, sending him crashing into the narrow aisle.

The plane's confined space worked in Anne's favor as she used the seats and narrow aisles for cover and leverage. Her training allowed her to incapacitate the remaining guards with rapid, effective strikes. Within moments, the once-imposing security team lay scattered and subdued.

Diane and I watched in astonished relief as Anne cleared the area. Her determination and skill had transformed our desperate situation into a glimmer of hope. The Queen, who had been momentarily distracted by the commotion, snapped her attention back, her face contorted in fury.

"What are you doing?" the Queen shrieked, her voice a blend of outrage and disbelief. "You're ruining everything!"

Anne, breathless but resolute, shot a defiant look at the Queen. "I'm taking back control," she declared, her voice steady despite the chaos. "We're not playing your game any longer."

The Queen's expression twisted into a devilish smile. "I knew there was a reason I liked you," she purred, clearly enjoying the spectacle.

At that moment, more henchmen emerged from hidden compartments, surrounding Anne and overwhelming her with their sheer numbers. More henchmen emerged from hidden compartments, surrounding Anne and overwhelming her with their sheer numbers, despite her formidable skills, making the situation grow increasingly dire. As the plane lurched, her attackers gained the upper hand. Anne was punched, kicked, and stabbed multiple times, her fight becoming increasingly desperate.

Amid the chaos, Diane had spotted the blade kicked toward her during the initial scuffle. With quick reflexes, she grabbed it and darted into the fray. The Queen's men were too busy subduing Anne to noticed Diane's approach. Anne, fighting valiantly, had knocked the gun from one of the henchmen's hands, but the third man brandished a firearm, aiming directly at her.

Seeing an opportunity, Anne wrestled the gun away and, with a swift, determined motion, aimed it at the Queen. The Queen's eyes widened with sudden fear as she swiftly ducked, narrowly avoiding the bullet. The shot instead struck the captain, who was seated behind her, causing the plane to immediately nose-dive.

The sudden jerk of the plane threw everyone off balance. With Anne temporarily stunned by the impact, the remaining henchmen overpowered her.

As the plane continued its violent descent, the chaos reached a fever pitch. The sheer number of henchmen increasingly overwhelmed Anne as she fiercely fought, still reeling from the previous attacks. During her struggle, one attacker broke through her defenses. He lunged forward with a knife, and before we could react, the blade sank deeply into Anne's stomach.

Anne's eyes widened in shock and pain as she staggered back, clutching her wound. Her breath came in ragged gasps, and blood seeped through her fingers as she tried to stem the flow. The sight of her suffering fueled our urgency.

Diane and I pushed through the remaining henchmen, our desperation turning into raw determination. Diane's face was a mask of fear and fury as she fought to reach Anne, her blade flashing with lethal precision. I aimed for the attackers closest to Anne, trying to keep them at bay.

The henchmen, now more focused on us, made it difficult to get to Anne. Despite our efforts, she was in a precarious state, and the fight seemed to drag on interminably. Anne, her face pale and sweat-drenched, struggled to stay on her feet. Her body swayed, weakened by the loss of blood.

"Anne, hold on!" Diane shouted; her voice choked with emotion as she finally reached her sister. She kneeled beside her, trying to help as best as she could amidst the chaos. "We're going to get you out of this!"

Anne's eyes glimmered with pain, but she managed a faint, determined nod. "Just… keep fighting," she whispered, her voice barely audible over the roar of the plane's engines.

With renewed resolve, Diane and I pressed on, our fight becoming more frantic. We pushed back the remaining henchmen, creating a small, chaotic path toward Anne. As I fought off the last of the attackers, the Queen's cruel laughter echoed through the cabin, her delight clear even amid the chaos. The worsening turbulence abruptly interrupted her, gloating as the plane continued its perilous descent.

Anne, barely conscious but still fighting, looked at us with eyes filled with gratitude and pain. There was a profound connection between the sisters, a silent communication that suggested they knew something no one else did. Diane, staring deeply into Anne's eyes, hugged her close, her tears flowing uncontrollably.

I realized at that moment—Anne would not make it. The realization hit me like a sledgehammer, and the laugh surrounding us felt like a dark, mocking specter. As I ran over to Anne, I put my arm around her and Diane, who clung to her sister with desperate, tearful resolve.

The henchmen, relentless and merciless, showed no signs of letting up. They pressed forward, their cold eyes fixed on us as they continued their assault. Their numbers seemed endless, their attacks unyielding.

The roar of the plane and the thud of fists and feet against flesh muffled Diane's sobs. She held Anne tightly, whispering broken promises of safety and love. Anne's breathing grew shallower, her strength waning.

"Anne, stay with us," Diane pleaded, her voice breaking. "We're going to get through this. I won't let you go."

Anne's weak hand reached up, brushing against Diane's cheek as if trying to offer comfort despite her own suffering. Her eyes were glassy, the pain clear but also a resigned acceptance.

The sound of more men approaching snapped me back to the grim reality. I fought with renewed desperation, my blows landing with a ferocity born from the need to protect Diane and Anne. Despite my efforts, it felt like a losing battle.

The turbulence grew worse, and the plane's shaking made every movement more difficult. The Queen's laughter continued to pierce through the chaos, a haunting reminder of the twisted game we were trapped in.

"Hang on, Anne!" I shouted over the cacophony, trying to keep my voice steady despite the fear and frustration clawing at me. "We're almost there. We'll get through this!"

But as I looked at Anne's pale, bloodied face, the harsh truth sank deeper in. The fight was far from over, and we were facing stacked odds. The plane continued its descent, the roar of engines and the Queen's malevolent laughter blending into a nightmarish symphony as we fought desperately against the encroaching darkness.

Diane and I caught a brief reprieve. As Diane and I rushed toward the exit, the chaos in the plane seemed to blur around us. The fight had left us exhausted and desperate, but the sight of the parachutes gave us a glimmer of hope. We grabbed one each, our hands shaking with the intensity of our fear.

"Jack, we have to get out now!" Diane's voice was a frantic whisper, her eyes darting around, desperate for a way out.

Before we could reach the exit, the Queen's imposing figure blocked our path. "Not so fast," she said with a cruel smirk. Her superhuman speed and strength made every attempt to get past her futile. The Queen's presence was a wall of invincibility, mocking our efforts.

A sudden, almost surreal calm descended when the Queen's laughter was abruptly silenced. Anne, barely clinging to life, smiles in defiance. Her blade, grimy and bloodied, was driven deep into the Queen's neck. The Queen gasped in shock; her smirk fading as Anne's hand grasped her head and smashed it against the wall.

Diane's eyes went wide, a mixture of horror and relief flooding her features. She dropped to her knees beside her sister, who lay struggling on the floor, a dark pool spreading beneath her.

"Anne!" Diane cried out, her voice cracking with raw, unrestrained pain. "Please, you have to come with us!"

Anne's gaze, although weak, displayed fierce determination. Her voice was barely a whisper, but each word was heavy with meaning. "No, Diane… I'm not going to make it. This is it for me."

Diane's sobs became more intense, her hands gripping her sister's shoulders with desperate strength. "No, Anne! You can't leave me! You have to come with us! We're family!"

I placed a steadying hand on Diane's shoulder, trying to pull her back. "Diane, she's right. She won't survive this. We have to go now, or we'll all be lost."

Anne's eyes shifted to me, a fleeting smile touching her lips despite the pain. "Besides," she said with a faint chuckle, "I know Jack never chose the better-looking twin." Her voice was laced with bittersweet nostalgia. In that moment, it was a poignant reminder of their fractured but unbreakable bond.

The tearful laughter shared between the three of us was short-lived. Anne coughed violently, her strength faltering. "Go!" she shouted through her gasps, her eyes locked on Diane's with a mix of love and sorrow. "Now!"

Diane's face crumpled; her body wracked with uncontrollable sobs. "Anne, please!" she cried out, clinging to her sister in a desperate grip. "I can't… I can't lose you!"

The Queen, recovering from her wounds, rose, her rage clear. Anne, with her last ounce of strength, reached for a grenade hanging from a strap. Her movements were slow, but purposeful. "I've got this," she said, her voice steady despite the turmoil. "Go now! Don't look back!"

Diane and I exchanged one last heart-wrenching look before we turned and bolted for the exit. I could hear Diane's anguished cries and the sound of the Queen's enraged scream as we leaped out of the plane.

As we descended, the wind roaring around us; I glanced back once again. The plane erupted in a brilliant, fiery explosion, the intense heat and light casting a harsh glow on the wreckage. I looked at Anne, her hand gripping the grenade, her face a mask of resolute sacrifice. Her testament to her unyielding courage and love.

The roar of the explosion was deafening, and the plane's wreckage fell away into the distance. Diane's tears flowed freely, mixing with the wind as she clung to the parachute. The raw emotions of loss, desperation, and hope intertwined, leaving us both with the weight of Anne's sacrifice heavy on our hearts.

CHAPTER 31

As we plummeted toward the ground, the fiery wreckage of the plane exploded above us, sending shockwaves through the sky. Debris rained down like shrapnel from hell.

"Hold on!" I shouted to Diane, my voice nearly drowned out by the roar of the wind and the crackling inferno overhead.

We descended fast, but just as I thought we were clear, a sharp piece of debris sliced through the straps of my parachute. I felt the violent jolt as it tore away from my body. The next thing I knew, I was spinning wildly, tumbling uncontrollably toward the ground. Panic clawed at my chest.

"Jack!" Diane's scream reached my ears as she struggled with her own parachute, debris slicing through the fabric and pulling her off course.

Forced To Fight: Trials of the Chosen

I fought with everything I had, trying to regain control, but gravity had me in its grip. With a desperate lurch, I angled myself toward a patch of scorched earth below. The landing was hard—my body slammed into the ground with bone-rattling force, pain shooting through me as I rolled across the terrain. I gasped for air, trying to shake off the impact.

Diane hit the ground a few moments later, her parachute tangled but mostly intact. She landed with more control, though the rough descent had clearly taken its toll.

We both lay there for a moment, catching our breath, our bodies aching from the fall. The heat from the flaming debris still hung in the air, and the distant roar of the burning plane was deafening. The worst of it, however, was far from over.

Above us, the remains of the plane continued to fall apart in the sky, the twisted metal skeleton groaning as it finally lost the battle with gravity. With a monstrous crash, the burning hulk of the aircraft collided with the earth behind us. The explosion sent a fresh wave of fire and destruction surging outward, and we both shielded ourselves from the searing heat and flying wreckage.

Panting and shaking, Diane and I pushed ourselves to our feet, our hearts racing as we took in the wreckage. Twisted metal and flames filled the area, turning it into a graveyard of wreckage. We had barely survived the crash—but the worst was yet to come.

Out of the smoldering wreckage, a figure emerged. Unharmed, untouched by the destruction. The Queen. Her appearance was immaculate, as if the inferno and explosion had been nothing more than an inconvenience. Her clothes were pristine, her hair only slightly tousled, a chilling testament to her unearthly power.

"How is this possible?" I whispered, my voice trembling with disbelief and anger.

Diane's eyes were wide with shock, her breath coming in shallow gasps as the horror of our situation sank in.

The Queen's laughter rang out, sharp and mocking, cutting through the crackling flames like a blade. "Oh, I'm so pleased to see you're still alive," she said, her voice dripping with sadistic amusement. "But don't think for a second that this is the end."

Diane clenched her fists, a fierce anger flaring in her eyes. "Fuck!"

The Queen's smile only grew, her eyes gleaming with cruel, sinister satisfaction. "You've done well to survive this long. In fact, I'm so impressed that I've decided to skip the fifth Trial entirely and move straight to the final one."

The weight of her words slammed into us like a hammer. I felt my throat tighten as I tried to process what she was saying.

"What's the final trial?" I asked, my voice rising in a mix of fear and disbelief.

The Queen stepped forward, her cruel smile widening with pleasure. "The final Trial," she said slowly, savoring every word, "is a battle to the death. No more games. No more tricks. One of you will die, and only one of you will emerge alive."

Diane's face paled, her body trembling as the reality of it sank in. "No... there has to be another way. You can't force us to do this."

The Queen's smile widened, her eyes dancing with malicious glee. "Oh, but I can. You have until dawn to prepare."

She gestured toward a massive, foreboding building in the distance, its dark silhouette looming ominously against the burning sky. It stood like a dark sentinel over the desolate landscape, a harbinger of the final trial that awaited us.

"Be there by dawn," the Queen commanded, her voice ice-cold and unwavering. "Or face the consequences."

With a final, mocking glance, she turned and began walking away, her footsteps echoing ominously as she disappeared into the smoke. Her laughter lingered in the air, a cruel reminder of the nightmarish reality we were now forced to confront.

We stood there in the aftermath, the wreckage of the plane still smoldering behind us, the heat from the flames searing our skin. The Queen's words hung in the air like a death sentence. The final trial awaited, and there was no escaping it. One of us would have to die. And the countdown to dawn had already begun.

With a final, mocking glance, she turned and began walking away, her footsteps echoing ominously as she disappeared into the smoke. Her laughter lingered in the air, a cruel reminder of the nightmarish reality we were now forced to confront. The realization hit us with crushing weight: we had moved from one trial to the next, and now faced the ultimate confrontation.

The enormity of our predicament hit Diane and me with full force, leaving us standing in stunned silence. The building seemed to grow larger and more menacing as we stared at it, a looming reminder of the challenge that lay ahead.

"Jack," Diane said, her voice trembling with a mix of fear and resolve. "What are we going to do?"

Still staring at the massive building in the distance, Diane's resolve crumbled. She broke down, her sobs wracking her body as she sank into my arms. "Anne is gone. Why did this have to happen?" Her voice was a shattering blend of grief and frustration.

I held her tightly, feeling the weight of our shared loss. The wreckage from the crash cast eerie shadows, a grim reminder of the life we had hoped to build. We stumbled through the debris until we found a small cave hidden behind a curtain of dense foliage. The entrance was narrow but just wide enough for us to squeeze through.

Inside, the cave was cool and damp, its walls were slick with moisture. We quickly gathered fallen branches and dry leaves to start a fire. I struck a match, and soon the crackling flames provided a small, comforting glow in the darkness. As the fire crackled, we noticed an unusual draft coming from deep within the cave. Curious and desperate for any advantage, we followed the draft and discovered a hidden passageway. Ancient drawings, aliens, covered the walls. Strange, twisted figures danced across the stone, depicted in scenes of otherworldly battles and unimaginable creatures. The air grew colder as we ventured deeper, the alien symbols becoming more intricate and foreboding.

We uncovered an old scroll tucked away in a crevice, its surface brittle and yellowed with age. The alien script was barely legible, illuminated by the flickering firelight. As we deciphered the text, a chilling realization dawned on us.

"The Queen," I read aloud, my voice echoing off the cave walls, "is an alien from the planet Venus with supernatural powers. Every one hundred years, she comes to Earth and forces humans into a tournament designed only to create the ultimate champion for her army in a battle with another kingdom on Venus. Earth's atmosphere enhances humans in every way imaginable. The champion gains abilities to live longer and survive under the harsh conditions of Venus."

Diane's eyes widened as she listened, her breathing quickening with each word. "So, we're just pawns in her game to create the perfect soldier."

The scroll detailed the Queen's only known weakness. "It was used once about three thousand years ago," I continued, my voice trembling, "but with the primitive weapons humans had, the Queen didn't feel its full effects. It was enough to injure her and drive her away, at least for another 100 years. Since then, she has kept it well-guarded in her ship."

"What is it?" Diane asked, her voice a mix of hope and desperation.

"The weakness is an artifact made from raw materials deep within the Earth," I explained. "It's a mystery how it was found or made, but it was forged into a weapon that can not only injure her but can kill her if used correctly."

Diane's expression hardened with determination. "We have to find this artifact. It's our only chance."

I looked at her, a sudden thought crossing my mind. "The scroll said it's kept in her ship. What if that massive building we saw is actually her ship in disguise?"

Diane's eyes widened in realization. "It makes sense. It's the perfect cover. No one would suspect it."

"We'll need a plan," I said, looking at her with renewed resolve. "If we can find a way to get into that building and retrieve the artifact, we might stand a chance."

Diane nodded, her eyes blazing with determination. "Yes, babe." Once satisfied with their findings, they returned to the fire they had made.

Diane slumped against the cave wall, pulling her knees to her chest. "I never imagined it would end like this," she said, her voice heavy with despair. "We had so many plans..."

I sat beside her, wrapping an arm around her shoulders. "I know. It feels like everything we dreamed of is slipping away."

The fire's flickering light cast moving shadows on the cave walls, creating a small oasis of warmth in the cold, dark space. Diane leaned into me, her head resting on my shoulder as the warmth from the fire contrasted with the chill of the cave.

Diane's voice trembling, she said, "We had plans to get married." "We talked about a big garden... growing our own vegetables, flowers. We even picked out names for our future kids. And now…"

Her voice cracked, and I tightened my grip on her. "We were so close. We had everything planned. I remember picking out the dress you loved. We imagined our house, our family. It was all within reach."

Diane's eyes filled with tears as she looked at me. "Now we're being forced to fight each other. It's like everything we dreamed about is being ripped away from us. How can we go from planning a future to... this?"

"I don't know," I said, my voice breaking. "The thought of being forced to kill each other is unbearable. All our dreams... they feel so distant now."

Diane's face was a mix of hope and sorrow. "Promise me something, Jack. Promise me that we won't let this end define us. That somehow, we'll find a way to hold on to our dreams, even if it's just a memory."

"I promise," I said firmly, though my heart ached with the weight of the promise. "We may not have the chance to live those dreams now, but they're a part of us. We'll remember them, and they'll give us strength."

Diane nodded, her tears mixing with a faint smile. "We had so much more to experience together. I wanted to grow old with you, to see our children play in the garden. I wanted to share those moments with you."

"I wanted that too," I said, my voice thick with emotion. "We were so close. But even if we don't get to live out those dreams, we can carry them with us. They're a testament to what we had and what we could have been."

Diane's eyes were misty as she clung to the memory of our plans. "I just want one more moment to remember what we had. To hold on to those dreams, even if we can't see them come true."

I squeezed her hand, looking into her eyes. "We can do this, Diane. We have a chance. The scroll said the artifact could kill her. If we find it and use it right, we can end this. We can defeat her."

Diane's expression shifted from despair to determination. "You're right. We have to try. For us, for everyone who's suffered."

"We'll find that artifact," I said, my voice resolute. "We'll defeat the Queen. And then, we'll have our chance at the life we dreamed of."

Diane nodded, a fierce determination in her eyes. "Yes, Jack. We'll do this together."

We sat in the dim light of the fire, sharing our last night together in the warmth of our memories. The cave became a sanctuary where our dreams, no matter how distant, blazed against the darkness of our reality.

The firelight danced across our faces, and the warmth of the flames enveloped us as we drew closer. The cave's coolness contrasted sharply with the heat between us. Diane's hand traced gentle patterns on my chest, and I cupped her face, gazing deeply into her eyes.

"Let's make tonight count," Diane said softly, her voice a whisper against the crackling fire. "Let's hold onto each other, even if it's just for a little while."

I nodded, feeling the same intense need for connection. "Yes, let's hold onto this moment. No matter what happens, we'll always have this."

We moved closer, our lips meeting in a slow, tender kiss. The kiss deepened, becoming a passionate exchange that conveyed all our emotions—fear, love, and a desperate longing for normalcy. Diane's hands roamed over my back, pulling me closer, while I caressed her skin with gentle, reassuring strokes.

We moved slowly and desperately as we took off our clothes. We had gathered a bed of leaves and twigs to soften the rough cave floor, but it was our shared warmth that truly provided comfort.

We made love with a mixture of tenderness and urgency. Each touch, each caress, was a reaffirmation of our commitment to each other and the life we envisioned. The fire's glow illuminated our bodies, adding to the intimacy of the moment. Diane's moans were soft and filled with emotion, and I responded with equally fervent touches, making every moment count.

As we reached the peak of our intimacy, we held each other tightly, savoring the connection and the warmth of our shared embrace. The love we shared was palpable, each kiss and touch a testament to the depth of our feelings. We whispered sweet nothings, promising each other a future filled with hope and love, despite the uncertainty that lay ahead.

When we finally lay back, spent and satisfied, Diane rested her head on my chest. We were both silent for a while, simply enjoying the closeness and the warmth of each other's presence.

"I love you so much," Diane murmured, her voice a mix of exhaustion and adoration.

"I love you too," I replied, kissing her forehead. "No matter what happens tomorrow, know that you're my everything. We'll get through this, and we'll have the life we dreamed of."

We fell asleep wrapped in each other's arms, the fire slowly dying down as the night deepened. The cave, though cold and dark, felt like a sanctuary as long as we were together. Our final battle awaited us at dawn, but for now, we clung to each other, finding solace in our love amidst the chaos.

CHAPTER 32

The first light of dawn seeped into the cave, casting a pale, haunting glow on our faces. The warmth of the fire had long since dwindled, replaced by the chill of the morning air. Diane and I stirred from our uneasy sleep, our dreams troubled by the events of the previous night.

Diane sat up, her face etched with exhaustion and worry. She gazed at me with a mixture of fear and determination. "Jack, it's time," she said her voice heavy with the weight of our situation. "We need to get ready."

I nodded, stretching and shaking off the remnants of sleep. "Yeah, let's prepare ourselves. We know what's at stake."

We gathered our things, each movement deliberate and filled with purpose. The cave, which had offered us a brief sanctuary, now felt like a prison, the calm before the storm amplifying our anxiety. The reality of what's ahead was pressing heavily on our minds.

Diane took a deep breath as she looked at the entrance of the cave, where the morning light was filtering through the foliage. "I keep thinking about everything we've lost. Anne… our plans… our future. It's hard to believe we're here, facing this."

I reached out and took her hand, squeezing it gently. "I know. We had so many dreams, our home, our family. It feels like it's all slipping away. But we can't let that break us. We have to fight for everything we've ever wanted."

Diane's eyes glistened with unshed tears. "We've been through so much, and now we're being forced to fight each other. It's not what Anne would want. It's not right."

I pulled her into a tight embrace, my heart aching with the weight of her words. "We're not going to fight each other. We're going to face this together. We'll show her that she can't tear us apart. Our love and our dreams—they're worth fighting for."

Diane looked up at me, her expression a mix of hope and resolve. "You're right. We need to stick together, no matter what. We'll face the Queen together and end this."

We stood up, our movements resolute as we extinguished the remnants of the fire and gathered our few belongings. The cave, once a brief respite, was now a reminder of what we stood to lose if we failed.

As we stepped out of the cave into the early morning light, the imposing structure of the building in the distance loomed larger and more foreboding. The terrain was rugged, the air thick with tension. Every sound seemed amplified, every shadow a potential threat.

Diane reached out and took my hand, her grip firm and reassuring. "No matter what happens, remember we're soulmates. Nothing can tear us apart."

Her words, simple yet profound, bolstered my spirit. "I wouldn't want to face this with anyone else. We'll fight together, and if it comes to it, we'll die together."

We shared a brief, tender kiss, drawing strength from each other before we continued toward the building. The Queen was waiting, but we were ready. Our love, forged through pain and sacrifice, was our greatest weapon.

As we approached the entrance of the massive building, an eerie silence filled the air, only interrupted by the distant sounds of the wind and the crackling of burning debris. We took a deep breath, our hearts pounding with a mix of fear and determination.

"This is it," Diane said, her voice steady despite the danger ahead. "Let's end this."

We nodded in unison, bracing ourselves for whatever awaited us inside. Our love and resolve were our shields, and together, we would confront the Queen and her twisted games, no matter the cost.

We approached the massive building with a mix of trepidation and resolve. The entrance loomed before us, its imposing structure, a stark reminder of the battle that awaited inside. I took a deep breath and stepped through the threshold, Diane right behind me.

The alien nature of our surroundings immediately struck us. Emitting a creepy, glossy sheen, the walls and floor were sleek and wet-looking. The black surface seemed to absorb the light, creating an oppressive atmosphere. Intricate white carvings of alien language covered every inch of the walls and floors, their strange symbols twisting and turning in patterns that were both mesmerizing and unsettling.

"Look at this place," Diane whispered, her voice echoing slightly in the vast, empty hall. "It's like nothing I've ever seen."

I nodded, my eyes scanning the alien carvings. "This must be the ship. The scroll said it would be well-guarded. We need to be careful."

We moved forward cautiously, our footsteps echoing in the quiet. The air was thick with tension, every sound amplified in the strange, otherworldly environment. As we ventured deeper, the alien symbols seemed to pulse and shimmer, as if alive.

"We need to find the artifact," Diane said, her voice steady despite the fear in her eyes. "It's our only chance."

I squeezed her hand, offering a reassuring smile. "We'll find it, and defeat her. We have to."

We continued through the labyrinthine corridors, our resolve unshaken despite the overwhelming odds. The sleek, wet-looking walls seemed to close in around us, but we pressed on, determined to end the Queen's reign of terror once and for all.

As we moved through the dimly lit corridors, the alien symbols on the walls seemed to grow more intricate, their patterns shifting in the low light. The air grew colder, and an oppressive silence enveloped us, broken only by our footsteps and the occasional drip of moisture from the ceiling.

Diane and I exchanged anxious glances. "We're getting close," I said, my voice barely more than a whisper. "Stay alert."

A vast, cavernous space opened up from the corridor. The room was enormous, its high ceiling lost in shadow. The same slick, black material covered the floor, and the walls displayed glowing alien symbols that pulsed rhythmically, casting eerie shadows across the room.

At the far end of the chamber, a raised platform held an imposing throne. The throne itself was a dark, crystalline structure, adorned with more alien carvings that seemed to throb with a life of their own. Seated upon the throne was the Queen, her presence dominating the room. A flowing, dark robe adorned her, shimmering with an otherworldly light.

As we stepped into the room, the Queen looked up, her eyes gleaming with malevolent satisfaction. Her laughter echoed through the chamber, a chilling sound that reverberated off the walls.

"Oh, how delightful," she purred, her voice dripping with mockery. "You've made it just in time for the grand finale."

Diane and I stood at the entrance, the enormity of the room and the sight of the Queen on her throne, a heavy weight on our shoulders. My heart pounded as I took in the scene. The Queen's laughter continued, a harsh reminder of the battle that lay ahead.

"Are you ready to fight each other?" the Queen taunted, her voice dripping with malice. "Isn't that what you've been waiting for?"

She fixed her gaze on us, her eyes gleaming with cruel anticipation. Diane's face was a mixture of defiance and fear as she looked at me. I clenched my fists, trying to keep my voice steady despite the oppressive atmosphere.

"We're not here to fight each other," I said firmly. "We're here to end this madness. We've come for the artifact, and we're taking it from you."

The Queen's laughter grew louder, filling the chamber with an eerie echo. "How noble," she said, her tone dripping with contempt. "But do you truly believe you can defy my will? The artifact is well-guarded, and even if you find it, you'll have to defeat me first."

Diane and I exchanged one last determined glance. The Queen leaned back on her throne, her laughter reverberating through the chamber as the space seemed to grow darker and more foreboding.

As the Queen's laughter echoed through the cavernous chamber, her form descended from the throne with an eerie grace. Her robe flowed around her like dark liquid, its edges rippling with unsettling energy. The moment her feet touched the slick, black floor, Diane and I sprang into action.

We charged at her with synchronized precision, each of us moving with a fluidity that spoke of countless hours of training and trust. Diane launched the first attack, her fist arcing toward the Queen's head. The Queen's movements were a blur of speed; she ducked effortlessly, the air brushing against her face as Diane's punch missed by mere inches.

I followed up with a spinning kick aimed at the Queen's midsection. Again, the Queen's reflexes were uncanny. She sidestepped with a speed that defied logic, her laughter ringing out mockingly. Diane and I moved as one, our strikes a continuous stream of motion, each attack flowing seamlessly into the next.

We expertly timed every punch and kick, showcasing our years of training and shared battles. Yet the Queen's agility was extraordinary. She ducked under Diane's left hook, twisted away from my high kick, and even caught my roundhouse kick with a casual shift of her body. She executed each dodge with an almost preternatural grace, her movements flowing and unnervingly precise.

The chamber's ambient light cast shifting shadows across her form, making her seem like a wraith, dancing just out of reach. Diane and I grunted with exertion, our breaths coming in ragged gasps. The Queen's speed was taking its toll on us, our attacks growing increasingly desperate and our defenses more strained.

A powerful kick from the Queen connected with Diane's ribs, sending her sprawling across the floor. I rushed to Diane's side, only to be met with the Queen's swift counterattack. Her foot connected with my shoulder, and I was thrown backward, crashing into the cold, slick wall.

Diane struggled to her feet, her face set in a determined grimace. She and I exchanged a brief look, a silent agreement forming between us. We knew we had to change our strategy if we were to stand a chance.

The environment around us offered an array of possible weapons. Strange, protruding alien machinery adorned the walls, and debris from previous confrontations littered the floor. With a nod, Diane and I split up, moving to opposite sides of the chamber.

I grabbed a large, jagged piece of alien metal, its surface sharp and uneven. Diane collected a length of metallic tubing, its ends barbed and twisted. We approached the Queen from different angles, our weapons ready. The Queen watched us with a cold, calculating gaze, her confidence seemingly unshaken.

Diane struck first, her makeshift weapon swinging toward the Queen. The Queen ducked and rolled, but Diane's attack was a feint. As the Queen recovered, I launched my assault with the jagged metal, aiming for her midsection. The Queen barely deflected the attack with a sweeping motion of her arm, but the force of the blow drove her backward.

Seizing the opportunity, Diane and I coordinated our movements with practiced precision. Diane swung her metal tubing, catching the Queen off-guard with a solid hit to her side. The Queen staggered; her regal composure momentarily shattered.

I followed up with a rapid series of strikes, driving the Queen toward a large, protruding piece of alien machinery. Diane's attacks kept the Queen off-balance, her strikes landing with increasing force. The Queen struggled to keep up, her movements growing more erratic as the combined assault took its toll.

In a final, desperate maneuver, Diane and I moved in tandem. Diane threw her metallic tubing with a powerful overhand swing, forcing the Queen to duck and stumble. I followed with a swift, calculated strike from the jagged metal, slashing across the Queen's shoulder.

The Queen collapsed onto the floor; the pain clear in her face. Diane and I wasted no time. We grabbed the Queen and pinned her down, using the surrounding debris to bind her limbs and restrict her movement. The Queen's eyes blazed with fury as she struggled against our hold.

Just as we thought victory was within reach, the Queen's laughter returned, now tinged with a sinister edge. Her eyes glowed with an otherworldly light, and her body convulsed, a dark energy swirling around her.

"You think you've won?" the Queen hissed, her voice distorted and menacing. "This is only the beginning. I have more in store for you than you can imagine."

Diane and I tightened our grip, our sweat mingling with the slick, alien surface beneath us. The Queen's convulsions intensified, the dark energy enveloping her form, growing in strength and darkness.

At that moment, the cavern seemed to pulse with a malevolent force; the walls vibrating with the Queen's otherworldly power. We held our breath, preparing for whatever was to come next.

With a swift, brutal swipe of her hand, the Queen sent Diane and me crashing against the floor. The impact left us gasping for air, our bodies aching from the force. I struggled to get up, my vision blurring as I tried to focus on Diane. By the time I regained my footing, the Queen was already standing. Her wounds healed and her presence more menacing than ever.

Before I could react, a dark energy shot from the Queen's hand, striking Diane. She fell to one knee, her body trembling as she faced away from me. Panic surged through me as I rushed over to her. "Diane!" I called out, my voice trembling with concern.

I approached cautiously, my heart pounding in my chest. I placed a hand on her shoulder, feeling the chill of the alien energy. "Diane, are you okay?" I asked, my voice strained.

The Queen's laughter filled the chamber, a cruel and maniacal sound that echoed off the walls. As Diane slowly turned her head to look at me, I felt a wave of horror when I saw her eyes were now completely black, devoid of any humanity. Her voice came out distorted, metallic, and unsettlingly cold. "Diane is no longer here," she said, her tone laced with a demonic edge.

Without warning, Diane, now a vessel for the Queen's malevolent influence, struck me with a backhand. The force of the blow sent me flying, crashing into the slick floor with a bone-jarring thud. Pain exploded through my body, and I struggled to catch my breath.

When I stood, my heart sank as I realized the full scope of the Queen's plan. This wasn't just a battle; it was a twisted game designed to break me. The Queen had manipulated everything, turning Diane into a weapon against me. I felt a surge of anguish, anger, and helplessness all at once.

My gaze locked onto Diane, or the empty shell of her that had become a puppet for the Queen. "Diane, please don't do this," I pleaded, my voice breaking with emotion. "It's me, Jack!"

Diane's eyes, now pools of darkness, stared back at me with an eerie calmness. Her expression was distant, devoid of the warmth and love that had once been there. The Queen's laughter continued to ring in the background, a haunting reminder of the victory she had achieved.

CHAPTER 33

The chamber seemed to pulse with a malevolent energy as Diane, now a vessel for the Queen's twisted will, stood before me. Her once-familiar eyes were now black voids, and her expression was cold and devoid of any trace of the woman I loved. With inhuman force, she infused every movement, delivering each punch and kick with a brutal efficiency that left no room for hesitation.

I could barely keep up with her speed as she launched a series of powerful strikes. Her fists pummeled me, each blow reverberating through my body. The impact of her kicks was like being struck by a freight train, and every hit felt like it was stripping away a piece of my soul. Her eyes were lifeless, and Diane was no longer in control. The Queen's dark will had replaced the person I had known, loved, and fought alongside with a relentless force.

Each time Diane struck, I could feel my heart breaking a little more. My movements were hesitant, my punches held back. I tried to dodge her attacks, but her speed and strength made it almost impossible. Every time I evaded a blow, it was only to be met with another fierce assault. The pain was almost secondary to the emotional torment I was experiencing. Fighting Diane was like fighting a shadow of what she once was—a ghost of the love we shared.

I caught her fist in mid-air, trying to hold it there. "Diane, it's me," I pleaded, my voice cracking with desperation. "I'm not here to hurt you. I'm here to save you. Please, fight it. You have to fight it!"

Her eyes met mine briefly, but there was no recognition there—just the cold emptiness of the Queen's control. Diane twisted her arm free and struck me again, the force of the blow sending me reeling. I fell to my knees, gasping for breath, tears streaming down my face.

The chamber around us seemed to close in, the walls lined with alien symbols pulsating with an eerie glow. The sounds of our battle echoed through the space, a brutal symphony of combat and despair. My body endured battering and bruising, but the emotional pain overwhelmed me. Every hit Diane landed was a reminder of what was at stake, of how far we had fallen from the dreams we once shared.

Despite the ferocity of her attacks, I continued to hold back by striking light and aimed more at defense than offense. Each time I got a punch in, I was hoping somehow, somewhere inside her, Diane would recognize me and fight back against the Queen's control. I saw glimpses of her former self in the brief paus between her attacks, moments when her face softened, but they were fleeting and quickly replaced by the hard, unfeeling mask imposed by the Queen.

Diane's relentless assault continued, her attacks more savage and unrestrained. The pain was excruciating, both physically and emotionally. I wanted to fight back with everything I had, but the thought of truly hurting Diane was unbearable. My heart ached with each punch she threw, each kick she landed. The internal conflict was tearing me apart—my duty to fight and protect, pitted against my love and desire to save her from the Queen's grasp.

Finally, after what felt like an eternity of relentless combat, I saw an opportunity. The chamber had become a chaotic whirlwind of alien symbols and flashing lights, the very walls seeming to close in on us. As Diane charged at me with fierce, unrelenting fury, I knew I had to decide. My resolve hardened as I prepared for a final, desperate maneuver.

I waited until Diane's next attack was imminent. With a deep breath, I used her momentum against her, guiding her into a trap of our surroundings—a makeshift cage formed by the debris and broken structures littering the room. It was a last-ditch effort to subdue her without causing fatal harm.

The struggle was brutal and exhausting, but with every ounce of strength and willpower, I restrained Diane, pinning her down momentarily. The Queen's laughter echoed in the background, a cruel reminder of the battle we were fighting. Diane's form lay beneath me, her breathing harsh and labored.

"Diane," I said, my voice trembling with exhaustion and sorrow. "Please, if there was any part of you left in there, fight back. We can get through this. We can beat her."

Diane's body writhed beneath me, but the black voids of her eyes remained unchanging. It was as if the Queen's control had turned her into a mere puppet, devoid of any true agency. The emotional weight of the battle, the love and pain intertwined with each punch and kick, made every moment feel like a lifetime.

The Queen's sinister plan was unfolding perfectly, but I refused to give in. I knew that this battle wasn't just about physical strength; it was about reaching Diane's heart and breaking the Queen's hold. Even if it seemed like an impossible task, I was determined to fight for the woman I loved and to reclaim the future we had once dreamed of.

I turned to the Queen, my breath ragged and my body aching from the relentless battle. "That's it—I won!" I shouted, my voice filled with exhaustion and desperation. "Stop this madness now!"

The Queen's laughter echoed around us, cold and mocking. "Oh, is that so? Only I can decide when it's over, foolish human."

My heart sank as Diane, still under the Queen's malevolent influence, crashed through the remains of her temporary cage. She brushed herself off and resumed her fighting stance with a grim determination that mirrored the Queen's own. This battle was far from over, and the weight of my impending decision bore down on me.

I looked at Diane, my beautiful fiancée, now a puppet of the Queen's dark will. The thought of fighting her was almost unbearable, but I knew I had no choice. My heart ached with the realization that to save her, I would have to do something I never wanted to do. The love I had for Diane clashed with the necessity of defeating the Queen once and for all.

"Diane," I whispered, my voice breaking, "I'm so sorry."

With a heavy heart, I steeled myself. I couldn't afford to hesitate. I had to fight the Queen with every ounce of strength I had, not Diane. My mind was a tumult of anguish and resolve as I readied myself. The battle was no longer just about survival; it was about ending this nightmare and reclaiming the future we had lost.

I took a deep breath and entered a fighting stance; my movements deliberate and focused. The Queen watched with a sadistic smile, her eyes glinting with malevolent anticipation. Diane stood ready, her expression devoid of emotion, a cruel reflection of the Queen's control.

With a tear sliding down my cheek, I launched myself at the Queen. My attacks were fierce and unrelenting, fueled by a mixture of desperation and a burning desire to end this once and for all. I powered each strike with the anguish of knowing that Diane, my soulmate, was trapped within this nightmare. I could feel my strength waning, but the thought of Diane's suffering drove me forward.

The Queen was fast, her movements fluid and almost inhuman. She dodged and countered with terrifying speed, her laughter ringing through the chamber. Her twisted glee at our struggle only fueled my resolve. I had to keep fighting, had to keep pushing through the pain, because the alternative was unthinkable.

Diane's eyes, though black and empty, seemed to follow my movements. I fought with all my might, each punch and kick aimed with precision and force, determined to break the Queen's hold. The battle was a chaotic dance of power and desperation, the chamber a battleground of light and shadow.

Despite my best efforts, the Queen remained a formidable opponent. Her speed and agility were almost supernatural, and every time I landed a blow, she seemed to recover instantly, her malevolent grin never faltering. Diane continued to stand as the Queen's weapon, her every movement, a reflection of the dark will be controlling her.

I felt my strength waning, my body screaming in protest with every move. But even as my physical energy depleted, my resolve remained unshaken. I had to defeat the Queen, had to find a way to end this nightmare and free Diane from the darkness that had consumed her.

With a final, desperate surge of energy, I unleashed a series of rapid, powerful strikes, my movements fueled by a mixture of love and sorrow. I fought with the intensity of someone who had everything to lose, my every action driven by the hope that somehow this would end the Queen's reign of terror and bring Diane back to me.

As the battle raged on, my heart ached with every move, knowing that I was fighting not just for my survival but for the future I had dreamed of with Diane. The tears continued to fall as I fought with every ounce of strength I had left, determined to end this madness and reclaim the life we had once envisioned.

The chamber seemed to close in on us; the walls lined with alien symbols casting an eerie glow over our desperate struggle. Through the space, the Queen's laughter, cold and cruel, echoed, serving as a haunting reminder of the darkness we confronted. But even in the face of such overwhelming despair, I fought on, my love for Diane, driving me to push through the pain and fear.

This was the culmination of our struggle. I had to defeat the Queen, no matter the cost, and free Diane from the nightmare that had torn our world apart. With a final, anguished cry, I launched my most powerful attack, hoping against hope that it would be enough to end this torment and bring Diane back to me.

With all my remaining energy, I swung with all my might, aiming for the Queen's mocking face. My fist hurtled through the air, powered by every ounce of desperation and hope I had left. But with a swift and effortless motion, she caught my fist mid-swung. The cold, unyielding grip of her hand sent a shockwave of pain up my arm.

Before I could react, she twisted my arm with a sickening crunch. The excruciating pain shot through my body, and I screamed as my arm broke. In the next instant, she delivered a devastating roundhouse kick to my head. The force of the blow sent me flying, and I crashed to the ground, my vision blurring as I tried to hold on to consciousness.

The cold, hard floor felt unforgiving beneath me as I struggled to breathe. My mind swam in a haze of pain and despair. I could barely make out Diane's form through the haze, still standing rigidly under the Queen's control.

The Queen's laughter filled the chamber, a chilling symphony of malice and triumph. "Oh, you thought you could defeat me? Foolish human."

I tried to push myself up, but my broken arm refused to cooperate, and the pain was overwhelming. My head throbbed from the impact, and I tasted blood in my mouth. Everything was slipping away. The future we had dreamed of the life we had planned all seemed to fade into darkness.

As I lay there, struggling to hold on, I looked up at Diane. Her eyes, now black and soulless, stared down at me with an empty, detached expression. The woman I loved was gone, replaced by this unfeeling puppet of the Queen's will.

Tears welled up in my eyes as the full weight of our situation bore down on me. I had failed. The Queen had emerged victorious, and I had lost Diane. The pain in my heart was almost as unbearable as the physical agony. I had fought with everything I had, but it hadn't been enough.

"Diane," I whispered, my voice breaking, "I'm so sorry."

The Queen approached, her movements graceful and menacing. She stood over me, her eyes gleaming with triumph. "Now, watch as your beloved finishes you off," she sneered.

Diane stepped forward, her movements robotic and precise. The Queen had complete control, and there was nothing I could do to stop her. I closed my eyes, bracing myself for the end. My heart shattered at the idea of losing Diane forever.

Diane picked up a jagged piece of metal from the debris, her movements slow and deliberate. She walked toward me, her eyes still devoid of emotion, the blackness within them reflecting the abyss I felt swallowing my hope. As she stood over my prone body, I looked up at her, my vision swimming with tears and pain.

"Diane, please," I begged, my voice barely a whisper. "It's me, Jack. Don't do this. Fight it. I know you're in there."

But my words fell on deaf ears. With cold, mechanical precision, she raised the piece of metal and plunged it into my stomach. The pain was immediate and excruciating, a searing agony that ripped through my body. I screamed, a raw, primal sound that echoed through the chamber.

The physical pain was unbearable, but the emotional torment was even worse. The woman I loved, my soulmate, had just stabbed me. Blood gurgled in my throat as I struggled to breathe, the metallic taste filling my mouth. My vision blurred, the edges darkening as my strength ebbed away.

Through the haze of pain, I heard the Queen's triumphant voice. "And now, the winner and new champion: Diane."

The Queen's control over Diane lifted, and I saw the instant recognition and horror flood her eyes. She looked down at me; her face twisting in a mask of grief and anguish. "Jack!" she screamed, dropping the metal and collapsing on her knees beside me. "Jack, no!"

She tried to reach out to me, her hands trembling, but the Queen intervened. "Oh, no dear. You're mine now."

Before Diane could touch me, a small portal opened up behind her. She was gone in a flash, disappearing into the void with a scream of despair.

I lay there, blood pooling around me, the world growing dim. The Queen's laughter echoed in the chamber, a cruel symphony to my final moments. As darkness closed in, the image of Diane's horrified face was the last thing I saw.

451

CHAPTER 34

As I lay on the cold, hard ground, bleeding out and struggling to breathe, the Queen approached, her malevolent grin widening. She towered over me, her presence an oppressive force that seemed to suck the remaining life from my body.

"You pathetic fool," she sneered. "Did you really think you were ever in control? Every moment of your life, every ounce of suffering, has been by my design."

I glared up at her, my vision swimming, but my anger began to ignite. "What... what are you talking about?" I gasped.

She laughed, a chilling sound that echoed through the chamber. "It was I who influenced your stepfather, Kyle, to murder your father. It was I who orchestrated the events that led your mother to meet him and fall in love, sealing your fate. Every beating, every moment of fear and pain... it was all me."

Her words sent a shockwave through my mind, igniting memories of my tortured past. I saw my father's murder, my mother's anguish, and Kyle's brutal attacks. This monstrous being filled me with such intense rage that it burned through my pain, as I realized that all of it had been manipulated.

"You're lying," I hissed, my voice trembling with fury.

"Oh, but I'm not," she replied, her eyes glittering with sadistic delight. "I've been pulling the strings all along. Your suffering has been my entertainment, your pain my masterpiece."

The anger surged within me, overriding the agony of my wounds. I couldn't let her win. I couldn't let her revel in my defeat. As I lay there, memories flashed before my eyes — moments of love, hope, and resilience. I saw Diane's face, filled with sorrow and love, and knew I couldn't give up.

With a guttural scream, I pushed myself up, my muscles protesting, the wound in my stomach sending waves of searing pain through my body. "It can't end like this," I growled, my voice filled with determination. "Fuck that bitch! You'll have to kill me yourself."

The Queen's laughter faded as she watched me rise, her expression shifting to one of mild surprise. "You're still defiant?" she mused. "Interesting. But futile."

I forced myself to my feet, every movement a battle against pain and blood loss. "You think you can break me?" I spat, staring her down with every ounce of defiance I had left. "You think you can control me? You're going to have to try harder than that."

My vision blurred, but I locked onto her, my resolve unyielding. I staggered toward her, my body screaming in protest, but my mind and heart burning with a singular purpose. If this was the end, I would face it on my terms.

"Come on," I snarled, standing tall despite the pain. "Fight me yourself, you coward."

The Queen's eyes narrowed, and for a moment, I thought I saw a flicker of uncertainty. "Very well," she said, her voice cold and calculating. "If you wish to die by my hand, so be it."

As I prepared myself, she continued, her voice dripping with malice. "You think you're the only one I've manipulated? Every person in this tournament, every one of your friends and enemies – I shaped their lives, their pain, their struggles. I had to make sure they were ready to fight, to survive, to do whatever was necessary to win. Their agony was the crucible that forged them into warriors for my entertainment."

My heart pounded with a mix of horror and fury. She had twisted not just my life but the lives of everyone here, turning us into pawns for her sick games. "You're a monster," I spat.

She laughed again, a cruel, mocking sound. "A monster? Perhaps. But I am also your master, and you will die knowing that every moment of your life was under my control."

With my one good arm, I swung weakly at the Queen, the effort futile. She easily pushed it aside and grabbed my neck, lifting me off the ground as if I were weightless. Her eyes bore into mine, filled with cold malice.

"When will you understand that you cannot win!" she hissed, her grip tightening.

Choking, I rasped out, "Love... always... wins!" I tried to laugh, but it came out as a strangled gurgle.

Annoyed, she hurled me through a wall with a force that shattered my neck and body. I crashed into another wall lined with glass vials filled with a strange yellow substance. The glass shattered around me, and I lay motionless on the ground, covered in the mystery liquid. My blood mixed with the yellow fluid pooling beneath me.

I could hear the Queen's triumphant, mocking laughter as I drifted in and out of consciousness. So, this is what dying is like? I thought.

Memories flashed before my eyes–Diane's smile, the warmth of her embrace, the dreams we had shared. The pain was overwhelming, but it was the thought of her that kept me clinging to the last threads of consciousness. The Queen's laughter echoed in my ears, a cruel reminder of her victory.

I lay there, feeling the life ebb from my body. The yellow substance seeped into my wounds, causing a strange burning sensation that only added to my agony. The Queen's footsteps drew closer, her laughter growing louder and more triumphant.

But as I lay there, broken and defeated, a new sensation spread through me. The yellow liquid, mixed with my blood, seemed to do something—something unexpected. It was as if it was reacting with my body, creating a strange, tingling warmth that spread through my veins.

The Queen's laughter suddenly stopped, replaced by a gasp of surprise. "What... what is this?" she demanded, her voice wavering for the first time.

I could feel the yellow substance coursing through me, merging with my blood, my pain subsiding just a fraction. It wasn't healing me, but it was giving me a strange sense of clarity and strength. My body, broken and bleeding, was still a vessel for something greater—something the Queen hadn't expected.

With a monumental effort, I pushed myself up, my vision clearing despite the agony. The Queen stared at me, her eyes wide with shock and fear.

"You..." she stammered, stepping back. "How are you still alive?"

I locked eyes with her, feeling the strange substance pulse through my veins. "You underestimated the power of love," I said, my voice gaining strength. "And now, you're going to pay for everything you've done."

The Queen's expression twisted with rage and fear as she realized she was no longer in control. I didn't know what this yellow substance was or how it kept me alive, but it didn't matter. All that mattered was that I had one last chance to end this.

I felt power surge through me, a strength I had never felt before. My body healed, my bones becoming like steel. My anger, frustration, and violent vengeance hit me like a shotgun blast. I became a vessel for an uncontrollable, rage-filled monster bent on the Queen's destruction. It felt like my eyes were on fire, and I screamed with unrelenting determination.

With a roar, I rushed at the Queen, taking her completely by surprise. I slammed into her with all my might, sending her flying. She crashed into another wall, hitting it with a bone-jarring impact before landing face-first on the cold floor. For the first time, the Queen had the wind knocked out of her.

She struggled to rise, her eyes wide with shock and anger. "Impossible," she hissed, blood dripping from her mouth. "You should be dead!"

I advanced on her, my steps steady and filled with purpose. "You took everything from me," I growled, my voice echoing with raw emotion. "You ruined my life, my family, my love. Now, it's time for you to feel the pain you've inflicted on others."

The Queen got to her feet, her movements slower, more deliberate. She tried to gather her power, but I could see the fear in her eyes. She knew she was no longer invincible.

With a primal scream, I lunged at her again. We clashed in brutal hand-to-hand combat, the sound of our struggle echoing through the vast chamber. Each punch, each kick, was a testament to my fury and desperation. The Queen dodged and parried, but she was no match for my newfound strength and determination.

I could feel her weakening with each blow. Her movements became sluggish, her defenses crumbling. I was relentless, fueled by a mixture of rage and sorrow. I had to end this—for Diane, for my father, for everyone who had suffered because of her.

She lashed out with a wild swing, but I caught her wrist, twisting it sharply. She cried out in pain; her face contorted with anger and disbelief. "You think you've won?" she spat, blood flecking her lips. "This is just the beginning. You have no idea what you've unleashed."

Ignoring her words, I tightened my grip, feeling the bones in her wrist crack under the pressure. "You've taken everything from me," I said, my voice trembling with emotion. "But you won't take anything more. This ends now."

With one powerful punch, I sent the Queen crashing to the ground. She lay there, gasping for breath, her once-imposing presence reduced to a vulnerable, broken figure.

I stood over her, my body trembling with exhaustion and adrenaline. "It's over," I said, my voice cold and resolute. "You won't hurt anyone ever again."

The Queen looked up at me, her eyes filled with hatred and desperation. "You think you've won?" she hissed. "This is just the beginning. You have no idea what you've unleashed."

Ignoring her words, I raised my fist for the final blow, determined to end her reign of terror once and for all. This was for Diane, for my father, for every life she had destroyed. And as my fist descended, I knew that love, in the end, would be our salvation.

My punch was so hard it crushed her entire head against the floor with a sickening burst of blood and bone, her skull squishing under my might. I stood there, panting, staring at the grotesque remains of the Queen. The silence was deafening, and the realization of what I had just done washed over me like a tidal wave.

I fell to my knees, the adrenaline fading, but the powerful liquid still surged within me, numbing any pain. My body trembled as I screamed, a raw sound of mental torment that echoed through the chamber. I had finally done it—the Queen was dead—but the victory felt hollow. Everything I had fought for, everything I had lost—it all came crashing down around me.

Tears mixed with the blood on my face as I sat there, my mind reeling. Diane was gone, taken by the Queen in her last act of cruelty. My father was dead, my childhood shattered, and now, even my sense of self felt broken. I had done what needed to be done, but at what cost?

The surrounding room was a testament to the brutality that had consumed my life. Blood stained the walls, with debris scattered everywhere. I could still hear the echoes of our battle, feel the impact of every blow. But now, there was only silence, and the weight of my grief threatened to crush me.

Then, like a lightning strike through the haze of my despair, I remembered—the relic. The commander had told me it was the only thing that could ensure the Queen's death was final. My heart raced as I realized I hadn't seen it during the battle. Where was it? My mind scrambled to recall anything that might give me a clue.

The liquid coursing through my veins kept the pain at bay, but it did nothing to quell the mounting fear and urgency. I stood, my movements quick and driven, feeling no exhaustion or ache. I needed to find that relic, or everything I'd fought for would be in vain.

I moved through the wreckage, my eyes scanning every inch of the ruined chamber. The chaos of the battle had scattered everything, and the relic could be anywhere. It had been hidden, that much I knew, but its exact location eluded me. My thoughts raced, piecing together fragments of memory, trying to remember where it could be.

I tore through the debris, my hands moving with a desperate speed. The liquid's power surged within me, pushing me onward, keeping my mind sharp even as my emotions threatened to overwhelm me. The Queen's death meant nothing if I didn't find the relic and use it.

Time felt like it was slipping away as I searched, my mind consumed with the need to find the relic. Every moment wasted was a moment closer to losing everything. The relic was my only hope, the last piece of this horrific puzzle that would ensure the Queen's end.

Finally, I stopped in the middle of the room, my eyes scanning the destruction around me. I knew it was here, hidden somewhere within the remnants of our battle. The powerful liquid kept me moving, kept my senses heightened, but even that couldn't dull the growing panic inside me.

I had to find it. I couldn't let Diane's sacrifice be in vain. With a final, deep breath, I steeled myself and walked, determined to search every inch of this place until I found the relic and ended the Queen's reign for good.

CHAPTER 35

Just as I was about to leave, a chilling sensation crawled up my spine. I thought I heard it—a faint, sinister laughter echoing through the chamber. At first, I dismissed it as a trick of my mind, a remnant of the trauma I had endured. But the laughter grew louder, more insistent, until it filled the entire room with its malevolent tone.

My heart raced as I turned back, fear and confusion clawing at me. The Queen's body trembled, her form shifting and distorting. What I saw next made my blood run cold. Her body expanded, grotesquely twisting, as if reshaping itself into a nightmarish new form. Tentacles sprouted from her back, writhing and slithering with a life of their own. Her once humanoid face was elongated and warped, turning into a grotesque mask of alien terror.

Her hair, which had once been like real dark hair, now grew into thick, serpentine strands that coiled and twisted around her head, adding to her monstrous appearance. Sharp, clawed appendages emerged from her hands and feet, each one glistening with a predatory sheen. Her mouth stretched wide, revealing rows of razor-sharp teeth that could make even the most fearsome predator seem tame.

The laughter grew louder, more echoing, as she completed her transformation. It was a sound that gnawed at the edges of my sanity, a cacophony of triumph and derision. She stood before me now as a towering, alien horror—a being of unimaginable power and malice.

"Did you really think you could defeat me so easily?" The Queen's voice boomed, now a deep, resonant growl that seemed to reverberate through the very air. "You've only scratched the surface of my power."

My breath came in ragged gasps as I faced this new abomination. My hands clenched into fists, my resolve hardening despite the dread that gripped me. The Queen's mockery stung deep, igniting a fresh wave of anger and determination. I had fought too hard, lost too much, to let this monster break me now.

I took a deep breath, steeling myself for the battle ahead. The Queen was no longer just a cruel, manipulative force; she was an embodiment of pure, alien terror. But I had come this far. I had survived so much. I would not falter now.

"I'm not done," I declared, my voice rough but resolute. "You may have revealed your true form, but you've only made me more determined to end this."

The Queen's laugh roared again, a sound that seemed to shake the very foundations of the chamber. Her monstrous form loomed over me, but I refused to back down. This battle was far from over, and despite the odds, I would fight until my last breath.

The air was thick with the stench of blood and sweat, the once-glorious hall now nothing but a battlefield littered with the broken bodies of those who had fallen before me. The Queen stood at the center of it all, her massive form towering over me, her eyes glowing with a malevolent light that seemed to pierce through my very soul. This was the end. The culmination of every battle, every sacrifice, every step that had brought me here. But as I stood there, facing the monstrosity that had terrorized not only me but countless others, I couldn't help but feel the weight of everything that had led to this moment.

My heart pounded in my chest; each beat a drum of impending doom. I could feel the sweat trickling down my back, mixing with the grime and blood that coated my skin. My muscles ached; my body battered from the relentless battles that had preceded this one. But there was no room for doubt, no time for hesitation. This was the endgame, and I was the only one left standing.

The Queen let out a low, guttural growl, her lips curling back to reveal rows of razor-sharp teeth. Her massive, clawed hands flexed as she readied herself for the fight, her body radiating a palpable aura of power. The ground beneath her seemed to tremble with every movement, as if the very earth itself feared her wrath. Her once-regal form was now twisted, grotesque, a monstrous parody of the being she had once been. The crown she had worn was long gone, shattered in chaos, leaving only the raw, unbridled fury of a cornered beast.

Fueled by a renewed surge of anger and the pulsating power from the mysterious liquid, I charged at the Queen with all my might. My steps were like thunder, shaking the ground as I raced toward her monstrous form. She raised her massive arm to swat me away, and the impact was like a tidal wave crashing against me. The impact threw me violently through another wall, slamming me hard into the debris-littered ground.

But this time, there was no pain. No sting or ache as I hit the floor. My body felt invincible, every bruise and wound healed almost instantly by the energy coursing through me. I pushed myself up, my eyes scanning the wreckage. Amid the rubble, my gaze locked onto something glimmering—a faint, golden light shining through the debris. It was the artifact!

I stumbled toward it, every step driven by fierce determination. As I reached the artifact, I could feel its power thrumming in my hand. This was the key to ending her reign of terror once and for all.

But as I turned to face the Queen, I saw her massive form shifting and reacting, her eyes gleaming with malignant amusement. The sheer size and power of her were daunting, and I knew getting close would be a challenge.

I tightened my grip on the artifact, the only weapon that had a chance of defeating her. It pulsed with energy, the light it emitted casting eerie shadows across the room. But even with its power, I knew this would be no easy fight. The Queen was no ordinary foe, and she had already proven time and time again that she was more than capable of killing those who stood in her way.

Without warning, she lunged at me, her massive form moving with a speed that belied her size. I barely had time to react, throwing myself to the side as her claws slashed through the air where I had just been standing. The force of her attack sent a shockwave through the ground, the impact reverberating through my bones. I rolled to my feet, narrowly avoiding a second swipe as her claws gouged deep furrows into the stone floor.

I retaliated, swinging the artifact in a wide arc, the blade glowing with a fierce, blinding light as it connected with her side. The Queen let out a roar of pain, but the wound was shallow, barely scratching the surface of her thick hide. She spun on me, her eyes blazing with fury, and I barely had time to brace myself before she was on me again, her claws tearing through the air with lethal precision.

The next few moments were a blur of violence and pain. We clashed again and again, each strike more brutal than the last. The artifact cut through the air with a whistling sound, its blade glowing as it met the Queen's flesh. But no matter how many times I struck her, she seemed to shrug off the blows as if they were nothing more than insect bites. Her claws raked across my chest, leaving deep, burning gashes that sent waves of agony through my body. Blood flowed freely, staining my clothes and the ground beneath me.

She was relentless; her attacks coming faster and harder with each passing second. I could feel my strength waning, the adrenaline that had carried me this far faltered. But I couldn't afford to slow down, couldn't afford to give her even a moment of advantage. Every second counted, every breath I took, bringing me closer to either victory or death.

The Queen's eyes gleamed with a savage joy as she pressed her assault, sensing my exhaustion. She lashed out with a backhanded swipe that caught me across the face, sending me sprawling to the ground. Stars exploded in my vision, pain lancing through my skull as my head struck the stone floor. I struggled to rise, but she was already upon me, her massive foot coming down on my chest with crushing force.

I gasped for air, my ribs creaking under the pressure. The Queen loomed over me, her eyes narrowing as she studied me, her lips curling into a cruel smile. She wanted to savor this moment, to drag out my suffering before delivering the final blow. Her claws hovered above me, poised to strike, and for a moment, I thought it was over.

But something deep within me refused to give in. I had come too far, lost too much to be defeated now. With a surge of strength I didn't know I had, I twisted my body, the artifact still clutched in my hand and drove the blade upward with all my might.

As the artifact's blade pierced the Queen's foot, the light flared upon touching her flesh. The Queen let out a scream of rage and pain, her foot jerking back instinctively. The pressure on my chest eased, and I rolled away, gasping for breath. Despite my blurred vision and my body screaming in protest, I stood up and confronted her once more.

The Queen staggered back, the wound on her foot seeping a dark, viscous fluid that hissed and steamed as it touched the ground. She glared at me with a hatred that seemed to burn hotter than the fires of hell, her claws flexing as she prepared to launch another attack. I knew I had only moments to act, to take advantage of her momentary distraction.

Summoning every ounce of strength I had left, I lunged at her, swinging the artifact with all the force I could muster. The blade sliced through the air, aimed at her chest, but the Queen was faster. She swatted me away with a backhanded blow that sent me crashing into the wall. The impact drove the air from my lungs, pain exploding in my back as I slumped to the ground.

She was on me in an instant, her claws wrapping around my throat as she lifted me off the ground. My feet dangled helplessly above the floor, my hands clawing at her grip as I struggled to breathe. The Queen's face was inches from mine, her breath hot and fetid against my skin. Her eyes bored into mine, and I could see the sadistic pleasure she took in watching me struggle.

"This is where it ends," she hissed, her voice a low, venomous growl that sent chills down my spine. "You thought you could defeat me? You are nothing but a worm, a pathetic little insect trying to play the hero. I will crush you like all the others, and your world will fall to my rule."

I could feel the darkness closing in at the edges of my vision, my strength fading with each passing second. The Queen's grip tightened, her claws digging into my flesh, and I knew that if I didn't act now, it would be over. With the last of my strength, I reached down, my fingers brushing against the hilt of the artifact still clutched in my hand.

The blade pulsed with a fierce light, its power surging through me as I raised it high. The Queen's eyes widened in surprise, but it was too late. With a desperate cry, I drove the blade into her chest; the light flaring as it pierced her flesh. The Queen let out a bloodcurdling scream, her grip on my throat loosening as she staggered back, the blade buried deep in her chest.

I fell to the ground, gasping for air, my vision swimming as I struggled to stay conscious. The Queen clutched at the artifact, her face contorted in pain and fury as the light spread through her body, consuming her from within. Her skin began to crack and blister, the dark fluid pouring from her wounds as she stumbled backward, her massive form shaking with the force of the energy coursing through her.

But even in her final moments, she did not feel defeated. With a roar of defiance, she lunged at me one last time, her claws outstretched, determined to take me with her. I barely had time to react, throwing myself to the side as her claws slashed through the air, missing me by inches. She crashed to the ground; the impact sending a shockwave through the room as the light from the artifact consumed her completely.

For a moment, everything was still. The Queen's body remained motionless, and the light dimmed as the last of her life force drained away. I stood there, panting and bleeding, my body trembling with exhaustion and adrenaline. It was over. The Queen was dead, and the nightmare was finally at an end.

But as I looked down at her lifeless form, I couldn't shake the feeling that something was wrong. The air was thick with oppressive energy, a dark, malevolent force that seemed to seep into every corner of the room.

Once a symbol of the Queen's dominion, the chamber now appeared unfamiliar and icy. Debris and devastation reduced the grandeur that had once filled this space, with the walls scorched and scarred from the battle. The very air felt different, as if the defeat of the Queen had drained the life from this place, leaving behind only emptiness and echoes of what once was. I tried to process the enormity of what had just happened, but before I could, an alarming sound sliced through the silence—the shrill, persistent blare of alarms.

The noise was jarring, reverberating through the chamber and drawing my attention to the flickering, ominous lights that began flashing in an erratic pattern. They bathed the room in harsh, strobe-like pulses, casting eerie shadows that danced across the broken remains of the Queen's throne. Each flash seemed to illuminate the destruction, highlighting the shattered pillars, the crumbled statues, and the fallen relics of the Queen's rule.

Alien voices, distorted and incomprehensible, echoed through the chamber. They were frantic, laced with a sense of urgency and alarm, as if the very structure of the building was crying out in despair. The messages were foreign, their meanings lost to me, but the intent was clear: something was very wrong. The voices overlapped and melded together, creating a cacophony that set my nerves on edge, heightening the sense of impending doom.

Panic surged through me as the ground trembled beneath my feet. It started as a faint vibration, barely noticeable, but quickly intensified into a violent shaking that rattled my bones. The building's structure was on the verge of collapsing as the walls, previously sturdy and unyielding, began to crack and groan under immense pressure. The intensity of the tremors increased. Dust and debris rained down from above, and the ceiling collapsed in slow, catastrophic chunks.

My instincts screamed at me to move, but for a moment, the sheer scale of the destruction paralyzed me, unfolding around me. The ground beneath me buckled and heaved, sending me stumbling as I fought to regain my balance. I could hear the deep, thunderous creaks of the building's foundations shifting, the walls cracking open like eggshells under the immense pressure. The once-majestic chamber was disintegrating before my eyes, transforming into a deathtrap from which there seemed no escape.

I had no time to think. Adrenaline surged through my veins, pushing me into motion as I sprinted toward the exit, navigating through the crumbling structure. The walls seemed to close in around me, their once-smooth surfaces now jagged and dangerous, protruding with sharp edges and splintered stone. I dodged falling debris, my movements fueled by sheer survival instinct. Each step felt like it could be my last, the ground unstable and treacherous beneath my feet.

The shaking intensified, the entire structure groaning as it threatened to come down around me. I could hear the distant roar of machinery struggling against the collapse, the grinding of gears and the snapping of cables echoing through the chamber. The ground quaked so violently that it was a struggle to maintain my footing, every step a battle against the forces tearing the building apart. I could see the exit ahead, a flickering light barely visible through the dust and chaos. It was my only chance.

With every ounce of strength left, I pushed forward, my heart pounding in my chest like a drumbeat of survival. The collapsing building seemed determined to take me with it, the walls and ceiling crumbling in a slow-motion descent into ruin. I could feel the heat of the destruction at my back, the oppressive weight of the debris pressing in on me from all sides. My lungs burned with the effort, my muscles screaming in protest as I forced my body to keep moving.

As I approached, the flickering light became more intense, and the exit loomed closer. Filled with the dust and smoke of the collapsing chamber, the passageway was narrow, barely wide enough for me to squeeze through. The air was thick and choking, each breath a struggle as I fought to reach the outside. The noise was deafening, a cacophony of destruction that drowned out everything else, the sound of the world collapsing in on itself.

With a final burst of speed, I hurled myself toward the exit, diving through the crumbling passage just as the chamber behind me gave way in a thunderous explosion of dust and debris. The force of the blast propelled me forward, and I tumbled out into the open air, the fresh breeze hitting me like a wave, a welcome relief from the choking dust and oppressive heat of the collapsing chamber.

I collapsed on the ground, gasping for breath, every muscle in my body screaming in protest from the intense battle and escape. My body was a tapestry of pain and exhaustion, my skin was slick with sweat and grime. The weight of what I had endured, the knowledge that I had barely escaped with my life, overshadowed the relief of being outside.

The chamber I had fought so fiercely to escape was now a smoldering ruin behind me, the last remnants of its structure collapsing in on itself with a final, thunderous roar. The dust and debris hung in the air like a grim reminder of the chaos I had just escaped, the sky above obscured by the thick clouds of smoke rising from the wreckage. I could barely lift my head to look back. My vision blurred and my strength waning.

As I lay there, gasping for breath, the battle's aftermath was more punishing than the fight itself. My body was a mess of pain, and I could feel the yellow substance forced into me surging back up. I retched violently, expelling the vile, viscous liquid onto the scorched ground. Each heave was a brutal reminder of how narrowly I had escaped death, and it left me feeling even more drained and exposed.

My muscles ached with exhaustion, and the cold ground against my side was a stark contrast to the intense heat of the battle. Every nerve in my body frayed, trembling uncontrollably as the adrenaline of survival faded. The reality of my situation crashed over me like a relentless tide. I had survived, but the victory felt hollow, overshadowed by the emptiness left by Diane's absence.

Tears streamed down my face, mingling with grime and blood. I lay there, overwhelmed by the weight of my grief, sobbing uncontrollably. Though the battle was over, my heart was shattered and weighed heavily on me. Diane's memory, her laughter, and the weight of her loss consumed me with an almost unbearable sorrow. I felt completely alone.

The distant blaring alarms from the wreckage added to the eerie desolation of the scene. The sound was a harsh reminder of the chaos I had just endured. But as I lay there, trying to accept my fate, a glimmer of hope emerged. I saw Diane's body crumpled near the debris, partially obscured by the wreckage. With my heart pounding in a mix of fear and desperation, I stumbled toward her. I collapsed beside her, pushing aside debris with shaking hands. Her chest rose and fell with shallow breaths, but she remained unconscious.

"Diane!" I shouted, my voice cracking with emotion. I shook her gently, my fingers brushed against her cold skin. "Please, wake up!"

Slowly, her eyes fluttered open. Relief surged through me as I saw her stir, but it was short-lived. Her gaze was blank, unrecognizing. She looked at me with confusion and fear, and the words she uttered hit me like a blow to the chest.

"Who are you?" she asked, her voice weak and trembling.

Her words took me aback, causing my heart to ache. "Diane, it's me. It's Jack."

But she shook her head, her expression growing more bewildered. "I don't... I don't know you," she murmured. "I don't know anything. Who am I? Where am I?"

My heart shattered, the weight of her words cutting deeper than any wound I'd suffered. "It's me," I said, choking on the lump in my throat. "It's Jack."

But there was no recognition, no spark of the woman I loved. She pulled away slightly, her gaze darting to the alien ships overhead. I reached for her hand, desperate for any connection, and for a moment, her fingers tightened around mine. It was a brief flicker of something human—before she turned away.

I looked up at the sky, the massive ships blotting out the sun. The Queen was dead, but her army was here. The fight wasn't over. It was just beginning.

The artifact, still clutched in my trembling hand, began to pulse with light. Cracks spread across its surface, glowing with an intensity that made my heart skip a beat. I barely had time to drop it before it shattered, the shards dissolving into a brilliant cascade of light. The energy lingered in the air for a moment before fading, leaving behind only silence.

I stared at the spot where it had been, my mind racing. It was over. The Queen was gone. But as I looked at the ships descending around us, I realized the artifact had been just a tool—a crutch. There would be no more ancient weapons or hidden relics to save us. It was just me, Diane, and whatever strength I could find to keep going.

I stood, pulling Diane to her feet as the first ship landed with a deafening roar. She flinched at the sound, her grip on my arm tightening instinctively. "I don't know who you are," she whispered, her voice shaking, "but don't leave me."

I looked into her eyes—lost, frightened, but alive. "I won't," I promised, my voice steady despite the storm of emotions inside me. "Not ever."

The ship's doors began to open, and I positioned myself in front of Diane, shielding her with my body. The fight wasn't over. But as long as I was breathing, I wouldn't let her face it alone.

ACKNOWLEDGMENTS

I want to express my deepest gratitude to my mother, Susan Nelson, whose unwavering support and encouragement made this book possible. To Dianna Grace, whose wisdom, feedback, and inspiration shaped the heart of this story—your influence is woven into every page. Diane, a character so central to this book, carries the strength, resilience, and compassion I've always admired in you. Thank you for your endless support and belief in my journey as a writer.

And to my readers—thank you for giving this story a home in your imagination. It is because of you that these words come to life.

ABOUT THE AUTHOR

Stephen Snyder is a debut author of the Forced to Fight series, a thrilling science fiction saga born from a lifelong passion for storytelling. He began writing stories at the age of 11 and has since been inspired by vivid dreams and real-life challenges to create imaginative worlds that entertain and inspire. Drawing heavily on personal experiences, Stephen blends themes of resilience, hope, and overcoming adversity into his work—values that resonate deeply with his readers and reflect the journey of his protagonists.

When he's not writing, Stephen enjoys wrestling, playing video games, and listening to music that motivates and inspires him. He lives in upstate New York in a very small town with his two kids, a dog, and a large collection of graphic novels and books.

Readers can connect with Stephen on several social media platforms:
Facebook: Stephen Snyder - Author
Instagram: @sjosephsnyder
TikTok: @s.js.s

SNEAK PEAK

Forced to Fight Book Two

The sky was on fire. Alien ships blotted out the sun, their massive forms hovering like storm clouds over the broken remains of the battlefield. The air crackled with energy, thick with the acrid stench of smoke and burning metal. Every breath I took felt like inhaling ash.

Diane clung to my arm, her steps unsure, as though every movement might send her tumbling into the chaos around us. Her wide, frightened eyes darted from one shadow to the next, her grip tightening with every distant explosion.

She hadn't spoken much since waking up, and when she had, her words were hesitant, fragile. Each question she asked felt like watching someone piece together shards of a broken mirror. But the memory of her earlier words lingered in my mind, gnawing at me.

Who are you?

I stole a glance at her now, watching as her gaze flickered over the ruined landscape. She slowed suddenly, tugging lightly at my arm.

"J…" She hesitated, her brow furrowing in frustration. "Jack, right?" Her voice wavered, unsteady, like she was testing the word for the first time.

"Yes," I said softly, steadying her with a firm grip. "You remembered."

Her face clouded again. "Barely. It doesn't feel… real." Her voice dropped to a whisper. "You said I'm Diane, but I don't even know who that is."

"You're Diane," I said firmly. "And you're with me. That's all you need to know right now."

She nodded, though her confusion was written plainly in her features. She didn't argue, but the way her eyes darted back to the horizon told me she was still searching for answers I couldn't give her.

A distant explosion shook the ground beneath us, sending a column of fire and debris into the air. The horizon was a patchwork of destruction. Alien crafts streaked across the sky, their weapons carving into the Earth below. From where we stood, the wreckage of human cities stretched out in jagged outlines—collapsed skyscrapers, shattered highways, and streets buried under rubble.

The invasion wasn't just here. It was everywhere.

"Where… are we?" Diane asked, her voice trembling.

I hesitated, scanning the devastation around us. "I wish I knew," I said quietly. "It doesn't even look like Earth anymore."

I scanned the landscape again, searching for anything that resembled safety. That's when I saw them—figures moving through the smoke, sharp silhouettes against the flickering fires. For a moment, I thought they were survivors, but as they stepped closer, the truth hit me like a fist.

They weren't civilians. The uniforms were unlike anything I'd seen—sleek, tactical, and impossibly clean despite the chaos. They moved with a precision that felt unnerving, each step measured, their coordination almost inhuman.

"Who are they?" Diane whispered, her voice barely audible. She pressed closer to me, her unease palpable.

"I don't know," I said, pulling her behind a crumbling wall. "But they're not here to help."

The figures fanned out, their movements deliberate and practiced. One knelt by a pile of debris, a faint blue glow emanating from a device in their hands. Another raised a hand, signaling to the others. They regrouped quickly, their helmets gleaming faintly in the firelight as they advanced.

"What do they want?" Diane asked, shrinking back.

"Not us," I muttered. "I don't think they even know we're here. Let's keep it that way."

The ground trembled beneath us, the vibration building into a steady rumble. Diane flinched as another explosion ripped through the distance, showering sparks into the already darkened sky. She grabbed my arm tightly, her breathing quick and uneven.

"Jack," she said, her voice raw with fear. "I don't understand any of this. What's happening? What do we do?"

I met her eyes, trying to anchor her in some semblance of stability. "We keep moving," I said firmly. "We don't stop until we're somewhere safe."

Her expression was tight with fear, but she nodded. There was trust in her grip, even if her memories were gone.

Ahead, the figures disappeared into the smoke, their shadows melting into the haze. My gut twisted, unease gnawing at me like a warning I couldn't ignore.

"We'll find a way through this," I said, though the words felt more like a promise to myself than to her.

But as I led her forward, I couldn't shake the feeling that surviving this might be impossible.

Jack's journey continues in Forced to Fight Book Two! Coming soon in 2025—stay tuned for the next chapter in the battle for survival.